# MEXICAN PUBLIC INTELLECTUALS

# LITERATURES OF THE AMERICAS

**About the Series**

This series seeks to bring forth contemporary critical interventions within a hemispheric perspective, with an emphasis on perspectives from Latin America. Books in the series highlight work that explores concerns in literature in different cultural contexts across historical and geographical boundaries and also include work on the specific Latina/o realities in the United States. Designed to explore key questions confronting contemporary issues of literary and cultural import, *Literatures of the Americas* is rooted in traditional approaches to literary criticism but seeks to include cutting-edge scholarship using theories from postcolonial, critical race, and ecofeminist approaches.

**Series Editor**

**Norma E. Cantú** is Professor of English and US Latino Studies at the University of Missouri, Kansas City and Professor Emerita from the University of Texas at San Antonio. Her edited and coedited works include *Inside the Latin@ Experience* (2010), *Telling to Live: Latina Feminist Testimonios* (2001), *Chicana Traditions: Continuity and Change* (2000), and *Dancing Across Borders: Danzas y Bailes Mexicanos* (2003).

**Books in the Series:**

*Radical Chicana Poetics*
Ricardo F. Vivancos Pérez

*Rethinking Chicano/a Literature through Food: Postnational Appetites*
Edited by Nieves Pascual Soler and Meredith E. Abarca

*Literary and Cultural Relations between Brazil and Mexico: Deep Undercurrents*
Paulo Moreira

*Mexican Public Intellectuals*
Edited by Debra A. Castillo and Stuart A. Day

*TransLatin Joyce: Global Transmissions in Ibero-American Literature*
(Forthcoming)
Edited by Brian L. Price, César A. Salgado, and John Pedro Schwartz

# Mexican Public Intellectuals

Edited by
Debra A. Castillo and Stuart A. Day

palgrave
macmillan

MEXICAN PUBLIC INTELLECTUALS
Copyright © Debra A. Castillo and Stuart A. Day, 2014.

All rights reserved.

First published in 2014 by
PALGRAVE MACMILLAN®
in the United States—a division of St. Martin's Press LLC,
175 Fifth Avenue, New York, NY 10010.

Where this book is distributed in the UK, Europe and the rest of the world, this is by Palgrave Macmillan, a division of Macmillan Publishers Limited, registered in England, company number 785998, of Houndmills, Basingstoke, Hampshire RG21 6XS.

Palgrave Macmillan is the global academic imprint of the above companies and has companies and representatives throughout the world.

Palgrave® and Macmillan® are registered trademarks in the United States, the United Kingdom, Europe and other countries.

ISBN: 978–1–137–39228–2

Library of Congress Cataloging-in-Publication Data

    Mexican public intellectuals / edited by Debra A. Castillo and Stuart A. Day.
      pages cm.—(Literatures of the Americas)
      ISBN 978–1–137–39228–2 (hardback : alk. paper)
      1. Mexican literature—20th century—History and criticism.
2. Mexico—Intellectual life—20th century. 3. Intellectuals—Mexico—History—20th century. I. Castillo, Debra A., editor of compilation.
II. Day, Stuart A. (Stuart Alexander) editor of compilation.

PQ7154.M49 2014
860.9'97209051—dc23                                2013040047

A catalogue record of the book is available from the British Library.

Design by Newgen Knowledge Works (P) Ltd., Chennai, India.

First edition: April 2014

10 9 8 7 6 5 4 3 2 1

*To our families*

# Contents

| | |
|---|---|
| *Acknowledgments* | ix |
| Introduction: A New Kind of Public Intellectual?<br>*Debra A. Castillo and Stuart A. Day* | 1 |
| Chapter 1<br>The Democratic Dogma: Héctor Aguilar Camín, Jorge G. Castañeda, and Enrique Krauze in the Neoliberal Crucible<br>*Ignacio M. Sánchez Prado* | 15 |
| Chapter 2<br>Engaging Intellectuals: Andrés Henestrosa and Elena Poniatowska<br>*Debra A. Castillo* | 45 |
| Chapter 3<br>Monsiváis in a Nutshell<br>*María Cristina Pons* | 71 |
| Chapter 4<br>Guadalupe Loaeza's Blonded Ambition: Lip-Synching, Plagiarism, and Power Poses<br>*Emily Hind* | 95 |
| Chapter 5<br>It's My (National) Stage Too: Sabina Berman and Jesusa Rodríguez as Public Intellectuals<br>*Stuart A. Day* | 117 |
| Chapter 6<br>From Accounting to Recounting: Esther Chávez Cano and the Articulation of Advocacy, Agency, and Justice on the US-Mexico Border<br>*María Socorro Tabuenca C.* | 139 |

Chapter 7
Mayan Cultural Agency through Performance:
*Fortaleza de la Mujer Maya–Fomma*   163
Elvira Sánchez-Blake

Chapter 8
María Novaro: Feminist Filmmaking as Public Voice   181
David William Foster

Chapter 9
The Masked Intellectual: Marcos and the Speech of
the Rainforest   197
Oswaldo Estrada

Chapter 10
Javier Sicilia: Public Mourning for the Sons of Mexico   217
Javier Barroso

*Notes on Contributors*   237

*Index*   241

# Acknowledgments

It has been a few years since we sat down in a café in El Paso, Texas, to discuss a book on public intellectuals in Mexico. With the exception of a graduate student we had not yet met, we knew who needed to be on our list of contributors, and we are profoundly grateful for their willingness to join us on this project. In the end, their own work says as much about the future of intellectuals as the figures they treat in the chapters that follow.

We are also indebted to the series editor, Norma E. Cantú, and to our external reviewers, who provided detailed suggestions to improve the manuscript, and to Pam LeRow, the Digital Media Services guru in the College of Liberal Arts and Sciences at the University of Kansas. Without Pam's help many a project would never come to fruition—including this one.

The same goes for the outstanding editorial team at Palgrave Macmillan, especially Brigitte Shull (Senior Editor), Ryan Jenkins (Editorial Assistant), Devon Wolfkiel (Production Assistant), and the production team led by Deepa John at Newgen. At every step of the process they lived up to their reputation—and more. They are friendly, fast, and have a collective eye for detail that is, to say the least, impressive.

# Introduction: A New Kind of Public Intellectual?

*Debra A. Castillo and Stuart A. Day*

Already in late 2011 things were heating up, a year away from the elections of 2012, one of those unusual years in the political cycle in which citizens of both the United States and Mexico were voting in presidential contests. Candidacies were bruited about, and the press lamented the anti-intellectualism pervading so-called political debates. On the ground, locally, things often looked somewhat different. In early November of 2011, the international hackivist group "Anonymous" backed off its promise to publish names and personal data of Mexican drug cartel members—an Internet action that would have been effectively a declaration of war, with real rather than video-game kills on both sides (revealing the locations of known cartel members would effectively target them for rival cartels; drug trafficking organizations had already murdered numerous Internet journalists and incautious users of social media). That same day, poet Javier Sicilia, the subject of the last chapter in this volume, was leaving *cempazuchitl* flowers at the Angel Monument in Mexico City for Day of the Dead, promising to lead a new caravan, this time from the US side of the border, to Washington DC, to protest the US counter narcotic strategy. The reelection of Obama has done little to stem the anti-intellectualist tide in US politics; that of Enrique Peña Nieto in Mexico seems a worrisome return to the PRI-dominated stagnation that marked most of the twentieth century.

This is the age that has seen a significant, more than rhetorical intellectual turn from scholarly publication to scholarly communication, where writers and scholars and thinkers express themselves in tweets and blogs, appear on video on the Internet, and establish dialogue through social media like Facebook. Occupy/Indignados movements swept across both countries, their multifarious voices including demands for increased support for Dream Act youth cut short from the promise of the American dream by their irregular immigration status, support for beleaguered university students in general, burdened with crushing debt in their bids to achieve class mobility through education. These movements met with the attendant small victories and inevitable harsh repression. UAM-Azcapotzalco economist Edur Velasco Arregui declared victory and ended his 41-day hunger strike in front of the Bolsa de Valores on November 22, 2011 in response to the November 15 action in the Mexican Congress to increase support for higher education. Meanwhile, on November 15 in New York City, police and homeland security agents dismantled the Occupy Wall Street installations, arrested several hundred people, and destroyed computers as well as thousands of books in "the people's library."

Across the country, California police actions against peaceful student protests in Oakland and Davis sparked national outrage. Likewise, protestors everywhere took inspiration from the brave activists in the Middle East, many of whom are recognized scholars and engaged public intellectuals in the strongest sense. All of these examples, and many more, point to locations in which intellectuals are putting their bodies on the line and their minds at the service of public issues, in print and online publications, on the streets, and in the plazas. If in certain US academic circles the idea of the public intellectual may seem "a soft oxymoron" (Garber), a subject for knowing snickers among the US-centric theory heads, throughout the hemisphere the concept is regaining the immediacy and vitality that had been slowly eroding since the late 1960s in the United States and the heyday of the Zapatista movement in Mexico in the mid-1990s.

In this respect, Mexico has often been ahead of the thinkers to the north. Indeed, one can argue that the term "public intellectual" is redundant in Mexico because Mexicans often mention, when defining the role of intellectuals, the importance of meaningful participation in the public sphere. A generation ago, in his 1985 book *Intellectuals and the State in Twentieth Century Mexico*, Roderic Ai Camp concluded that "the majority of public figures [argue] that the intellectual can and should be a public actor. Those Mexicans most involved in public life vigorously believe the two roles not only are interchangeable, but are one. They do not believe that all public figures are intellectuals, but rather that all intellectuals *should* be public figures" (45). In Mexico, the participation of intellectuals in public life has always been extraordinary in comparison to the United States, and for many of these intellectuals—especially those who cross traditional lines either to protest or to engage a larger circle of the public—the price of this public presence and participation can be high.

The year 2011 was rocked by the brutal drug cartel response to internet tracking of their activities (yes, they too have their well-trained technologists, as well as their intellectuals); two young people were mutilated and hung from a Nuevo Laredo traffic overpass with a sign that read: "This is what happens to people who post funny things on the internet. Pay attention" (Burnett). By May 2013, the 20-something administrator of the infamous "Blog del Narco" had, astonishingly, been revealed to be a woman, forced out of Mexico when her identity was uncovered. In contrast, in the United States, where opposition is a safer (if no less well-monitored) game, such participation by intellectuals in the public life of the nation has often been downplayed, mocked, or ignored. Thus, for example, writing at the same time as Camp, poet Adrienne Rich explores the implications for the United States of very different expectations about an intellectual's responsibility to society. The first paragraph of her famous essay, "Blood, Bread, and Poetry," written during the height of the devastating civil wars in Central America, is worth citing in full:

> The Miami airport, summer 1983: a North American woman says to me, "You'll love Nicaragua: everyone there is a poet." I've thought many times of that remark, both while there and since returning home. Coming from a culture (North American, white- and male-dominated) which encourages poets to think of ourselves as alienated from the sensibility of the general population, which casually and devastatingly marginalizes us (so far, no slave labor or torture for a political poem—just dead air, the white noise of the media jamming the poet's words)—coming from this North American dominant culture which so confuses us, telling us poetry is neither economically profitable nor politically effective and that political dissidence is destructive to art, coming from this culture that tells me I am destined to be a luxury, a decorative garnish on the buffet table of the university curriculum, the ceremonial occasion, the national celebration—what am I to make, I thought, of that remark? *You'll love Nicaragua; everyone there is a poet.* (Do I love poets in general? I immediately asked myself, thinking of poets I neither love nor would wish to see in charge of my country). Is being a poet a guarantee that I would love a Marxist-Leninist revolution? Can't I simply travel as an American radical, a lesbian feminist, a citizen who opposes her government's wars against its own people and its intervention in other people's lands? And what effectiveness has the testimony of a poet returning from a revolution where "everyone is a poet" to a country where the possible credibility of poetry is not even seriously discussed? (167–68)

Thus, in contrast with Camp's argument that Latin American intellectuals are expected to have a public projection, Rich describes an anti-intellectual bias in mainstream US culture—one that many would agree has continued to the present day. Not only do intellectuals go unheard, more crucially, they are also expected to inhabit a frivolous corner of high culture as a luxury item. There is a certain echo here with Marjorie Garber's throwaway line, her comment (presumably speaking of US academic circles) that the concept of a public intellectual is a soft oxymoron, and that humanities in general have come to serve as mere decoration or fashion accessories to more crucial areas of study. Garber's argument in "After the Humanities," in effect, follows the chain of reasoning from Rich's earlier piece—that in the United States, the humanities have devolved into "accessories" in the double sense of fashion and crime, and that given this fact, business as we knew it for the last one hundred years of academic study is now effectively over. It is no wonder, then, that casually marginalized academics located in US institutions of higher education have been energized by Occupy Wall Street and images of brutalized students across the hemisphere, that we are fascinated by the idea of the Mexican intellectual: a central figure in the life of the nation, someone who is taken seriously—so seriously, in fact, that his or her words can become literally a matter of life and death.

The following chapters feature prominent public intellectuals in present-day Mexico and, in doing so, (re)affirm the roles they and others play in Mexican sociopolitical life. As public intellectuals they reach out to a wide audience, share their opinions and knowledge, and, in questioning (and at times reinforcing) the status quo, provide a critical stance that often influences the actions of the Mexican people and/or the government. Public intellectuals can be artists, activists, professors, performers, politicians, and/or writers. For our purposes, what unites them—in addition to living in and engaging with what Yvon Grenier calls "the only country in the Americas where intellectuals have had significant and sustained role in the political arena during the twentieth century"—is social commitment, in its myriad and sometimes contradictory forms, coupled with influence in spaces well beyond the ivory towers of academia or the salons of the (literary) elite. The transformation (some would say expiration) of traditional public intellectuals, the aristocratic figures who continue to haunt these pages, is, to be sure, not lamented in the pages that follow. The threat of figures like Octavio Paz is reduced—his writing simply does not have the power to combat the *chingonas* that assert their presence on the national stage, and Mexico is a more inclusive society (especially Mexico City), more apt to accept (and read, or watch) the work of unlikely public intellectuals.

The people we highlight range from the internationally known (Elena Poniatowska, Subcomandante Marcos, Enrique Krauze), to those who are well-known in Mexico and among specialized audiences outside their country (Sabina Berman, Jesusa Rodríguez, Carlos Monsiváis, Jorge Castañeda, Guadalupe Loaeza, Andrés Henestrosa). We give particular attention to those who are recognized for their human rights work (Esther Chávez, Petrona de la Cruz, Isabel Juárez Espinosa, Javier Sicilia) but are not necessarily household names in Mexico or beyond, even if their stories tend to be the most compelling because of the extent of their commitment to social causes combined with a sense of awe that people like this are out there—they are peaceful *comandantes* without as much media attention. All but three (Andrés Henestrosa, the Zapotec intellectual who died in 2008; Esther Chávez, who fought for human rights in Ciudad Juárez and died in 2009; and the chronicler Carlos Monsiváis, who died in 2010) are living and active in their respective endeavors. Taken together, this group of unique yet integrally linked intellectuals paints a picture of the ever-changing context of Mexican intellectualism. If there are absent figures that haunt this book they are, without a doubt, Carlos Fuentes and Octavio Paz. They remain key touchstones who are admired (they were, after all, the consummate twentieth-century intellectuals) and refuted—almost always with a respectful tone, especially in the eulogies after their deaths: Paz in 1998 and Fuentes more recently in 2012. To a lesser but important degree, people like Salvador Novo, Andrés Manuel López Obrador, and numerous others remind us that the intellectuals in this volume, despite their different circumstances, share a tremendously rich and overlapping cultural tradition. Enrique Krauze stands out for the degree to which those of us in the US academy rely on his work: he has replaced Paz in our love-hate relationship with those who at once make Mexico accessible and challenge our views by not (always) towing the party line—foreign-located academics can also get entrenched in both the progressive and stagnant remnants of the 60s. Like many Mexicans, readers in the United States rely on intellectuals who bridge cultures—Paz, Fuentes, Poniatowska, Castañeda, and the occasional *New York Times* or *Los Angeles Times* correspondent. And, while the authors of the following chapters (not to mention the public intellectuals we write about) at times critique these powerful public figures, we also recognize the impact they have had on us and on other intellectuals in Mexico.

It is therefore fitting that while an intellectual like Poniatowska (with her cats, Monsi and Vais) can be criticized, she nonetheless stands out as a major touchstone in the project: her influence comes through in many sections of the book, for example in chapter 5 when Stuart A. Day asks Sabina Berman if Poniatowska, and specifically her testimonial work on the October 2, 1968 massacre of students, influenced her book on the 2006 elections, *Un soplo en el corazón de la patria*. Berman responds: "I believe that if I had not read *La noche de Tlatelolco*, possibly it wouldn't have occurred to me [to write this one]...it's the same type of book. And, curiously, it finds Elena and me, who I have read and admire, on opposite sides of a political debate" (interview). What the reader will soon note, however, are not the differences among the people we write about, though there are many, but the cross-references that allow us to discover crucial points of contact, including the one that has made each person highlighted in the book relevant: Edward Said's idea that if we are not being polemical we are probably not having much of an impact on the powers that be. Sadly, one way to know that intellectuals have effectively communicated their ideas at the right time and to the right people is if their opponents strike back, in some cases physically. Over the years, several of the intellectuals profiled here have told stories of threats—outright death threats, more subtle threats, threats that result in a lost position or a loss of freedom.

Readers will no doubt compose mental lists of well-known and up-and-coming intellectuals who should be in this book—and we encourage you to do so. Our purpose is not to be all-inclusive but to be more inclusive, and along the way open up a space—beyond that of the surprisingly agile transformations of former old-school intellectuals who have adapted to, and to some degree influenced, new realities and as such remain relevant—to recognize what Mexicans already know: there is a new kind of Mexican public intellectual who can be found on the shelves of a Gandhi bookstore (and not always in the literature section), in the streets, or on TV. Those who are most successful in today's media and political climate have taken on new formats, even if the written word is often still the basis of most of their activities. Ignacio M. Sánchez Prado, in his chapter on Enrique Krauze, Aguilar Camín, and Jorge G. Castañeda (chapter 1), affirms "the need of intellectuals to rapidly adapt to new forms of discourse and practice, particularly considering that the three prevailing intellectual figures in 1980s Mexico—Carlos Fuentes, Carlos Monsiváis, and Octavio Paz—were all members of the lettered city whose claim to knowledge and authority came from granting literature a status of epistemological privilege and from literature's consecration in the mid-twentieth century as the discourse for the exploration and exposition of the national self." Sánchez-Prado works toward a definition of public intellectuals firmly grounded in Mexico, and along the way shows how intellectuals can be at once barometers and instigators of social change. Key to his argument is (1) that intellectuals like the three he treats remain relevant precisely because of their ability to evolve; (2) that as writers they have embraced a nonexclusive but significant move from literature to historiography as the preferred mode of reaching the reading public; and (3) that, as all other authors in this volume also contend, explicitly or implicitly, public intellectuals in Mexico are relevant because, though some lean more toward the Left and some toward the Right, they eschew dogmatism (which at times, of course, means that they will accuse each other of being dogmatic).

Sánchez Prado's discussion of former president Carlos Salinas de Gortari also takes up the latter's elastic use of the term "organic intellectual," the Gramscian concept that Adam David Morton studies in his 2003 article titled "The Social Function of Carlos Fuentes: A Critical Intellectual or in the 'Shadow of the State'?" published in the Bulletin of Latin American Research. Morton asks the question that underlies several chapters in this book: To what extent are public intellectuals co-opted? He writes: "Whilst the social function of Carlos Fuentes has been ambivalent, consisting of a mixture of critical opposition and accommodation, the overriding interpretation is that such intellectual agency has predominantly performed a function organic to dominant social forces within the state. The social function of the intellectual in this case is therefore certainly cast within the 'shadow of the state'" (48). Here we see the less commonly considered type of organic intellectual, who represents the "caviar left" (Morton, 46) and who, in doing so, often legitimizes dominant powers.

In chapter 2, Debra A. Castillo also treats the concept of complicity, noting—in her discussion of the framing of the so-called matriarchal Juchitán, a city of 60,000-plus residents in the state of Oaxaca—that "the uniqueness the country has to offer ironically comes from the vital indigenous cultures and languages that are consistently devalued both at home and abroad except as tourist sites or anthropological subjects." Castillo questions the role of intellectuals in selling "deep" Mexico nationally and internationally. Indeed, the public that public intellectuals engage often unwittingly includes providing local color for tourists. Andrés Henestrosa, the notable Zapotec intellectual and politician, played an important role in the construction of a utopian Juchitán in the international imaginary. In the next generation, Elena

Poniatowska visits Juchitán, producing the accompanying 1988 text to Graciela Iturbide's photographs. Henestrosa's and Poniatowska's texts closely mesh with many different needs: local, national, and international. The Mexican public intellectual in this case is balancing centripetal and centrifugal forces that on the one hand pull all cultural products and producers toward Mexico City, and on the other define deep national culture by the peripheries, a centrifugal movement out of the cosmopolitan center to the "untouched" indigenous past/present. In her analysis, Castillo also turns the table on readers, reminding us of the need to recognize the combination of fact and fiction in much of Poniatowska's writing.

In the third chapter, we see that public intellectuals in Mexico—this time with the beloved Carlos Monsiváis—can and do become household names. When the author of the chapter, María Cristina Pons, told a taxi driver the address where she was headed to interview this public figure (affectionately and widely called Monsi) who explained Mexican life to so many, the driver asked: "Ah, you're going to visit Monsiváis, the writer, right?" This chapter explains Monsiváis's theorizing of the concept of *relajo* within the context of the chaos of Mexico City—in a chapter that would no doubt please Monsiváis for its combination of "low" and "high" culture, for its artful weaving of anecdote and analysis. Monsiváis was at once accessible (and recognizable, perhaps more widely than anyone treated in this book) and, as Pons highlights, very difficult to read—especially for foreigners or others not in the know. Monsiváis was so unique that he was considered by Paz, as Pons notes, to *be* a genre of his own, and for Krauze, Monsiváis is "unrepeatable." Despite his immense popularity in Mexico, in some ways Monsiváis does not translate well. It is easy to find books in almost any US bookstore by Fuentes (both fiction and nonfiction), Paz, and Castañeda. Monsiváis is present, too, but not as often and with fewer titles. What Pons makes clear to an audience less familiar with Mexico is the degree of Monsiváis's commitment to all aspects of society—to the marginal in myriad forms—and the impact of his uncanny ability to "walk the streets of the city and allow the reality he witnesses to invade his text."

Pons's chapter on Monsiváis is followed by Emily Hind's analysis of another master of irony, Guadalupe Loaeza (chapter 4), who translates much easier in terms of both syntax and content. Hind writes about Loaeza and, among other topics, the gendered boundaries of intellectuals in Mexico and the trap (for women) of writing about popular culture: "Because she wasn't supposed to be an intellectual in the first place and because she writes about topics that lend themselves to frivolity, it is not surprising that Loaeza wrestles with a girlish media label, 'la eterna niña bien' (the eternal rich girl)." Hind's analysis of the way being in the spotlight, especially on television, feminizes the subject draws on two personal interviews with Loaeza and aid from Loaeza's political campaign manager. She provides an original understanding of Loaeza's career trajectory as a femininely styled television personality, newspaper columnist, essayist, and fiction writer. The idea of packaging, or marketing, runs through this and other chapters: intellectuals who are successful must market themselves and be cautious about how others portray them (think of the political commercial that twisted Poniatowska's words in support of Andrés Manuel López Obrador, and her effective if not game-changing counterattack). In combining a bit of Loaeza-style irony with academic analysis, Hind both reminds the reader of the real impact of machismo in the intellectual community and beyond and, more importantly, the savvy (and sassy) ways that women can and do win the spotlight.

In chapter 5, Stuart A. Day treats two figures from the world of theatre and performance—Sabina Berman and Jesusa Rodrígez—who, beginning with the 2006 elections, left the dramatic stage to take their places on the national stage, performing new roles as public intellectuals. Day recognizes the value and influence of theatre—especially when it comes to Berman and Rodríguez, two of Mexico's most successful theatre/performance practitioners—yet draws a line between the stage and the world of politics. The latter, to be sure, is theatrical, but personal interviews with these artists make it clear that their roles on the national stage superseded previous work. This includes Berman's role as cohost and now host of the TV Azteca program *Shalalá*, where she has interviewed everyone from presidents to the mothers of the young men and women who were kidnapped in the nightclub Heaven and murdered; and Rodriguez's work with the Andrés Manuel López Obrador's campaign team. In an interview with Day, Rodriguez speaks about leaving the comfort of her posh political cabaret space in the equally posh Coyoacán district of Mexico City:

> More than an extension, I would say that it's an absolute change to go beyond the cabaret—political farce created in an enclosed stage—and to take this work to its true setting, which is the street and the plaza. Then we can really say that it passes from one plane to another—completely different—where theater has direct political consequences, something that, as much as one tries, is not going to happen in the enclosed space of the cabaret. It's like talking about the map and talking about the land; we have now moved to the land. (Interview)

Of course, there are those who, while also feeling compelled to act, took a more circuitous and surprising (to them) route to public prominence. Such was that case of Esther Chávez Cano, an accountant who became a political activist (and a main character in Sabina Berman's movie *Backyard/Traspatio*) in Juárez, a city that has experienced tremendous violence related to the drug war and neoliberalism, the ideology that puts trade and privatization above social investment.

The author of the chapter on Chávez Cano (6), María Socorro Tabuenca Córdoba, is also a resident of the El Paso / Ciudad Juárez border region, and her work on Chávez Cano helps explain the call to action that many people who never thought of themselves as public figures experience when faced with an eroding social landscape. While many of the authors of this collection have firsthand experience with the public intellectuals about whom they write, Tabuenca's collaboration with Chávez Cano and other activists on the border offers a powerful example of the forays authors in this study make into the world beyond our classrooms. Chávez Cano became an intellectual as she became a public figure. Tabuenca writes, "Like a prophet, she anticipated the future and registered the present. Her pen never stopped documenting injustices and her voice—as low as it was—remained strong until the day she could not utter a sound. Esther never stopped denouncing impunity and demanding justice; never stopped articulating advocacy, agency, and justice on the US-Mexico Border." The sword is not always mightier than the pen, especially in Ciudad Juárez, but there are times worth studying and emulating where voices, especially unified voices, can be more powerful than governors, transnationals, and narcotraffickers.

The next two chapters (7 and 8) also treat people who engage in intellectual endeavors that place women at the center of social and artistic change: the work of Petrona de la Cruz and Isabel Juárez from the collective, women-based troupe Fortaleza de la Mujer Maya / Strength of Mayan women is treated by Elvira Sánchez Blake, who focuses on the use of theatre and performance to promote social equality; and that of the Mexican feminist filmmaker María Novaro who—as David William Foster underscores in his analysis of her films—challenges the male-centered action movie and in doing so achieves international recognition. These chapters highlight the different roles intellectuals can play, from the small stage, working one-on-one and in small groups to empower women, to the big screen, where masculinist, Hollywood narratives are undermined. Sánchez-Blake reminds the reader that the audiences of public intellectuals can vary in size and composition, arguing that "following the central theme of this book, Juárez and de la Cruz can be considered alternative public intellectuals because their influence reaches a non-traditional audience on one hand, and the broader circles of Mexican mestizos and intellectuals on the other," while Foster shows that Novaro stands alongside Mexican feminist intellectuals who have used powerful academic and political forums to express their understanding of women's lives in Mexico. If Juárez and de la Cruz are unique in their local (but internationally respected) work as indigenous playwrights, Novaro is unique in crafting a film career that has enabled her, through a very public and influential medium of cultural production, to articulate persuasive interpretations of women's issues on the national (and sometimes international) screen.

Chapter 9 by Oswaldo Estrada takes an unusual literary look at Subcomandante Marcos, noting that it is crucial to study "his literary communiqués because they embody the historical experience of the Zapatistas with an aesthetic touch that will certainly pass the test of time." The idea that literature can buttress and extend a social movement becomes clear through the analysis of two of Marcos's characters, Don Durito de la Lacandona, a beetle, and the Mayan Old Antonio (one surely fictitious and the other potentially so), as well as the collaborative novel that Marcos penned with Paco Ignacio Taibo II. Estrada's defense is twofold: he defends Marcos against those who, especially upon reading the coauthored mystery *Muertos Incómodos*, questioned Marcos's aesthetic and revolutionary staying power; and he defends the written word as a valuable mode for waging and sustaining a revolution. By studying Marcos's fiction, Estrada takes a different and less glamorous route to show that "Marcos behaves like an intellectual endowed with a faculty for representing the indigenous *Other*, or those who are routinely forgotten by the Mexican government."

The volume ends with a chapter (10) on Javier Sicilia, the poet who became a prominent voice for change upon the murder of his son. Javier Barroso paints a complex picture of this poet who leads the Movimiento por la Paz con Justicia y Dignidad, a movement that has seen a number of its members murdered and disappeared—yet another reminder of the potential dangers of being an engaged intellectual in Mexico. While Barroso notes that the worldwide movement for peace and democracy had a high point in Arab Spring (2011), he is clear, as is Sicilia, that Mexico's homegrown movement was instigated first and foremost by the murder of his son. As with many other intellectuals profiled in this book, Sicilia was surprised to find himself in the spotlight. Barroso traces, in work of Sicilia and others, the emergence (here Barroso works with Raymond Williams's concept of structures of feeling) of a more generalized feeling on the part of Mexicans that they must act out and speak up, despite the odds, in order to combat impunity. Barroso argues that the anarchist Christian poet turned his mourning into a national cause, and that his nonconformist attitude has made him an uncomfortable figure to both conservatives and liberals in Mexico.

There are, of course, other publications that treat the topic of public intellectuals in Latin America and beyond, indicating a heightened interest in the topic. The role of intellectuals in Latin America has also been studied, for example, in a noteworthy volume edited by Mabel Moraña and María Rosa Olivera-Williams (*El Salto de Minerva*). And recent, more general books like *Public Intellectuals: A Study of Decline* (Posner), *Public Intellectuals: An Endangered Species?* (Etzioni and Bowditch), and *Where Have All the Intellectuals Gone?* (Füredi) highlight anxiety at the seemingly reduced importance of intellectuals, in contrast with the case of the Mexican intellectuals engaged in this volume. They have all made unique and compelling incursions into central issues in Mexican life: elections, strikes, human rights, foreign policy, the drug war, among many other topics facing Mexico. And in many cases they venture well beyond the production of rarified knowledge to take to the streets, literally and figuratively.

Yet not all of these sociopolitical incursions, despite a general leaning toward progressive trends, are seen as exclusively so, making a nuanced reading of their engagement critical. A few examples: Jorge G. Castañeda was shunned by many when he took a position in President Vicente Fox's cabinet; Carlos Fuentes and Elena Poniatowska were criticized for not supporting students on strike at the National Autonomous University of Mexico at a crucial moment before armed government intervention; and Sabina Berman elicited passionate responses to her book *Un soplo en el corazón de la patria*, in which the leftist author refused to conclude prematurely and without further evidence that the 2006 election of Felipe Calderón had been achieved through fraud. It is the blurring of binaries (Left/Right, religious/secular, past/present, traditional/progressive) that enriches the chapters in this study, decentering our preconceptions and allowing us to promote meaningful dialogue in an ever-changing context. As noted above, one of the main currents in debates regarding public intellectuals, whether explicitly stated or not, is that of the organic intellectual. Stuart Hall notes, "Gramsci had a notion of two types of intellectual. 'Traditional intellectuals' merely refine existing knowledge as it is; they produce rarified and expanded knowledge but for the sake of the powers and structures that currently exist. In contrast, 'organic intellectuals' are those who are working critically and whose work is in some way aligned with emerging oppositional social forces" (de Peuter, 113). Whether these social forces in the end favor *los de abajo*, the underdogs, or not is one of the questions that makes it worthwhile to study the role of intellectuals in Mexico.

**Works Cited**

Berman, Sabina. Personal interview. June 24, 2008.

———. *Un soplo en el corazón de la patria: instantáneas de la crisis*. Mexico, DF: Planeta, 2006. Print.

Burnett, John. "Mexican Drug Cartels Now Menace Social Media." National Public Radio. September 23, 2011. http://www.npr.org/2011/09/23/140745739/mexican-drug-cartels-now-menace-social-media .Web.

Camp, Roderic Ai. *Intellectuals and the State in Twentieth-Century Mexico*. Austin: University of Texas Press, 1985. Print.

de Peuter, Greig. "Universities, Intellectuals, and Multitudes: An Interview with Stuart Hall." *Utopian Pedagogy: Radical Experiments against Neoliberal Globalization*. Edited by Mark Coté, Richard J. F. Day, and Greig de Peuter. Toronto: University of Toronto Press, 2007. 108–28. Print.

Etzioni, Amitai and Alyssa Bowditch. *Public Intellectuals: An Endangered Species?* New York: Rowman and Littlefield, 2006. Print.

Furedi, Frank. *Where Have All the Intellectuals Gone?: Confronting 21st Century Philistinism*. London and New York: Continuum, 2004.

Garber, Marjorie. "After the Humanities." Cornell University, Ithaca, NY. November 14, 2011. Lecture.

Grenier, Yvon. *From Art to Politics: Octavio Paz and the Pursuit of Freedom*. Lanham, MD: Rowman and Littlefield, 2001. Print.

Moraña, Mabel, and María Rosa Olivera-Williams. *El salto de Minerva: intelectuales, género y estado en América Latina*. Colección Nexos y Diferencias. Madrid; Frankfurt am Main: Iberoamericana/Vervuert, 2005. Print.

Morton, Adam David. "The Social Function of Carlos Fuentes: A Critical Intellectual or in the 'Shadow of the State'?" *Bulletin of Latin American Research* 22.1 (2003): 27–51. Print.

Posner, Richard A. *Public Intellectuals: A Study of Decline with a New Preface and Epilogue*. Cambridge, MA: Harvard University Press, 2003. Print.

Rich, Adrienne. "Blood, Bread, and Poetry: The Location of the Poet." *Blood, Bread, and Poetry: Selected Prose, 1979–1985*. New York: Norton, 1986. 167–87. Print.

Rodríguez, Jesusa. Personal interview. June 19, 2008.

## Chapter 1

# The Democratic Dogma: Héctor Aguilar Camín, Jorge G. Castañeda, and Enrique Krauze in the Neoliberal Crucible

*Ignacio M. Sánchez Prado*

One of the salient traits of Mexico's unfinished transition to democracy is the ubiquity of its intellectuals across mediascapes. All major radio and television networks recruit intellectuals as opinion makers and as hosts of nightly news shows, while local and national newspapers grant them a daily forum in their op-ed sections. The country has many leading magazines and newsweeklies (from *Letras Libres* and *Nexos* to *Metapolítica* and *Proceso*) where intellectuals play predominant roles and where their voices are heard alongside those of the politicians who seek to position themselves in the media and the journalists who report on the country's daily life. Intellectuals have even reached high spheres of government and civil society: many founding figures of the Federal Electoral Institute (IFE) came from intellectual ranks, and writers, critics, commentators, and scholars have served in positions ranging from diplomatic outposts to local and federal cabinet offices. As I write this article, poet Javier Sicilia (the subject of chapter 11) is leading a nationwide caravan for peace in the wake of his son's murder in the city of Cuernavaca, representing those who have been affected by the government's war on drugs. The fact that a poet, of all people, is able to attain such a public status in a country where most relatives and loved ones of the thousands of victims of crime and drug violence have been silenced, ignored, or even criminalized, attests to the power and the symbolic aura still enjoyed by the intellectual class.

In this chapter, I will argue that this constant presence in the public sphere, or in civil society, results from a major transformation in the notion of the intellectual and her perceived responsibilities in Mexico since the 1980s. Among the factors that contributed to this transformation, I will underscore three: the decline of the traditional "literary" intellectual (embodied by figures like Octavio Paz and Carlos Fuentes)[1] in favor of the rise of an intermedial intellectual, who combines the practices of the "lettered city"[2] with other forms of media and with intellectual disciplines beyond the humanities; the emergence of practices of journalism and communication in post-1988 media, which allows intellectuals to become communicators and opinion leaders in a much wider sense of the term; and the reconfiguration of traditional functions of the literary intellectual ("legislation" and "interpretation," to use Zygmunt Bauman's terms[3]) in the post-NAFTA cultural landscape, in relation to the emergence of the figure of the technocrat. I will analyze this process through the work of three leading intellectual figures—Héctor Aguilar Camín, Jorge Castañeda, and Enrique Krauze—who, in my view, represent the most important aspects of this transformation. To be sure, the topic is vast and it is not my intention to exhaust it in any way. Instead, I will try to point out the ways in which the trajectory of these three figures, particularly in the wake of the 1988 presidential election, provide important issues through which the very concept of public intellectuals in Mexico may be rethought, and their complex institutional articulation of that concept, which goes beyond the limits established by twentieth-century theories of the intellectual.[4] Rather than trying to confine Castañeda, Aguilar Camín, and Krauze to defined notions of the public intellectual, I will invoke the term as a notion in constant redefinition. The three authors studied here, therefore, construct their own practice as "public intellectuals" on the basis of their self-fashioning *vis-à-vis* the public and the specific ideologies and theoretical genealogies deployed in their work. In adopting this approach, I hope to demonstrate that the prevalence of the intellectual as a key figure in Mexican public life—in contrast to the proverbial decline of the public intellectual in countries like the United States[5]—rests on the basis of historical specificities that redefined intellectual work in the early 1990s.

Considering the role played by public intellectuals in Mexico, it is not at all surprising that even the most powerful men and women in the country engage with intellectuals in quarrels and controversies. One recent and notable example of such engagements takes place in former president Carlos Salinas de Gortari's book *Democracia republicana* (2010). The book is a manifesto in favor of what Salinas de Gortari terms "social liberalism," the doctrine he claims to have developed as president and that, in his narrative, was betrayed and dismantled by his successors' neoliberal policies. We may leave aside, for now, the fact that Salinas de Gortari is a reviled figure in Mexico, credited mostly with introducing the very neoliberal reforms he now claims to reject and with leading the country into disaster in 1994, when Mexico faced the assassination of two major political figures, the Zapatista rebellion, the implementation of NAFTA, and the worst financial crisis in recent history. *Democracia republicana* is a telling document not only because a figure identified with him, Enrique Peña Nieto, won the 2012 presidential election, but also because it provides a unique reading of Mexico in the wake of neoliberalism.

For my purposes, I want to point out that Salinas devotes one of his chapters to a critique of what he calls Mexico's "organic intellectuals" (541). Not surprisingly, three of Salinas de Gortari's targets are Krauze, Castañeda, and Aguilar Camín. In the former president's words, "Enrique Krauze is at the top of the list of organic intellectuals sympathetic to the neoliberal governments that have ruled the country in recent presidential terms, certainly with the reservations implied in the certainty that there exists, among today's Mexican intellectuals, the clear inclination to be carried away by the winds of the government at hand" (549. My translation). Salinas thus attacks Mexican intellectuals like Krauze and Castañeda on the grounds that they were supportive of his reforms in the early 1990s, and that Krauze became an "enthusiastic" supporter of the subsequent "neoliberal" governments. In his telling, Castañeda experienced a similar conversion, from his ardent opposition to NAFTA in the early 1990s to his alleged support of pro-American policies, such as Mexico's vote for the war in Iraq in the UN Security Council (569–70).[6]

The notable thing about Salinas de Gortari's argument is that, behind the superficiality of his critique and the many half-truths that sustain his contentions, his assessment of Krauze, Castañeda, and others accurately identifies a major switch in Mexican intellectual work in the wake of the 1994 crisis. However, Salinas de Gortari errs in his interpretation of the underlying causes. It is true that many Mexican intellectuals have intermittently supported state policies from all the post-1988 administrations, and that in some cases one can read their support as instances of political accommodation. Nonetheless, the alleged complicity of intellectuals with power is too simplistic an explanation because, even in the cases in which an intellectual is effectively "organic," there is usually an underlying doctrine to justify such a choice. Part of the problem is that Salinas de Gortari's Gramscian framework of analysis, one that remains quite popular in the successive reconstitutions of the theories of the intellectual, either leads to the easy disqualification of any engagement with the State as "complicity," or idealizes 1960s forms of engaged intellectualism over perceived ideas of the "institutionalized" intellectual prevalent from the 1980s onward.[7] Furthermore, it is important to remember that the Gramscian model of analysis itself has deep roots in the distinction between an intellectual engaged with society and one who chooses independence and autonomy from the social, as well as in the definition of the "organic intellectual" as the philosopher in the service of the people, not of the ruling order (Fontana, 24–34).

All these limitations heighten the need for an understanding of the intellectual in a transitional setting, such as the one experienced by Mexico in the 1990s, which leaves aside value judgments and assessments of individual intellectuals' affinity with power. The crucial issue, rather, is that major changes in the ideological paradigm of a country's intellectual class and the corresponding change in function of intellectuals *vis-à-vis* the public sphere signal a major transformation in the very logic of political and social knowledge. In these terms, I would contend that the iconic roles played by Castañeda, Krauze, and Aguilar Camín in post-1988 Mexico stem from their ability to register dramatic changes in the episteme that configures the fabric of discourse upon which the Mexican transition was fashioned. In other words, their trajectories represent three distinct ways of successfully reinventing the relationship between intellectuals, power and civil society in a context where the prevailing definitions of all three of these categories experienced dramatic changes. One could indeed locate this change somewhere in between the mid- and late-1980s, when the PRI's stronghold in Mexican society was undermined by the early instances of social organization unleashed by the 1985 earthquake[8] and by the crisis of legitimacy caused by the questioned 1988 election. The depth of the epistemic change faced by Mexican intellectuals in this period resulted from the historical coincidence of three seismic shifts in the ideological basis of the nation's polity: the defeat of the old nationalist revolutionary ideals embodied by the Cárdenas candidacy; the apparent (though not lasting) success of *Salinista* policies, based on the mixture of neoliberal economic reform and in the cooptation of citizenship organization into state organized structures of decentralized social policy; and the emergence of a new class of knowledge producers—technocrats, economists—who competed with traditional intellectuals in the definition of policy and public discourse.

This last point is particularly crucial to understand the need of intellectuals to rapidly adapt to new forms of discourse and practice, particularly considering that the three prevailing intellectual figures in 1980s Mexico—Carlos Fuentes, Carlos Monsiváis, and Octavio Paz—were all members of the lettered city whose claim to knowledge and authority came from granting literature a status of epistemological privilege and from literature's consecration in the mid-twentieth century as the discourse for the exploration and exposition of the national self. Furthermore, regardless of the many differences and quarrels among them, Paz, Fuentes, and Monsiváis operated within a liberal paradigm that, following models like Isaiah Berlin and Julien Benda, predicated the role of culture and the humanities as platforms of autonomy *vis-à-vis* the state and as strategies of construction of a civil society—or an "open society," to use the Karl Popper term favored by Paz—to independently organize the citizenry.[9] One of the early effects of liberalism was the vertiginous rise of economics as an alternative regime of knowledge and expertise that directly challenged lettered city models of intellectual practice. As Sarah Babb (171–98) and Roderic Ai Camp (*Mexico's Mandarins*, 2002) have aptly documented, a new generation of economists with doctoral degrees from US universities joined the political fray as Mexico negotiated its opening to international trade with the World Bank in 1986. This generation would go on to shape the core of subsequent governments. This exclusive and highly educated elite created an alternative regime of knowledge that had nothing to do with the "civil society" advocated by literary intellectuals, one that favored quantitative social-scientific knowledge over ideological and cultural discourses. This type of knowledge was not exclusive to economists and invaded even the very territory where lettered intellectuals thrived throughout the twentieth century: print media. As José Antonio Aguilar Rivera recalls, "the rise of pollsters and efforts to measure public opinion on contemporary issues seems to be undermining one of the historical roles of Mexican public intellectuals: to be the interpreters of civil society" (103). The emergence of quantitative measurement of public opinion in the mid-1990s, and the important role that polling played in creating conditions of credibility in electoral processes, allowed for the incorporation of discourses outside of the intellectual sphere into Mexico's public conversation (Camp, *Polling*,1996).

This neural period became crucial in redefining the intellectual work of Aguilar Camín, Krauze, and Castañeda, each of whom published works between 1988 and 1994 that represented major turning points in the very nature of intellectual practice in Mexico. Aguilar Camín was an early interpreter of this phenomenon, as shown in his book *Después del milagro* (1988). The book is an in-depth analysis of two sets of trends. On the one hand, Aguilar Camín defines four "superstructural" trends, namely "transformations in the system of political domination": the decline of the state and the rise of civil society; the breakup of the relationship between government, labor, and capitalist organizations; the loss of state control in the countryside and the cities; and the transition from "absolutist presidentialism" to "constitutional presidentialism" (16–17. My translation). On the other, Aguilar Camín highlights four "structural" trends, that is, "civilizational transitions of a wider historical horizon": the shift from being a rural country to becoming an urban one, and the corresponding decentralization of the state apparatus; the country's integration into the world economy; a strengthening social inequality; and the emergence of a "new people," that is, a "new national mental, social and political majority" (17. My translation). If we read this diagnosis carefully, it becomes clear that Aguilar Camín is identifying the opening of a radically new terrain for intellectual action. If the state declines to the benefit of an expanded society, which results from the "structural" emergence of a "new people" that presumably overrides the national subject constructed by postrevolutionary ideas and processes, it follows that public intellectuals have an obligation not only to be interpreters of this change, but also to contribute to the very constitution of the new order. In fact, some of the other trends in Aguilar Camín's narrative favor a potential new role for public intellectuals: the shift from rural to urban populations brings more citizens under the aegis of intellectual action, while the breakup of corporate and labor organizations creates an opening for new forms of social movement organization.

*Después del milagro* is a book that seizes the opportunities created by the questioned 1988 election to argue for a change in the very nature of the political system. Aguilar Camín implicitly refuses to endorse the idea of electoral fraud—by saying that voters "renewed the mandate of continuity to the regime [ ... ] as someone who grants a last chance"—and his recognition of Cuauhtémoc Cárdenas's candidacy walks a fine line between praising his role in the country's democratization and rejecting the content of his political platform: "Under the *cardenista* convergence, the July voters questioned the modernizing path of the current government and sought in the past—in the populist and inefficient past remembered, regardless of everything, as better—a way less alien to the country's history and traditions" (293. My translation). In claiming that the alternative to the PRI is in fact not a modern alternative, and that the political system does not represent the "structural" changes experienced by Mexican society, Aguilar Camín opens the path for public intellectuals to conceive of and define new forms of citizenship. Aguilar Camín is particularly drawn to the idea of recognizing the cornerstone issue of the Mexican Left, the country's chronic economic and social inequality, and situating it within a paradigm of thinking that renounces Marxist notions of revolution in favor of a more institutionalized idea of social transformation. Aguilar Camín clarifies that, while he "never was a Marxist [ ... ], [t]he only discourse that, in Mexico, really posed the question of inequality and justice, besides the PRI rhetoric, was the discourse of the left" (Toledo and Trejo, 18. My translation). One could argue that *Después del milagro* foresees a paradigmatic change in the discourses of non-regime Mexican intellectuals in some portions of the Left, where the goals of justice and equality would be reached not by traditional socialist dogma but by the construction of a new paradigm of modernity that would respond to the new historical conditions of a country that had been structurally transformed.

The point in identifying long-term structural changes underlying the more obvious superstructural ones, and by doing so coyly invoking Marxist terminology for non-Marxist ends, is that received political paradigms are no longer adequate to respond to the country's new modernity. The intellectual thus emerges as an agent capable of performing "silent subversions," a term that Aguilar Camín borrows from French historian François Xavier Guerra's 1985 book *Le Mexique*. Guerra argues that the 1910 revolution was the result of the accumulation of changes performed under the Porfirio Díaz regime, showing a particular interest in the interaction between tradition and cultural elites. This interest, as well as his interpretation of the revolution as the passage from a traditionalist *Ancien Régime* to a modern country, makes Aguilar Camín's adoption of his term quite meaningful. He interprets the potential democratic transformation of Mexico as the result of long-term "silent subversions" (his "structural" changes) as opposed to outbursts of popular mobilization, like the 1985 protests, which would fall under the "superstructural" category. In following Guerra's concept, Aguilar Camín finds a blueprint for a particular kind of intellectual action. In a 1992 text included in *Subversiones silenciosas*, Aguilar Camín asserts that free-market reforms constitute a "new international paradigm," which may potentially result in the demand for more political competition (178–84). If democratization is the space of action of the intellectual, and if economic reform is a path to it, it follows that the public intellectual must craft an alliance with the emerging technocratic class in order to push for the "structural" changes needed in Mexico.

One simply has to take a look at Aguilar Camín's editorial vehicles, his monthly magazine *Nexos* and his book publishing company Cal y Arena, to see such an alliance in action. If one revisits Cal y Arena's catalog in the 1988–1993 period, one can find, alongside the house's tradition of publishing literary fiction and criticism, an interesting set of books that showcase the coexistence of intellectual assessments of Mexico's historical legacy, claims for democracy from Mexico's political class and an interest in economic reform. In the first category, we find Aguilar Camín and Lorenzo Meyer's landmark reassessment of the Mexican revolutionary process, *A la sombra de la Revolución Mexicana* (1989), as well as Castañeda's first major assessment of Mexican foreign policy, *La casa por la ventana* (1993). In the second, we see Raúl Trejo Delarbre's reflection on the relationship between democracy and the media in *La sociedad ausente* (1992), as well as PAN operative Juan Molinar Horcasitas's *El tiempo de la legitimidad* (1991), which was an argument for the reform of the Mexican electoral system. Finally, the third category is represented by books squarely focused on economic policy, such as Guillermo and Jones's *Contra la pobreza* (1992), which compiles articles by noted economists and political scientists, or Edna's *Lo hecho en México* (1993), an argument for free trade.

This balance between literature and economic and political issues is also clear in *Nexos*' editorial line. Unlike *Vuelta*, which always gave literature the central role in its intellectual constellation, *Nexos* gradually developed an editorial profile that privileged major features on politics and economics. According to Maarten Van Delden, the two magazines are characterized by their distinct notions of the public intellectual. On the one hand, *Nexos* is devoted to the idea that, even though the intellectual belongs to the social elite, her work must be in service to society. Conversely, Van Delden argues, *Vuelta*'s main commitment was to the idea of intellectual freedom and the intellectual's resistance to represent or advocate any predefined political program. This, Van Delden concludes, led to a major difference in political attitudes, since Aguilar Camín was "irritated" by Octavio Paz's pessimism and sought to place the intellectual in a more positive social role ("Conjunciones y disyunciones," 108–9). Predictably, the *salinista* period generated major conflict between the two magazines, particularly because of Paz's reluctance to embrace the type of transformational discourse advocated by Aguilar Camín. This was proven, for instance, by Paz's rejection of the major conference organized by Aguilar Camín, the famous *Coloquio de invierno*, an attempt to identify and push forward social and political reforms.

Perhaps the most surprising and original trait of Aguilar Camín's work in the period stems from the fact that, of all the members of the new cadre of public intellectuals in the late 1980s, he is the only one with a prolific and acclaimed trajectory as a novelist. One should remember here Aguilar Camín's major novels of the period: *Morir en el Golfo* (1989), which focused on a fictional leader of Mexico's oil labor union, and *La guerra de Galio* (1991), a voluminous exploration of the political legacies of the 1968 massacre. Besides the commercial success reflected in the many reprints of both books, literary critics have widely praised Aguilar Camín's fiction as a major instance of political literature. Alberto Moreiras, for instance, has stated that "both novels theorize a crucial moment of decision, beyond any program, and it is a moment that in each case sutures the relationship between ethics and politics" (78). In other words, Moreiras argues that Aguilar Camín's fictional work resists the temptation to praise things such as "democratic volunteerism" and that his characters' inability to complete their sociopolitical decisions gives literature the ability to reflect on politics proper rather than on the virtues of any specific political standpoint. Moreiras thus concludes: "That literature, in these two texts by Aguilar Camín, finds itself at the service of politics, means that literature, in this case, reclaims its undeniable privilege as a means of thinking about democracy, which is also, or above all, a means of imagining the possibility of a decision outside of any calculating reason" (82). In my view, this analysis closely mirrors Aguilar Camín's claim of "structural changes" as the proper space for intellectual reflection, signaling that fiction works as a staging of the dilemmas faced by intellectuals in a moment of deep paradigmatic change. Moreiras's insistence on the idea of a decision "outside of any calculating reason" as the condition for using literature to "think about democracy" aptly illustrates Aguilar Camín's attempt to position his own work as transcending the inherited paradigms of revolutionary nationalism. Another literary critic, Ryan F. Long, advances a similar point. For Long, *Morir en el Golfo* is "a text that helps explain why appeals to the national totality could no longer support an inclusive ideology that concealed political domination once the national-popular state's hegemony was irreparably damaged by the oil bust and the devastating debt crisis it produced" (54). By addressing the failure of one of Mexico's cornerstone revolutionary achievements, the nationalized oil industry, Aguilar Camín uses fiction to ponder the exhaustion of the postrevolutionary paradigm, and to explain his reticence to praise Cuauhtémoc Cárdenas, the son of the president who nationalized the oil industry, in *Después del milagro*. Paradoxically, the novel puts Aguilar Camín in the same ideological territory as many of the technocratic reformers, who saw the privatization of national industries as a central component of their reform agendas.

In spite of the importance of Aguilar Camín's fiction in the formation of his identity as a public intellectual, the late 1980s are in fact a period in which literary fiction as an instrument of societal interpretation is in frank decline. The gradual erosion of revolutionary discourse in the wake of the 1982 debt crisis and the 1985 earthquake resulted in the emergence of history as the central discursive site of intervention for public intellectuals. Fiction itself registered that process. As many critics have noted,[10] the most important literary works of the period, including Fernando del Paso's *Noticias del Imperio* and Rosa Beltrán's *La corte de los ilusos*, were historical novels. This meant that many emerging public intellectuals, including Héctor Aguilar Camín and, of course, Enrique Krauze, wrote major history books and developed highly personal forms of historiography to accompany their ideological and social agendas. Aguilar Camín, for instance, wrote major revisions of accepted paradigms of Mexican revolutionary history, including *La frontera nómada* (1977), which highlights the role of Sonora and northern Mexico in the revolution against the grain of centralized accounts of the event. More importantly, Aguilar Camín authored two major books, *Saldos de la Revolución* (1982) and the aforementioned *A la sombra de la Revolución Mexicana*, which displace the interpretation of the revolution from a reminiscence of the revolutionary war to a *long durée* understanding of its consequences spanning the entire twentieth century. The essential point here is that, in gradually positioning the lettered aspects of public intellectual work away from literature and closer to history and historiography, Aguilar Camín and Krauze open the door for more interdisciplinary and intermedial pursuits, which are crucial to the survival of intellectuals as public figures in the neoliberal period.

One of Krauze's early works, *Caras de la historia* (1983), laid some of the groundwork for history's emerging centrality in Mexican public discourse. In the brief prologue, Krauze explains his preference for biographical history by arguing against an impersonal and structural understanding of history. In these terms, Krauze sustains that eschewing the role of the individual in history "denies liberty and leads, in the end, to historical impunity" (10. My translation). This historiographical axiom is as consistent with two central values of Mexico's democratizing process—individual agency and accountability—as it is a diagnosis of Mexico's historical tradition of embodying the sovereign and the popular in iconic figures or *caudillos*: Hidalgo,

Madero, Zapata, and so on. *Caras de la historia* also vindicates an interpretive and public notion of history based on the right to use history for contemporary causes (16). Krauze's method is based on the idea that history must seek to be a public discourse and resist what Herbert Butterfield called "The Whig Interpretation of History" (17), namely, the transformation of the present's reflection of the past into "historiographic technique" (17–18). Krauze also adopts Luis González's idea of "Bronze History" to designate and reject institutional understandings of history in the service of state power (18). The neural role these notions play in Krauze's positioning within Mexico's intellectual field is such that he devotes the first section of a recent book, *De héroes y mitos* (2010), to attacking both state-oriented history and academic history. Krauze's long-running critique of academia's opaque prose and his skeptical views on theory are based on the idea that "history is not, cannot be, a discipline for the initiated, an impenetrable writing" (*Entre héroes*, 52. My translation). History, for Krauze, is meaningful only if it reaches a wider audience and if it contributes to the reconfiguration of civil society's relationship to power. This is why Krauze developed an entrepreneurial dimension in his intellectual work very early on, which he then used to construct one of Mexico's most notable media ventures: Editorial Clío.

Given Krauze's insistence on infusing history into public discourse, it is important to recall that the turn to history resulted from the public intellectuals' newfound access to electronic media. Paz, Fuentes, and other writers had been able to develop a media presence, but it was mostly in the context of strictly cultural television shows, like the 1988 TV series *México en la obra de Octavio Paz* or Fuentes's landmark mini-series *El espejo enterrado* (1994). It is important to note that both these series were in fact of a historical nature. While Aguilar Camín would have major forays into media, including his literary show *Los libros tienen la palabra* (in the late 1980s) and a political show entitled *Zona abierta* (in the early 2000s), Krauze is the leading figure of the transition to history and the full-fledged entrance to media. In direct reference to Krauze, Claudio Lomnitz has discussed the role of history during the "neoliberal moment." According to Lomnitz, Mexico experiences "an excess of historical invocation—or historical obsession—[as] a diagnostic sign of failed modernities" (39). In other words, the rise of history results from the failure of the modernizing project of the revolution and the need to reinterpret the past in a context where that project no longer needs to be legitimized. Another important insight in Lomnitz's article rests on his insistence on linking journalism to history, since the "excess of historical invocation" is only possible when it resonates beyond academic and lettered circles. Randal Sheppard has recently expanded Lomnitz's thesis by arguing that nationalism and history were not only used by the State, but also as "a shared framework for communicating opposition to the state to a national audience" (515). The emergence of historical discourse and its subsequent articulation to media takes place mostly due to the fact that public intellectuals are able to reinterpret widely known frameworks of public historical knowledge into the emerging ideological paradigms of civil society and democratization. Here, one could revise Bauman's idea that intellectuals evolve from modern "legislators" of culture and taste to "interpreters" of the world at large, by pointing out that Mexican intellectuals work in the simultaneous operation of both paradigms: interpretations of history that result in a legislative role in civil society. The wide resonance of historical interpretations put forward by intellectuals like Krauze allowed them to play a major role in the formation of Mexico's ideas of civil society and democratization.

Krauze's major interventions in this process are registered in his 1992 book *Textos heréticos*, a gathering of texts written in the 1980s and the second of the three iconic books of the period. The book's ample scope covers Mexico, Latin America, and the global transformations brought about by the decline of the Soviet Union. The main narrative is centered upon the idea of the end of the three "creeds" that sustained Mexico throughout its postindependence history: the nineteenth-century clerical/conservative creed, the revolutionary creed of the twentieth century and the Marxist creed long thought of as the alternative to the *status quo*. In a way, this work is aimed at clearing the sociopolitical and ideological terrain of hegemony[11] toward the construction of a new liberal ideal. I have argued in detail elsewhere[12] that Krauze's main influences—Isaiah Berlin and Edmund Wilson, among others—led him to a particular idea of liberalism as the ideology that upholds freedom over right-wing and left-wing "tyrannies," as well as to a practice of historiography focused on a biographical approach based on ideas of individualism. Furthermore, his influences convinced him of the importance of unique transformational figures in historical processes. This latter understanding of history is at the base of Krauze's media success. His first major foray was as a writer of documentaries based on major figures of the Mexican Revolution, along with books on those figures in the mass distribution market. This would, in turn, give Krauze the ability to construct a major media company by way of his Clio publishing house, which includes books, two long-running television series on Mexican history, the magazine *Letras Libres* that took over the legacy of Octavio Paz's *Vuelta*, and even a stint as a writer for the historical soap opera *El vuelo del águila*. Part of this success undoubtedly corresponds to Lomnitz's diagnosis of a need for history in a country too aware of its failed modernity, but another fundamental part of Krauze's major role in the media undoubtedly comes from his prescient understanding of the ideological frameworks of the Mexican transition and his ability to take over from Carlos Fuentes and Octavio Paz in shaping major interpretive spaces of the country's history.

The starting point of Krauze's success is his famously scathing attack on Fuentes, "La comedia mexicana de Carlos Fuentes," included in *Textos heréticos*. Part of the resonance and visibility of this text was due to Krauze's ability to publish it not only in *Vuelta*, which perhaps was aided by Paz's own fallout with Fuentes, but also in *The New Republic*, a magazine that shares major affinities with Krauze's work and where he is currently credited as a contributing editor. The text can be read as Krauze's attack on the epistemological privilege of literature among intellectual discourses through an indictment of what, in his view, is a problematic complicity with outdated ideologies stemming from the Cuban Revolution. Krauze's core attack focuses on what he deemed Fuentes's inability to read the values of democracy: "[to Fuentes,] democracy does not reveal the *whole* history of a community, only the fragmentary will of its citizens" (53. Emphasis in the original, my translation). Furthermore, Krauze argues that Fuentes has an "identity scar" that produces a "love-hate feeling toward the United States," which preempts "any intrinsic understanding of Latin American phenomena" (53. My translation). In attacking Fuentes, Krauze achieves three fundamental goals in his positioning as a public intellectual. First, following the lead of Octavio Paz, he declares the exhaustion of any form of political and cultural imagination resulting from both nationalism and Cuban-inspired Latin Americanism, thus opening the space for his brand of liberalism as an instrument of modernization. Second, by attacking Fuentes's infamous defense of Luis Echeverría in spite of Echeverría's role in the 1968 massacre, and the accompanying diagnosis of Mexico in Fuentes's 1971 book *Tiempo mexicano*, Krauze is able to portray Fuentes as a man with an uncomfortable relationship with power, against which Krauze (and Aguilar Camín) could fashion themselves as representatives of civil society in its struggle against a nondemocratic state. Finally, and perhaps most meaningfully, Krauze questions Fuentes's idea of literary totality by sustaining that his fiction falls short of its ambition to represent history due to his characters' proclivity to reflect his personal self. By attacking Fuentes's political credibility and the paradigm of fiction he represents, Krauze is able to construct himself as a model for an intellectual removed from the seduction of state-centric tyranny and to favor historical work over fiction as the privileged intellectual activity in a democratic society. It is thus central here that Fuentes's purported affinity with power and his individualistic notion of the novel in spite of its historical claims—which, interestingly, were the same attacks that intellectuals directly tied to the Cuban Revolution levied at him (Fernandez Retamar, 71–82)—are consistent with the legacies both of the PRI and the Cuban Revolution. In the task of creating a new kind of intellectual practice in Mexico, Krauze deftly embodies in his account of Fuentes all the elements he regards as outdated, outmoded, and even immoral.

The concept behind the book's title and the tone of his many attacks against conservatism, the clergy, Marxism, and nationalism show the central axiom behind Krauze's notion of critique. By invoking the idea of heresy to define his stance against what Krauze calls "dogmas," *Textos heréticos* operates under the idea that the role of the intellectual is to question accepted frameworks of political and social discourse by exposing their inner contradictions and their historical aporias. Furthermore, his work implicitly defines this essential task against a Marxist notion of critique, where the study and exposition of the inner contradictions of capitalism ultimately serve Marxist dogmas. Krauze's liberalism understands critique as part of a civil society in which democracy is measured by the plurality of voices within it. It is thus crucial that there is no preexisting ideological paradigm in the act of critique: the freedom of the critic is a function of her commitment to expose the contradictions of power and of her reluctance to put her intelligence at the service of dogma. While this stance is not far from the *ethos* behind many concepts of the intellectual—one can think here of Edward Said's imperative of "speaking truth to power" (Said, *Representations*)—it is important to keep in mind that the ultimate result of Krauze's work was his emergence as a major hegemonic figure within Mexico's cultural field. Krauze's impeccable command of the public uses of history, both in book form and in electronic media, particularly in contrast with Carlos Fuentes's gradual exit from Mexico's intellectual spotlight, is a testament of how transformational his work was in the very construction of cultural capital in contemporary Mexico.

It is important to note here that, even though Krauze and Aguilar Camín may have differences of opinion, their work ultimately rests on a very similar concept of democracy as a modern form of polity that overrides revolutionary nationalism and grants relief from twentieth-century authoritarian ideologies. Krauze's work's core principle is the idea of democracy as the necessary starting point to overcome the outdated political programs of the twentieth century. Krauze proposed this concept in a 1983 essay and developed it into the book *Por una democracia sin adjetivos* (1986). Krauze contends in this book that "democratic liberalism" was never accepted in the twentieth century due to the "prestige of the State as a lever for modernization, equality and justice" (11. My translation). This idea may not sound different from the points advanced by Aguilar Camín in *Después del milagro*. However, *Por una democracia sin adjetivos* boldly advances the critique of the state as an instrument of modernity by arguing that, in every major variant of political and economic discourse—from the welfare state and Keynesian economics to fascism and Stalinism—the strengthening of the state was the central result. In other words, Krauze defines liberalism in opposition to what he considers the authoritarian strand underlying every major political and economic program of the twentieth century. While Krauze would probably not deny the major differences of degree between Keynesian regulation and Stalinist purges, his point is that the faith in the state severely undermined democracy's role in constructing a functional polity. Thus, when turning to Mexico, Krauze claims that the problem is that postrevolutionary nationalism, as an idea well inscribed into the paradigms of the twentieth century, followed the same pattern and gradually annulled democratic participation. The key conclusion in this book is that liberalism is not a political position in itself, but the defense of freedom, plurality, and democracy, understood as a form of social "coexistence" (14). The political program put forward by *Por una democracia sin adjetivos* was in fact simple: the limitation of government action, the emergence of a viable political party system and the existence of a press independent from the State (74). Krauze's contribution in this regard is that his work represented one of the earliest formulations of the agendas for democratization that would define Mexican civil society as late as the 2000s. To be sure, Krauze himself remains committed to the ideas advanced in his works in the 1980s. When he gathered his most important political writings in his book *Tarea política* (2000), published on the eve of the presidential election in recognition of the upcoming end of the PRI regime, Krauze placed his 1986 book within a timeline of writings that repeat the same principles: a suspicious view of political authoritarianism, an antagonical vision of left-wing nationalism, and a credo centered on democracy as the ultimate value. That these ideas have become central to major segments of Mexico's *intelligentsia* shows the impact Krauze has had in defining the ideas of post-PRI Mexico.[13]

While Aguilar Camín and Krauze set the stage for a new generation of intellectuals focused on the democratic transition, a third book, Jorge Castañeda's *La utopía desarmada* (1993), provided the language that allowed Mexican—and many Latin American—intellectuals to overcome the imperatives of twentieth-century leftism. Castañeda's work embodies one of the most astonishing and drastic evolutions in personal ideology in the entire Mexican intellectual field. The son of one of Mexico's top diplomats, Castañeda's early books were written well within the paradigms of Latin American dependency theory. His 1980 book *Nicaragua: Contradicciones en la Revolución* was an early assessment of Sandinismo on the basis of the contradiction between the movement's emancipatory nature and its economic dependence on foreign powers. His second book, *Los últimos capitalismos*, is undoubtedly paradoxical from a contemporary perspective. In this book, Castañeda assesses the perceived decline of US capitalism and the emergence of "Southern" capitalist economies like South Korea and Brazil, mounting an argument that is not too different from the mainstream diagnosis around the US economic decline and the rise of BRIC countries in today's print media,[14] fully argued through a revised Leninist framework. Castañeda's work starts distancing itself from his earlier dogmas and begins to shift toward the ideas that would define the latter part of his career in the late 1980s. This transformation is due to Castañeda's emerging role as a transnationalized interpreter of Mexican reality, whose work on Mexico is constructed upon his dialogues with European and North American academic and journalistic circles. In *México: El futuro en juego* (1987), a compilation of his journalistic writings from the mid-1980s, Castañeda sheds the Leninist terminology and adopts issues of diplomacy to assess Mexico's political and social transitions. Castañeda is particularly interested in Mexico's role in the wake of Central America's conflicts, which, in turn, shook Castañeda's initial enthusiasm regarding the Sandinista project. By 1986, in an article published in *Foreign Affairs* and in *Nexos*—following the same blueprint of binational public interventions used by Krauze in his polemic with Fuentes—Castañeda joins the intellectual chorus asking for democratic and economic reform and criticizing the entrenched structures of the PRI. Interestingly, by this point, Castañeda's assessment is not too different from the one advanced by Aguilar Camín in *Después del milagro*, as both argue in favor of pro-market economic reform and political democratization. The key book in Castañeda's intellectual evolution, however, is *Limits to Friendship* (1988). Coauthored with Robert Pastor, this book is Castañeda's first major assessment of the US-Mexico relationship, a topic central to his intellectual work from this point on. I would argue that, in writing this book, Castañeda departs from the dependency theory that still plagued *México: El futuro en juego*, recognizing for the first time the crucial role that the United States has in understanding Mexico. Given that NAFTA was around the corner, Castañeda identifies in *Limits to Friendship* a way to overcome the militant nationalism of the Mexican intellectual class, as he became one of the first major intellectuals to come out in favor of privileging the relationship with the United States over the Latin Americanist fidelities developed in connection with the Cuban and the Sandinista revolutions. It is also important to point out that Castañeda published the book simultaneously in English and in Spanish, something that sets the stage for a unique trait of his intellectual practice: his willingness to dialogue with the distinct audiences on both sides of the border. By 1993, in *La casa por la ventana*, Castañeda developed an original stance in the Mexican Left: the book advocates both for a reconsideration of the role of the state in national development—something that distances him starkly from Krauze—and for the serious and critical engagement with the United States. In the intersection between these two points, *La utopía desarmada* produces an epistemic change as the first theorization of Castañeda's influential democratic advocacy in the 1990s.

While Aguilar Camín flirted with the idea of modernizing the Mexican Left, *La utopía desarmada* truly led the way for the Left to extract itself from 1960s paradigms and directed it toward the democratic imperatives of the 1990s. The book was the subject of an intense debate in major journals of international issues, from the right-leaning *Foreign Affairs* to the *New Left Review*.[15] The book's central contention is that, even though the Latin American Left won two revolutions, in Cuba and in Nicaragua, the movement's ability to make an impact on the contemporary world depends on its ability to adapt itself to the democratic framework. In Castañeda's assessment, one of the main limitations of the Left comes from its attempts to govern through the support of relatively small segments of the electorate. Therefore, Castañeda suggests, the only viable path is for the Left to seek wider coalitions with groups beyond its core in order to use democracy as a vehicle for entering the state. Along with this contention, Castañeda claims that the Left must also come to terms with some elements of the market economy and use the state and fiscal policy, along with some of the changes brought about by neoliberal reform, to address the increasing inequality produced by Latin America's entry into globalization. Castañeda's work put on the table, in the Latin American context, the painful idea that the Left had to adapt to the political ways of democracy and break away from armed struggle. Furthermore, as Francisco Panizza argues in a recent article, the most successful manifestations of the Latin American Left (like Brazil's Lula da Silva), have succeeded through the compromises with the market economy prescribed by Castañeda in his book (730). Still, beyond Castañeda's prescient understanding of the roads that the Latin American Left would eventually travel, one of the big omissions of the debate on *La utopía desarmada* was the influence of the 1988 election in the book and the role Castañeda's ideas would play in Mexico's intellectual world.

One of the most significant passages of *La utopía desarmada* is the one dedicated to the analysis of Cuauhtémoc Cárdenas's candidacy and the emergence of the PRD. According to Castañeda, the underlying architecture of Cárdenas's coalition was doomed from the start, since he opted to build a coalition of "small, traditionally corrupt and co-opted parties" (188. My translation) such as the PPS, which was created in the 1940s precisely to deactivate the radical elements in Mexico's labor movement. When many elements of Cárdenas's coalition melded into the PRD, they failed in the task of maintaining the electoral base constructed in 1988, mostly by losing the middle class. The PRD thus became a perennial third force in Mexican electoral politics, unable to win elections—either due to a legitimate loss or to electoral fraud—and fragmented due to the inherited ideological divisions and petty interests of the small parties that formed it. To this day, the PRD remains divided into ideological and political "tribes" who spar constantly for candidacies and leadership positions.[16] Castañeda's deep differences with the PRD, a party that, in theory, should be able to appeal to a left-wing reformist intellectual like himself, became the major propelling force of his call to renew the Left. Castañeda, however, did not share Aguilar Camín's view that Cárdenas's reformism was hopelessly outdated. In Castañeda's view, the central issue was the inability of the PRD to compete in a legitimate democratic space and to emerge as a political party by itself, which resulted in Cárdenas's decision to join the truly outdated minority parties to take advantage of their existing electoral registration.[17]

The truly meaningful development behind *La utopía desarmada* in the Mexican context is that the PRD's ultimate configuration into a fragmented nationalist-popular party divided the Mexican left-oriented intellectual class. While intellectuals belonging to different forms of the nationalist Left, such as Carlos Monsiváis and Elena Poniatowska, remained faithful to the PRD, a cosmopolitan figure like Castañeda could not identify with a party that still operated, both ideologically and electorally, within a discourse nostalgic of twentieth-century populism. The rise of the idea of civil society in Mexico and the proliferation of middle-class political associations is a direct result of the PRD's chronic inability to capture a coalition larger than its 15–30 percent electoral base. Castañeda became one of the founders of an influential political group, the Grupo San Ángel, which he describes as "a group of academics and writers, as well as system politicians and activists from social and citizen-based movements," who tried to enact a political transition in Mexico (*Sorpresas*, 77. My translation). In Castañeda's account, the Grupo San Ángel came to be as a result of the disappointment over the way in which the PRI chose its second candidate for the 1994 election—through the presidential single-handed designation of yore[18]—and on Cárdenas's poor performance in the first presidential debate. Grupo San Ángel became a meaningful component of the redefinition of the public intellectual class because it established democratic reform as a concern beyond issue of Right and Left, and as a common language for Mexico's *intelligentsia* precisely at the moment when left-wing intellectuals like Castañeda lacked a clear party articulation and right-leaning figures like Enrique Krauze were emerging as major forces in the public debate. Not surprisingly, Krauze, Aguilar Camín, and Monsiváis became involved with Grupo San Ángel. To be sure, Grupo San Ángel was unable to achieve its short-term goal of a 1994 transition due to Ernesto Zedillo's unimpeachable victory in the presidential election. Still, for many left-wing figures, including Castañeda and his close friend Adolfo Aguilar Zínser, a major political operative of the PRD, the truly important consequence is that the Grupo San Ángel displayed the ability to create bridges and consensus outside the historical Left and, at least in theory, to participate in the type of wide social coalition advocated by *La utopía desarmada*. By allying himself with figures from completely different parts of the spectrum, including major PAN elements like Vicente Fox and Tatiana Clouthier, the powerful leader of the teachers' union, Elba Esther Gordillo, and leaders of major center-to-right intellectual groups like Krauze and Aguilar Camín, Castañeda was able to establish himself as an independent political and intellectual figure whose advocacy for a pragmatic and democratic Left put him at odds with the PRD's nationalist Left. Castañeda's farewell to the twentieth-century Left took place in his 1997 biography of Che Guevara, *La vida en rojo*, where he unsentimentally concludes: "Che is precisely where he belongs: in the niches reserved for cultural icons, for the symbols of social movements that, once filtered into the bedrock of society, are sedimented into its most intimate corners and cracks" (498. My translation). By placing the most iconic figure of the 1960s paradigm in a "niche" that exists solely in the "bedrock" ("*subsuelo*"), Castañeda concludes his own path toward the privilege of democracy over ideology. When Castañeda threw his support behind Vicente Fox in the 2000 election and accepted the position of secretary of External Affairs, his break with Mexico's imperfect institutional Left became definitive.

Beyond his role within Mexico's democratic process, Castañeda has also been a pioneer in the construction of a binational intellectual identity. *Limits to Friendship* was in fact the first of some important books geared at engaging the US audience in a conversation with Mexico. Castañeda makes it a point to issue most of his US-published writings in Mexico in order to show the ways in which the Mexican public sphere can construct frameworks of dialogue beyond the paralyzing nationalism and anti-Americanism inherited from the twentieth century. Castañeda argues as much in his 1996 book *The Estados Unidos Affair*. Clearly intended for a Mexican audience, the book consists of an essay in Spanish about the United States, two lectures given to Mexican and US audiences, and the Spanish translations of two essays originally published in *The Atlantic* and *Foreign Affairs*. The *ethos* behind Castañeda's book is to show the workings of binational intellectual action by exposing his Mexican readers not only to the arguments about the United States developed by his own experiences in the country but also to the language he uses to engage Americans regarding Mexico. Perhaps the most meaningful book in Castañeda's US trajectory is *The Mexican Shock* (1995), a detailed account of the US-Mexico relationship in the wake of NAFTA, the 1994 crisis, and the US-backed bailout of Mexican financial institutions. Castañeda openly admits that his goal is to "fill those blank spaces for the American reader" (3), given that NAFTA and the bailout created great interest in Mexico but the American public and government lacked important knowledge of the country. Castañeda is clear in recognizing that his point of view was "counterintuitive" under the heyday of the Salinas presidency, and that he believed that Mexico's "absence of democracy" and the "cold-turkey, free-market" policies implemented through PRI authoritarianism were counterproductive (3). In this, Castañeda became a leading voice in articulating what may be called a "Mexican perspective" of binational affairs. This perspective is nonetheless characterized by its departure from the inherited *doxa* of postrevolutionary foreign affairs and by the transformational role he played as Mexico's top diplomat, revising the country's protective relationship with Cuba and reengaging the United States as Mexico's priority in the hemisphere. The "Mexican perspective" fashions itself as representative of the views of Mexico's citizenry, as opposed to the state, and through an informed understanding of the viability of Mexico's position in relation to American public opinion and policies. This allowed Castañeda to publish the most important account of the immigration issue from Mexico's perspective, *Ex-Mex* (2007), and, more recently, *Mañana Forever* (2011), a book aimed at explaining the contemporary Mexican self and its attitudes toward democracy and the world to an American audience.

Castañeda is also distinct from Aguilar Camín and Krauze in his consistent assertion that the true democratization of Mexico requires a full break with existing political parties. While Krauze does not have an organic relationship with any party, he did side with some aspects of the Calderón presidency, in part due to his skepticism regarding both the PRI and the PRD, and in part because of his belief that the PAN has contributed enough to sustain Mexico's institutions. However, Krauze himself has expressed doubts regarding the struggle of the PAN to find a "good politician" to embody its civic legacy and values (*Para salir de Babel*, 58). On the other hand, Aguilar Camín withdrew from openly supporting active politicians after being criticized for his support of many *salinista* reforms. Aguilar Camín's turn to journalism not only led him to adopt political positions removed from the ideologies of the political parties but also to (mostly) refrain from writing openly political books for much of the 2000s.[19] Conversely, Castañeda attempted to become a presidential candidate as an independent. In preparation for his run, Castañeda published *Somos muchos* (2004), a book detailing his campaign platform. The book revolves around four major proposals: rule of law, educational reform, the reinvention of Mexican institutions, and a fiscal reform aimed at the elimination of special tax regimes (16–17). The concepts laid out in *Somos muchos* are, in my view, the most developed version of the ideas of democracy and governance of what we may term the "technocratic turn" of the Mexican public intellectual. Reversing the process described by Bauman, Castañeda gradually transformed himself from interpreter to legislator, and his presidential platform marks the end point of the twentieth-century tradition of literary intellectuals with an autonomous relationship to power—the last of whom are perhaps Aguilar Camín and Krauze—and proposes the emergence of an intellectual class clearly entrenched in the political realm. Many figures of the Grupo San Ángel followed similar paths: Santiago Creel and Alonso Lujambio sought the PAN presidential nomination. Still, Castañeda's decision to run outside of the system—avoiding Cuauhtémoc Cárdenas's "mistake"—preempted him from being able to participate in the 2006 election, and the political parties in Mexico have gradually passed reforms aimed at excluding candidacies outside the party system and at creating insurmountable requirements for the recognition of any emerging political party. In my view, *Somos muchos* represents the last stage in the transformation of the very regime of knowledge to which public intellectuals belong, leaving traditional cultural discourses and even historiography behind for the sake of the direct production of political discursivity. Still, if one looks at contemporary Mexico, it is clear that Castañeda's book identifies four crucial concerns that no political party has been able to truly embody. No party has been able to govern under a fully functional rule of law; the educational system is in shambles; the institutions built in the 1990s, like the electoral institute, have lost credibility in the eyes of many citizens; and the tax system remains burdensome, convoluted, unfair, and inefficient. Beyond the merits of Castañeda's proposal, the point is that his presidential run takes the ideologies of independence and democracy developed in the 1980s and 1990s and turns them into a proposal for governance, while breaking away from a political party system stuck in the twentieth century.

Today, as Mexico is mired in an apparently unwinnable war against organized crime, and as general disappointment with the democratic transition resulted in the PRI's return to the presidency in 2012, the challenges faced by the intellectuals discussed here seem even larger. The Mexican Left suffered two major losses in 2010, with the passing of Carlos Montemayor and Carlos Monsiváis, two of its foremost intellectual figures, and faces a void of intellectual discourse as the PRD suffered a schism after López Obrador's decision to create his own political organization. On the other hand, the PAN's two terms in the presidency have taken their toll on that party as well, and it faced a major internal crisis in 2013. Furthermore, President Enrique Peña Nieto is backed by one of the PRI's most entrenched political operations, the Grupo Atlacomulco. Facing what Arturo Anguiano has recently called the "endless twilight" of "the Mexico of broken changes" (*Ocaso*), Krauze, Aguilar Camín, and Castañeda remain the three major intellectual figures in the country and the future of Mexico's public sphere will at least be influenced by their interventions. While it remains urgent to shape a new paradigm to replace the one created in the 1980s, *Letras Libres* and *Nexos* continue to act as two important and controversial vehicles for public debate in Mexico. Castañeda and Aguilar Camín engaged in a new attempt to guide the public conversation, titled *Un futuro para México*, which includes a series of books,[20] articles in *Nexos*, and conversations on *Milenio Televisión*. *Un futuro para México*, like *Para una democracia sin adjetivos* or *Después del milagro*, continues to advocate the need for a democratic future, and for Mexico to break free from its twentieth-century anchors. The survival of this idea is as much a testament to the weight that Krauze, Castañeda, and Aguilar Camín have in steering the public conversation as it is to the ongoing success of the Mexican political regime in preempting democratic transformations.

## Notes

1. For reasons of space, I will avoid spending too much time in characterizing Fuentes and Paz as paradigms for twentieth-century intellectual work in Mexico. Nonetheless, it may be useful to point out that excellent scholars have already worked on this topic. For Octavio Paz, see Grenier, *From Art to Politics*. For Fuentes see Van Delden, *Carlos Fuentes, Mexico and Modernity*. Van Delden and Grenier developed their ideas on Paz and Fuentes further in their coauthored *Gunshots at the Fiesta*.
2. I invoke Ángel Rama's influential term to distinguish between the Latin American intellectual tradition of literary intellectuals, which, in his analysis, spans from colonial times to the twentieth century, and the new regime that I will be analyzing here. Rama's widely accepted description of the intellectual class across Latin American history as a cultural episteme is a useful shorthand to avoid explaining twentieth-century paradigms of intellectual practice. See Rama, *The Lettered City*. Besides Rama, readers interested in pre-neoliberal intellectual practice in Mexico may also consult Camp, *Intellectuals and the State in Twentieth Century Mexico*.
3. Bauman's book, to which I will refer later in the chapter, argues that in the transition from modernity to postmodernity, intellectuals evolved from "legislators"—men of knowledge who sought to "interfere directly with the political process through influencing the minds of the nation" (2)—to "interpreters" whose work consists in "translating statements, made within one communally based tradition, so they can be understood within the system of knowledge based on another tradition" (5). In the analysis that follows, I will question some elements of this model while borrowing others.
4. In their article "The Sociology of Intellectuals," which in my view offers the best theoretical taxonomy of the subject, Charles Kurzman and Lynn Owens identify three paradigms from the twentieth century: the intellectuals as "a class in themselves" (i.e., the idea that they

are an autonomous and identifiable social group), as "class-bound" (i.e., that intellectuals are representative of their respective social classes or sectors) and as "class-less" (i.e., as figures that transcend social groups to pursue intellectual ideals). An underlying point raised by Kurzman and Owens is that the theorists that defined all three approaches—authors like Pierre Bourdieu, Antonio Gramsci, Edward Shills, Michel Foucault, and Karl Mannheim—constructed their theory of the intellectual on the basis of their own intellectual practices. My argument throughout this article will imply the need to redefine a notion of the "public intellectual" that specifically accounts for the practices of intellectuals in Mexico, or for their specific genealogies, rather than accepting a predefined notion of the intellectual.

5. This, of course, is an issue that exceeds my scope, but it is interesting to note that at the very same time that Roderic Ai Camp wrote his field-defining book on intellectuals and the state in Mexico, which attested to the important and visible role played by intellectuals in the country, many US critics and scholars were lamenting their invisibility and growing irrelevance in the United States in the wake of the Reagan revolution. See Jacoby, *The Last Intellectuals*, for a symptomatic example of this issue from the late 1980s.

6. Which is in fact a half-truth, since Mexico, following Castañeda's own position as minister of Foreign Affairs, adamantly opposed the United States' first resolution for the war. It was only after the United States and Britain presented resolution 1441, a much more limited proposal based on inspections, that Mexico joined all other countries in the Security Council for a unanimous vote.

7. While Salinas de Gortari provides a crystal clear example of how to dismiss intellectuals on accusations of complicity, the second case can be also pervasive. In their book *US Hegemony under Siege*, James Petras and Morris Morley suggest that professionalized intellectuals—namely academics and people working at think tanks—"abdicate their responsibility as critical intellectuals" (156). The problem with an assertion like this is that it fails to historicize intellectual action and to consider that intellectuals are in part a product of the structures of production of discourse and knowledge.

8. This historical moment is registered by Carlos Monsiváis (the subject of chapter 4) in his book *Entrada libre*.

9. I have written extensively in support of the idea of this brand of liberalism as the key defining factor of mainstream Mexican intellectuals on the Left and the Right. See Sánchez Prado, *Naciones intelectuales*, Chapter 2, for the introduction of Benda's ideas in Mexico; "Carlos Monsiváis" and "La batalla del liberalismo" for studies on Monsiváis and nationalist liberalism; and "Claiming Liberalism" for a study of the "open society" strain inaugurated by Paz and transformed by Krauze.

10. See Guerrero, *Confronting History and Modernity*; Coira, *La serpiente y el nopal*; Taylor, *The New Narrative of Mexico*; and Price, *Cult of Defeat*.
11. Here I am thinking of "hegemony" in Ernesto Laclau's sense of an open signifier whose meaning is a site of contention among different interests and ideologies. See Laclau, *Emancipation(s)*.
12. See Sánchez Prado, "Claiming Liberalism." Most of my analysis of Krauze in that text is focused on *Siglo de caudillos*, *Biografía del poder*, and other works focused on his view of Mexican historical figures. To avoid redundancies with that text, in the present essay I focus on Krauze's notion of democracy, but my arguments here rely on the ones I made in "Claiming Liberalism." Beyond my own analysis, one can also find Krauze's assessment on many figures he admires in his book *Travesía liberal*, where he profiles and interviews people like Berlin, Leszek Kolakowski, Paz, and John Ellott.
13. A good testament of Krauze's influence may be found in García Ramírez, *El temple liberal*, which gathers the proceedings of a 2007 conference organized to honor Krauze. The texts offer little in academic analysis, and they are mostly praiseful commentaries on his work. However, the astonishing spectrum of intellectuals and politicians participating in the book, and the common recognition of Krauze's commitment to liberalism and democracy, shows the deep penetration of the ideas he formulated first in the 1980s.
14. See, most particularly, the two books that have taken this topic into the mainstream, Thomas Friedman's *The World is Flat* and Fareed Zakaria's *The Post-American World*, which, of course, do not share Castañeda's Leninism.
15. And perhaps the most lucid commentary in this regard is that of James Dunkerley in the *New Left Review*. He, in my view, accurately assessed the merits of Castañeda's argument in modernizing the Left in Latin America. See Dunkerley, "Beyond Utopia." On the other hand, perhaps the most suggestive attack on Castañeda's book is that of James Petras, who accuses him of an excessive pragmatism that prevents him from fully recognizing the role of the Left in the resistance against issues such as state terror. See Petras and Vieux, "Pragmatism Unmasked."
16. For accounts of the history and development of the PRD, see Bruhn, *Taking on Goliath* and Wuhs, *Savage Democracy*.
17. Significantly, Krauze's assessment of the PRD on the eve of the 2006 election shares this very idea. Krauze in fact asserts that the "remainders of the antidemocratic and revolutionary traditions of the PRI and the Communist Party [...] have relegated the genuinely progressive and liberal sectors of that political institution" (*Para salir de Babel*, 55. My translation).
18. It is important to recall here that the PRI's first candidate, Luis Donaldo Colosio, was murdered during a campaign event in Tijuana.

While he was also personally chosen by Salinas de Gortari as his successor, Colosio was seen as turning to the Left and as a man with the ability to democratize the PRI and to moderate neoliberal reforms. After his passing, Salinas designated Ernesto Zedillo, a technocratic economist, as a candidate, a choice that disappointed many people who saw in Colosio a force of change. The Colosio murder became a major point of interest of the Mexican intellectual class, and Aguilar Camín himself wrote what remains the definitive account of the event, *La tragedia de Colosio* (2004), which reconstructs the event through the testimonies published by Mexico's law enforcement agencies. Castañeda himself became obsessed with the process of presidential designation and wrote the most important study of it, *La herencia*, where he managed to interview four former presidents and the losers of the designation process in elections dating back to 1970.
19. The only two significant exceptions to this were *México, la ceniza y la semilla* (2000), a history of the Mexican State published on the eve of Fox's election as president, and *Pensando en la izquierda* (2008), a brief book on the modernization of the Mexican Left.
20. See Aguilar Camín and Castañeda, *Un futuro para México* and *Regreso al futuro*.

## Works Cited

Aguilar Camín, Héctor. *Después del milagro. Un ensayo sobre la transición mexicana.* Mexico City: Cal y Arena, 1988. Print.

———. *La frontera nómada. Sonora y la Revolución Mexicana.* Mexico City: Siglo XXI, 1977. Print.

———. *La guerra de Galio.* Mexico City: Cal y Arena, 1991. Print.

———. *La tragedia de Colosio.* Mexico City: Alfaguara, 2004. Print.

———. *México. La ceniza y la semilla.* Mexico City: Cal y Arena, 2000. Print.

———. *Morir en el Golfo.* Mexico City: Cal y Arena, 1989. Print.

———. *Pensando en la izquierda.* Mexico City: Fondo de Cultura Económica, 2008. Print.

———. *Saldos de la Revolución. Cultura y política de México 1910–1980.* Mexico City: Nueva Imagen, 1982. Print.

———. *Subversiones silenciosas. Ensayos de historia y política de México.* Mexico City: Aguilar, 1993. Print.

Aguilar Camín, Héctor and Jorge G. Castañeda. *Regreso al futuro.* Mexico City: Punto de lectura, 2010. Print.

———. *Un futuro para México.* Mexico City: Punto de lectura, 2009. Print.

Aguilar Camín, Héctor and Lorenzo Meyer. *A la sombra de la Revolución Mexicana.* Mexico City: Cal y Arena, 1989. Print.

Aguilar Rivera, José Antonio. *The Shadow of Ulysses. Public Intellectual Exchange across the U.S.-Mexico Border.* Translated by Rose Hocker and Emiliano Corral. Lanham, MD: Lexington Books, 2000. Print.

Anguiano, Arturo. *El ocaso interminable. Política y sociedad en el México de los cambios rotos.* Mexico City: Era, 2010. Print.
Babb, Sarah L. *Managing Mexico. Economists from Nationalism to Neoliberalism.* Princeton: Princeton University Press, 2001. Print.
Bauman, Zygmunt. *Legislators and Interpreters. On Modernity, Postmodernity and Intellectuals.* Ithaca, NY: Cornell University Press, 1987. Print.
Beltrán, Rosa. *La corte de los ilusos.* Mexico City: Planeta, 1995. Print.
Bruhn, Kathleen. *Taking on Goliath. The Emergence of a New Left Party and the Struggle for Democracy in Mexico.* University Park: The Pennsylvania State University Press, 1997. Print.
Butterfield, Herbert. *The Whig Interpretation of History.* London: G. Bell and Sons, 1931. Print.
Camp, Roderic Ai. *Intellectuals and the State in Twentieth-Century Mexico.* Austin: University of Texas Press, 1985. Print.
———. *Mexico's Mandarins. Crafting a Power Elite for The Twenty-First Century.* Berkeley: University of California Press, 2002. Print.
———, ed. *Polling for Democracy. Public Opinion and Political Liberalization in Mexico.* Wilmington, DE: SR Books, 1996. Print
Castañeda, Jorge G. *The Estados Unidos Affair. Cinco Ensayos sobre un "amor" oblicuo.* Mexico City: Aguilar, 1996. Print.
———. *Ex-Mex. From Migrants to Immigrants.* New York: Norton, 2008. Print.
———. *La casa por la ventana.* Mexico City: Cal y Arena, 1993. Print.
———. *La herencia. Arqueología de la sucesión presidencial en México.* Mexico City: Alfaguara, 1999. Print.
———. *La utopía desarmada. Intrigas, dilemas y promesa de la izquierda latinoamericana.* Barcelona: Ariel, 1995 [1993]. Print.
———. *La vida en rojo. Una biografía del Che Guevara.* Mexico City: Alfaguara, 1997. Print.
———. *Los últimos capitalismos. El capital financiero. México y los "nuevos países industrializados."* Mexico City: Era, 1982. Print.
———. *Mañana Forever? Mexico and the Mexicans.* New York: Knopf, 2011. Print.
———. *The Mexican Shock. Its Meaning for the United States.* New York: The New Press, 1995. Print.
———. *México: El futuro en juego.* Mexico City: Joaquín Mortiz, 1987. Print.
———. *Nicaragua. Contradicciones en la revolución.* Mexico City: Tiempo Extra, 1980. Print.
———. *Somos muchos. Ideas para el mañana.* Mexico City: Planeta, 2004. Print.
———. *Sorpresas te da la vida. Mexico 1994.* Mexico City: Aguilar, 1994. Print.
Castañeda, Jorge G. and Robert Pastor. *Limits to Friendship. The United States and Mexico.* New York: Knopf, 1988. Print.

Coira, María. *La serpiente y el nopal. Historia y ficción en la novelística mexicana de los 80*. Mérida, Venezuela: El otro el mismo, 2009. Print.
*Coloquio de invierno. Los grandes cambios de nuestro tiempo*. 3 vols. Mexico City: Consejo Nacional para la Cultura y las Artes/Fondo de Cultura Económica, 1992. Print.
Del Paso, Fernando. *Noticias del Imperio*. Mexico City: Diana, 1987. Print.
Dunkerley, James. "Beyond Utopia. The State of the Left in Latin America." *New Left Review* I.206 (1994): 27–43. Print.
Fernández de Castro, Rafael, coord. *Cambio y continuidad en la política exterior de México*. Mexico City: Planeta, 2002. Print.
Fernández Retamar, Roberto. *Todo Calibán*. San Juan, Puerto Rico: Callejón, 2003. Print.
Fontana, Benedetto. *Hegemony and Power. On the Relation Between Gramsci and Machiavelli*. Minneapolis: University of Minnesota Press, 1993. Print.
Friedman, Thomas L. *The World Is Flat. A Brief History of the Twenty-First Century*. New York: Farrar, Strauss, and Giroux, 2005. Print.
Fuentes, Carlos. *Tiempo Mexicano*. Mexico City: Joaquín Mortiz, 1971. Print.
García Ramírez, Fernando. *El temple liberal. Acercamientos a la obra de Enrique Krauze*. Mexico City: Fondo de Cultura Económica; Tusquets, 2009. Print.
Grenier, Yvon. *From Art to Politics. Octavio Paz and the Pursuit of Freedom*. Lanham, MD: Rowman and Littlefield, 2001. Print
Guerra, François Xavier. *Le Mexique. De l'Ancien Régime à la Révolution*. 2 vols. Paris: L'Harmattan, 1985. Print.
Guerrero, Elisabeth. *Confronting History and Modernity in Mexican Narrative*. New York: Palgrave Macmillan, 2008. Print.
Jacoby, Russell. *The Last Intellectuals. American Culture in the Age of Academe*. New York: Basic Books, 1987. Print.
Jaime, Edna, coord. *Lo hecho en México*. Mexico City: Cal y Arena; CIDAC, 1993. Print.
Krauze, Enrique. *América Latina. El otro milagro*. Bogotá: Fundes, 1991. Print.
———. *Biografía del poder. Caudillos de la Revolución Mexicana (1910–1940)*. Mexico City: Tusquets, 1997. Print.
———. *Caras de la historia*. Mexico City: Joaquín Mortiz, 1983. Print.
———. *De héroes y mitos*. Mexico City: Tusquets, 2010. Print.
———. *El poder y el delirio*. Mexico City: Tusquets, 2008. Print.
———. *Para salir de Babel*. Mexico City: Tusquets, 2006. Print.
———. *Por una democracia sin adjetivos*. Mexico City: Joaquín Mortiz Planeta, 1986. Print.
———. *Siglo de caudillos*. Mexico City: Tusquets, 1994. Print.
———. *Tarea política*. Mexico City: Tusquets, 2000. Print.
———. *Textos heréticos*. Mexico City: Grijalbo, 1992. Print.
———. *Travesía liberal*. Mexico City: Tusquets, 2003. Print.

Kurzman, Charles and Lynn Owens. "The Sociology of Intellectuals." *Annual Review of Sociology* 28 (2002): 63–90. Print.
Laclau, Ernesto. *Emancipation(s)*. New York: Verso, 1996. Print.
Lomnitz, Claudio. "Narrating the Neoliberal Moment. History, Journalism Historicity." *Public Culture* 20.1 (2008): 39–56. Print.
Long, Ryan F. *Fictions of Totality. The Mexican Novel, 1968 and the National-Popular State*. Purdue Studies in Romance Literatures 44. West Lafayette, IN: Purdue University Press, 2008. Print.
Molinar Horcasitas, Juan. *El tiempo de la legitimidad*. Mexico City: Cal y Arena, 1991. Print.
Monsiváis, Carlos. *Entrada libre. Crónicas de una sociedad que se organiza*. Mexico City: Era, 1987. Print.
Moreiras, Alberto. "Ethics and Politics in Héctor Aguilar Camín's *Morir en el Golfo* and *La guerra de Galio*." *South Central Review* 21.3 (2004): 70–84. Print.
Panizza, Francisco. "Unarmed Utopia Revisited. The Resurgence of Left of Centre Politics in Latin America." *Political Studies* 53 (2005): 716–34. Print.
Petras, James and Morris Morley. *US Hegemony under Siege. Class, Politics and Development in Latin America*. London: Verso, 1990. Print.
Petras, James and Steven Vieux. "Pragmatism Unmasked: History and Strategy in Castañeda's *Utopia Unarmed*." *Science and Society* 60.2 (1996): 207–19. Print.
Price, Brian L. *Cult of Defeat. The Historical Novel in Contemporary Mexico*. New York: Palgrave Macmillan, 2012. Print.
Rama, Ángel. *The Lettered City*. Translated by John Charles Chasteen. Durham: Duke University Press, 1996. Print.
Said, Edward W. *Representations of the Intellectual. The 1993 Reith Lectures*. New York: Pantheon, 1994. Print.
Salinas de Gortari, Carlos. *Democracia republicana. Ni Estado ni mercado: una alternativa ciudadana*. Mexico City: Debate, 2010. Print.
Sánchez Prado, Ignacio M. "Carlos Monsiváis: crónica, nación y liberalismo." In *El arte de la ironía: Carlos Monsiváis ante la crítica*. Edited by Mabel Moraña and Ignacio Sánchez Prado. Mexico City: Era; UNAM, 2007. 300–36. Print.
———. "Carlos Monsiváis. La crónica como narrativa pública." In *Doscientos años de narrativa mexicana vol. II. Siglo XX*. Edited by Rafael Olea Franco. Mexico City: El Colegio de México, 2010. 385–402. Print.
———. "Claiming Liberalism. Enrique Krauze, *Vuelta*, *Letras Libres* and the Reconfigurations of the Mexican Intellectual Class." *Mexican Studies / Estudios Mexicanos*. 26.1 (2010): 47–78. Print.
———. "La batalla del liberalismo. Notas sobre la ensayística reciente de Carlos Monsiváis." In *La consciencia imprescindible. Ensayos sobre Carlos Monsiváis*. Edited by Jezreel Salazar. Fondo Editorial Tierra Adentro 369. Mexico City: Consejo Nacional para la Cultura y las Artes, 2009. 127–42. Print.

———. *Naciones intelectuales. Las fundaciones de la modernidad literaria mexicana (1917–1959)*. Purdue Studies in Romance Literatures 47. West Lafayette, IN: Purdue University Press, 2009. Print.
Sheppard, Randal. "Nationalism, Economic Crisis and 'Realist Revolution' in 1980s Mexico." *Nations and Nationalism* 17.3 (2011): 500–19. Print.
Taylor, Kathy. *The New Narrative of Mexico. Subversions of History in Mexican Literature*. Lewisburg, PA: Bucknell University Press, 1994. Print.
Toledo, Alejandro and Pilar Jiménez Trejo. *Creación y poder. Nueve retratos de intelectuales*. Mexico City: Joaquín Mortiz, 1994. Print.
Trejo, Guillermo and Claudio Jones, coords. *Contra la pobreza*. Mexico City: Cal y Arena, 1992. Print.
Trejo Delarbre, Raúl. *La sociedad ausente. Comunicación, democracia y modernidad*. Mexico City: Cal y Arena, 1992. Print.
Van Delden, Maarten. *Carlos Fuentes, Mexico and Modernity*. Nashville, TN: Vanderbilt University Press, 1998. Print.
———. "Conjunciones y disyunciones. La rivalidad entre *Vuelta* y *Nexos*." In Kristen Vanden Berghe and Maarten Van Delden. Edited by *El laberinto de la solidaridad. Cultura y política en México (1910–2000)*. Foro Hispánico 22. Amsterdam: Rodopi, 2002. 105–20. Print.
Van Delden, Maarten and Yvon Grenier. *Gunshots at the Fiesta. Literature and Politics in Latin America*. Nashville, TN: Vanderbilt University Press, 2009. Print.
Wuhs, Stephen T. *Savage Democracy. Institutional Change and Party Development in Mexico*. University Park: The Pennsylvania State University Press, 2008. Print.
Zakaria, Fareed. *The Post-American World*. New York: Norton, 2008. Print.

## Chapter 2

# Engaging Intellectuals: Andrés Henestrosa and Elena Poniatowska

*Debra A. Castillo*

What public do public intellectuals engage? What aspect of their intellectual work finds the most resonance with their audiences? One surprising answer might be that they provide local color for tourists, where the public intellectual, often unwittingly or unwillingly, collaborates in creating/producing the exportable veneer of an authentic, folkloric deep Mexico for an international consumer market. In some cases, this convenient alliance of intellectuals with local people and the international audiences intrigued by their unique cultural expression (and their reasonably priced tourist trinkets) has very deep roots. "Las mujeres de Juchitán," muses David Foster, asking the rhetorical question: "¿hay una frase en la cultura mexicana—por lo menos en la cultura mexicana femenina/feminista—que evoque más resonancia que ésta?" (181). (Is there a sentence in Mexican culture—at least in the feminine/feminist Mexican culture—that evokes more resonance than this one?)

Undoubtedly, Andrés Henestrosa (1906–2008), the notable Zapotec intellectual and politician, has been one of the native informants who has played an important role in the construction of a utopian Juchitán de Zaragoza in the international imaginary, partly by guiding a star-studded cast of visitors to his hometown—his wide circle of friends and acquaintances included figures ranging from José Vasconcelos, Tina Modotti, Frida Kahlo, and Diego Rivera to Miguel Covarrubias, Pablo Neruda, Antonin Artaud, Langston Hughes, Paul Strand, and Henri Cartier Bresson. In the next generation, Elena Poniatowska (1932– ), daughter of Polish royalty and Mexican aristocracy, herself tours Juchitán, citing Henestrosa's work and producing in the wake of her visit the accompanying 1988 text to Graciela

Iturbide's stunning and exoticizing photographs of (mostly) Juchitecas (and, in this small world of the Mexican intelligentsia, Iturbide was also a close friend of Henestrosa). This study will return to these two authors whose work has been so important for the iconicity of the Juchiteca as symbol of the timeless, nonthreatening, exotically beautiful deep Mexico. They are, of course, a pair of public intellectuals trailing their own stereotypes.[1] Both Poniatowska and Henestrosa remain in some sense outsiders to Mexico, though both spent most of their lives in the Mexico City cultural orbit: Henestrosa, the perfectly assimilated Indian, and Poniatowska, aristocratic and gracious, the politically sensitive chronicler of Mexico City's people and paroxysm; public intellectuals but not overly scholarly, good mother and father figures for the nation.

The point of this chapter is not to parse out truth claims about the presumed matriarchal utopia of Juchitán, but to note the consistency of their construction, and how closely they align with a structure of desire and anxiety evoked in Henestrosa's and Poniatowska's texts, an ethos that closely meshes with many different needs: local, national, and international. To use another metaphor: the Mexican public intellectual in this case is balancing centripetal and centrifugal forces that on the one hand pull all cultural products and producers toward Mexico City, and on the other define deep national culture by the peripheries, a centrifugal movement out of the cosmopolitan center to the "untouched" indigenous past/present. For these writers, located within Mexico City, there is another axis as well, deriving from Mexico's anxiety about its place in the West and its rank in the hierarchy of nations. Thus, Mexico anxiously touts its modern developments while recognizing—and officially celebrating—that the uniqueness the country has to offer ironically comes from the vital indigenous cultures and languages that are consistently devalued both at home and abroad except as tourist sites or anthropological subjects.

Public intellectuals writing on Juchitán de Zaragoza, therefore, serve as a case study to look closely at structures of nostalgia (or desire) and alienation (or anxiety) in their discussions. In these texts, written from the heart of Mexico's love affair with Western modernity, we see the deep nostalgia for a preindustrial culture, along with a realization that modernity makes Mexicans less beautiful, and even terrifyingly dangerous. Understandably, then, these intellectual works rely less on a standard Western academic model of argument, but rather operate on an emotional level, and speak to the power of affect, in a register that constantly reminds us of the foreignness of these supposed native informant texts.

## Touring Juchitán

In the proliferating and promiscuous world of Oaxaca tourist sites, uncited quotes from Elena Poniatowska abound,[2] and in their turn jostle with uncredited photographs by Gabriela Iturbide. Juchitán has become a destination for independent women of means and gay travelers curious about this seeming paradise. These images and text have taken on an important life of their own: "In macho Mexico, the extraordinary Zapotec Indian women of Juchitán dominate their men, celebrating fatness and fertility" (blurb for Jocasta Shakespeare's essay in *Journeywoman*), or "Here, the sun is a smudge of red lipstick in the sky and time seems to walk on high heels. In Juchitán, Oaxaca, years of history and the conditions of a matriarchal society have placed the inhabitants in a unique world where gays and transvestites live with complete tolerance" (Clement). British journalist Jocasta Shakespeare's flinch-worthy flights of invention (for which she has been the defendant in a legal suit; see Acosta), include describing a community of "quiet and henpecked men" who do what their much larger women say, while the women sit around the market eating aphrodisiac iguana meat and admiring their strings of "medieval gold coins, symbolizing [their] erotic merit." Clement and Gage are less hyperbolic, but point to the same underlying structure: a pure matriarchy and utopia of sexual tolerance, distant in space and harking back to an earlier time, albeit sporting metaphorical high heels. Similar stories, including her curiosity and indignation sparked by reading Shakespeare's article, inspired San Francisco Bay area filmmaker Maureen Gosling to revisit the myth of Juchitecan matriarchy in her under-focused documentary *Blossoms of Fire*, which, she emphasizes, was ten years in the making, and hence is no simple or superficial view (Acosta).

One of the most often reproduced, now iconic, images from Iturbide's sequence on the women of Juchitán is the striking low-angle photograph of an unsmiling market woman with a live-iguana headdress.[3] It is certainly one of the eagerly sought-after references that tourists hunt out in the market and in celebrations, or *velas*. Gage celebrates her own version of this encounter with a vivid image in her tourist article, one upping Iturbide in the process by combining a muxe with the famous hat. She reports that a teenage girl in one of the *velas* asked for a picture of the author. Gage was first surprised, then quickly came to her own interpretation of the request: "I couldn't understand why she would waste film on me when there was a transvestite with three live iguanas on her head nearby. Then I realized that in Juchitán, a blonde in a traje...was a more unusual sight than either a man in drag or a live iguana" (Gage). Here, concisely, is the perfect tourist encounter: a muxe, iguanas, and the blonde tourist in gaudy Zapotecan garments, at a local party.

The Mexican national tourist plots and popular culture recuperations of Zapotec culture are not exempt from these stereotypes of fiery, powerful women. Thus, for instance, the life of the nineteenth-century Istmeña *cacica* from nearby Tehuantepec, Juana Catarina Romero (1837–1915) was controversially reinvented in *El vuelo del águila*, a 1994 telenovela (soap opera) starring Salma Hayek. A fascinating historical figure who rose from cigarette vendor to powerful businesswoman and political figure in her own right, in the telenovela she appears merely as the beautiful young woman who attracts the eye of a young Porfirio Díaz while selling her ribbons (more politically correct than cigarettes) in the market. Outraged Istmeños protested the portrayal of this prominent figure as little more than a sexually voracious mistress to the handsome young Captain Díaz, and Televisa responded with an apology. Interestingly enough, as Francie Chassen-López observes in her article on this telenovela, both the protest and the response were framed in terms of men's protectiveness about the honor of their women and a recognition of that right—neither the outraged Istmeños nor the Televisa authorities were much concerned about remedying the lack of attention to Romero's historical role as a public figure (119). Like the familiar images derived from tourism sites, or from works like those of Poniatowska and Henestrosa, which have been borrowed and repurposed for tourist consumption, the telenovela, the protest, and the response to the protest all privilege the image of the exotic preindustrial beauty, differing only in whether we see her as touchingly innocent or as voraciously sexual, in need of protection by her macho counterpart or disdainful of men's role in society.

Inevitably, traveler's panegyrics like Poniatowska's have sparked anger at what many Istmeños see as a gross misrepresentation of their culture. Thus, for instance, the protest registered with Televisa on behalf of women's honor, thus the legal suit against Jocasta Shakespeare for her description of Juchitecas as sexually open and indiscriminate in their choice of partners. For his part, Rasgado González takes on Elena Poniatowska's discussions of Juchitán, both in her famous travelogue to accompany the Iturbide pictures, as well as in her more recent articles in the Mexico City newspaper *La jornada* (Spring 2007) on the COCEI (Coalición Obrera, Campesina, Estudiantil del

Istmo) movement, which he accuses of being so unprofessional as to give rise to a breach of ethics:

> ¿Cuál es la ética de los investigadores? ¿Cuál es la ética de los creadores literarios? ¿La tienen?...[Elena Poniatowska] escribe lo que sus amigos le dictan sin importarle en ningún momento la veracidad de esos dictados. Sin importarle las mentiras, las falacias que ostenta con su pluma, no importando que esa pluma mienta y haga daño a terceros. Doña Elena, noto, no tiene mucha idea del contexto sociocultural del Istmo sobre el cual escribe, y no sé por qué lo hace, o sólo transcribe lo que le dicen, pues tiene prisa en irse de shoping en el centro de Juchitán.
>
> (What are the researchers' ethics? What are the ethics of literary creators? Do they have any?...[Elena Poniatowska] writes what her friends dictate to her without caring at any moment about the truth of these commentaries. Without caring about the lies, the falsehoods that her pen flaunts, not caring that her pen lies and hurts third parties. Doña Elena, I notice, doesn't have much of an idea about the sociocultural context of the Isthmus she writes about, and I don't know why she does it, or if she is just transcribing what people tell her because she's in a hurry to go shopping in downtown Juchitán.)

One might share Rasgado's frustration with the inaccuracies in travelogue accounts, or critique Poniatowska's inaccuracy in the florid prose that surrounds her citations of native informants like Henestrosa: and indeed, other studies, like those of Chassen-López and Taylor, are clearly framed by an ethical imperative akin to that called for in Rasgado to set the record straight.

At the same time, it is important to recognize that the core myth of Juchiteca exceptionality is not the result of a one-way imposition of outsiders' superficial reactions onto an unfamiliar culture and language. Local intellectuals, emphasizes Mary Kay Vaughn, have long participated "in the construction of a Juchitecan history of heroic independence defended by ferocious men and sensuous, militant women" (291). It is also a matter of documented historical fact that Juchitán, dramatically unlike the case of many other indigenous communities, has nurtured a very deep and respected tradition of sponsoring important intellectuals and political figures at the national level, beginning during the early years of the Porfiriato, when recognition for their support of the national struggle against the French gave them certain privileged access and sponsorship to elite circles in Mexico City (Vaughn, 290). Andrés Henestrosa is certainly one of more well-known of these intellectuals in the twentieth century, but his situation is by no means unique.[4]

Perhaps the most amazing quality of the community is that despite this unusual level of access to central Mexican political circles and a constant flow of international tourists, for almost one hundred years Juchitán has been able to maintain its image as a quaint, isolated culture, relatively untouched by Spain or central Mexican national culture. During this time, Taylor says, this city has come to represent, and remains "the promise of what Mexico would be like if it had not been conquered and what it might be like if the promise of the revolution is fulfilled" (835). This idiosyncrasy gives pause, and suggests at the very least that the Juchitecos are highly able managers and manipulators of their international cultural capital, a necessary talent in a community where 54 percent of the population is employed in tourist-related enterprises (Gobierno).

The core of this myth—ferocious men and sensuous women—has necessarily been pared down for tourist consumption, eliminating from sight the conceivably more dangerous aspect (warrior men), leaving as the dominant image that of a nonthreatening and accessible matriarchal society where straight men have little relevance except for their sexual prowess, while women and muxes, their highly prized gay sons—"las auténticas buscadoras del peligro" (the authentic seekers of danger) in a purely metaphorical sense—live in a perpetual party featuring gloriously elaborate clothing. This emphasis on the striking beauty, sensuality, and independence of the women is so foregrounded, Poniatowska insinuates, that it makes them irresistible to outsiders: "los extranjeros (y en el Juchitán todos salvo los del Istmo son extranjeros) se escandalizan o se fascinan para siempre" (84). Foreigners (and in Juchitán everyone except those from the Isthmus are foreigners) are scandalized or fascinated forever.

## A Women's City

Andrés Henestrosa first came to Mexico City from Juchitán in 1922 at age 16 with 30 pesos to his name and wearing his first pair of shoes, speaking little to no Spanish. By the end of his life, he was much traveled, a multiple Guggenheim award winner who had worked with scholars in Stanford, Berkeley, the University of Chicago, and Tulane during his years in the United States. In his over 30,000 articles,[5] Henestrosa's work ranges widely across many genres, including journalism, poetry, scholarly studies, ethnography, and autobiography. His work represents, then, the very epitome of a highly prized form of cultural globalization, in the form of indigenous research projects that gain an extra glow of authenticity from the combination of the author's Zapotec background and his Western educational institution credentials. He is, then, ideally positioned to confirm or to refute descriptions of his homeland that come from outsiders. At the same time, it is important to underline the complexity of his own position, which includes not just his recollections of his youth, but also the wide range of metropolitan, westernized experiences he has had since then.

As Henestrosa says in one of his articles, and repeats in similar forms elsewhere, "Muy pobre fui de niño, de joven y de hombre. Si algún bienestar logré más tarde, pienso siempre que será pasajero...Yo vengo de muy lejos, de muy abajo" (*Andrés Henestrosa*, 144). (I was very poor as a child, a youth, and a man. If I achieved some better quality of life later, I always think it will be transitory....I come from very far away, very far down.) It is immediately obvious that the message is aimed not at his community, but at outsiders, to give them a context for his autobiographical account. "Muy pobre," "muy lejos," "muy de abajo" (very poor, very far away, very far down) are all implicitly comparatist terms, reflecting a more ample and nuanced contemporary perspective that holds together in the mind past poverty and contemporary well-being, as well as considerations of a distance that is not just spatial, but also cultural, involving western and nonwestern understandings, and an awareness of hierarchies of class.

In a short piece called "Los cuatro abuelos," Henestrosa weaves the story of his immediate family in the last three generations, then deftly hints at another, more literary genealogy. He playfully makes allusion to the coincidence of sharing the same patronymic as a distinguished group of important literary and cultural figures in the Spanish literary canon: the Toledan poet Garcilaso de la Vega (himself a descendent of the poet-soldier Marqués de Santillana, Íñigo López de Mendoza), and the eighteenth-century viceroy of New Spain, Antonio María de Bucareli y Ursúa, Hinistrosa y Lasso de la Vega. He recounts, only to immediately refute, Huave stories that his father's people originally came from Perú, and mentions as well the common patronymic with El Inca Garcilaso de la Vega (*Andrés Henestrosa*, 146–47). This double genealogy—of illiterate Huave "white Indians" and highly aristocratic Spaniards—meets in the intentionally spurious reference to the disproven indigenous legends of the Peruvian origins of the Huaves and the unsustainable hint of shared blood with the most famous cultural figure of all the royal Incan descendents. The point of Henestrosa's comment in these pages is not to draw a realistic family tree, or not only that, but rather to suggest, more complexly, that through assertions of this double heritage his indigenous forefathers and he himself have an equal and legitimate claim to Western attention, in the very terms that define the most sacred of Western canons. And, at the same time, he can assert the illegitimacy of such Western forms of thought and remind us of the arbitrary nature of an argument from genealogy. An analogous conclusion might be drawn from his comment, made elsewhere: "I consist of at least five races: Huave, Zapotec, Spanish, black, and even a little Jewish" (Bach, 40). Notable here is Henestrosa's implicit definition of "race," which includes three languages (Huave, Zapotec, Spanish), where standard Mexican racial discourse would define two ethnicities—indigenous and white; he follows this series of languages with one ethnicity (black), and a religion (Jewish). Here, Henestrosa lays out a very different understanding of indigeneity than that adopted by central, mestizo Mexico, while still evoking the terms of José Vasconcelos's "raza cósmica."[6]

One of most famous and much reprinted of his autobiographical (or auto-ethnographical) short pieces, the focus of this study, is his 1937 "Retrato de mi madre," originally written as a letter to his friend, the pianist Ruth Dworkin. This short, lyrical portrait of his mother, Martina Man,[7] describes a strong, twice-widowed woman who worked her land and raised her children during the worst years of revolutionary violence in the early twentieth century. While a loving and devoted wife to her two husbands, she came into her own fully only when left widowed: "amparada en los brazos del marido, su voluntad, su energía, su coraje, no pudieron manifestarse mientras el esposo vivió. Pero los tenía cabales" (134). (Harbored in her husband's arms, her will, her energy, her strength could not manifest themselves while her husband was alive. But she had them fully.)

Henestrosa begins his portrait with a paragraph on her family background, then describes a pair of photographs of her. She was a lovely young girl, he says, "la flor del pueblo" (flower of her village) who never needed makeup to enhance her beauty. Later, she develops another, more intangible quality that photographs can only hint at—a mature beauty that comes from her energy and strength. Thus, in reference to a photograph of her from 1917, he says: "se la ve con esa arrogancia que siempre adorna sus actos y su andar. Lo que un día dije de las tehuanas y juchitecas que caminaban en verso, que su andar era la poesía del movimiento, me lo sugerió ella." (One can see the arrogance that always adorned her acts and her walk. What I said one time, that the Tehuana and Juchiteca women walk poetically, that theirs was a poetry in movement, was suggested by her). As he describes it, a later photograph, from 1932, shows her as an elderly woman, but still "conserva en todas ellas ese gesto altivo que en tí sugirió la idea de indominabilidad" (*Andrés Henestrosa*, 132). (Maintains in all of them that haughty gesture that suggested to you the idea of undominability.) This pair of photographs, then, serves as a register of her character rather than her physical appearance, and evokes her grace in motion rather than a static pose for the camera.

One of the anecdotes Henestrosa tells about his mother is that she gave away all her belongings during the revolution. He asks, echoing the inevitable query of the reader: "Pero, ¿por qué repartía Tina Man de aquella manera sus pequeñas riquezas? ¡Ah! Lo hacía porque estaba segura de que más tarde o más temprano todo aquello iba a acabarse" (*Andrés Henestrosa*, 138). (But why did Tina Man give away all her small riches that way? Ah! She did it because she was sure that sooner or later all that was going to come to an end.) She had two reasons, he alleges. During the revolution, he explained, every few days armed men came to the house, robbing money or food, so she preferred to give her belongings away to friends and family; second, she was already widowed and wanted to marry again, but did not want anyone to say that a man married a young woman with children for personal gain (139). This simple but terrible story, as Henestrosa intended, demonstrates his mother's indomitable character. She is haughty, shrewd, and generous at the same time.

Henestrosa's portrait of his mother ends with a reference to her famous, widely traveled son: "Cuando le preguntan por mí responde, como poniendo en duda el tamaño del mundo, que estoy en un lugar que nombran Berkeley, Chicago, Nueva Orléans. Y agrega, '¡Al saber si es verdad que existen esos lugares!'" (143). (When they ask after me, she answers, as if doubting the size of the world, that I'm in some place called Berkeley, Chicago, New Orleans. And she adds, "Who knows if those places really exist!"). Her response (and Henestrosa's citing of it) has little to do with her supposed ignorance about world geography, and more a sense that this is a woman who has a strong sense of place and knows what is of value and what is not, and who is quick to depress her son's pretensions. Her dismissal of those northern intellectual centers comes with the author's own ironic wink as well as, of course, the same sharp and gentle satire that we saw in his other, genealogical mediation of an Istmeño versus northern pride in heritage: he wrote the letter to Ruth Dworkin (who he met in Chicago) when he was working in New Orleans. Thus, Henestrosa once again plays off the centripetal and centrifugal forces of center and margin, where the center could be alternatively Mexico City or Chicago or Juchitán itself, succinctly pointing to the changes of perspective that each shift of orientation and vision would provide.

Poniatowska, for her part, while picking up on Henestrosa's quote about the women of Juchitán as poetry in motion, focuses more intensely on two other aspects: their role as business administrators and their sexuality. She cites Henestrosa: "en las juchitecas no hay ninguna inhibición ni cosa que no pueden decir, nada que no puedan hacer" (77). (The Juchitec women have no inhibitions and there is nothing they cannot say, nothing they cannot do.) Where Henestrosa's work contextualizes this forwardness as a sign of women's independence and strength, he is also clear that the juchitecas are loving, faithful partners to their men. Sexuality is a natural part of life in Henestrosa's description of this culture, nothing to be either particularly remarked, or avoided, very unlike the case for his presumed audience of central Mexican and North American readers, for whom he writes these comments in his acquired second language of Spanish, and in an awareness of Western mores that would circumscribe or condemn sexual expression.

Poniatowska's article has a very different spin, though it seems as if she has picked up her point of departure from the Juchitecan scholar, who notes in one of his articles, calmly: "muy niño, tuve conocimiento de la mujer, lo que nunca, en ninguna circunstancia, creí un pecado en fuerza de ver engendrar a animals y gentes" (124). (I had physical knowledge of women as a very small child, something I never, in any circumstance, thought a sin, since it was how I saw people and animals reproduce.) Where the earlier writer is circumspect and matter-of-fact, if highly aware of different traditions among his audience members for whom sexuality and sin are closely tied, ladylike Poniatowska is provocatively excessive and erotic, speaking from the context of a conventionally more restrained center toward this periphery.[8] She chooses hyperbole when she quotes Henestrosa in her article: "Los juchitecos son unos extraordinarios fornicadores, ¿verdad?, increíbles. Somos encarnizados, desesperadamente fornicadores. A la mujer la montamos a todas horas para que a todas horas tenga a un hombre encima" (82). (People from Juchitán are extraordinary fornicators, right? Incredible. We are fierce, desperate fornicators. We mount women every hour of the day and night so that she always has a man on top of her.) No doubt the combination for the Mexican reader of an awareness of Poniatowska's aristocratic background and her lyric outpouring of what can only be called erotica has been part of the titillating attraction of this essay; for the tourist reader the vivid depiction of a strange sensual utopia likewise compels attention.

The original title of her essay in the Iturbide album was "El hombre del pito dulce" (The man with the sweet penis), a highly charged and misleading title for a portrayal that in the end has little to do the title's announced pornographic slant, or even with men at all for that matter. She begins her piece with the provocative statement: "los hombres no encuentran dónde meterse si no es en las mujeres" (men don't know where to put themselves except in women, 77), before turning to the discussion of the women who enjoy them: "los hombres del pito dulce o salado según se apetezca" (men with sweet or salty penises, according to taste). After a long, digressive celebration of the women of Juchitán, she ends her article by returning to the erotic premise of the opening lines in the last paragraph, with the piling up of sensual detail and a vast orgasm, "esa inacabable actividad sexual...una catarata de semen" (this unending sexual activity...a cataract of semen, 95), involving people, horses, cattle, dogs, burros, goats, pigs, turtles, monkeys, shellfish, birds, frogs, iguanas, and coyotes, all brought to a frenzy of desire by the salty air: "Sobre la tierra de Juchitán esparecen los vientos sus olores marítimos, aquellos que encienden el deseo" (95). (Winds with maritime fragrances scatter over the earth of Juchitán, inciting desire.) How does she get away with it?

Irene Matthews points to a playfulness in Poniatowska's language that undercuts the explicitness, such that the erotic element becomes less offensively direct. This quality is paired with the author's typical style of piling on a rich excess of details, making the text at the same time overblown and presumably factual, a mythic tale of long ago and far away that resonates with Henestrosa's plaintive "Yo vengo de muy lejos" (I come from very far away.) There is an unequivocal, if equally playfully obscured, feminist thrust to this writing as well. Matthews argues that in the combination of a lush, excessive language and "a functional and startlingly feminist social rubric,"[9] Poniatowska very deftly creates a seductive, accessible critique of heterosexist mores, where those elements of social exchange "which in other women writers' words are rendered grim and vengeful,...in this essay become ironic, playful, innocently melodramatic" (235–36). Thus, says Matthews, Poniatowska's pose of playfulness allows her to breach the normative bounds of propriety without losing her ladylike decorum, while the very knowing melodrama of her prose resonates with the structure of myth, drawing the reader into a wistful longing for an almost certainly imaginary past: "Poniatowska's essays on photographs often romanticize an earlier Mexico, when living was simpler, more honest, more communal, more fun....[T]he tone of nostalgia in her writings hauls the most attractive elements of those earlier periods out of the simply specular and onto a platform of contemporary desires" (238). Poniatowska says it openly and more simply: "Juchitán es un espacio mítico en donde el hombre encuentra su origen y la mujer su esencia más profunda" (83). (Juchitán is a mythic space where man finds his origin and woman her most profound essence.)

The Juchiteca women in Poniatowska's article are the "guardianas de los hombres" (guardians of the men) and "dueña[s] del mercado" (owners of the market, 82), a symbolic stature much greater than the merely economic one, following the tradition in Juchitán that women administer the family money. In one much cited quote from this essay, they impose themselves on the landscape, where Poniatowska's words match Iturbide's monumentalizing low-angle camera shots: "hay que verlas llegar como torres que caminan" (82). (You must see them arrive like towers that walk.) Here, as elsewhere, Matthews would say that Poniatowska's most effective journalistic writing depends on a kind of photographic analogy: cropping and framing her referent, in this case focusing on the market women and leaving out the heavy labor of farming and fishing where the men are employed, creating emotional responses through specific uses of angles/interpretations and shadings of light and dark, then producing meaning "from the cumulative, metonymic effect of 'simple' contiguity" (22).

Even their language, says Poniatowka, conspires to keep men in their place: Zapoteco "es un idioma mujer" (a woman's language, 92) with its softened, drawn-out vowels. The implicit contrast is clear in her references to the local musical tradition. If stereotypical Mexican Spanish can be distilled into the sound of machista mariachi gritos and women's weeping, in Zapoteco the language itself enforces other forms and other sounds, though the musicality she evokes is through familiar Spanish language songs from the Isthmus: "La llorona," "Sandunga." Thus, while the central Mexican musical and social cliché involves the man with the wandering eye and the self-sacrificing woman who loves him, the Juchiteca sings softly, in the feminine, but she stands tall, proud of her independence and her accomplishments: "ellas no, nada de abnegadas madrecitas mexicanas anegadas en el llanto" (84).[10] (Not them, no, they have nothing of the self-sacrificing Mexican mommies, negating themselves in their weeping.)

A natural corollary of this tale of a woman-centered culture is the story about Juchitán's unusually open attitude toward gays and lesbians, a highlight of all the tourist sites, and one of the ways Poniatowska helps anchor her argument about the Juchitecan difference from the dominant Mexican culture, and indeed, from Western cultures in general. Poniatowska ponders: "quizás porque la madre tiene tanto peso en la comunidad, es aceptado el homosexualismo porque el muchacho ayuda al quehacer. Una madre siente gusto por tener un hijo homosexual porque jamás se va" (83–84). (Maybe because the mother is such a force in the community, that homosexualism is accepted, since the young man helps with the domestic work. A mother feels pleased to have a homosexual son since he never leaves home.) This feature of Juchitecan culture, more than any other, has sparked national and international tourism to the community, and uncovering the "reality" of the extraordinarily tolerant relation toward gays and lesbians is the topic on everyone's mind.

A significant portion of "Blossoms of Fire" is dedicated to this question of alternative gender roles, with a group of Juchitecos commenting in round table fashion on the acceptance of (or even preference for) gay sons.[11] One speaker says it directly, in a form very similar to Poniatowska's paraphrase above, perhaps even inspired by the same source: "Todo el mundo se casa, él que se queda con la mamá es el homosexual... Por eso las mamás dicen a veces, 'Ay, ojalá Dios me concediera la dicha de tener un homosexual en mi casa.'" "Pero no son todos" (Everyone gets married. The only one who stays with his mom is the homosexual... That is why the moms sometimes say, "Oh, I wish God had given me the happiness of having a homosexual in my house." "But not all of them"), responds one man immediately, while the rest of the participants at the table interrupt to insist that yes, a good many families are completely open and accepting. In most of the anecdotes, the gay child is eventually accepted, but not without resistance. One wife says of her husband's attitude, speaking in Zapoteco: "Before it bothered him a lot, but he's tired of being angry." Another young man tells his story of coming out to his parents: "pensaba que me iba a dar un bofetón pero no me lo dio" (I thought he was going to punch me, but he didn't), indicating that he is perfectly aware than even in Juchitán, gayness is not universally celebrated.

Nevertheless, the bulk of Poniatowska's essay, like Gosling's film and unlike Islas's more sobering depiction, gives an impression of celebrating powerful women and their gentle gay sons at the expense of their weak, almost invisible male partners. In contrast with the statement that "los hombres no encuentran dónde meterse si no es en las mujeres" (the men don't know where to put themselves except in women) (which completely leaves out the muxes who become so definatory a bit later in the text), Poniatowska also writes, albeit more briefly, of Juchitán's famously aggressive past, which carries over to the present day. The Zapotec speakers may be soft-spoken, but "en Juchitán no hay hombre que sea más hombre que otro, imposible, todos son igualmente temerarios" (94). (In Juchitán there is no man who is more masculine than another. It's impossible. They are all equally bold.) She speaks also of the familiar patriarchal cult of virginity, and emphasizes that a woman's chastity (and, as is expected, not the man's[12]) is a matter of great importance to family pride (88, 90). Thus, Poniatowska's article pulls two ways: toward the women who dominate in this presumably matriarchal society and, in a minor key, toward patriarchal values that dominate in the rest of society; that is, toward the men who even in the context of Mexican machista ideals, are famously brave, worthy inheritors of the warrior tradition that impressed military leaders from Porfirio Díaz to the present.

Carlos Monsiváis is far more skeptical than Poniatowska in his parallel discussion of Juchitán, also written with a consciousness of the community's role in the national imaginary, particularly during the COCEI demonstrations in the 1980s. This is a history Poniatowska discusses as well in a much less cited section of her essay (79–82), a section of the article that perhaps is less commented internationally because, for foreign feminists, this political movement seems too confusingly local. In his contextualization, Monsiváis notes the role of Juchiteco intellectuals in Mexico City, but insists on their marginality to the concerns of centrist political and cultural circles. Monsiváis argues that these Juchitecan intellectuals were mostly decorative additions to the more influential cultural tastemakers: "por años, los escritores indígenas son en la capital demonstraciones 'exóticas', emblemas de un México anterior a México" (162). (For many years, indigenous writers in the capital city have been exotic demonstrations; emblems of a Mexico before Mexico.) When pondering the COCEI movement itself, Monsiváis asks the fundamental question about the influence of women on social and political systems, looking beyond the superficial, easily consumable, photogenic images of women in the market, with their beautifully hand embroidered huipiles and necklaces of gold coins. What, he asks, is the real incorporation of women in social and political struggles? He finds that, disappointingly, "tampoco ratifican aquí la leyenda del matriarcado, tan grata a todos los sectores de Juchitán, tan desmenuzable en anécdotas...tan nítida en su concesión de sitios de honor en la marginalidad" (164). (Nor do they ratify here the legend of the matriarchy, so pleasing to all the sectors in Juchitán, so deconstructable in anecdotes...so clear in its concession to the honorable sites of marginality.)

There are other dissonant notes as well in Poniatowska's overflowing panegyric to a nostalgically framed matriarchy. In another passing allusion, she briefly points to the vexed issue of the relation between indigenous communities and the markers of progress that define modernity: "los juchitecos no se sienten fuera de la modernidad como otros que hablan el idioma entre ellos. Ser zapoteco es un privilegio" (79). (Juchitecans don't feel that they are outside of modernity, like others who speak their language among themselves. To be Zapotec is a privilege.) Here she raises in passing the question of Juchitán's relation to modernity. Certainly, common markers—cars, televisions, refrigerators—are absent or mostly excluded from the frame of Iturbide's images and Poniatowska's text, and there are rather significant reasons for this choice, if we consider that the task of the beautifully produced book is to sell Juchitán, and Mexico, to national and international tastemakers. Scholars like Quetzil Castañeda and Claudio Lomnitz have pointed to the negative response from the mainstream culture when indigenous communities adopt signs of progress, such that the communities are divided into "good" and "bad." The good community retains a folkloric, pre-Columbian veneer; the bad community adopts Western labor-saving devices and entertainments. Thus, for example, in Castañeda's discussion of communities near the anthropological zone of Chichén Itzá, it is just such visible adoption of Western commercial products that made Pisté what he calls a "scandal...erased from anthropological memory" (43). Lomnitz describes in similar terms the negotiated modernity of Tepoztlán, where community cultural values include stereotypical calendar images of Aztec clichés, along with carnival costumes in the form of Donald Duck (190), to the dismay of international tourists.

Yet to be fair, at the time of the writing of this article, even Poniatowska notes that in this matriarchal utopia there are significant disadvantages, including isolation and extreme poverty. She cites fellow chronicler José Joaquín Blanco who says that in the mid-1980s there was still no potable water, no sewage or waste disposal, no paved roads, and no health-care providers or clinics in Juchitán (86). It was a town, moreover, with an evidently severe alcoholism problem. Says Poniatowska: "toman los viejos, toman los jóvenes, toman mucho, antes licor y vinos, ahora cerveza....Mucha cerveza. Muchísima. Hasta el vértigo" (90). (Old people drink, young people drink, they drink a lot, in the past liquor and wine, now beer....A lot of beer. A huge amount. Until they collapse.) More recent data from the state of Oaxaca shows considerable improvement in regard to infrastructure. What is striking, however, is the persistence of the desire, as expressed in Poniatowska's narrative and the many tourist sites and films that continue to express a similar nostalgia, to find in Juchitán a primitive community completely isolated from modernity and exempt from its stifling rules, downplaying the hardships and suffering the people face because they seem to us so picturesque.[13] It is worth pondering the sadness we westerners feel when we see Juchitecos driving cars, playing video games, or watching television, while at the same time we tourists to the area want to enjoy easy access from nearby airports, good roads, hot baths, safe water, and medical care, if needed. We want to go to their parties and not worry about their alcoholism rates; to celebrate their muxes and ignore their poverty.

## Useful Fictions

There is a strange moment in Poniatowska's essay, when among her references to people like Andrés Henestrosa, fellow cronista José Joaquín Blanco, Harvard political scientist Jeffrey Rubin, and ethnographer and painter Miguel Covarrubias, she suddenly cites her own fictional character, Jesusa Palancares:[14] "Son los hombres los que mueren de amor. Ninguna se deja, o como dice Jesusa Palancares, 'allá no hay lugar para las dejadas que han de estarse quemando en el infierno, puros tizones en el fundillo'" (83). (The men are the ones that die of love. No woman is left behind, or as Jesusa Palancares says, "there is no place for single women, who have to be burning in hell, pure smut in the ass.") While Poniatowska has elsewhere admitted to confusing the names of her informant with her character ("cuando pensaba en ella pensaba Jesusa" [when I think about her I think of her as Jesusa, 56]), the alert reader is justified in seeing in this unusual allusion a reminder of the constructedness of all literary essays. Like much of her best work, Poniatowska's essay on the women of Juchitán combines a fiction writer's sensibility to thick description with a journalist's attention to reputable source material. The result is a compelling exercise, too often read as unedited truth telling by incautious outsiders.

Graciela Iturbide, for her part, likewise insists on the error of attributing facticity to her work: "la fotografía no es la verdad. El fotógrafo interpreta la verdad" (Bradu, 59). (Photography is not truth. Photography interprets truth.) Her interpretative selection, cropping, and framing of the stunning photographs of Juchitecas, abstracting them from conventional referents of modernity, creates opportunities for the viewers of her photographs, in their implicit invitation to fantasize and create myths derived from our engagement with her work. She explains her famous picture of the woman with the iguanas in just such a manner, between canny and disingenuous: "Es una foto que tomé casualmente en el mercado" (It's a photo that I casually took in the market). It was also a staged picture to some degree, she relates, since she asked the market woman to put the iguanas back on her head and pose, and after taking a sequence of shots, she adds, "Una sola fotografía de las doce que le saqué, quedó bien" (Only one photograph of the dozen I took turned out well). In the majority of the shots, the iguanas were moving and the woman was laughing; only in the famous low-angle shot did the woman look more serious and the iguanas more alert (Bradu, 61). An earlier interview, also with Bradu, describes the combined effect of her photograph and Elena Poniatowska's highly subjective text, as together generating the opportunity that resulted in this specific image being turned into an international icon such that "many feminists in Japan or England, following the text of Elena Poniatowska, believed in the existence of a matriarchy in Juchitán and went there to interview the lady of the iguanas" (cited in Brandes, 99). Iturbide, of course, intimates a far more nuanced context for understanding the relation of her chosen photographs to some abstract concept of truth, and her remark to Bradu suggests as well that the idea of a matriarchal utopia exists primarily as an invention of foreign feminists.

With Andrés Henestrosa, it would seem that the intervention of a central Mexican eye and voice is eliminated, such that the reader might happily presume that we are privy to a native informant's direct and unmediated accuracy. This certainly seems the case for Luis Cardoso y Aragón's reading, in his introduction to the 1945 edition of Henestrosa's first book, *Los hombres que dispersó la danza*, which was originally published in 1929. In this introduction, Cardoso points to the difference between what he calls "arte auténtico" (authentic art) and literature, where the latter is the product of Western, educated intellectuals. Authentic art, like Henestrosa's work in this book, he argues, "exige el despojo absoluto de todo artificio" (demands the absolute stripping away of all artifice); it correlates, he says, with "el mundo de la niñez, la propia y la del nuestro pueblo" (xvii). (The world of childhood, my own, and that of our people.) While readers today would wince at Cardoso's description of Zapotec authenticity as childlike, I am by no means convinced that the sentiment he expresses has vanished.

At any rate, there is a startling disjunction between Cardoso y Aragón's description of an authentic art, naturally stripped of artifice, and the stories he prologues. In his notes to the stories, Henestrosa makes clear that his work is not simple at all, but highly crafted. A law student and collaborator with José Vasconcelos at the time he wrote/recreated these folktales, Henestrosa was very aware of the anthropological and literary context for the ongoing recuperations of indigenous tales in post-revolutionary Mexico, as well as contemporary conflicts about claims to authenticity, originality, and accusations of plagiarism for written transcriptions of oral stories. Henestrosa warns in his notes to the volume: "la mitad del material con que están compuestas estas leyendas fue inventada por los primeros zapotecos. La otra mitad la inventé yo.... Cuando alguien ha vuelto a contar alguna de estas leyendas, aunque la transcriba, no me llamo a plagiado, ni me duelo" (half of the materials are composed of those legends invented by the first Zapotecs. I invented the other half.... When someone retells one of these legends, or even transcribes it, I don't call it plagiarism, nor does it pain me.) In the same discussion, he defends himself against charges of having plagiarized from Wilfrido Cruz, who collected and transcribed many of the same Zapotec legends for a book published five years previously (*Hombres*, 131–33).

Bach reminds us of another context as well. By his own account, when he arrived in Mexico City, Henestrosa barely spoke Spanish, but by the late 1920s he was living at Antonieta Rivas Mercado's house, working for Vasconcelos, and studying law. He buried himself in Rivas's extensive library, and was particularly taken with Rudyard Kipling's *Jungle Book* and Frobinius's collection of African folktales, which became important inspirations for him as he retold/invented his own versions of tales from the Zapotec oral tradition—a highly literary structure of influence and buried allusion. Furthermore, Antonieta Rivas Mercado encouraged him to write down the oral stories, and, says Henestrosa, "volunteered to take dictation and polish passages because my written Spanish was far from perfect" (42). We are, thus, invited to see in *Hombres* a form adapted from his readings in authors who register western encounters with a nonwestern storytelling tradition, along with the superimposition of a more standard Spanish than he possessed at that time.

The crucial role of invention, whether by his ancestors or by himself, remains a thread running through Henestrosa's auto-ethnographic discussions in general, and he frequently aligns truth with lie. Thus, in a letter to Estela Shapiro, he confides: "hay una sola manera de decir las cosas cuando están hondamente sentidas, cuando son verdaderas, aunque técnicamente sean mentiras" (*Remoto*, 62). (There is only one way to say things that are deeply felt, when they are true, even if technically they are lies.) Elsewhere, he gives an example of the working of this truthful lie in the local Zapotec context. He first tells a story of the death of Chinto Pineda, as related to him by Lorenzo

Fuentes, the accidental murderer, before Fuentes flees to Chiapas and disappears from the story. Henestrosa, who was still a young boy at the time, helps take the body to town for burial, and then in his turn relates what happened to Chinto to a group of women:

> Era de ver a las mujeres que estaban más próximas a mí que hacía la crónica, tomar la noticia y transmitirla agrandada a las otras que estaban más retiradas. Hablaba yo.... En boca de cada una de aquellas mujeres la noticia se complicó con nuevas circunstancias. Tan alterada, tan desfigurada la dejaron, que ahora que refiero aquel terrible percance, no sé si así ocurrió o como la oí la mañana siguiente, una vez que fue del dominio público. (*Andrés Henestrosa*, 23)
> (It was something to see the women who were nearest to me and what they did with the story, taking the news and transmitting it in longer form to those who were further away. I spoke.... In the mouths of each of these women the news became more complicated with additional circumstances. They left it so altered, so disfigured, that now when I refer to that terrible event, I don't know if it happened that way, or the way I heard it the next day, once it was in the public domain.)

Henestrosa's point by point account of the sad story has already convinced us of it veracity; it is only when we reach the end of the tale that we are made aware of the layers of artifice that already shape his and our understanding of the events. Eyewitness Fuentes tells him the story, in great emotional distress; Henestrosa retells it to the community women, who retell it to each other adding details; by the next day, Henestrosa no longer recognizes the story or knows what is true or false. And yet, he convinces us, unlike Western testimonial truth, the importance of the narrative lies not in the authenticity of details, but in the highly elaborated and complex emotional truth at the narrative's core.

In his portrayal of his mother, Henestrosa adds at least one other layer. He recalls (and what does that mean, in this context?) Martina Man's recitation of a ballad in Spanish, which he cites in full in the text, commenting: "la oí recitar un romance que sólo más tarde supe que no era de nuestra invención, y que ni siquiera sabíamos bien a bien lo que las palabras significaban, porque el romance memorizado sirvió, sirve aún entre nosotros, para ocultar la pena de que no podamos expresarnos fluidamente en español" (137). (I heard her tell a ballad that I only later found out was not our invention, and that we didn't even really know for sure what the words meant, because the memorized ballad served—and still serves us—to disguise the pain that we cannot express ourselves fluently in Spanish.) Here the idea of invention is central, as is the question of the usefulness of a text memorized in a foreign language. The story encoded in the ballad tells one tale, unknown and inaccessible; the speaker uses it to express a different kind of pain.

The ballad, coincidentally, also has to do with a man's violent death, focusing on the reaction of the sorrowful widow. The central idea he conveys here is that the poem transmits a powerful emotion, even though the words are imperfectly understood, with the exception of the final line, the only one in Zapoteco. The reader of Henestrosa's Spanish language text (whether we consider that reader to be Ruth Dworkin, as the specific destinatory of the letter, or any of the many readers since who have had access to the reedited essay in Henestrosa's published work) necessarily comes to the ballad and the story of his mother from a very different linguistic and cultural competence, where Martina Man is an exotic character and the ballad structurally part of a familiar literary history. We are likely, for example, to have a repertoire of similar, familiar ballads in our own experience, but are equally likely to need Henestrosa's helpful note that the Zapotec word, "iquedée," substituted for the Spanish "quedé" as the last word of the ballad, means "junto al fogón" (138). (Near the hearth.) Then we step back to the other story, and must remember that the death of Chinto Pineda would necessarily have been told and retold in Zapoteco, but when that tale reaches us, seemingly so ballad-like in its formal qualities, it acquires yet another gloss, recalled many years after the event, and retold once again, this time in Spanish.

Asks Analisa Taylor, "What might be gained or lost if we buy into the idea of an alluring gynocentric paradise in the Isthmus of Tehuantepec?" And what, furthermore, does this suggest about the imaginary construction of Mexican national identity? (817). Her lucid and convincing study argues that promoting the image of the Juchitec matriarchy contrasts with the hoary founding myth of the Malinche, offering a model for an active indigenous woman who is not a traitor to her nation, while at the same time reinforcing that myth by insisting on Juchitecan exceptionality (819). Succinctly, here she describes the emotional charge of what I have described as centrifugal and centripetal forces shaping our reading of the Juchitán presented in these public intellectuals' narratives.

Transnational and national culture industries collude in marketing images of pre-Hispanic survival as a way to define the modern Mexican difference. For Matthews as well, Poniatowska's work in general is compelling because it has cannily been able to capture Mexico in the "moment of crisis, of being undone." In this specific essay, rather than depicting them as backward, Poniatowska redefines indigenous Mexico as picturesque, but always and only in the context of an urgency about its current crisis, its projected future loss: "Poniatowska looks for the evidence of vitality in a culture she feels is losing its urgency, its sense of pride, and its sense of self" (Matthews 238), thus encoding a structure of nostalgia as its necessary adjunct. This strategy, which we have been at pains to trace in both public intellectuals discussed here, accords well with the structure described by Lomnitz: "The elevation of traditional culture for the consumption of elite classes" (250), leaving intact the prejudice of dominant society: "The view of the current population as degenerate, as having been made to depart from the best developmental possibilities of its race" (252).

Inevitably, then, these texts by Poniatowska and Henestrosa engage questions about the role of the public intellectual in Mexican society, as well as their function as mediators of the very rich discussion involving the West and the rest. On the one hand, Henestrosa and Poniatowska, despite their adoption by the international academy, share a fundamental inclination to popular and middlebrow media, forms, and audiences that they share with other cronistas, and that to some extent competes with the more obtruse analyses of academic disciplines. This reflects, of course, a social commitment and a political one. Even Octavio Paz, with all his highbrow inclinations, argues that "hay que devolverle a la imaginación la función que le ha sido usurpada por los profesores y los teóricos" (Revel, 32). (One must return to imagination the role that has been usurped by professors and theorists.) In both these authors, the newspaper article or letter and the rich details of a storytelling form are deployed to define for mainstream audiences cultural practices that would otherwise remain unreadable, unsymbolized, inaccessible to the central Mexican or international imagination.

On the other hand, Mexico enters this discussion as a western and nonwestern country at the same time, where the state and its two others are seen both from abroad and at home as inhabiting both modernity's shoals and its evil twin: alternatively the positive image of quaint primitivism, and that of underdevelopment. Thus, on the one hand, Mexico sells itself through images of pyramids, beaches, and exotic people in fancy clothes while on the other, the news media focus on more intractable problems of transnational globalized economies: infrastructure problems in the world's largest city, drug-related violence in the northern deserts, undocumented immigration to the United States caused by extreme poverty in the south. Meanwhile, according to Islas, many of the more activist muxes in Juchitán have repurposed the group that organizes what is for international tourists one of the most famous *velas* in Juchitán: "Las intrépidas buscadoras del peligro" (the intrepid seekers of danger) are now "Las intrépidas de la lucha contra la SIDA" (the intrepid fighters against AIDS), a much more sobering social project.

**Notes**

1. Poniatowska in particular has been the subject of many studies; see Bencomo, Jörgensen, Hind, and Schuessler for classic studies of her life, her fiction, and her contributions to the Mexican chronicle tradition, especially in her more urban-oriented work. In looking at a specific case study, this chapter also opens a window onto the transnational debates around the promotion of Mexican-ness that inevitably come to the fore in the discussion of these two authors.
2. See for example, Clement, "Juchitán and the Authentic Searchers for Danger" (an uncited borrowing from the title of Islas's film): the first page has an inset uncredited quote: "On the Isthmus of Tehuantepec, every family considers it a blessing to have a gay son" (a quick search will find the sentence credited to Oaxacan chef Susana Trilling in Gage's *Travel and Leisure* article on Juchitán); in the main text of Clement's article: "for many mothers it is much better to have a gay son than to have a daughter who will sooner or later leave the family. For the mothers of Juchitán, gay sons promise eternal company and support in household duties and family businesses" (compare to Poniatowska, "una madre siente gusto por tener un hijo homosexual porque jamás se va. La hija se casa y se muda y el hijo apegado a la madre cuida a la familia, el fogón, agarra la escoba" (a mother is pleased to have a homosexual son because he never leaves home. A daughter gets married and moves, and the son attached to the mother takes care of the family, the hearth, grabs the broom," 83–84).
3. Snow comments that the image has appeared "in dozens of books and articles on Latin American photography. She's appeared on a best-selling postcard. And a copy of the still photography played a pivotal role in the movie *Female Perversions*" (22).
4. For example, the influential lawyer, politician, and founder of the "Científicos" Rosendo Pineda, one of six Juchiteco children Porfirio Díaz brought with him to Mexico City to educate in 1867 (Gobierno del estado de Oaxaca).
5. Henestrosa gives this figure in his interview with Caleb Bach, also saying that still, at age 98, he writes at least one, and as many as four articles a day (45).
6. Vasconcelos was a personal friend and mentor to Henestrosa. Further development of the implications lie outside the purview of this study.

7. Elsewhere he clarifies his family tree: his maternal great-grandfather, Germán Henestrosa, was called "Man" and the name stuck with succeeding generations. His mother's first husband, Andrés's father, was a Huave named Arnulfo Morales (Bach, 40). Alternatively, he says the nickname comes from his grandfather, Fernando Henestrosa, called "Stiano Man" (Cristiano Man): "diminutivo que los indios hicieron de Fermán or Fermando" (a diminutive that the Indians made from Fermán or Fermando) (*Andrés Henestrosa*, 146). The author has always used his maternal last name (Henestrosa) rather than his father's (Morales).
8. I am indebted here to two brilliant readings of Poniatowska: Irene Matthews and Emily Hind.
9. Foster would agree, adding that the relative absence of men in Iturbide's photographs and the accompanying article provide a certain strongly feminist corrective balance to more familiar urban studies where the emphasis has been precisely on men (188).
10. Taylor makes the excellent observation that the celebration of the Juchiteca's strength and independence reinforces rather than undercuts the Marianist stereotype: "Isthmus Zapotec culture then becomes that indissoluble element, that other against which Mexican national identity may be defined" (836).
11. Released five years apart, the films by Gosling and Islas interview many of the same muxes. It is tempting to theorize that the difference in tone derives partly from the international versus national origins of the interviewers/filmmakers.
12. Islas's film points out that one of the important roles for muxes in Juchitán society is to provide a sexual outlet for straight men, who will later marry virgin women.
13. Such films would include the documentary by Maureen Gosling.
14. "Jesusa Palancares" is the fictional protagonist of Poniatowska's novel *Hasta no verte Jesús mío*, based on a series of in-depth interviews with a transplanted Istmeña, Mexico City laundrywoman Josefina Bórquez (Poniatowska, 56).

## Works Cited

Acosta, Belinda. "An Indomitable Culture: Maureen Gosling on the Zapotecas of Juchitán and 'Blossoms of Fire,' the Documentary She Made About Them." *The Daily Hustle*. May 4, 2001. June 10, 2010. Web.

Bach, Caleb. "Andrés Henestrosa: From Fables to Fame." *Américas* 57.2 (2005). 38–45. Print.

Bencomo, Anadeli. *Voces y voceros de la megalópolis: La crónica periodístico-literaria en México*. Frankfurt: Vervuert, 2002. Print.

*Blossoms of Fire*. Dir. Maureen Gosling. 2000. Film.

Boyce, Anya Peterson. *Prestigio y afiliación en una comunidad urbana: Juchitán, Oax*. Mexico: Instituto Nacional Indigenista, 1975. Print.

Bradu, Fabienne. "Ojos para soñar." *Revista de la Universidad de México* 72 (February 2010). June 26, 2010. Web.
Brandes, Stanley. "Graciela Iturbide as Anthropologial Photographer." *Visual Anthropology* 24.2 (2008): 95–102. Print.
Castañeda, Quetzil E. *In the Museum of Maya Culture: Touring Chichén Itzá*. Minneapolis: University of Minnesota Press, 1996. Print.
Chassen-López, Francie R. "Distorting the Picture: Gender, Ethnicity, and Desire in a Mexican Telenovela (*El vuelo del águila*). *Journal of Women's History* 20.2 (2008): 106–29. Print.
Clement, Jennifer "Juchitán and the Authentic Searchers for Danger." *Vuelo*. October 2002. Oaxacaoaxaca.com. June 10, 2010. Web.
Foster, David William. "Género y fotografía en *Juchitán de las mujeres* de Graciela Iturbide." In *Ensayos sobre culturas homoeróticas latinoamericanas*. Ciudad Juárez: University Autónoma de Juárez, 2009. 181–96. Print.
Gage, Eleni N. "Oaxaca's Alternative Lifestyle Scene. *Travel and Leisure*. November 2005. June 10, 2010. Web.
Gobierno del estado de Oaxaca. "Juchitán de Zaragoza." *Encliclopedia de los municipios de México*. 2009. June 23, 2010. Web.
Henestrosa, Andrés. *Andrés Henestrosa*. Mexico: Editorial Novaro, 1969. Print.
———. *Los hombres que dispersó la danza*. 1929. Mexico: Imprenta Universitaria, 1945. Print.
———. *El remoto y cercano ayer*. Mexico: Editorial Porrúa, 1979. Print.
Hind, Emily. *Femmenism and the Mexican Woman Intellectual from Sor Juana to Poniatowska: Boob Lit*. New York: Palgrave Macmillan, 2010. Print.
Jörgensen, Beth E. *The Writing of Elena Poniatowska: Engaging Dialogues*. Austin: University of Texas Press, 1994. Print.
Lomnitz, Claudio. *Deep Mexico, Silent Mexico: An Anthropology of Nationalism*. Minneapolis: University of Minnesota Press, 2001. Print.
Matthews, Irene. "Woman Watching Women, Watching." In *Reinterpreting the Spanish American Essay: Women Writers of the 19th and 29th Centuries*. Edited by Doris Meyer. Austin: University of Texas Press, 1995. 227–41. Print.
Monsiváis, Carlos. "Juchitán: ¡Ay zapoteco, zapoteco, lengua que nos das la vida!" In *Entrada libre: Crónicas de la sociedad que se organiza*. Mexico: Era, 1987. 151–66. Print.
*Muxes: auténticas, intrépidas y buscadoras del peligro*. Dir. Alejandra Islas Caro. IMCINE 2005. Film.
Poniatowska, Elena. "Juchitán de las mujeres." (1988). In *Luz y luna, las lunitas*. Mexico: Era, 1994. 77–95. Print.
Rasgado González, Abraham. "Los intelectuales pro COCEIstas y sus falsedades." Revolucionemosoaxaca. February 14, 2010. June 21, 2010. http://revolucionemosoaxaca.org/articulo/los-intelectuales-pro-coceistas-y-sus-falsedades.html. Web.
Revel, Jean François. "Miradas sobre el mundo actual" (interview with Octavio Paz). *Vuelta* 114 (May 1986): 29–32. Print.

Schuessler, Michael Kart. *Elena Poniatowska: An Intimate Biography.* Forward by Carlos Fuentes. Tucson: University of Arizona Press, 2007. Print.

Shakespeare, Jocasta. "Mexico's Red Hot Mamas." *Elle* 1994. *Journeywoman.* June 10, 2010. Web.

Snow, K. Mitchell. "Lens of Ritual and Revelation." *Américas* 51.1 (1999): 22–29. Print.

Taylor, Analisa. "Malinche and Matriarchal Utopia: Gendered Visions of Indigeneity in Mexico." *Signs* 31.3 (2006): 815–40. Print.

Vaughn, Mary Kay. "Cultural Approaches to Peasant Politics in the Mexican Revolution." *Hispanic American Historical Review.* 79.2 (1999): 269–305. Print.

## Chapter 3

# Monsiváis in a Nutshell

*María Cristina Pons*

*In Memoriam*

*Monsiváis is one of the last public writers of this country and perhaps one of the last names that the Mexican masses will be able to recognize.*
Castañón, "Un hombre llamado ciudad"[1]

Carlos Monsiváis Aceves, born in Mexico City on May 4, 1938, was one of the most prominent and influential leftist intellectuals in Latin America. Unique and extensive, his body of work is as vast as it is hard to classify. The very figure of Monsiváis as a writer is equally hard to define; therefore, writing about him is never an easy task. So perhaps it is best to simply start at the beginning, my beginning, or "my Monsi." I guess many people have a "Monsi" of their own.[2] I personally met him at his home in Colonia Portales. His chronicles, sharp, different, clever, and full of humor, had dazzled me. I wanted to meet him. So I came up with an interview, which was never fully completed that day. We finished it years later at a coffee shop in Los Angeles, the last time I invited him to come to UCLA. I did not know then that it would be the last time I would ever see him.

Coincidentally (or not), on every one of those occasions, some casual interchange would confirm Monsiváis's stature as a renowned intellectual and public figure. That first time I went to visit him at his home, I caught a cab by San Jerónimo, which was quite far from my destination. As I got into the cab, I said, "62 San Simón Street, Colonia Portales." The driver immediately said to me: "Ah, you're going to visit Monsiváis, the writer, right?" I could not believe it, because Mexico City may be a *big hell* for many people, but no one can say it is a *small town*. Even more surprising was that something similar happened the last time he came to Los Angeles. I was having lunch with Monsiváis and some friends, when suddenly the waiter approached us, asking permission for him and his coworkers to greet the "Maestro" (Teacher). In addition to the waiter, the busboy and a kitchen helper also came over. That happened in Westwood, near the university. The next day I drove him to the airport, and, to my surprise, he was approached twice by people wanting to greet him to express their love and admiration. The first time it was a family from Los Angeles, and the second, a middle-aged woman on her way back to Guadalajara, her hometown. I share these occurrences because they highlight one crucial, distinctive feature of Monsiváis: his widespread popularity. Monsiváis was one of the few writers who, according to the poet José Emilio Pacheco, people would easily recognize on the street.

His popularity was partially due to his undeniable and legendary omnipresence, which would gradually form the foundation of the "Monsiváis" myth. Elena Poniatowska, one of his closest friends, recalls: "Adolfo Castañón used to think of him as a one-person news agency and called him 'the last public writer.' 'Ask Monsi,' we would advise each other. 'Monsi is the one who knows.' 'No one knows what Monsi knows.' 'Monsi has already analyzed this'" (n.p.). Monsiváis's intellectual versatility and ubiquity were intimidating but, at the same time, also irresistibly fascinating. With an astounding intellectual clarity and his usual irony and humor, he was able to expound on any subject and attract the masses like many a celebrity.

From a very young age he contributed to the most important Mexican cultural and journalistic media. For instance, he worked as a columnist for the Mexican newspapers *Novedades*, *El Día*, *Excélsior*, *El Universal*, and for magazines such as *Eros*, *Vogue*, and *El Norte*. He was also a contributor to *Debate Feminista*, *Proceso*, *Uno más uno*, *Nexos*, and *La Jornada*, and director of *La Cultura en México*, a supplement of the magazine *Siempre!*. Authors like Carlos Fuentes, José Luis Cuevas, and Fernando Benítez collaborated with Monsiváis on this supplement, forming an intellectual elite known as "la Mafía." This avant-garde group functioned as an agent for the process of cultural modernization, opposing Mexican chauvinism with their cultural cosmopolitanism (Mudrovcic, "Carlos Monsiváis," 296). By 1964, the influence of the group was already notorious; Mudrovcic quotes the following comment by Agustín: "[They] controlled, directly or indirectly, the supplement of *Siempre!*, *Revista Mexicana de Literatura*, *Revista de la Universidad*, *Revista de Bellas Artes*, *Cuadernos del Viento*, *Diálogos*, *Radio UNAM*, *Casa del Lago*, and various cultural promotion offices, along with their payrolls" (qtd. in Mudrovcic, "Carlos Monsiváis," 296).

One of Monsiváis's most popular journalistic columns is *Por mi madre, Bohemios*, whose publication spanned four decades. From 1972–1987 it appeared in *La Cultura en México* and from 1989 to 2001 in *La Jornada*.[3] Beginning in 2006, it was published in *Proceso* by invitation of its founder and current director, Julio Scherer. The column, mainly dedicated to political satire, constituted a privileged space for the display of irony; but above all, observes Villamil, *Por mi madre, Bohemios* represented a forum for reflection, remembrance, and Monsiváis's encounters with journalistic investigation and the discourse of power:

> [The] contrast between a culture of tolerance and secularism, deeply rooted in civil society, and the vulgarity, cynicism, tackiness, prejudice, or compulsive ignorance of the governors, legislators, bosses, bishops, and moral leaders—whatever that can possibly mean in a country of impunity—constitutes the core of the Monsivarian irony that has been published every week in *Proceso*. (Monsiváis and Villamil, n.p.)[4]

Beyond his journalism, Monsiváis is considered one of the greatest chroniclers of contemporary Mexico. Comprising over a dozen books, his chronicles document and interpret diverse aspects of the political, social, and urban popular cultural life of Mexico City. Most of his chronicles are compiled in books such as *Días de guardar* (1970), *Amor perdido* (1977), *Entrada libre* (1987), *Escenas de pudor y liviandad* (1988), *Los rituales del caos* (1995), *Mexican Postcards* (1997), *"No sin nosotros": los días del terremoto 1985–2005* (2005), and *Apocalipstick* (2009). In addition to chronicles, Monsiváis published one piece of fiction, *Nuevo catecismo para indios remisos* (1982), written in the form of parables, and in 1996 he published a self-parodying autobiography: "I took on this sort of autobiography [says Monsiváis] with the petty goal of making myself look like a mixture of Albert Camus and Ringo Starr" (*Carlos Monsiváis*, 56). He has also published biographies, anthologies, and essays on poetry, literature, and culture. Most salient, and just to name a few, are his works on Octavio Paz and on the chronicler Salvador Novo, his predecessor, as well as pieces such as *La poesía mexicana del siglo XX. Antología* (1966), and *Aires de familia: Cultura y sociedad en América Latina* (2000), in which he analyzes the cultural heritage of the continent and for which he received the Anagrama Essay Award (2000). Of his latest titles, we could mention *Las tradiciones de la imagen* (2003), which is an approach to the most emblematic poets in Mexican literature, and *Las alusiones perdidas* (2007).[5] There are also three posthumous publications worth mentioning: *Maravillas que fueron, sombras que son: La fotografía en México* (2012); *Que se abra esa puerta: Crónica y ensayos sobre la diversidad sexual* (2010); and *Las esencias viajeras: Hacia una crónica cultural del Bicentenario de la Independencia* (2012). In these latter chronicles, Monsiváis revisits themes, events, artistic movements, and trends of thought in Latin America of the past two centuries "whose first and last *raison d'être* was the will of independence, autonomy, and liberation in everything that relates to culture or the 'life of the spirit'" (Monsiváis, *Las esencias viajeras*, 25).

It is fitting that more than a journalist, chronicler, and unsparing critic, Monsiváis defined himself primarily as a cat and movie lover, and as an avid reader. "It would be impossible for me to live without my books and my cats [he says in one of his famous aphorisms]. Books do not meow and cats do not provide wisdom, and that is why I could never choose between them. I would rather live without me [preferiría vivir sin mí]." The names of some of his cats were: "Longing for Belonging," "Meow Tse Tung," "Miss Oginia," "Wonderful Myth," "Gatzinger," "Fray Gatolomé de las Bardas." His love for cats led him to become a cofounder of the "Forgotten Cats" Civic Association. Today, Monsiváis rests in the "Gaturna," the urn the artist Francisco Toledo created for him in the shape of a cat.[6]

## Monsi, the Unrepeatable

The above (Monsi, the Unrepeatable) is how Enrique Krauze entitled his tribute to Monsiváis, published the day after his death. The note reads:

> He was a unique and original intellectual character in Mexican cultures. I use the plural because the peculiar genius of Monsiváis consisted precisely in his ability to inhabit, encourage, nourish, transform, and connect the most diverse areas of our heritage. He felt equally comfortable within popular culture and high literary culture, urban culture and pop culture, leftist culture and Protestant culture... He breathed culture. (n.p.)[7]

Monsiváis was a voracious reader since early childhood and his defense of reading was a constant in his life. According to Monsiváis, the lack of reading is more and more evident as conversations become structured like television dialogues: "Public language is declining and the effects of it are clearly visible in the construction of referential points. Talk-show and reality-show language is predominant, and trampling upon respect for speech is clearly visible there." This process, in which verbal coherence is diluted and words are thoughtlessly rushed through, is also noticeable in political discourse: "The vulgarization of public affairs [Monsiváis asserts] is a way to disaggregate authority and trivialize power, presenting politics as a show and the politician as a showman" (qtd. in Pons, "Carlos Monsiváis," 48).

Monsiváis read and observed everything—and what he read and observed he processed, assimilated, and remembered. Indeed, his memory was prodigious and, being an irredeemable movie lover, he was a walking encyclopedia of cinematic history. He could also recite entire poems by both sixteenth-century poets and contemporary ones, along with passages from Mark Twain, Oscar Wilde, Borges, or Charles Dickens. His erudition was unquestionable.[8] One of the books he read throughout his childhood and adolescence was the Bible. Monsiváis used to quote passages from the Bible by heart; he admired it mostly because of its rhetoric and as bookish, literary knowledge. Sergio Pitol recounts that because both of them were widely read they would have conversations about British and North American authors, and would always unerringly coming back to the conclusion that "Borges's writing constitutes the greatest miracle for our language in this entire century" ("Carlos Monsiváis," 343). At that moment, "Monsiváis [would] pause for a second and add that one of the high points for the Castilian language is thanks to Casiodoro de Reina and his disciple, Cipriano Valera." When Pitol, clueless about those names, asks him: "And who are those?" Monsiváis answers, shocked: "They are none other than the very first to translate the Bible into Spanish" (Pitol, "Carlos Monsiváis," 343).

With his sharp pen, pithy phrases, and humor *a la* Groucho Marx, Monsiváis was able to generate both scathing critical pieces and memorable poetic encounters. An example of the latter is recounted by Carlos Fuentes in one of the many funerary tributes dedicated to Monsiváis. It happened in Paris, when the two intellectuals went to visit Pablo Neruda at the hotel where he was staying. The Neruda-Monsiváis conversation was quite unusual, recalls Fuentes:

> "How are you?" Neruda asked Carlos [Monsiváis].—"It so happens that I am growing tired of being a man [*Sucede que me canso de ser hombre*]"—replied Carlos. At first, Neruda did not notice the quote.—"So, what are you doing in Paris?"—asked Pablo.—"I play every day with the sea of the Universe [*Juego todos los días con la mar del*

*universo*]," quoted Monsiváis. And Neruda, finally noticing the game, laughed and decided to play along, asking him:
- So, tell me, what are you writing now?
- The saddest of all verses [*Los versos más tristes*].
- When?
- Tonight. [*Esta noche*]. (n.p.)

Today, Monsiváis is undoubtedly a cultural institution and recognized as such by his peers. In addition to chronicling the country's cultural and political life for over 50 years, Monsiváis was considered the intellectual who best interpreted the pulse of contemporary Mexico. For Poniatowska, "Carlos's mind was a guide for the intellectuals of this country." For others, Monsiváis himself turned into a cultural phenomenon in his own right (Salazar Escalante, 75) and can even be considered the embodiment of a new literary genre, as suggested by Paz:

> I am thrilled by the case of Monsiváis: he is neither novelist nor essayist, but rather a chronicler, yet his extraordinary prose, rather than constituting the dissolution of those genres, combines them. A new language appears in Monsiváis's work—the language of the street boy from Mexico City, a brilliantly intelligent boy who has read every book, every comic, and has watched every movie. Monsiváis: a new literary genre. (331)

Perhaps Monsiváis as a new literary genre is simply part of the construction of the myth. It is interesting, though, that Monsiváis himself defined the chronicle as "That point of contact between the essay, journalism, and even poetic prose" (qtd. in Pons, "Carlos Monsiváis," 41). Heterogeneity, versatility, complexity, and the masterful use of the language and irony are some of the shared characteristic of his chronicles. They incorporate various types of discourses and voices (including popular jargon, song lyrics, poems, monologues, biblical and mythical references). They also display Monsiváis's extensive knowledge of *refranes* (Mexican popular sayings), proverbs, and myriad other aspects of Mexican culture and politics. In his chronicles Monsiváis also comments on almost everything from the intransigence (as a sign of incompetence) of the ruling classes to social movements, the *jipitecas* (hippies) of the 60s and literature, María Félix and rock music, cinema, and wrestling (e.g., the wrestler *el Santo*), and Televisa.[9]

The incorporation in his chronicles of the different manifestations of Mexican popular culture prompted some to consider him the precursor of the theoretical-critical revolution of cultural studies in Latin America, whose founding figures (Néstor García Canclini and particularly Jesús Martín-Barbero) would take Monsiváis's chronicles as the basis for their work (Sánchez Prado, "Otra conciencia," n.p.). The characteristics and institutionalization of cultural studies would, in turn, position Monsiváis as a postmodern intellectual. Sánchez Prado, however, offers a different perspective. According to this scholar, Monsiváis is not interested in perceiving the chronicle as a postmodern and hybrid genre, but in aligning himself as part of "a genealogy that goes back to the sixteenth century chronicles and was amply cultivated by the nineteenth-century writers. In other words, Monsiváis is not interested in the chronicle as a novel genre, but as an intellectual exercise with a long tradition of *political* functions"; a nonconformist political tradition within the lettered city ("Crónica, nación y liberalismo," 309, 333).[10] The cultivation of this genre, the chronicle, certainly situates Monsiváis far from the classic figure of the traditional intellectual. While the traditional intellectual might be seen to interpret reality from his distant and secluded position, and to produce a monologist and didactic interpretation of the world (often through the analysis of "high" culture), the chronicler/journalist rejects this distance. He walks the streets of the city and allows the reality he witnesses to invade his text (Mudrovcic, "Carlos Monsiváis: Un intellectual post," 68; Riebová, "Metáfora e ironía").

It should be noted, however, that in the case of Monsiváis's chronicles, references to daily life and the incorporation of popular culture does not mean that everybody could easily read them, that they were always accessible. The "rejection of distance" exercised by the chronicler/journalist seems to be more nominal than real when it comes to reading Monsiváis's chronicles. This is not to imply that Monsiváis emphasizes the traditional hierarchical relationship between the author in his ivory tower (who has the knowledge) and the reader (who does not). Yet, it is important to note that his chronicles can be quite demanding on the reader. They are, like the reality that he witnesses and allows "to invade the text," overwhelmingly vast, slippery, and difficult to apprehend. It is certainly the inexorable critical eye and sharp pen of Monsiváis that creates the effect, the illusion of "the reality invading the text." His chronicles are more than a mirror in which Mexican society can recognize itself. They are an exercise in interpretation composed of multiple "ingredients" (including fiction), by which Monsiváis turns "an image in the mirror" into an X-ray of Mexican society. Thus, Monsiváis's complex style, along with the constellation of references found in his chronicles (from local culture and politics, to mythical, biblical, and the like), require significant work digesting and decoding from the (well informed, educated) reader in order to make sense of the whole, and to appreciate the critical power of his irony and sarcastic humor. For those readers who are not familiar with Mexican social, cultural, and political daily life, reading Monsiváis's chronicles is particularly difficult. To read Monsiváis, says Linda Egan, represents a challenge to any scholar, reader, or translator.[11] Jean Franco has pointed out how difficult it is to translate Monsiváis, mainly because of his deft use of the language and irony. It is very difficult to translate him without betraying him, which explains, according to Franco, why this Mexican intellectual is not so well-known internationally, particularly beyond the Spanish-speaking world. Indeed, only two of his books have been translated into English.

These observations do not make him less "un-repeatable" (that is, less unique) or less a public intellectual *par excellence*. Monsiváis's intellectual contribution to and participation in the understanding of the political, social, and cultural life of Mexico was not confined to his chronicles. Nor are his writings limited to the local realities of Mexico. He wrote and spoke more generally about Latin American culture, literature and history, social movements, indigenous uprisings, women and gay rights, sexual diversity, neoliberalism, globalization, and so on. Moreover, Monsiváis was not just a writer; he was a free thinker and committed intellectual in the full sense of the word. To be sure, Monsiváis was part of the Mexican intellectual elite, despite the fact that he might have had a hard time acknowledging it, but he was physically, emotionally, and intellectually much closer to the people than any typical traditional intellectual. Quite telling are the words written by Mexican actress Marichuy in an online forum when Monsiváis passed away: "Monsi (as he was also known) belonged to a kind they don't make anymore. This country needs more people like him and fewer self-absorbed, pretentious, elitist, and old-fashioned 'intellectuals' like those that abound" (qtd. in "México se despide de Monsiváis," n.p.).

Monsiváis's critical readings of the world reach people through different means, for example his writings in newspapers, his participation in conferences and roundtables, or his appearances in videos, television, and radio shows. Omnipresent and indefatigable, as Poniatowska describes him, Monsiváis could also be seen "Visiting Ciudad Juarez to denounce the murder of young women; taking another plane to Hermosillo to show solidarity with the parents of the 44 children burned to death in the fire at the ABC Daycare Center; going out at dawn to collect the testimonies of those injured by the San Juanico gas explosion; living in the streets for thirty days after the earthquake of 1985" (n.p.). He could also be found surrounded by renowned writers, eminent politicians, or celebrities, just as he could be seen side by side with neighbors from the lower classes, or marching along with the people in defense of all human rights. As Marta Lamas comments in her prologue to *Misógeno feminista*,[12] "[Monsiváis] put his celebrity, like a political strategist, at the service of activist groups. His fame opened doors for us that, without him, we would've never been able to enter" (n.p.).[13]

Monsiváis's defense of minorities and his unconditional alliance with social movements, his struggle for equality and social justice, his constant wandering throughout the city and frequent appearances in the media, all help explain why he was not only popular but also loved by the people, who considered him one of their own. When he died, an immense crowd showed up to say goodbye, wanting to stand beside the casket and guard it (a position that had originally been assigned to select guests), while voicing their appreciation for him: "Monsi lives forever!" "Long lives the man of the people!" "We love you, Monsi, we love you!" "Monsi is the people!" "Monsi was the voice of the people!" "Monsi is not a VIP!" In short, it might not be easy for the general public to read or have access to some of Monsiváis's works, but his ideas and his words were very much present and heard in the public arena.

### The Quixote of the Left

If there is one thing for which Carlos Monsiváis will always be known and recognized, it is his relentless criticism of intolerance and his consistent and deep commitment to the idea of social justice. He has been called "the Quixote of the left," "the critical conscience of the country," "the moral leader of the city," and an "intellectual whose rebellious spirit never left him," as Herralde asserts. At the commemoration of the first anniversary of the writer's death, gathered for a roundtable called "Lost love (Amor perdido): A year without Monsi," Jenaro Villamil emphasized how Carlos Monsiváis was always on the side of minorities: "To begin with, he was born poor, he was a Protestant in a Catholic society, he was gay without labels in a country full of homophobia" (n.p.). In *Mexican Postcards*, Monsiváis clearly and succinctly states his position:

> What social and cultural spaces have been made available for Mexican dissidents, fighting for democracy or . . . for alternative lifestyles? Prisons,

silence, negation, clandestine lives, ridicule by the mass media...confinement, and the asphyxiating alleys in which the hopes and illusions of bohemians, feminists, radicals, homosexuals, have been born, and—rebels or not—have found it possible to disaffiliate themselves from the State, Society, the System, Convention and Moral Prejudice, Machismo, all abstractions that name everyday oppression. (22–23)

He dedicated a number of his writings to dismantling homophobic and sexist prejudices as part of his defense of human rights. Many of these writings are reproduced in *Misógeno feminista,* as well as in the posthumous publication *Que se abra esa puerta.* Throughout the chronicles and essays collected for these volumes, Monsiváis not only aims to dignify the struggles of gays and women, but also to point out the high cost of both self and societal incrimination (namely, hate crimes against homosexuals, transvestites, and women). The introduction to *Que se abra esa puerta* (by Marta Lamas) could not bear a more appropriate title: "The Door to Dignity." The first part of this collection mainly includes Monsiváis's reflections on the life and social expressions of the Mexican gay community. As Brito points out, in the chronicles and essays included in this volume Monsiváis makes the effort to describe and make visible a world that remained hidden and at the margin of any social and institutional acknowledgement in Mexico (*Que se abra esa puerta*). But Monsiváis also reflects on the close relationship that exists between misogyny and homophobia (Villamil, n.p.).[14] We cannot dissociate one from the other, he suggests. Without a doubt, the rejection and hostility toward homosexuals, observes Monsiváis, belongs to the social construction of the feminine, and the infinitesimal place granted to women in our societies: "A gay voluntarily degrades himself when he resembles women, and the *machista* condemnation is the public and private registering of that degradation" (Monsiváis, *Que se abra esa puerta,* 59).

For Monsiváis, Salvador Novo's savage and insolent humor allows him to create a distance from the bitterness of reality. Novo, says Monsiváis, is a practitioner of "effeminacy," and "by underscoring it he satisfies the expectation of moral voyeurism" (*Que se abra esa puerta,* 65). While Novo was probably the first public figure to openly accept his gayness in an intolerant society, he opted for "the valiant and humorous" cynical exhibition of his homosexuality to protect himself from the machismo and nationalism of his time.

In his essay "De la marginalidad sexual en América Latina," Monsiváis perceives a change in the tradition as a result of the self-mocking that Novo cultivated to protect himself, a change seen in the awakening of a new wave of Latin American gay writers like the

Argentineans Néstor Perlongher and Manuel Puig, the Puerto Rican Manuel Otero, the Cubans Reynaldo Arenas and Servero Sarduy, and the Mexican Joaquín Hurtado. In them, Monsiváis perceives a "literature of the indignation (Perlongher, Ramos Otero, Arenas, Hurtado), of radical experimentation (Sarduy), of the playful and victorious incorporation of the proscribed sensibility (Puig). For all of these authors gayness is not artistic identity but an adjacent attitude that affirms a cultural trend and consciousness raising movement" (*Que se abra esa puerta*, 188). The second part of *Que se abra esa puerta* specifically includes chronicles and essays in which Monsiváis locates gay and sexual diversity advocates within the framework of his defense of human rights and of their marginal and dissident position. He also reflects on the changes regarding sexuality and sexual practices taking place in Mexican society in particular, and in Latin America in general.

His enthusiasm for the indigenous struggle in Chiapas was notorious, but he idealizes neither the indigenous people nor the Chiapas insurgency. He admits that even though it did prompt a generation to reevaluate their idea of the country, it was also evident that, while the presence of indigenous populations was now taken into account, their demands were still not met. At one point, Monsiváis even openly criticized Subcomandante Marcos when the latter expressed his support for the Basque separatist movement.[15] While he always identified with the political left, he never hesitated to criticize its dogmatic positions. He was one of the first to distance himself from Cuba when it started to show traces of inflexibility and a lack of individual freedom, just as he later distanced himself from Hugo Chávez. "What interests me of the left," he told journalist Jorge Ricardo of the newspaper *Reforma*, "is the need for it to stay critical, not blindly admiring Fidel Castro's dictatorship; to put into perspective the often unacceptable authoritarianism of Hugo Chávez; to oppose the right; to denounce corruption without compromise; to draw conclusions from the failure of real socialism; to be deeply anti-racist, to defend national interests without being nationalistic, to oppose inequality, the biggest problem in the country" (n.p.).

Iconoclastic as few can claim to be, Monsiváis was also a fierce critic of religious dogmatism, a defender of the secular state who fought against religious instruction in public schools, as well as a harsh critic of the effects of any religion that induces idiocy and lethargy. The common bonds between religious excess and social marginalization are also prone to cause blind belief in the miracles of the Virgin of Guadalupe or the exaltation of mystic individuals such as Niño Fidencio, the folk saint and *curandero* (healer) who "perfectly symbolizes a level of popular, self-denying religiosity, violent in its self-flagellation, incapable of despondency and hopelessness, that is reborn in every cult or ritual. The story of Fidencio pertains to this extreme vision of the vanquished, which is the disease of the poor" (*Los rituales*, 104). Monsiváis was equally merciless toward the solemnity, vulgarity, and greed of politicians, officials, and rulers and against any form of authoritarianism:

> Mexican authoritarianism, which is what I have experienced, is unbearable in all of its manifestations, not only in the PRI, but also in the socially-applauded cruelty, the slavery of housewives, the rejection of the different, etc., of daily life. These are the issues that, if I were to compile them by simply stating them, I would not be creating a chronicle but an election campaign without a candidate. (qtd. in Pons, "Carlos Monsiváis," 44)

Against the solemnity he criticizes, Monsiváis uses one of his best weapons: irony. In the Mexican leftist environment of the 50s in which he was educated (he says), the lack of irony was astounding; everything was seriousness, rigidity, demagogy, inflexibility of the worst kind. For Monsiváis, irony is a form of protection against these ills:

> I wanted to immunize myself from the atmosphere of pompous discourses, from turning everyday experiences into sculptures...Many people used to speak as if they were victims on the gallows who must pronounce their last words to mankind before the blade falls on their neck...*MANKIND... WHEN YOU LEAVE THE HOUSE, DON'T FORGET TO TURN OFF THE STOVE!!* (qtd. in Pons, "Carlos Monsiváis," 43)

His irony spared no one, not even Paz. It is noteworthy, however, that Monsiváis admired and greatly respected Paz as a poet and an intellectual. He never ceased to recognize the influence the Nobel laureate had on his own conception of prose, the influence of the man who, without neglecting scholarly rigor, was able to make poetry in his critical work and essays. That famous gesture by Paz of renouncing his position as cultural attaché in India after the student massacre at Tlatelolco was of particular relevance for the progressive intellectual community to which Monsiváis belonged. Nevertheless, the ideological differences that would lead to an inevitable distance between them were soon to become increasingly evident. Paz defended his position as a liberal and independent intellectual, while Monsiváis identified with the socially committed intellectual community.[16]

The figure of Monsiváis as a committed intellectual reaches greater heights with his chronicles of the Tlatelolco massacre in 1968, compiled in his book *Días de guardar* (1970). It is in these chronicles and those of Elena Poniatowska that the Mexican left finds its voice.[17] Moreover, in Krauze's opinion, Carlos Monsiváis was an icon of the years 1968 and 1985, and the leader of a broad sector of the civil society. In many ways, Monsiváis is the intellectual who emerges from 1968 with the idea that political resistance must arise from civil society and culture.

Monsiváis was equally ruthless in revealing the fraud of Mexican cultural nationalism and its definition of the national identity, which he saw as an imposition and a case of "symbolic domination" (to use Karl Kraus's concept). He dismantles the symbols and figures glorified by the Mexican State, from the Mexican muralists and the narrative of the revolution, to the melodramatic narrative of Pedro Infante's films and *The Labyrinth of Solitude* by Paz. For Monsiváis, popular culture is what will define an unofficial, alternative form of nationalism in which national identity is defined in the sphere of everyday life (Monsiváis, "Muerte y resurrección," 20). The relationship and distinction that Monsiváis establishes between "*nationalist culture* (or what is perceived as a monolithic cultural identity imposed from above) and *national culture* (or the many different cultural identities defended from below)," examined by Mudrovcic, is one the constant aspects that can be observed throughout his chronicles ("Cultura nacionalista vs. Cultura nacional" 125). For Sánchez Prado, the manifestations of popular culture that interest Monsiváis are those that would allow us to glimpse an "authentic" people, and thus an alternate history, rejecting those histories that mimic the rituals of power ("Crónica nación y liberalismo," 313). This explains to a certain degree the ambivalent love/hate relationship, the attraction and rejection of the cultural and social manifestations of the popular classes that Monsiváis expresses throughout his chronicles. Very often, these aspects of popular culture that are vindicated and defended by Monsiváis are referred to as "Chaos/Relajo."

### Chaos/"Relajo": The Alpha and the Omega

*Without a doubt, "relajo" is the permanent mood of Monsiváis:*

*—I insulted you the other day—he says on the phone, distressed.*
*—What did you say?*
*—I quoted you.*
*(Laughter)*

Mejía Madrid

Monsiváis's concept of *relajo* can mean several, usually interrelated, things. It may refer to a sense of humor and playfulness that imply an enjoyment of language; spontaneous fun; any kind of carnivalesque expression, either in the form of a big mess, a rowdy party, or a social gathering; a purposeful avoidance of schedules and all types of conventions; anything implying real or symbolic excess that would defy the *status quo* or the ruling order. Essentially, *relajo* would be all that happens outside the limits of any given order, or within a spontaneous, changing, unpredictable, or absurd kind of order. This term, *relajo* usually appears in Monsiváis's chronicles associated with "chaos." The chaos/order relationship is one of the biblical/mythical references we find throughout his chronicles, often in relation to culture and the urban landscape as the privileged site where society's real and symbolic struggles take place.[18]

In general terms, one might say that in the chronicles previous to *Los rituales del caos*, the notion of order is represented specifically by hegemonic power groups in Mexican political and social life—the institutionalization of the Mexican Revolution; the authoritarianism of Porfirio Díaz, the PRI, and those occupying the pinnacles of political power; the sentimental and demagogic legacy of nationalism imposed from above; and the morality and "good manners" of the bourgeoisie, the dictates of "refined" taste of that set of "human decorations" ("The Beautiful People," "the jet set representatives," "The Happy Few," or "the Favorites of Fate"). That is, it is always a question of an identifiable order in terms of politics, class, and/or gender. Similarly, in general terms, one could say that in the chronicles before *Los rituales del caos*, the notion of chaos is rather a rupture with, or a challenge to the hierarchies imposed by that same political and social order by means of scandal, countercultures, and, mainly, through a demand for "free access to the history" of different social movements. Whether these ruptures and challenges to the social order triumph or are repressed, what is relevant is that in the earlier chronicles, the notion of chaos (linked to these gestures of defiance) is not critiqued but vindicated in that they propose options and a space for questioning or even altering hierarchies.

In *Los rituales del caos*, however, the concept of chaos/*relajo* is no longer associated with defying norms and hierarchies, with rebellions or insurgencies, or with disturbances to the social order. In these chronicles, under the section titled "Parable of the end. Where, due to a lack of signs, the alpha and the omega are confused," the notion of chaos (which takes here the name *Relajo*) is presented, on the one hand, as in mythology: "*Relajo*: the alphabet of origins"

(*Los rituales*, 134). On the other hand, Monsiváis alludes to those "disarrays/relajos" that lead to, and are part of, the final disorder, the Apocalypse: "In the Last Moment of all living beings, when severity and excess combine, *Relajo* will be the language at hand to foster the dictatorship of uniformity...When everything is over, a racket and an eternal minute of silence will be the same, and *Relajo* (with its speakers, proclamations, orchestras, horns, chain explosions) will be that effective method for providing a homely warmth to the massive generalization of agony" (*Los rituales*, 134).

Monsiváis uses the parabolic language of the Apocalypse in order to point out that that inevitable "massive generalization of agony" is a result of the uncontrolled processes of globalization and neoliberal policies. From the start, *Los rituales del caos* declares that this final disorder has to do with the demographic overflow, the urban disorder, and the society of the masses proper of Mexico City—a city of apocalyptic characteristics where urban vitality turns into a suffocating dead end and traffic jams or a ride on the subway are nothing but "chaos in a nutshell, so to speak" (111). "In my commute on the Periférico highway, [says Monsiváis on another occasion], I was able to listen to the complete nine symphonies of Beethoven. Do you know what I felt? That true leisure time is that of traffic jams" ("Del cultivo del alma en los embotellamientos," n.p.).

In addition to this condition of urban apocalyptic chaos, Monsiváis exposes the rituals of (false) chaos that are both the product of an imposed order, and the best guarantee of its continuity. In these chronicles it is suggested, thus, that chaos and order are nothing but two sides of the same coin. It is a more ubiquitous, penetrating, and totalizing order: one generated by the process of modernization and the excesses of advanced capitalism (represented in these chronicles by the dictates of marketing and consumption, and technology, "the true driving forces of society").

For Monsiváis, one of the ultimate dangers underlying these driving forces is that they are not just the "generators of false satisfiers for illusory needs" (207); they became, above all, a monologist dictatorial system of social organization and the rationale regulating the way society thinks and behaves, nullifying all alternatives (Monsiváis, *Los rituales*, 205). On the back cover of *Los rituales del caos*, we read that these later chronicles describe "chaos not, in this case, as the alteration of hierarchies, but as a desire to live as if those hierarchies were not here, upon and within oneself." In fact, there are no references to social movements or any other social actors in these chronicles. As Zermeño observed, "What in Mexico has been called modernization since the 1980s (defined as globalization and transnational insertion) resulted in a furious attack against social actors" (11), among them: union leaders, the universities, the autonomous media, the social movements, and the like. The few "liberating forces" mentioned in *Los rituales del caos* are represented by popular cultural manifestations, which are perceived not as rupture with, or a challenge to any imposed repressive order, but as survival strategies during economic crisis: "To a great extent the economic crisis *is* the urban popular culture in that it adapts everything (life styles, manners, desires, uses of leisure time) to the logic of survival" (122).

### From Chaos to *Apocalipstick*

The Apocalypse, says Monsiváis in *Los rituales del caos*, is a moment of extreme decadence, and when the time of Apocalypse comes, "the most atrocious nightmare" is to be "definitively excluded" (*Los rituales*, 250). Recently, in response to the question of whom or what are the great plagues of the urban centers today, Monsiváis uses again the metaphor of the Apocalypse:

> If we want to draw upon the images of science fiction films and we talk of the Four Horsemen of the Apocalypse, we have to select among unemployment, urban violence, domestic violence, the disaster of schooling, the sub-employment, exploitation, the time invested in transportation and commute, the shortage of water in the city and the country, contamination, and *ni modo* (there is no way we could deny it), the gross stupidity of the right. It doesn't matter if there are more than four horsemen, after all...they don't have any more room to ride. (qtd. in Mateo-Vega, n.p.)

In spite of his critical and assertive perception of our times, I believe that Monsiváis never lost his optimism. In *Mexican Postcards*, he points to forms of social action that speak of the utopias of our days, as he says, including the defense of human rights, the fight against AIDS, the struggle for ecological preservation, and indigenous movements (140).

In *Apocalipstick*, Monsiváis returns to the critical view of the city as chaotic, disperse, fragmented, and inhospitable, as well as to the omnipresence of the technology and power of the media: from the reality shows, YouTube, the web social networks, cellular phones and the addictive need to be connected, to the ambition to appear on camera. "In the future everybody will have the right to 15 minutes of anonymity," sentenced Monsiváis in another of his aphorisms. However, he also dedicates a number of chronicles in this volume to the social movements, marches, and other expressions of dissident and counter-hegemonic groups, and analyzes the changes he perceives that have taken place in Mexico, particularly those concerning sexuality and the manifestations of the body. Very telling in this regard is the cover of the book: it is a picture of a Spencer Tunick performance with 20,000 naked bodies covering the Zócalo (the central plaza of Mexico City). As mentioned before, in the second part of *Que se abra esa puerta*, we also find chronicles and essays in which Monsiváis locates advocates of gay and sexual diversity not only within the framework of their marginal and dissident positions, but also in relation to the above mentioned changes in the sexual practices and beliefs in Mexican society, including the new spaces and types of nocturnal life. It is interesting that in relation to these latter issues, Monsiváis comes back to what he calls "the geopolitics of *relajo* and desire," in which he describes one night in the nightclub El14, including the parade of the different "tribes of urban-gay" *habitués* of the place. For him, this is an example of a refreshing change or redefinition of Mexican nightlife.

This permanent desire of Monsiváis to locate social behaviors that could eventually counter an oppressive order is another constant aspect in his chronicles. "The exercise of writing chronicles," says Monsiváis, "takes me to the certitude of all singularities, of the worth of locating between the poles of life (the good and the bad): the vitality, the originality, the creative powers of the minorities and majorities" (qtd. in Mateo-Vega, n.p.). These words are consistent with Monsiváis's position as an intellectual whose role, as suggested by Sanchez-Prado, is to discern which manifestations of social mobilization are characteristic of civil society and which ones correspond to the "society of spectacle" that mimic the rituals of power. All the forms of social action characteristic of civil society, says Monsiváis in *Mexican Postcards*, propose opening a space for a greater humanism and social justice, even if they do not intend to change the totality of the system or the human being as a whole.

Monsiváis never abandoned his belief (and hope) that political resistance and social change must and would arise from the civil society, and never stopped supporting and accompanying those social actions that would lead to it. His deep sense of social ethics reminds me of the distinction between individual morality and social ethics that was brought about during the Civil Rights Movements in the United States. One of the examples used to illustrate this distinction was the view that John Adams, the second president of the United States, had on slavery. Adams opposed slavery, considering it to be an abhorrent practice, but he was not an abolitionist. Thus, prompted by his sense of individual morality, he refused to employ slaves "in times when the practice of slavery was not disgraceful," as he proudly said. He failed, however, to recognize that social ethics would have demanded from him support of the abolition of slavery altogether. Monsiváis's moral responsibility as an intellectual was never divorced from his social ethics. His implacable criticism of all forms of oppressive, dehumanizing powers always goes hand in hand with the consistent effort to locate and support social actions that could lead to a more just and humane society.

## Monsiváis: The Myth, the Void, and the Challenge

"What are we going to do without you, Monsi, how are we supposed to go on?" This is the question with which Poniatowska titled and opened her tribute speech to Monsiváis on the day of his funeral service at the Palacio de Bellas Artes. Without a doubt, the death of this great Mexican intellectual leaves an irreparable void in the Mexican and Latin American intellectual communities alike. "Fast wit, deep culture, a piercing gaze, timely reference, hidden melancholy, forever joyous. How we are going to miss all those characteristics of the great and unique Carlos Monsiváis!" Fuentes grieves (n.p.). For his part, Pitol remembers him this way: "Carlos was many things, but above everything, he was our most lucid and incisive conscience. His figure and work became a moral compass for traveling through this Mexico that he wrote so much about and was able to see so clearly...With his death, there is a sense of abandonment floating in the air, there will be no one to take his place" (qtd. in Aguilar Sosa, *El Universal*, n.p.).

The void left by Carlos Monsiváis, however, while helping feed the legends and myths surrounding his figure, also poses a challenge for all Latin American intellectuals: a challenge to further develop or reinvent their own roles as intellectuals. To summarize what Collazos said: if there was anything that linked those two great writers, Monsiváis and Saramago, who died just two days apart from each other, it is that they both lived the ethical and political dimension of the intellectual, that invention of the late nineteenth century that the neoconservative cynicism of the twenty-first century has not yet managed to destroy. The challenges of the twenty-first century, says Monsiváis in *No sin nosotros*, are huge: to humanize politics and society in order to humanize the economy (52). Keeping that dream alive, and the intellectual ethical, social, and political commitments afloat could be an answer to Poniatowska's question, as well as the challenge of our century.

## Notes

1. All translations are my own.
2. One of the many ceremonies to honor him on the anniversary of his death was held in the Museo del Estanquillo, which he founded, where a collective reading was announced as such: "To each his Monsi."
3. In the first stage, Monsiváis wrote this column in collaboration with Alejandro Brito, the current coordinator of the supplement *Letra S*, and in the second stage, with Jenaro Villamil.
4. For his journalistic endeavors, Monsiváis received, among others, the National Journalism Award (1977 and 2009), the Manuel Buendía Award (1988), and the Journalism Award of the Club de Periodistas de México (1995).

    He received various prizes and awards for his work as a chronicler and essayist, too numerous to mention here.
5. For a more complete list of his essays and chronicles, see Moraña and Sánchez Prado.
6. The urn is kept in the reading room of el Museo del Estanquillo. This museum was founded in 2006 following Monsiváis's wishes to share his collection of more than 20,000 pieces of various kinds: historical documents, paintings, photos, engravings, miniatures, and so on.
7. On similar lines, Castañón states that the figure Carlos Monsiváis "is unexplainable if we fail to take into account that he is one of the best informed men in Mexico. A constantly mobile and fresh network of contacts, relationships, friendships, meetings, references, readings, and records keep him always afloat on the sea of stressed but tireless Mexican humanity. No matter how much he may write and how much we may read him, we will never truly exhaust Monsiváis's knowledge of Mexico" (163).
8. Upon his death, a special space named "La Ciudadela" (The citadel) was built in one of the wings of Mexican library "José Vasconcelos" to host the 24,000 volumes of Carlos Monsiváis' personal library, now available to the public.
9. For a more extensive discussion of the characteristics of his chronicles as a hybrid genre, see the works of Egan and of Anadeli Becomo. For a genealogy of the genre, see Moraña. For a discussion of the chronicle and the popular cultures as a liberal project since the nineteenth century, see Sánchez Prado ("Crónica, nación y liberalismo").
10. Anadeli Becomo considers Monsiváis within the intellectual genealogy of Western modernity, but she does so in relation to his essayistic work, not necessarily in relation with the chronicle.
11. See "Traducir Monsiváis, el reto" by Yanet Aguilar Sosa. *El Universal. Cultura.*
12. *Misógeno feminista* is a collection of the essays that Monsiváis wrote about feminism, gender, and women's issues. The title of the volume is taken from the very definition that Monsiváis gave of himself

when asked to provide, as a collaborator of *Debate Feminista*, some autobiographical information. He wrote then, in the third person, "He alternates his misogyny with his passionate defense of feminism" (Lamas, "Prologue").

13. Referring to the supplement *Letra S*, published monthly by the newspaper *La Jornada*, featuring information for the lesbian-gay community and on AIDS-related subjects, Marta Lamas remembers that Monsiváis was the one who suggested the supplement's name to the editors. He said that the letter "S" stood for: AIDS (*SIDA* in Spanish), solidarity, sexuality, syndrome, sweat, society, blood (*sangre*), safe sex, health (*salud*), secretions, sexual services, system, sarcoma, HIV-positive (seropositivo), saliva, solution, serum, symptom, semen, solitude, supplement, sanity, suffering, supply, knowledge (*saber*), and so on.
14. See Villamil's wonderful introduction to *Que se abra esa puerta* in 2011.
15. See also the letter that Monsiváis wrote to Subcomandante Marcos in 1996, "Fábula del país de Nopasanada, carta dirigida al subcomandante Marcos en donde se encuentre, para notificarle acuerdos, discrepancias y modestas reflexiones." (Fables from the country of Nothinghappens, a letter addressed to Subcomandante Marcos, wherever he is, to notify him of some agreements, discrepancies, and modest reflections), published by *La Jornada Semanal*, January 14, 1996: 9-10.
16. For further information on the separation between Paz and Monsiváis, see Mudrovcic, "Carlos Monsiváis."
17. For Monsiváis, Poniatowska's *La noche de Tlatelolco* is "a masterpiece of participatory journalism." According to him, this text accompanied by photographs became a political act the moment it was published (*Entrada Libre*, 359).
18. For a more detailed elaboration and discussion of the dialectic relationship between chaos and order in Monsiváis's chronicles, see my work included in Moraña and Sánchez Prado. I would like to thank Mabel Moraña for giving me permission to reproduce part of this analysis in these pages.

## Works Cited

Aguilar Sosa, Yanet. "Monsi, el ciudadano que mejor denunció la codicia rampante." *El Universal*. Mexico, DF. June 20, 2011. http://mx.noticias.yahoo.com/monsi-ciudadano-denunci%C3%B3-codicia-rampante-050539851.html. Web.

———. "Traducir Monsiváis, el reto." *El Universal.Cultura*. June 19, 2013. http://www.eluniversal.com.mx/notas/930664.html. Web.

Becomo, Anadeli. "Carlos Monsiváis. Discurso a dos voces." *Textos Híbridos. Revista sobre la crónica latinoamericana* 1.1 (2011). Permalink: http://escholarship.ucop.edu/uc/item/901488gc. Web.

Castañón, Adolfo. "Un hombre llamado ciudad." *Vuelta* 163 (1990): 19–22. Print.
Collazos, Oscar. "Saramago y Monsiváis." *Fundaçaõ José Saramago*. June 6, 2011. http://www.josesaramago.org/detalle.php?id=872. Web.
Egan, Linda. *Carlos Monsiváis: Culture and Chronicle in Contemporary Mexico*. Tucson: University of Arizona Press, 2001. Print.
Franco, Jean. "Monsiváis, autor difícil de traducir." *El Universal*. June 19, 2013. http://www.eluniversal.com.mx/notas/930664.html. Web.
Fuentes, Carlos. "Monsiváis." *La Nación*. July 10, 2010. http://www.lanacion.com.ar/1283226-monsivais. Web.
Herralde, Jorge. "Nadie podrá olvidarte, Monsi." *Anagrama*. December 2010. n.p. http://www.anagrama-ed.es/agenda/11/2010. Web.
Krauze, Enrique. "Monsi, el irrepetible." *Letras Libres*. June 21, 2010. http://letraslibres.daniloblackusa.net/blogs/monsi-el-irrepetible. Web.
Lamas, Marta. Prologue. Monsiváis *Misógeno feminista* (e-book).
Mateo-Vega, Mónica. "Reportaje Monsiváis." *La Jornada*. February 15, 2010: 10. http://www.elsaborsaberdelpsicoanalisis.org/2010/02/15/reportaje-monsivais/. Web.
Mejía Madrid, Frabrizio. "Carlos Monsiváis: retrato en taxi. In memoriam: Carlos Monsiváis (1938–2010)." *Prodavinci*. May 4, 2011. http://prodavinci.com/2011/05/04/artes/carlos-monsivais-retrato-en-taxi/. Web.
"México se despide de Monsiváis," June 20, 2010. http://www.holaciudad.com/mexico-se-despide-carlos-monsivais-n88383. Web
Monsiváis, Carlos. *Aires de familia: Cultura y sociedad en América Latina*. Barcelona: Anagrama, 2000.
———. *Amor perdido*. Mexico: Biblioteca Era, 1977. Print.
———. *Apocalipstick*. Mexico: Debate, 2009. Print.
———. "Del cultivo del alma en los embotellamientos." *Nexos*, January 1, 2006. http://www.nexos.com.mx/?P=leerarticulo&Article=660400. Web.
———. *Días de guardar*. Mexico: Biblioteca Era, 1970. Print.
———. *Entrada libre. Crónicas de la sociedad que se organiza*. Mexico: Biblioteca Era, 1987. Print.
———. *Escenas de pudor y liviandad*. Mexico: Grijalbo, 1988. Print.
———. "Fábula del país de Nopasanada, carta dirigida al subcomandante Marcos en donde se encuentre, para notificarle acuerdos, discrepancias y modestas reflexiones." *La Jornada Semanal* (Mexico *La Jornada*), January 14, 1996: 9–10. Print.
———. *La poesía mexicana del siglo XX. Antología*. Mexico: Empresas Editoriales, 1966.
———. *Las alusiones perdidas*. Barcelona: Anagrama, 2007.
———. *Las esencias viajeras*. Mexico: Fondo de Cultura Económico, 2012. Print.
———. *Las tradiciones de la imagen*. Madrid: Fondo de Cultura Económica de España, 2003.
———. *Los rituales del caos*. Mexico: Biblioteca Era, 1995. Print.
———. *Maravillas que fueron, sombras que son. La fotografía en México*. Mexico: Era, 2012. Print.

———. *Mexican Postcards*. New York: Verso, 1997. Print.
———. *Misógeno feminista*. Selection and Prologue by Marta Lamas. Mexico: Oceano; Debate Feminista, 2013.
———. "Muerte y resurrección del Estado Mexicano," *Nexos* 109 (1987): 13–22. Print.
———. "No sin nosotros": los días del terremoto 1985–2005. Mexico: Era, 2005. Print.
———. *Nuevo catecismo para indios remisos*. Mexico: Siglo XXI, 1982.
———. *Que se abra esa puerta. Crónica y ensayos sobre la diversidad sexual*. Mexico: Paidós, 2010. Print.
———. "Respuesta a Octavio Paz." *Proceso* 59 (19 Dic. 1977): 39–41. Print.
Monsiváis, Carlos and Jenaro Villamil. "Las Cuatro Décadas de *Por mi madre, Bohemios*." June 6, 2010. http://pormimadrebohemios2.wordpress.com/. Web.
Moraña, Mabel. "El culturalismo de Carlos Monsiváis. Ideología y carnavalización en tiempos globales." Moraña and Sánchez Prado. 21–59. Print.
Moraña, Mabel and Ignacio Sanchez-Prado, eds. *El arte de la ironía: Carlos Monsiváis ante la crítica*, Mexico: Ediciones Era; UNAM, 2007. Print.
Mudrovcic, María Eugenia. "Carlos Monsiváis, un intelectual post-68." *Tradition y actualidad de la literatura iberoamericana. Actas del XXX Congreso del Instituto Internacional de Literatura Iberoamericana*. Edited by Pamela Bacarisse. Vol. 1. Pittsburgh: University of Pittsburgh-Instituto Internacional de literatura Iberoamericana, 1995. 295–302. Print.
———. "Cultura nacionalista vs. cultural nacional: Carlos Monsiváis ante la sociedad de masas." Moraña and Sánchez-Prado. 124–35. Print.
Paz, Octavio. "El precio y la significación." *Obras Completas*. Vol. 7 (Los privilegios de la vista II). Mexico: Fondo de Cultura Económica, 1994. 331–37. Print.
Pitol, Sergio. "Carlos Monsiváis, el jóven." Moraña and Sánchez Prado. 339–52. Print.
Poniatowska, Elena. "Carlos Monsiváis, el cronista." *El Puercoespín*. June 15, 2011. http://www.elpuercoespin.com.ar/2011/06/15/carlos-monsivais-el-cronista-por-elena-poniatowska/. Web.
Pons, María Cristina. "Carlos Monsiváis." Interview with Carlos Monsiváis. *Hispamérica* 101 (2005): 39–52. Print.
———. "Monsi-caos: la política, la poética o la caótica de las crónicas de Carlos Monsiváis." Moraña and Ignacio Sanchez Prado. 107–23. Print.
Ricardo, Jorge. "Carlos Monsiváis, el intelectual multitemático que aún se entusiasma por las causas perdidas." *El Sur*. Agencia Reforma. July 14, 2011. http://www.suracapulco.com.mx/nota1.php?id_nota=37570. Web.
Riebová, Markéta. "Metáfora e ironía. Tlatelolco en la obra de Octavio Paz y Carlos Monsiváis." *La palabra y el hombre. Revista de la Universidad Veracruzana* 14 (2010): 9–15. Print.
Salazar Escalante, Jezreel. "Carlos Monsiváis: de crítico heterodoxo a institución cultural." *Metapolítica* 24–25 (July–October 2002): 74–84. Print.

Sánchez Prado, Ignacio. "Carlos Monsiváis. Crónica, nación y liberalismo." Moraña and Sánchez Prado. 300–38. Print.

———. "Carlos Monsiváis. Otra conciencia perdida." Weblog entry. Ignacio M. Sánchez Prado blog. June 2010. http://ignaciosanchezprado.blogspot.com/2010/06/carlos-monsivais-otra-conciencia.html. Web.

Sotelo, Humberto. "Carlos Monsiváis: el último intelectual." *Reforma Universitaria*, Puebla. El Movimiento estudiantil. June 22, 2010. http://www.poblanerias.com/columnas/sotelo/31434-carlos-monsivais-el-ultimo-intelectual.html. Web.

———. "Pasado y presente." June 22, 2010. http://www.poblanerias.com/columnas/sotelo/31434-carlos-monsivais-el-ultimo-intelectual.html. Web.

Villamil, Jenaro. "*Que se abra esa puerta*. Presentación." January 26, 2011. In *Jenaro Villamil. Medios, Política y sociedad* http://jenarovillamil.wordpress.com/2011/01/26/que-se-abra-esa-puerta/. Web.

Zermeño, Sergio. *La sociedad derrotada. El desorden mexicano del fin de siglo*. Mexico: Siglo XXI, 1996. Print.

## Chapter 4

## Guadalupe Loaeza's Blonded Ambition: Lip-Synching, Plagiarism, and Power Poses

*Emily Hind*

*Thanks to Mary Vázquez Guizar, Sergio Almazán, Margarita de Orellana, and the always delightful Guadalupe Loaeza.*

When trying to think beyond the stereotypes about Guadalupe Loaeza that cast her as a ditzy *señora*, it proves helpful to place her in context with other femme intellectuals in the Mexican media. The genealogy begins at least with late nineteenth- and early twentieth-century feminized bohemian Mexican poets Amado Nervo and Ramón López Velarde, who helped to make the non-masculine endeavor of poetry writing more visible and even respected. Significantly for my argument, these poets paid homage to romantic themes in their poetry and cultivated a sort of noble aesthetic sensibility in their clothes. Decked out in a beribboned diplomatic jacket (think Michael Jackson's Sergeant Pepper wear) and a black dandy coat respectively, Nervo and López Velarde paved the way for other more extravagantly dressed writers to gain visibility as notable citizens. The successors include eccentric twentieth-century Mexican literary stars and television personalities Salvador Novo and Guadalupe Amor, and, some years later, Juan José Arreola. These celebrities' public appearances drew on varying combinations of outrageous femininity and blatant sexuality to support their claims of singular artistic ability and sparkling intellectual talent. Loaeza had in common with Arreola and Amor the struggle to define herself as a capable thinker who never attended a university. The feminized act attracted public attention, but came at the cost of reducing connotations of intellectual authority and depth. Mexican writers' lack of control over the reception of their performances leads me to Joseph Epstein's notion of the "publicity intellectual," who trades not on knowledge, but on self-exposure as a main source of power (21). This power flows along a two-way current.

The public figure at best manipulates the revelation of his or her self in the media, but cannot also determine the interpretation of that self-presentation. This incomplete control over one's own public image presents a special challenge to celebrities who would be famous for their brain work, because when playing to a general audience, it is best for those who want to be admired for their rational intellectual ability to style themselves in an image of reasoned control. Fame thus works to limit legitimacy when it comes to public thinkers' credibility as rational and exceptional minds. By contrast, fame works the opposite effect for "artistic talents," and perhaps deepens a popular conception that opposes artistic creativity to rational thought. Artists are often believed to be legitimately "crazy," and because their uncontrolled or "wild" public images can aid a creative reputation, they seem at home on television. The media, in turn, comes to favor heavily the presence of artists rather than intellectuals. It is germane to review the stereotypes that often cast masculine characteristics as linked to reason, authority, and control, while the feminine can connote the unreasonable and a lack of authoritative power. There is something feminizing about modern fame, then, and this renunciation of reason and control in one's public image works against a media personality who would wish to be recognized for his or her analytical abilities. This effect becomes even more pronounced for exposed personalities on television who lack (or disguise, in Novo's case) masculine-associated intellectual credentials such as a university degree or a legitimating job title.

An example of the humiliation that awaits the feminine-sympathetic and self-publicizing writer surfaces with Reyna Barrera's account of the sordid side of Salvador Novo's relationship with Jacobo Zabludovsky. Novo used to reminisce about a bygone Mexico City on Friday night newscasts of *24 Horas*—in much the same theme as Loaeza's later nostalgic pieces about the city and its famous occupants. Loaeza and Novo also share the feminine publicity act, which risks a compromised image. Take Novo's last days in 1973, when the newspaper columnist landed in the hospital due to fatal complications of a weight-loss treatment. Anchorman Zabludovksy burst into the hospital room with camera at the ready to film Novo live, and caught the writer without his toupee, without his habitual makeup, without proper clothing, and reaching with embarrassment for his dentures (Barrera, 253). Another tale of televised humiliation appears with Juan José Arreola's mortification before the pop singer Thalía on a live broadcast when she accused him of being a "rabo verde" (dirty old man).[1] In an interesting critique of the event, Jorge F. Hernández blamed Arreola for the misunderstanding, because he should never have accepted an appearance on television to talk about soccer (Muñetón Pérez, n.p.). The critic's disapproval of Arreola supports my suggestion that writers who would be "serious" cannot participate lightly in the dignity-stripping media realm that Daniel Howitz describes as "increasingly identical to the public sphere" (143). The conflict plagues the careers of artistic intellectuals who craft spectacular self-images to make it into the spotlight in the first place. Writers who would be public intellectuals must appear on Mexican television, and yet the feminized act that initially catches the public's interest complicates the effort to maintain a respectable image. This problem hints that writers who would be "hard-hitting" (masculinist) public intellectuals must shun publicity-seeking "light" (feminized) opportunities, such as providing color commentary during a soccer broadcast or waxing nostalgic about Mexican urban geography. But, to reject these opportunities is perhaps to forgo meaningful (i.e., highly rated) appearances on television. In fact, a vicious paradox seems to describe the relationship between media and thought: the more successful an intellectual, the more famous he is; with increased fame comes greater manipulation by the media, and thus increased feminization of the intellectual's image, which reduces the intellectual's reputation as respectable. The way to break this cycle would be to find greater respect for the feminine—a surprisingly difficult task. The very mention of Guadalupe Loaeza causes eyes to roll in academic circles. I don't think that this widespread rejection of Loaeza among elite readers has as much to do with her literary skills as it does with the unwritten understanding of what constitutes a "serious" intellectual performance.

Loaeza, faithful to a feminized intellectual performance, routinely accepts nonacademic jobs as a writer and interviewer, and she also cheerfully attends ribbon-cutting ceremonies, invitational breakfasts, and other sorts of promotional events for charities and businesses that end up with coverage in the social section of the newspapers and other forms of style reports. Loaeza continues to over schedule her days with these appearances, probably due to panic at the idea of fading from public attention and missing out on the material payoff. This suspected fear likely reflects the arbitrary nature of her rise to decades of stardom in the first place. Significantly, Guadalupe Loaeza was born María Guadalupe Loaeza Tovar to a socially elite, but financially declining Mexico City family in 1946, and she was never supposed to be an author, much less a public figure known for her witty observation of Mexican politics, history, and social custom. True to the connotations of the word "witty" (*ocurrente*) as an intrinsic sort of intelligence, humorous ideas simply seem to occur to the largely self-educated thinker. The trilingual sixth sister—of a family of seven girls and one boy—did not finish secondary school. After being dismissed from private Catholic school for her unwelcome attitudes and financial problems, Loaeza began work at age 15 as a receptionist in Mexico City for the fashion house Nina Ricci.[2] Two decades, one husband, and three children later, Loaeza decided to complicate her career as the public relations manager for Nina Ricci by trying her hand at writing. In quick succession, she enrolled in a workshop with Elena Poniatowska, won a writing award, and presented herself at the opposition newspaper *Unomásuno* as a chronicler in potential who could satirize the ways of the Mexican wealthy.

In retelling her audacious decision to ask for work at the paper, Loaeza voices her suspicion that onlooking journalists noted her lack of credentials: "¿Quién diablos era esa señora con boina roja a quien le parecía tan sencillo incorporarse en las planas del periódico, sin ser periodista, ni economista, ni tampoco politólogo, ni nada?" (*Por los de abajo*, 11). (Who the hell was that *señora* with a red beret who thought it was so simple to incorporate herself onto the pages of the newspaper, without being a journalist, or an economist, or a political scientist, or anything?) As Loaeza tells it, her pitch benefited from her attractive looks and her family's social connections, both of which appealed to Miguel Ángel Granados Chapa, the man who would become her editor and the second of three husbands.[3] Her decision to emphasize physical appearance and social status in her autobiographical comments reveal Loaeza's constant attention to a proper *señora* performance that values "decency." On this point, Loaeza differs from the more blatant sexuality projected by precursors Novo, Amor, and Arreola. By stripping her act of excessive sex appeal, Loaeza seems to avoid testing boundaries in the startling modes of the flirtatious writers who broke ground for her and who likely made it possible for us today to see the *señora* performance as more compatible with the tasks of a public thinker. In contrast to her appearance, however, in her writing Loaeza usually breaks with the rules of upper-class decency in two important ways: she spills intimate details about the habits of the rich and she adopts a leftist perspective to criticize social problems in Mexico.

Significantly, when she remembers that momentous day in the early 80s when Granados Chapa phoned her after receiving her first text, Loaeza takes care to include the fact that his enthusiastic call interrupted her soap opera (92). If she is telling the truth, I imagine that the context sticks in her memory because much of Loaeza's most regular calling circle would also have been watching the show, rather than telephoning her. Thus, the interruption may represent a dramatic moment of rupture with Loaeza's insular social class. At any rate, the anecdote of the soap opera anticipates the fact that a sincere taste for melodrama guides Loaeza's views on politics and lends a distinctively feminine flavor to her political analysis. Just as soap characters can turn from conniving schemers to admirable saviors and back again, the politicians in Loaeza's writing fall into unambiguous but potentially reversible categories of hero and villain.[4] This simplification welcomes readers who might not normally take an interest in political events. It also earns many literary critics' disdain. For a representative example of critical rejection, I cite Rafael Lemus's negative review of Loaeza's autobiographical novel *Las yeguas finas* (2003). According to Lemus's hyperbolic dismissal, "Escribe [Loaeza], como tantas otras, una literatura falsamente penetrante, falsamente frívola, falsamente femenina. No es, en rigor, una escritora" (n.p.). (Loaeza writes, like so many other women, a falsely penetrating, falsely frivolous, and falsely feminine literature. She is not, strictly speaking, a writer.) The idea that Loaeza is not a writer and—*and*—writes fallaciously as far as frivolousness and femininity go, designs a game too rigged to invite me to play. However, I will quote more of Lemus's critique because it covers all the bases at once when it comes to disliking Loaeza's work. The critic simultaneously accuses Loaeza of merely reflecting other books and consumer demands ("reflejos de otros libros, ecos a su vez de ciertas demandas comerciales") (reflections of other books, echoes in turn of certain commercial demands) and—*and*—of writing in a vacuum: "Escribe plantada en el vacío, ajena a su clase, a toda tradición literaria, a cualquier visión del mundo" (n.p.). (She writes situated in the void, removed from her class, from all literary tradition, from any vision of the world.) How Loaeza might write unoriginally *and* in ignorance of all literary tradition supplies another conundrum. Such vitriolic criticism of Loaeza's literary efforts demonstrates the ways in which readers can be seen to fall short of Loaeza's work. Of course, Lemus's success as a relatively popular critic in Mexican journalism sets up my suspicion that he in turn looks to the (feminized) irrational to gain a spot in the media in the first place. The femininizing effect of fame means that Lemus can find public success in artistic contradiction and can employ a spectacularly interesting but irrational argument to reject what he chooses to describe, by implicit contrast to his own work, as dully and illegitimately irrational.

But what, exactly, is Lemus's root problem with Loaeza? I suspect that her standing as an intellectual in the absence of a university degree irritates him. In general, critics disgruntled with Loaeza probably agree with a single petulant question posed by a woman critic for *Excélsior*: "¿Quién le habrá dicho a Loaeza que tiene la capacidad y el conocimiento suficientes para poder opinar sobre cualquier tema?" (Fong Robles). (Who in the world told Loaeza that she has sufficient ability and knowledge to be able to opine on any topic?) The answer for Loaeza probably lies in the authorization granted her by a mass audience. The public that responds to Loaeza's dramatically emotional and emphatically amateur style has helped keep her work in print. After leaving *Unomásuno*, she contributed to the founding of *La Jornada*—or "¡¡¡*La Jornada*!!!" as she puts it—and now she writes three times a week for *Reforma* (*Por los de abajo*, 53). Loaeza's nearly 30 books have achieved phenomenal sales for the Mexican book market with hundreds of thousands of copies sold, and with some titles reaching nearly 30 editions. As predicted from her columns in the newspaper, many of Loaeza's narrative strategies seem lifted not from sanctioned or "high" literary technique, but from the spontaneous conversation of upper-middle-class Mexican women. Loaeza herself identifies her narrative style as conversational: "Soy una platicadora por entregas. O sea que en lugar de platicar, escribo y escribo" (Loaeza, "Confesiones ante un espejo," 23). (I am a serialized chatterer. That is, instead of chatting, I write and write.) Characteristic literary tropes in her work include feigned innocence, unabashed punctuation marks, and word play that mixes Spanish with English and French. A representative example of this intentionally feminized wit appears in Loaeza's hilarious descriptions of grocery shopping from her first collection of newspaper columns, *Las niñas bien* (The good/wealthy girls) (1985). The essay, "Pagas el vino, las cerezas y el gruyere" (You pay the wine, cherries, and gruyère) takes place after the peso devaluation of the early 1980s and assumes the frazzled voice of a once financially comfortable wife who must explain to her suspicious husband the struggle to stretch the food budget:

> Ay, gordo, me deberías de haber visto frente al mostrador de los mariscos, no tienes idea lo que sufrí, para decidirme a comprar entre el camarón gigante a $3,999.00 y el chico de $1,749.00. Después de

mucho reflexionar, de plano me incliné por el grandote. Primero, porque sentía como que me hacía ojitos y me conquistaron ¿no? Y segundo, porque siendo más grandotes, pensé que nos íbamos a llenar más pronto, por menos. (56–57)

Ay, honey, you should have seen me in front of the seafood counter, you have no idea what I went through to make up my mind between buying the jumbo shrimp at $3,999.00 and the small ones at $1,749.00. After reflecting a lot, I finally went for the huge ones. First, because I felt like they were making little eyes at me and they won me over, no? And second, because they are so much larger, I thought that we would fill up faster, with fewer.

If readers smile at the notion of the jumbo shrimp "making eyes" at the housewife, they catch Loaeza's humorous, ground-level approach to dealing with the economic crisis. Many readers view this sort of humor as unsophisticated because it deals with the easily dismissed domestic crisis of consumer choice, rather than the serious problem of poverty or lack of choices.

Clearly, laughing along with Loaeza requires an adequate aesthetic, and only fans of the flirty and frivolous will enjoy her most original writing. As a litmus test of your sense of humor, consider my favorite line from "Miroslava," a text about the eponymous actress who committed suicide in Mexico City in the early 1950s: "Muchas horas después de que Miroslava había muerto, su lipstick seguía intacto" (*Primero las damas*, 126). (Many hours after Miroslava had died, her lipstick was still intact.) In criticism published in *La Jornada*, Elena Poniatowksa rejects the aesthetic of "Miroslava" as all research and no heart.[5] The aspects that bother Poniatowska might prove less aggravating for her if she read the short story as a narrative essay. A change in genre can shift the expectations from the desired suspense-building plots and emotive characters typical of short stories and instead embrace the non-plotted fiction of a well-researched narrative. Unlike the psychologically complex beings that would inhabit Poniatowska's ideal short stories, the characters in a narrative essay can illustrate thematic points without needing to mimic human emotional depth. And when speaking of something as selfishly superficial as a movie star's staged suicide, attempted complex sentiment might weaken the admiration for the subject's defense in femininely stylish self-destruction. The Miroslava of Loaeza's text tries to narrow her public interpretation to a single image of unassailable glamour. Ultimately, "Miroslava" narrates not the end of the subject so much as the subject's self-immortalizing ending. Poniatowska's preferred topics of social justice, which require poignantly empathetic readings, have little to do with Loaeza's aesthetic interest in catching the cold glamour of artistic success in death.

On this topic of genre, I propose that one key to understanding Loaeza's preference for the narrative essay relates to the notion of "public prose" proposed by José Antonio Aguilar Rivera as a mode of separating public intellectuals from mere academics (38). I wonder if, in her role as an accessible intellectual, Loaeza cultivates the narrative essay as a sort of user-friendly genre. The popularity of nonfiction in the late twentieth and early twenty-first centuries suggests that not every reader has the patience to develop a concern for plotted fictional characters' sentiments, although many readers take an interest in fact-based essays that ignore the contrivance of an overarching plot in favor of the immediate and discrete anecdote. Accordingly, the characters in Loaeza's books on problematic Mexican shopping habits appear almost as personalities in progress; *Compro, luego existo* (I buy, ergo I exist) (1992) and *Debo, luego sufro* (I owe, ergo I suffer) (2000) feature vaguely sketched figures, including the author's alter ego Sofía. Because the books shun a plot and leave the human figures in an anecdotal state, Loaeza allows the audience to engage with an almost "open source" character rather than a completed portrait of a human being. Aguilar Rivera illuminates one mechanism behind the accessible nature of Loaeza's public prose when he cites data suggesting that the "few books Mexicans buy will typically be only half-read" (52). Loaeza's work lends itself to an incomplete reading. She constantly recycles her prose, and thus her longest books contain sections lifted from other books she has written, which makes it possible to read only parts of several of her books and come to a coherent grasp of her views. On top of the repetitions, Loaeza further cultivates accessibility by fragmenting the page with lists, boxes of information, lengthy quotations from other sources, interviews broken up among questions and answers, illustrations and photographs, dictionary-style entries, and short journalistic pieces. Her books also reflect the brightly fluid style of self-help manuals and nonacademic journalism by avoiding page-clogging bibliographic citation.

This habit of unattributed citation occasionally enters the potentially copyright-infringing territory of full-blown plagiarism, a transgression that Guillermo Sheridan has publicized on his blog that is linked to the intellectually legitimizing magazine *Letras libres*—which incidentally also publishes Rafael Lemus's criticism. In an extraordinary coincidence, an interview with Loaeza from 1989 almost predicts this conflict; she picks Sheridan seemingly at random as her feared audience: "Si yo pensara en Guillermo Sheridan, por ejemplo, no escribiría.

No podría hacerlo, porque pensaría a cada línea: esto no le va a gustar a Sheridan, se va a burlar Sheridan" (García Hernández, 33). (If I thought about Guillermo Sheridan, for example, I wouldn't write. I couldn't do it, because I would think at every line: Sheridan isn't going to like this, Sheridan is going to make fun of me.) Loaeza correctly anticipates "qualified" intellectuals' skeptical attitudes toward her work, and hints that she views herself as an illegitimate public thinker if she ponders the matter. Loaeza's ability, up until now at least, to survive accusations of plagiarism corroborates Richard Posner's complaint about the "striking lack of accountability" that marks the performance of thinkers in the media today (382). Of course, it is possible that we do not feel the need to punish Loaeza severely since as a self-taught *señora* she isn't supposed to be able to think for herself in the first place. The issue of unaccountability relates to a scale of public lies. Importantly, Loaeza is not the worst liar out there; for instance, she has never knowingly published against fact. I realize the apologist nature of my thinking here, but after living through the consequences of George W. Bush's mendacious presidency, I gladly make the argument that Loaeza displays a certain "integrity in plagiarism" that in some ways combats anti-intellectual tendencies of the global media.[6] Loaeza never denies scientific or other grounded thought and instead disseminates it, albeit at times without recognizing the source and claiming it as her own.

Because she wasn't supposed to be an intellectual in the first place and because she writes about topics that are either borrowed or lend themselves to frivolity, it is not surprising that Loaeza wrestles with a girlish media label, "la eterna niña bien" (the eternal rich girl). That is, national newspapers tend to nickname Loaeza somewhat derogatorily after her star subject, the well-to-do young women or *las niñas bien* that give the title to her first book. It seems only logical that Loaeza's attempt to develop the persona of a *señora*-who-thinks-in-public ends up occasionally proving stereotypes of feminine stupidity; if she does not conform to these stereotypes at least once in a while, she will no longer be visible as a *señora*. Now in her mid-sixties, Loaeza comes to terms with her reputation as privileged and immature female by describing herself as an "ex niña bien" (former good/rich girl), a label that forms part of the subtitle, in fact, of her book about her failed bid for public office during the elections of July 2008.[7] When I chatted in May 2011 with the campaign manager, Mary Vázquez Guizar, about an impressively answered questionnaire on history related to Mexico City printed in *¿Quién?* for Loaeza's 2008 campaign, Vázquez explained the difference between

Gabriela Cuevas, the winner of the election, and Loaeza. In paraphrased translation, the political insider commented, "Gaby knows an answer about architecture in Mexico City because she read it in a book. Guadalupe knows the answer because she heard the architect talk at a dinner party." Perhaps predictably, many literary critics and political commentators reject this chatty manner of gaining intellectual authority. Certainly, this question of legitimacy describes the conflicting résumés held by Loaeza and her four-years-younger academic sister, Soledad ("Marisol") Loaeza.

The two sisters have not been on speaking terms for years, even though they both live in Mexico City. I suspect that the tension has something to do with rivalry sparked by their competitive struggles for intellectual authority. Soledad went to the trouble of backing her political writing with a doctorate from France, no less, and she works as a research professor at the prestigious Center for International Studies at the Colegio de México. Yet, compared to Guadalupe's public popularity, Soledad labors in the shadows. Possibly, Soledad's thoughtful, well-researched, properly documented, and poorly selling texts form a parallel with my present academic readers' careers. You poor Soledades. If you look up the academic Loaeza sister on YouTube, you will see a possibly familiar, undeniably soulless display of academic speak. Soledad talks stiffly, dresses stiffly, smiles stiffly, and gives a stiff message so correctly expressed that after the first few pronouncements, the viewer watches the time counter on the video frame. A simple comparison among clips on YouTube shows that Guadalupe's success does not stem from being better looking or smarter than Soledad, but from wielding greater charisma. In her warm style as a permanently amateur interviewer, Guadalupe does not lecture to the camera; she comes alive and emotes for it. The effect of Guadalupe's dazzling charm is even more powerful in person—but don't take my seduced word for it. Here is how Elena Poniatowska describes the magnetism wielded by her former workshop pupil: "La 'chispa' de Lupita no la tiene nadie. Su simpatía ejerce un poder hipnótico en sus interlocutores. Uno suplica que no deje de hablar, de gesticular, de hacer visajes mientras pasa la mano derecha por su cabello rubio" (Poniatowska, "Guadalupe [ ... ] Tercera Parte," 34). (No one has Lupita's [Loaeza's] "spark." Her affability works a hypnotic power over her interlocutors. We beg that she not stop talking, gesturing, grimacing while she runs her right hand through her blond hair.) Lest the reader believe that the presence of blond hair responds to simple racist rhetoric, I hasten to point out that Poniatowska is the natural blond. In fact, so was Soledad Loaeza as a child. By contrast, photos of Guadalupe in childhood show that she was actually a decided brunette—a detail that probably no one who watches her blonded public performance in the 80s and beyond would guess. The lesser respect paid to Guadalupe likely responds to Guadalupe's determination to take blond to its unnatural limits by exceeding what Poniatowska and Soledad Loeaza allow themselves in their more demur self-performance. In May 2011, I observed this femme exaggeration firsthand over several days while Loaeza filmed interviews for one of her many short-lived interview series on Mexican television. For her assorted appearances and recordings, Guadalupe wore a blond bobbed hairdo, red nails and red lipstick, fake eyelashes, big jewelry, high heels, flowing scarves, and generous cleavage. During my visit, she described how she has worked hard to leave behind the diminutive nickname "Lupita" used in the previous quotation by Poniatowska—that is, "Elenita" Poniatowksa, as some journalists call her. Bucking that ultimately disrespectful public convention and convincing others to address her as "Guadalupe" marks a hard-earned increase in status.

But there is no need to exaggerate the disparity between real and fake blonds, or among Poniatowska and Soledad Loaeza on the one hand, and Guadalupe Loaeza on the other. The invention of strictly disparate categories for the women intellectuals' public images contributes to false isolation of the most femme performances. Generally speaking, women writers in Mexico are more similar than different in large part because they come from comparable backgrounds and face analogous challenges in the effort to attain critical respect. For example, note Loaeza's recollections of all that she and Soledad shared in girlhood: "nuestra recámara, amigos, [...] pretendientes, monjas, lecturas, reseñas en el cine Roble, enojos y excentricidades de mi madre y los juegos olímpicos de 1968, ambas fuimos edecanes" (*Mujeres maravillosas*, 27–28). (Our bedroom, friends, [...] suitors, nuns, readings, reviews in the Roble theater, my mother's attacks and eccentricities and the Olympic games of 1968, we were both hostess-models.) Yes, you read that last detail correctly. Both girls spent time in late 1968 proudly strutting their stuff during Mexico's politically troubled Olympics as *edecanes*, a sort of sexist cross between a model valued for her looks and a more or less articulate presenter of a product, which in this case was Mexico for tourists. Soledad has managed to overcome this disqualification to serious intellectual status, perhaps by virtue of her foreign graduate studies. By contrast to Soledad's silence, Guadalupe reminisces proudly about her Olympic moment as a good-looking Mexican model, and she did not march in a political protest until she had already become a middle-aged writer.

Herrera's concluding remarks in a negative review of *Mujeres maravillosas* (1997) deliver a stern warning to Loaeza, supposedly drawn from Freud: "Para publicar se necesita pudor" (14). (To publish, one needs modesty.) Aside from the hypocrisy inherent in the fact that Freud was not particularly modest, this advice seems absurd because a truly self-effacing writer would lapse into silence. Fortunately, modesty is what Guadalupe Loaeza habitually sets aside in order to continue the lineage of published femme thinkers. Rather than modesty, Loaeza flaunts a kind of self-authorized pride that supports a will to doubled curiosity: as a femme thinker she is a curious creature to others and she delights at performing curiosity by, among other tactics, posing endless questions. This habit gains an audience at the cost of a more serious reputation. But the communal character of questions, as opposed to the more individual or copyrightable nature of answers, fits Loaeza's limitations as a self-taught intellectual. For fellow writer and activist Sabina Berman, Loaeza's main drawback is her lack of a proposed alternative, which causes her indignation at the status quo to stall in irony (5). In the end, Loaeza does not aim to make sense for her public so much as she encourages audience members to think for themselves through indignant questioning of Mexico's contradictions and injustices. If Loaeza were to volunteer answers instead of ironical questions, she would distract from that very goal. Furthermore, people wouldn't listen to her.

In point of the fact that when Loaeza does venture an answer, few listen to it, I cite the campaign materials from 2008. Loaeza turned in the first registered ideas in response to a call for citizens' political proposals put out by the Sistema de Obervación por la Seguridad Ciudadana, A.C. (SOS, System of Observation for Citizen Safety). I possess an official stamped copy of Loaeza's six suggestions, thanks to campaign manager Vázquez Guizar's archival generosity, and I find that the most significant proposal asks for a law that would allow citizens to participate in politics without the necessity of having a political party to back them. A second important proposition asks that politicians in Mexico City be eligible for one period of reelection so that elected officials may work with one another in a more coordinated manner. These unrealized and poorly disseminated plans have had little or no effect on the political landscape and are the exception in Loaeza's questioning performance as an intellectual. Her "fun" questions find more of an audience than her "serious" answers.

An example of Loaeza's questioning style appears in the two-volume *Manual de la gente bien* (1995, 1996), where she rewrites the famed *Manual de Carreño*, the late nineteenth-century guide to manners. The debate over the word "provecho," a term sometimes spoken in Mexico before mealtimes in the tradition of "bon appétit," supplied the initial inspiration for the guide to manners (Poniatowska, "Guadalupe [...] Primera Parte," 35). Yet, this foundational controversy does not receive definitive treatment in the guidebook, and after reviewing the sides of the argument, Loaeza leaves it to the reader to decide the propriety of wishing others "provecho" before a meal. The same DIY (decide it yourself) approach characterizes her handling of the character Sofía, who gives uncritical voice to what Loaeza haplessly thinks; as the author explains in an article for ¡Siempre!: "Debo decir que [Sofía] es un poco mi consciencia, mi otro yo. En su boca pongo todo lo que yo no quiero decir, pero que sí pienso. [...] Cuando escribo sobre ella es una forma de exorcizar todo lo que no me gusta de mi personalidad" ("Confesiones ante un espejo," 23). (I should say that she [Sofía] is a bit of my conscience, my other "I." In her mouth I put everything that I do not want to say, but that I do think. [...] When I write about her it is a way to exorcize everything that I don't like about my personality.) One characteristic that Loaeza does not want to confess but that Sofía easily admits is racism. That Sofía is racist surfaces upon her return to Mexico from a shopping binge in the United States, when she suffers the "usual" culture shock: "'La verdad es que son feos los mexicanos. Ya no me acordaba de que fueran tan morenos, ¡qué horror!', se dijo" (*Compro, luego existo*, 48). ("The truth is that Mexicans are ugly. I didn't remember that they were so brown. How awful!" she said to herself.) This insider approach to racism allows the audience to either identify with, or raise an alienated eyebrow at, the prejudice and then to arrive at an independent rejection of it. To conquer a personal prejudice, a bigot must first admit to the bias, and Loaeza manages to own up indirectly to the hateful racism that other wealthy Mexicans share but publicly deny. Importantly, Loaeza's readers must finish for themselves the critique of racism set up by Sofía's stupidity. Given the traditional social context for Mexican readers of authoritarian politicians who rarely admit the racist social structure that underlies the official rhetoric, this break from thought commandments may draw an audience eager for greater political participation.

The plucky but error-stricken protagonist Sofía, in the style of her creator, inevitably participates in the customs that she critiques. This hypocrisy reflects the double sense of *lo comprometido*: Sofía's act as a wealthy femme leftist is at once committed and compromised. For instance, Sofía, like Loaeza, cheerfully fails at self-improvement with endless (ergo unsuccessful) diets and eternally renewed resolutions to stop shopping.[8] Although Sofía and Loaeza amuse and exasperate by failing to improve on an individual level, they nevertheless expect change to occur on a national scale. In evidence of a decidedly romantic commitment to political change, Sofía finds refreshing escapism in the gossip magazines like *¡Hola!*, of the famous title *Confieso que he leído... ¡Hola!* (2006) (I confess that I have read... *¡Hola!*), and the alter ego reads the newspaper as a reality trip that almost always ends in furious disbelief (*Las obsesiones de Sofía*, [1999]). While some may view Sofía and Loaeza's overt inconsistencies as hypocritical, I see the obvious (i.e., not closeted) incongruence as a way of bringing shaming social problems to the discussible surface. Possibly, through the flexible help-yourself social definitions and unplotted characters like Sofía, Loaeza avoids the downfall of the contemporary intellectual as Aguilar Rivera fears it. Contrary to the alleged trend in specialization, Loaeza has not shrunk the role of intellectual to a narrow academic focus.

In fact, an interview from 2010 quotes Loaeza as wanting to be remembered in vague terms as a "communicologist of her time" ("comunicóloga de su tiempo") (Hernández, 31). The downside of versatility is that Loaeza acts with relative unaccountability, and I wonder if instead of "communicologist" the term "pop intellectual" might suit her better. Unfortunately, the pressure of deadlines on the media star means that even some of Loaeza's questions are half-baked, over and above her ghost-written or plagiarized answers. Fortunately for the sake of my analysis, Loaeza's preferred rhetoric of the question welcomes incongruence. The self-aware spirit of her inconsistencies strengthens Loaeza's appealing sincerity and increases the political relevance of her wit. Not surprisingly, given her public confession of flaws through Sofía and other, more direct autobiographical statements, Loaeza implicitly dismisses a possibly transcendental value inherent in the act of writing. It seems that for Loaeza, the written word serves to transmit ideas and to justify an extratextual performance of her media image. However, writing does not seem to serve as a supreme end in itself for her. This value suggests one likely reason why Loaeza has not bothered to imitate learned writers' fiction styles. This lack of pretension makes Loaeza an easy voice. Her freedom from pragmatic answers and solutions returns me to the matter of her popularity in a country that does not read much. Loaeza becomes "fun" and an author of texts ripe for casual consumption because she frames many social and political problems in terms of melodramatic conflict, and because she rarely bothers to invent a (boring) happy ending. This is not to say that she is satisfied with the approach.

As a lip-synching performer of public intellectuality, Loaeza feels guilty about her own habits and keeps tabs on the most appealing critiques issued by others, which only makes her that much more engaging and even useful for the general public. It bears emphasizing that Loaeza is not the shining example, but the flaming contradiction, and she consistently admits it. An interview published in 1994 has her respond to the one-word question of whether she is "¿Intelectual?" with a one-word denial: "Cero" (Zero) (J. Ortiz). She goes on to clarify "No tengo disciplina intelectual. [...] Soy la Gloria Trevi de las periodistas" (n.p.). (I do not have intellectual discipline. [...] I am the [pop star] Gloria Trevi of women newspaper reporters.) Contradictorily, in another interview Loaeza shrinks from an imagined reputation as "la Gloria Trevi de las letras" (the literary Gloria Trevi) (Poniatowska, "Guadalupe [...] Segunda Parte," 34). Although more substantially clothed than Trevi, Loaeza also rebels against mother's rules, a familiar feminism that does not end up proposing a new way so much as it satirizes the old one. Loaeza, perhaps predictably, vacillates as a labeled feminist. A conversation published in 1989 with Arturo García Hernández reports Loaeza denying a personal feminism: "No, yo no me considero feminista" (No, I do not consider myself to be feminist) (33). Nearly ten years later, during an unpublished interview with me in October 2008, Loaza gave a wavering answer to the same question that ultimately favored the label: "Sí, sí soy feminista." (Yes, yes I'm feminist.) In May 2011, she gave me another entertaining philosophical puzzle by defining her religious orientation as an atheist believer in the Virgin Guadalupe, which incidentally gives an ambivalent vote of confidence for her namesake ("Soy guadalupana atea").

Faithful to her flashy paradoxes as atheist believer in the supreme Mexican Catholic diva, Loaeza contradictorily defends both her love for shopping in a grossly inequitable capitalist society and leftist ideals for social justice. Official sources face a challenge when trying to co-opt Loaeza's message precisely due to her critical contradictions as an embodied femme thinker. I wonder if this unmanageability explains some of Loaeza's failure to attain significant party backing in the recent elections. Even though *Compro, luego existo* and *Debo, luego sufro* owe their existence to the Federal Consumer Protection Agency, la Procuraduría Federal del Consumidor (Profeco), Loaeza challenges the official call for fiscal responsibility that she helped to articulate, and continues to shop compulsively (*Debo, luego sufro*, 341). I cannot resist citing Loaeza's telling but nonsensical refusal to give up the credit card, as recognized in the acknowledgments of

*Compro, luego existo* when she thanks Casa Nina Ricci for teaching her to distinguish between "comprar y comprar" (buying and buying) (15). I leave it to the reader's sensibility to determine whether Loaeza has a valid point. Regardless of the interpretation of this paradox, the quirky statement exemplifies Loaeza's habitual technique of amusing absurdity.

Loaeza's act is most creative in these moments of passionate incongruence, which support her intellectual act as a media attraction. For example, she has adapted the upscale Palacio de Hierro department store slogan to cheer on the indigenous rebellion in Chiapas during the mid-1990s. From having bought into the famous advertising campaign and designed herself as "totalmente Palacio" (totally Palacio), she describes herself as turning "totalmente Chiapas" (totally Chiapas) (*Por los de abajo*, 295). This unexpected gesture of using an advertising slogan to characterize a civil war suggests the similarity of the consumerist ideals and the Chiapan movement for Loaeza; being totally in style relates to political taste. Since the consumer mentality fits with a significant portion of the media consuming public, Loaeza's femme fan base will probably take greater delight in chicly posing as "Totally Chiapas" than in declaring with rigid masculinity, "Todos somos Marcos." (We are all Marcos). This attention to individuality and shopping habits reflects a major current in the contemporary political spirit. As Bruce Robbins has pointed out, collective social identities today form around not so much the productive ideal of "Workers of the world unite," but a consumer call for shoppers to unite (39). Just as a savvy shopper wants a (feel) good transaction, so a savvy voter searches for the right (looking) candidate. In the long run, something does not quite work with this arrangement. Consumers might unite in Loaeza's implicit rallying cry to style themselves as leftist, but due to the individualistic and even unsustainable nature of the proposal, the readers can hardly react as an articulated unit. This individualistic disarticulation helps to provoke Loaeza's criticized lack of concrete answers. Her readers may value style over substance—or perhaps more accurately, they value style *as* substance. This obsession with design fails to supply a stable political platform for collective action beyond the marketplace. Unfortunately for Loaeza's political ambitions, the questions that fuel her literary appeal also constitute her limitation. Her methods prevent her from adhering to any one institution.

Not all of Loaeza's ineffectiveness when it comes to coordinating social change is the fault of her intellectual and performative contradictions, however. As I have tried to clarify, another serious shortcoming for Loaeza's political efficacy has to do with society's trivializing response to wealthy Mexican women's political protest. Loaeza reviews this problem somewhat impersonally in *Los de arriba* (The people on top) (2002), when she recalls twenty-first-century attempts at protest among the *señoras* who group at Rosario Castellanos Park in Mexico City only to attract smirking press coverage:

> Las mujeres "popis" del parque Rosario Castellanos fueron víctimas de un juicio terrible por parte de los medios de comunicación. Se burlaron de ellas. No recibieron el menor crédito. Las sentían falsas, ignorantes e incluso farsantes. Para colmo, pensaban que estas señoras eran incapaces de pensar por sí solas. [ ... ] "Mala onda, dicen los popis, Las Lomas contra los Pinos," se leía en la primera plana del *Ovaciones*. "Represión *light* contra los vecinos de colonias residenciales," se leía en *La Jornada*. "Los ricos también lloran," comentó, con una sonrisita tendenciosa Javier Alatorre en el noticiario de Televisión Azteca al presentar el reportaje de la marcha. (*Manual de la Gente Bien*, II, 276–77)
> 
> The preppy women of Rosario Castellanos Park were victims of a terrible trial on the part of the media. They were laughed at. They were not given the least credit. They were perceived as fake, ignorant, and even liars. To top it off, these *señoras* were seen as incapable of thinking for themselves. [ ... ] "Bad Vibes, Say the Preppies, Las Lomas [the ritzy neighborhood] against Los Pinos [the Presidential residence]," read the headline of *Ovaciones*. "Repression *Lite* Against the Neighbors of Residential Zones," read *La Jornada*. "The rich cry too," Javier Alatorre commented, with a biased little smile on the newscast of Televisión Azteca when presenting the report on the protest.

Loaeza regrets that the "alleged women citizens" ["estas supuestas ciudadanas"] only managed to provoke hilarity among the foreign correspondents and national reporters. Here, I adapt Gayatri Spivak's famous question, "Can the subaltern speak?" for the purposes of analyzing the "amateur" femme thinker: "Can wealthy women critique?" If we are accustomed to giving the poor a voice in the media (but wait a minute, wasn't *that* Spivak's critique? That we don't?), then how do rich *señoras* fail to assume the agency that is supposed to be inherent to their privileged social station? Who can speak authoritatively as intellectuals in the media besides the politicians, the police, and the PhDs? Or rather, whom can we hear?

This question is no joke, despite the seeming offense to Spivak's original concern with the disenfranchised who battle for agency under racist and classist repression. Perhaps unexpectedly to those critics who focus on the problems of representation for a majority of the population, a minority citizenship problem appears to exist among would-be liberal wealthy women living in sexist circumstances. George Yúdice has pointed out that in one sense agency is a "false concept" because just like language, power is never wholly one's own (668). According to Yúdice's proposals, Loaeza and other women would need to be granted agency in the media in order for them to exercise a Right to leftist political critique. Yet, the media does not seem to have much respect for rich women's political protests. This problem may have something to do with the framework in which entitled feminine voices usually appear. Entertainment, social, and style sections of the media feature wealthy women when the news is "good," but these same sections do not often cover feminine acts if they attempt to emit a "serious" (ergo "bad") message. Given the potential for wealthy women like Loaeza to effect positive political change, this mirthful media attitude toward them indicates an unsettling bias.

This media limitation did not always affect wealthy women's ability to be taken seriously as political and intellectual players. In an earlier, less democratic age in Europe some wealthy women's political decisions gained respect as matters of national policy and not insanely immodest attempts to "play serious," because the women held noble titles, such as "queen." In my final observation for this article, I suggest that the femme power granted by a noble title explains the curious and otherwise self-defeating tendency among feminized pioneers in the Mexican media to turn nostalgic. Loaeza has in common with Amor, Novo, Arreola, and even López Velarde and Nervo, the tendency to use her literature to cast an evocative glance back to times when some admirable members of society were also nobles. This look back reminds me of Peggy Phelan's discussion of Michael Jackson's moonwalk as an otherworldly logic "in which one advances by moving backward" (944). By playing the divo, Michael Jackson gave a consummate performance that blurred the artist with his art and proposed the culmination of a class act. I offer Loaeza's psychological dependence on shoulder pads as an equivalent to Jackson's eccentricities as the "King of Pop." As is evident from a smiling admission made to me by her personal assistant and from narrative attributed to Sofía, Loaeza requires that shoulder pads be sewn into every item of her clothing that could use it, including her nightgowns. The padding lends a sort of strength in costume that reminds me of the force granted in other times by a crown, and it is perhaps not utterly exaggerated to note the resemblance among the words "hombreras" (shoulder pads), "hombro" (shoulder), "hombre" (man), and "hombría" (manliness). Alongside these connotations of fake masculinity imparted by the shoulder pads, however, it is clear that Loaeza loves them for at least one other motive: they add visual structure that slims the waist.

In sum, Loaeza's feminized performance makes her more salient in the media, but that same performance subtracts from her intellectual credibility. Loaeza's blonded consumer act tries to communicate a "classy," even royal air in the midst of an argument for leftist democratic values, and possibly this contradiction means to establish her credibility by falsely "remembering" an innate right to rule. The notion of return to authority by intellectuals who stake a claim to nobility is as troublesome to me as the tendency for intellectuals who become successful media stars to suffer a decline in the public's estimation of their rational thinking abilities. To this end, I note that while contemporary Mexican journalists born in the early 1960s, such as Lydia Cacho, Denise Dresser, or Carmen Aristegui, might seem more "serious" as public intellectuals, they are standing on Loaeza's neurotic shoulder pads. When inventing how to be a woman public intellectual in an act that ultimately benefited the generation born after her, Loaeza used a conservative touch to restrain the sexuality of her predecessors while still cultivating a liberal blond ambition. I know of another Madonna, the one with the sometimes royal British accent, who might be impressed.

### Notes

1. All translations are mine.
2. In fact, the infamous compulsive shopper was initially paid in clothes: "Son ellos que me hicieron adicta," Loaeza explained in a personal interview in May 2011. (They made me an addict.)
3. Loeaza explains, "Iba guapísima. Yo entonces era delegada de la casa Nina Ricci. Lo que le interesó mucho [a Granados Chapa] es que era pariente de [expresidente] López Portillo, por el lado de mi mamá" (V. Ortiz, 91). (I went in gorgeous. Back then I was a delegate for the Nina Ricci fashion house. What interested him [Granados Chapa] a lot was that I was a relative of [expresident] López Portillo, on my mother's side.)
4. After losing her own election for federal political representative for a section of Mexico City in 2008, Loaeza seems to have lost her shine for Andrés Manual López Obrador, just as previously Cuauhtémoc Cárdenas fell from political perfection for her when she began to favor AMLO.
5. Poniatowska writes, "Bien documentado, sacado de la Hemeroteca, la investigación es acuciosa, pero el '*feeling*' brilla por su ausencia,

ninguna introspección, la escritura plana resulta enumerativa. Falta imaginación literaria" ("Tú tienes la culpa [...]: Tercera partes," 27) (Well-documented, extracted from the Journalism Archive, the research is thorough, but "feeling" shines by its absence, no introspection, the flat writing is enumerative. It lacks literary imagination.)
6. Recall Susan Jacoby's dismay that George W. Bush's support for the teaching of intelligent design failed to stir major critique: "But no one pointed out how truly extraordinary it was that any American president would place himself in direct opposition to contemporary scientific thinking" (28).
7. Loaeza's failed political campaign for federal representative labeled her the "ciudadana de bien" (good citizen).
8. A list of confessed faults from *Debo, luego sufro* has the aging Sofía take stock of her personal defects: "Tengo varices. Soy muy gastadora. Ya no tengo cintura. [...] Ronco por las noches. No tengo seguro de vida. No soy deportista. Tengo arrugas. No puedo dormir sin mis hombreras. Soy muy desorganizada...Pero mi peor defecto es mi ego. ¡Es enorme! [...] Aunque ya estoy madurita, no soy una persona madura. Sigo siendo la típica niña-mujer. Soy muy unilateral. Criticona. Chismosa. Frívola. Materialista. Ignorante. No sé cuántos ríos hay en la república. No me sé de memoria todas las estrofas del himno nacional. No sé cocinar. No sé quién es Caravaggio" (55). (I have varicose veins. I spend too much. I no longer have a waist. [...] I snore at night. I don't have life insurance. I am not athletic. I have wrinkles. I can't sleep without my shoulder pads. I am very disorganized...But my worst defect is my ego. It's huge! [...] Although I am getting up there, I am not a mature person. I continue to be the typical girl-woman. I am unilateral. Overly critical. Gossipy. Frivolous. Materialistic. Ignorant. I don't know how many rivers the republic has. I don't know by heart all the stanzas of the national anthem. I don't know how to cook. I don't know who Caravaggio is.)

## Works Cited

Aguilar Rivera, José Antonio. *The Shadow of Ulysses: Public Intellectual Exchange Across the U.S.-Mexico Border*. 1998. Foreword by Russell Jacoby. Translated by Rose Hocker and Emiliano Corral. Lanham, MD: Lexington Books, 2000. Print.

Barrera, Reyna. *Salvador Novo: Navaja de la inteligencia*. Mexico: Plaza y Valdés, 1999. Print.

Berman, Sabina. "Los de arriba." *Reforma* May 18, 2003: 5. Print.

Epstein, Joseph. "Celebrity Culture." *Celebrity Culture in the United States*. Edited by Terence J. Fitzgerald. New York: H. W. Wilson, 2008. 12–25. Print.

Fong Robles, Silvia. "El pequeño Loaeza (no) ilustrado." *Excélsior*. January 14, 1996. Print.

García Hernández, Arturo. "Escribo para darles sentido a mis días: Guadalupe Loaeza." *La Jornada* 7 (December 1989): 33. Print.
Hernández, Felipe. "Entrevista / Guadalupe Loaeza / Sin Concesiones." *Mural* 31. December 17, 2010. *ProQuest*. Web. January 24, 2014.
Herrera, Alejandra. "Escritura y poder: Lectura playera de *Mujeres maravillosas*." *Revista Mexicana de Cultura* 87 (1997): 14. Print.
Howitz, Daniel. *The Star as Icon: Celebrity in the Age of Mass Consumption*. New York: Columbia University Press, 2008. Print.
Jacoby, Susan. *The Age of American Unreason*. New York: Pantheon Books, 2008. Print.
Lemus, Rafael. Review of *Las yeguas finas* by Guadalupe Loaeza. *Letras Libres* (March 2004). http://www.letraslibres.com/index.php?art=9436. Web.
Loaeza, Guadalupe. *Compro, luego existo*. 1992. 2nd ed. 28th printing. Mexico: Océano, 2003. Print.
———. "Confesiones ante un espejo." *Siempre!* 57.3013 (2011): 23. Print.
———. *Confieso que he leído…¡Hola!*. Prólogo Nicolás Alvarado. Mexico: Ediciones B, 2006. Print.
———. *Debo, luego sufro*. Presentación de Pilles Lipovetsky. Mexico: Océano; Procuraduría Federal del Consumidor, 2000. Print.
———. *Ellas y nosotras*. Mexico: Océano, 1998. Print.
———. *La comedia electoral: Diario de una campaña de una ex niña bien*. Mexico: Planeta, 2009. Print.
———. *Las niñas bien*. 1985. 21st ed. Mexico: Cal y arena, 1997. Print.
———. *Las obsesiones de Sofía*. Prólogo Luz Emilia Aguilar Zínser. Mexico: Nueva Imagen, 1999. Print.
———. *Los de arriba*. 1ra edición Plaza y Janés, 2002. Primera edición en Debosillo [Random House Mondadori], 2004. Print.
———. *Manual de la gente bien. Volumen 2*. Mexico: Plaza y Janés, 1996. Print.
———. *Mujeres maravillosas*. Prólogo de Sealtiel Alatriste. Mexico: Océano, 1997. Print.
———. *Por los de abajo: Historia política de una <<niña bien>>….* Mexico: Plaza y Janés, 2005. Print.
———. *Primero las damas*. 1990. 3rd ed. 9th printing. Mexico: Océano, 2004. Print.
Muñetón Pérez, Patricia, Francisco José "Octavio Paz: la mente lúcida que hace falta para comprender nuestra realidad. *Entrevista con Jorge F. Hernández*." *Revista Digital Universitaria* 9.10 (2008). http://www.revista.unam.mx/vol.9/num10/art79/int79.htm. Print.
Ortiz, J. "Soy la Gloria Trevi de las periodistas." *Reforma*. May 23, 1994. Print.
Ortiz, Verónica. "Guadalupe Loaeza. 'Infancia es destino.'" *Mujeres de palabra: Rosa Beltrán, Fabienne Bradu, Laura Esquivel, Eladia González, Mónica Lavín, Guadalupe Loaeza, Silvia Molina y Rosa Nissán*. Prólogo de Elena Poniatowska. Mexico: Joaquín Mortiz, 2005. 86–108. Print.

Phelan, Peggy. "'Just Want to Say': Performance and Literature, Jackson and Poirier." *PMLA* 125.4 (2010): 942–47. Print.

Poniatowksa, Elena. "'Tú tienes la culpa por traer esa minifalda' o la prosa de Guadalupe Loaeza: Tercera de cuatro partes." *La Jornada*. December 16, 1989: 27. Print.

Posner, Richard A. *Public Intellectuals: A Study of Decline with a New Preface and Epilogue*. Cambridge, MA: Harvard University Press, 2003. Print.

Robbins, Bruce. *Secular Vocations: Intellectuals, Professionalism, Culture*. London: Verso, 1993. Print.

Yúdice, George. "Latin American Intellectuals in a Post-Hegemonic Era." *The Latin American Cultural Studies Reader*. Edited by Ana Del Sarto, Alicia Ríos, and Abril Trigo. Durham: Duke University Press, 2004. 655–68. Print.

## Chapter 5

# It's My (National) Stage Too: Sabina Berman and Jesusa Rodríguez as Public Intellectuals

*Stuart A. Day*

The fissure between past and present was defied by the woman who walked toward Mexico City's *zócalo*, the main meeting place for demonstrators who in this case had come (by foot, on the metro) to listen to Andrés Manuel López Obrador, the man who, for a time, and without irony, was considered by millions to be the "presidente legítimo de México," the legitimate president of Mexico, and who continues to be known as Peje or AMLO ("Te AMLO," a play on "I love you," reads a common slogan). The woman was clad as a nun, "suffering" silently in the heat as she played the role of seventeenth-century poet Sor Juana Inés de la Cruz. Her performance of resistance was a fitting combination of word and image: the many depictions of Sor Juana, often seated in her library, were recalled through the habit donned by the performance artist who marched assertively among a sea of yellow AMLO T-shirts, visors, and umbrellas; and the large placard she carried presented a productive parody of Sor Juana's untitled poem known as "Hombres necios" (Foolish men). The first four verses of the re-inscription read: "Foolish priests who accuse / Resistance in action / Knowing that it is you / Who are accomplices of corruption."[1] In this case, the ridiculous men of Sor Juana's iconoclastic poem are converted into present-day priests accused of active complicity in a web of corruption, among other key issues related specifically to the 2006 elections. More broadly, this Sor Juana, along with many other performance artists, represented a key moment in Mexican politics and theatre: during this time Mexican performers left the enclosed spaces, the multiple, many-sized theaters that dot Mexico City, where they often found their enthusiastic but limited audiences, in order to take to the national stage.

Two striking examples (Sabina Berman and Jesusa Rodríguez) serve to underscore the way major political events shape and are shaped by Mexican intellectuals, and the way politics, already containing its share of drama, can be infused with the power not of theatrics (the cynical fictionalization of reality for personal gain) but rather through the ability to envision a different reality—the lifeblood of the theatrical stage. During the 2006 elections and beyond, socially committed artists like Berman and Rodríguez claimed, not for the first time by any means, but much more visibly than in the past, a place on Mexico's national stage. Their contrasting incursions into the 2006 electoral debacle exhibit a multifaceted political left in Mexico—regardless of the questions concerning the legitimacy of the then-designated president, Felipe Calderón, which many people agreed was achieved through fraud[2]—and the enduring power of artists in Mexico to play a part in, and indeed stimulate, political action and dialogue; that is, to play the role of public intellectuals.

Agnes Lugo-Ortiz refers to this contemporary political reality, which can seem foreign to US artists who frequently remain on the periphery of the political arena:

> In 1945, Pedro Henríquez Ureña...had already noted the ties of singular intimacy between literature and politics that were constitutive of Spanish American processes of cultural modernization. Or, to say it differently, he noticed the porosity between these two realms in the formation of a modern public sphere (a process that later was so brilliantly analyzed by Angel Rama in his fundamental 1984 work *The Lettered City*). It could be argued that these ties may very well be in the process of dissolution, partly due to the rise of notions of technocratic intellectual/political authority linked to the neo-liberal projects of the last decades. Yet we only have to look at the recent Mexican electoral crisis to doubt the imminence of such an apocalypse. On the stage, shoulder to shoulder with López Obrador and addressing mass rallies at the Mexico City *zócalo*, we found writers such as Carlos Monsiváis and Elena Poniatowska and performing artist Jesusa Rodríguez. (1)

Berman and Rodríguez, since the July 2, 2006 presidential elections, have gained significant political exposure—as well as changes of venue. Mexicans looking for a good show, not to mention academics who study Mexico City theater and performance, had for many years been able to count on two things: a politically biting show at Jesusa

Rodríguez's cabaret space (El Hábito) in the posh Coyoacán district of southern Mexico City, and one or more plays by Sabina Berman on stage, whether at a small independent theater or at the theater complex of the National Auditorium. For years they had offered their public a bitter yet almost always humorous dose of ironic, impertinent commentary that many argued—though Berman and Rodríguez were rarely so arrogant as to do so—made a difference on Mexico's national stage. Rodríguez told Mark and Blanca Kelty, in 1997, that her work in political cabaret is "not an escape; on the contrary, it is confronting what you most wanted to elude, what you didn't want to look at, what you didn't want to notice. Cabaret theater makes you say, 'This is what you are living'" (124); while in 2004 Jacqueline E. Bixler wrote that Berman's theater wavers "between mockery and caustic criticism of the historical, political, cultural, and sexual status quo of her country" (21). As part of the Mexican mosaic their texts and performances contributed to genuine albeit tortuous sociopolitical change. Mexican audiences—not to mention students in US universities, who often read texts and view performances by these and other Mexican artists—might see in the art of these two women gender politics denaturalized on the page/stage, or experience the power of parody to debunk the mythical morass of official histories that confirm, conform, and deform the nation.

In the 1990s and early 2000s, for example, the public, including academics in search of good material, could turn to their work to see politicians parodied, the role of the church questioned, the enactment of a same-sex wedding (the stage is of course ideal for rehearsing future reality), or—in my case—a critique of neoliberalism, the conservative economic doctrine that posited the magic of the "free" trade, privatization, and a reduction in social spending. Mexican artists, it turns out, did not buy Francis Fukuyama's assertion that "while some present-day countries might fail to achieve stable liberal democracy, and others might lapse back into other, more primitive forms of rule like theocracy or military dictatorship, the *ideal* of liberal democracy could not be improved on" (xi. Original emphasis). They made this known through their plays and performances; audiences, including the occasional politician, might find solace (except perhaps for the occasional politician) in the scenes represented, and a community of like-minded intellectuals, through their work and that of others, was solidified. Berman's 1990 play *La grieta*, or the "crack," for instance, depicted the massive crevice of corruption on the part of the Partido Revolucionario Institucional (PRI) and President Carlos Salinas de Gortari. The seduction of Mexico by neoliberal forces was clear in this brutally comical play that combined documentary theater with the theatre of the absurd—a recipe for reality. I saw this play with a dozen other people in 1996 at the diminutive Foro de la Conchita, not far from Jesusa Rodríguez's bar El Hábito, where among many cabaret performances that critiqued the neoliberal order was the piece *Misa en Los Pinos*, which lampooned, through a mass performed on a stage designed to represent the presidential palace, the influence of two fundamental religions: conservative Catholicism and neoliberalism (Fox had recently asked the Mexican people to pray for the US economy). Rodríguez told me at the time, as she has often told others, that her two favorite targets were the church and the state; as of the 2000 elections, the Fox administration offered two for one.

During the last several theater seasons, however, Rodríguez bowed out of her political cabaret in the Coyoacán district in southern Mexico City (it is now in the hands of Las Reinas Chulas[3]), and one summer the only Berman plays on the Mexico City theater scene were the adaptation (produced by Berman, anonymously at first) of *Puppetry of the Penis* at the Foro Shakespeare, as well as a play for children.[4] Academics and others perceived that artists like Berman and Rodríguez had abandoned the performance of politics, yet this was hardly the case. In fact, they were rehearsing for their roles on the national stage, and the early years of the twenty-first century were by no means stagnant for the two artists: among many other projects, Berman conducted on-site research and wrote her screenplay *Backyard/Traspatio* on the murders of hundreds of girls and young women in Ciudad Juárez, while one of Rodríguez's multiple political incursions included her wedding to Liliana Felipe on the same day as hundreds of other gay and lesbian couples, in Valentine's Day ceremonies that at once parodied conservative politics and set the stage for sanctioned civil unions.

Notwithstanding their significant political participation in the past, the power of these two women on the national stage was realized most forcefully in their roles during and after the 2006 presidential elections: Rodríguez through increased political involvement with Andrés Manuel López Obrador (for whom she began to serve, shortly after the election, as stage director for numerous political events) and the Civil Resistance Movement; Berman through her initial work with an "independent" United Nations election watch group, and later in her 2006 book on the elections *Un soplo en el corazón de la patria: instantáneas de la crisis* as well as her television interview show *Shalalá*, which originally featured co-facilitator Katia D'Artigues. More than ever before, they took the stage (literally, figuratively) as public intellectuals, following trajectories that have been viable in part because of the aftershocks of the 1968 massacre of students and others in Mexico City—a massacre that was provoked, we now know, by government snipers (Preston and Dillon, 63-94).

In 1985 Roderic A. Camp wrote, and many would agree, that "the most important single event affecting intellectual-government relationships in the last twenty years is the government-ordered massacre of student demonstrators at Tlatelolco" (208). Camp goes on to note that "intellectuals did not have much influence on the state in the aftermath of 1968, which is important as an illustration of their lack of political clout" (209). The events of 1968, however, would lead to political organization (in and beyond the universities) by intellectuals and others: there would not be another major event in Mexico in which Mexican intellectuals did not play a significant role. In *Parte de Guerra*, a book that includes declassified documents and other information that clarifies some of the events surrounding the government's use of force during the peaceful demonstration on October 2, 1968, Carlos Monsiváis indicates that despite easily encountered views that the events of 1968 destroyed hope ("For some, the most cynical,... nothing was achieved, neither democratic gains nor organizational perspectives"), the fight against the official version of events has, in and of itself, been a positive incubator for opposition participation in the political process. Through an avalanche of dissembling, stalling, and manipulation, "abundant evidence was opposed by...almost the entire Media, the PRI machine, and inhibitions based on fear. For the last thirty years, the social and testimonial truth has come face to face, victoriously, with [official history]" (Scherer García, 124).

Perhaps it is this need to provide counter-histories that leads many public figures in Mexico to link their definitions of "intellectual" to a search for truth. Camp, in his book *Intellectuals and the State in Twentieth-Century Mexico*, writes of the "five most common characteristics" Mexican intellectuals identify as key to their varied vocations: "The use of the intellect to live, the search for truth, the emphasis on the humanities, the creative bent, and the critical posture" (38-39). Beyond the general definitions of intellectuals and the work they do, Camp, basing his research on numerous interviews, signals ideas that make the term "public intellectual," a useful and necessary lexical grouping in the Anglophone world, seem rather redundant: "The most striking feature of the Mexican intellectual's self-appraisal, as differing from that proposed by the North American, is his or her attitude toward the political activity or the involvement of the intellectual." He adds that "several individuals emphasized political activity as essential, and still others suggested that public involvement is necessary" (Camp, 42).[5] Thus, while I use the term "public intellectual" for reasons addressed in the introduction to this volume and that I will touch on briefly here, in Mexico intellectuals are often considered by definition to be political players.

In order to consider the work of Berman and Rodríguez and their "performances" on Mexico's national stage, I will begin on the day in 2006 that they coincided in Parque México, in Mexico City's Condesa district. Rodríguez had begun to speak regularly in this well-known, treelined park well before the election, and one day Berman went to listen. She was surprised to find a "humorless" Rodríguez (as I had been, after the 2006 elections, watching Rodríguez protest outside Calderón's transitional home before he moved to Los Pinos, the presidential residence). Berman, while affirming that she and Rodrígiuez both considered themselves leftists, stated: "I miss, hearing her that Sunday on the rotunda, as one misses the happiness of an infirm friend, her formidable sense of humor" (13). Rodríguez had indeed taken on a serious role, a role that proves once again that parody is not her only avenue of resistance. Recently, when asked if her various forms of humor were no longer part of her political repertoire, she commented: "No, no. On the contrary. And now, for example, our songs serve millions of people—earlier they were only for a few" (interview). It is true that their trademark dark humor can still be found, including in the songs that Liliana Felipe and Rodríguez create, for example the one that insists: "You have to decide who you prefer to be killed by: poverty, misery, the Free Trade Agreement, or the anti-hunger program." This song, "Tienes que decidir," which until a couple of years ago would have been for sale only at the entry to El Hábito, can now be found in various forms (including video) on the Internet, to give one example of their increased visibility. Notwithstanding new avenues for parodic social criticism, however, and the fact that Rodríguez continues to present some cabaret shows in Mexico and abroad, the tenor of her public discourse—and indeed the way she is portrayed by the leftist press—changed dramatically with her involvement in the 2006 elections and their wake.

One illustration of such a change can be seen in the two "wedding" pictures that *La Jornada* published of Liliana Felipe and Rodríguez: the first, playing up the parody, shows the couple dressed as traditional brides—gowns, veils, roses—in a perfectly posed embrace, with the "officiating priestess" in the background. The headline reads "Blissful and in Virginal White the Brides Joined their Lives Together: Nuptials of Liliana y Jesusa," and the text, which is itself a parody, continues: "It all started a few hours before with the official photo of the consorts: a chaste kiss for the lenses of Lourdes Almeida y Heriberto Rodríguez. The background of the photography studio—Mexican rose-colored cloth—highlights the dresses of the brides, designed and made-to-measure with India paper by the artist Humberto Spíndola—'the future of fashion is in paper.'" Then the "priestess" completes the union of the two members of the "rancid aristocracy": "*Consumatum est.* You may go in peace as soon as the political prisoners are freed, the Army withdraws, and the treaties of San Andrés are signed. Amen" (Vega). Rodríguez and her partner, in their bridal parody, at once embrace and mock nuptial traditions, as did the newspaper account of the event. Years later, at a mass wedding on Valentine's Day 2006, before the July elections, Rodríguez is quoted as saying, "We're a fucking homophobic country, and as long as that's the case we'll be shamefully Mexican" (Muñoz).

Contrast this with the second photo of the couple at their civil union in August 2007: they are dressed in modest attire, with Liliana Felipe wearing an H.I.J.O.S. T-shirt, linking her Argentine past to Mexico's own dirty war of the 1960s–1980s, and to the continued disappearance of political activists and others.[6] Rodríguez is wearing simple, elegant indigenous-influenced attire (Montaño Garfias). The couple had left the cabaret stage, where anything can be imagined, in order to stand firm in a city that recognized officially what previously had been a crime.[7] Their dress rehearsal had become a reality; anything but a farce, the new civil union law in the federal district, while not allowing adoption or other important rights, did represent an important move toward equality for same-sex couples. Yet, Rodríguez puts the law in perspective and subtly signals the federal government, which has been much less progressive than that of the federal district: "We see that these small steps are almost symbolic of a justice system that is becoming degraded, brutally, in other areas: in human rights, in everything that we are seeing, the repression of the entire country" (Montaño Garfias).[8]

The change in emphasis, from parody to gravity, has taken center stage for Rodríguez, especially when she is directing mass demonstrations.[9] Indeed, parody is not the most efficient mode of communication when more direct avenues for political change seem viable;

and perhaps the dangers of parody make a more explicit, direct message necessary. Linda Hutcheon, in *A Theory of Parody*, writes that parody "is a form of imitation, but imitation characterized by ironic inversion" (6); and in *Irony's Edge* she reminds the reader that irony is complex precisely because of the possibility that a message will misfire: "The major players in the ironic game are indeed the interpreter and the ironist. The interpreter may—or may not—be the intended addressee of the ironist's utterance, but s/he (by definition) is the one who attributes irony and then interprets it: in other words, the one who decides whether the utterance is ironic (or not) and then what particular ironic meaning it might have" (11). On the political stage, where the audience (live, or in the media) may easily surpass a million, a direct message is key—even if that message can be made ironic, as was the case when a direct statement by Elena Poniatowska in a campaign commercial for López Obrador was later used by the PAN in their own advertisement. As was widely reported, her words affirming López Obrador's honesty were ironically inverted through the use of controversial footage (of corruption and Las Vegas gambling) showing people who worked with Lopez Obrador when he was leader of the federal district.[10]

Parody and its counterpart, irony, are dangerous weapons. In the cabaret space, or even in the pages of *La Jornada*, the spectators or readers are in on the joke. Yet, beyond the walls of the theater, where irony is more likely to misfire—or backfire, seeming elitist—Rodríguez presents messages for broad consumption. Cabaret performances are serious business, but without the frame of the traditional stage, a reminder that words are in play (and playful), the rules change. Rodríguez is aware that different venues call for different methods but also that her contribution to López Obrador is based, in addition to her status as an intellectual, on her work in the theater. When she saw the people protesting what they assumed would be an official decision in favor of Felipe Calderón, on the part of the Federal Elections Tribunal, her path was clear: "I placed at the disposition of the resistance movement what I could, in particular for the large demonstrations in the *zócalo* that reached two million people. What I proposed to them was that I could oversee the scenic direction of the pavilion because, in general, the pavilion is seen as a political concern, but in the end it follows the same laws as any stage" (interview). From massive demonstrations to the protest where she and thousands of other Mexicans spent many nights camped out on Mexico City's Reforma Avenue, in a protest called the *plantón*, Rodríguez has, as she puts it, "diversified" her work (interview).

Rodríguez's ability to stage events, and to lead the crowd, was evident when she spoke to an estimated one million people in the center of Mexico City for the National Democratic Convention in September 2006, the massive extra official congress at which López Obrador was declared Mexico's legitimate president. This was a key moment, a key decision for the political left. The main question, to be asked by Rodríguez, was this: Should López Obrador be declared the coordinator of the Peaceful Civil Resistance, or "legitimate president of Mexico"? Shouts of "presidente" drowned out any possible dissent, though the crowd was clearly supportive. Rodríguez, now often pictured in the news alongside intellectuals like Poniatowska, if not López Obrador himself, was in a position to choreograph resistance. As Rodríguez read the lists of candidates for three commissions (with roles ranging from civil resistance to the organization of plebiscites), the members of the crowd, all convention "delegates," raised their hands to vote "Yes."

This scene is documented in many sources, including Berman's book *Un soplo en el corazón de la patria: instantáneas de la crisis*, which chronicles the 2006 elections. The book is comprised of Berman's own opinions, some published in periodicals like *Letras libres* and *El Universal*, as well as numerous of accounts of the experiences by people (at times anonymous; at times thinly veiled; at times named) with a variety of political positions. Berman's book reminds the reader of Poniatowska's *La noche de Tlatelolco*, a text that has influenced Berman's journalism, which includes columns in major news magazines, her *Mujeres y poder* series that won the 2000 National Journalism Award, the recent coauthored *Democracia cultural*, and, of course, *Un soplo en el corazón de la patria*. The subtitle of this book, "Snapshots of the Crisis," points to Poniatowska's writing on the 68 massacre as well as the pieces she wrote on the 1985 earthquake. Berman affirms the importance of Poniatowska's work: "I believe that if I had not read *La noche de Tlatelolco*, possibly it wouldn't have occurred to me [to write this one]...it's the same type of book. And, curiously, it finds Elena and me, who I have read and admire, on opposite sides" (interview). Poniatowska, widely recognized in Mexico as a prominent public intellectual, paved the way for artists like Berman and Rodríguez. One legacy of Tlatelolco is the power of publishing, the power to document—as Poniatowska did— events as they occur, and to do so in a way that challenges the status quo by presenting myriad viewpoints. She opened up an avenue for public expression, despite censorship, something Berman faces much less than her predecessor. Julia Preston and Sam Dillon explain that

Poniatowska still struggled with censorship in 1985, though from vastly a more powerful position:

> About a week after the quake [Poniatowska] had an experience of déjà vu. Her editor at *Novedades*, the same man who has suppressed her stories in 1968, instructed her to stop writing about the damage and the disarray. Word had come down from President de la Madrid, he said, that it was time for Mexico City to "return to normal." The editor told Poniatowska that her stories about the survivors' struggles were demoralizing the public.... She had not pressed the issue since 1968, but now she was an older and more accomplished journalist. She decided to take her stories across Calle Balderas to the offices of an upstart newspaper called *La Jornada*.... Poniatowska just left off her latest earthquake story at the front door and went back to *Novedades*. An hour later she got a call asking her for another story for the following day. She wrote reports for *La Jornada* every day for four months. (109)

In the history of public intellectuals in Mexico, the tenacity of this reporter, and the multiple progressive causes she has supported over the years, created a legacy that started the morning after Tlatelolco when she went to see for herself what had happened, and when she used her skills as a reporter to project what was, at the time, the most reliable public documentation of the massacre. *Un soplo en el corazón de la patria* is at once an exemplar of the literary legacy of Poniatowska (the book itself; the genre of documentary reporting in Mexico) as well as of the legacy of performing on the national stage—Rodríguez's performances are documented in Berman's book, as mentioned above, and Poniatowska also makes an appearance. As the elderly Doctora Hamlet, one of the book's thinly veiled characters, makes her way to one of the demonstrations on the *zócalo* she sees an unsavory character out of Mexican history, "the old PRI member who, in 1988, orchestrated the electoral fraud that brought Salinas de Gortari to the presidency" (33). Later that evening, however, she sees a more positive figure: "She saw Elenita Poniatowska pass by, diminutive, white hair and laughing out loud, and became happy when she saw her: in her she does have absolute confidence, she's an angel of God, a dove of peace" (35).

One of many other scenes Berman presents is that of La Actriz; this woman encounters a man who affirms: "Peje [López Obrador] and us, with the intermediation of Jesusa as the announcer, will put everything in order" (82). Yet the performances of Rodríguez, and that of López Obrador himself, after a sea of hands elected him "president," strikes the actress as a dangerous act: "'What the hell is going to become of us?,' she thinks. 'We'll have to create a theatrical country so that our symbolic "president" can give orders that will be carried out. A replica of a country.'" The actress also wonders if they can take over the *zócalo* in order to stage, daily, a play called *The Republic* (83). She decides that someone should create a new dictionary for the times: "People (*Pueblo*) of Mexico: Said of those of us who are in agreement with ourselves"; "Enemies of the country (*patria*): The stubborn people who don't agree with the Mexican *pueblo*" (82). The skepticism that Berman relays here and throughout the newspaper articles that make up much of her book leads to her own view of the of López Obrador's political party, of which she has been a supporter: "If the leadership of the PRD does not really believe there was fraud; if [alleging] fraud is their strategy and they are sacrificing their followers and passing by this historic opportunity for the left, it would be unpardonable" (70–71). Berman's preferred route, at the time of publication, would have been to avoid theater, to form a coalition government with the ruling party, and to prepare the political left to win 2012 elections. Perhaps Berman's views can be summed up in the testimony of one of her acquaintances, who calls himself a "damned reformer": "If you place the causes of the left before democracy, if first and foremost you are a leftist, then join the civil resistance. Not me" (91).

Rodríguez, of course, has done just this. She explains: "A year later, when the electoral fraud occurred, it was completely clear that those who dedicate ourselves to culture had to dedicate our work, or at least part of our work, to the Civil Resistance" (interview). That is, after years of political commitment often characterized (albeit not exclusively) by sharp criticism in the relative safety of her cabaret pieces, she decided to take to the streets—literally. An anecdote Augusto Boal recounts puts into perspective the leap from political play to the national stage into perspective. Jan Cohen-Cruz writes that while "performing for peasants in rural Brazil, Boal's middle-class actors ended an agit-prop play by lifting their prop rifles over their heads and calling for revolution. The peasant leader invited them all to eat together and then take up arms against the local landowner. Boal was ashamed; he and his actors were not prepared to fight but were telling others to do so (14). As would Boal, Jesusa has shown that she is willing to take to the streets, in political performances where words and images are peaceful proxies for the rifles of revolution.

In Rodríguez we also find the inspiration of Poniatowska, whose political activisim leading up to the present she credits for the political awakening that she and others experienced: "Her influence is like the air I breathe, without her I can't imagine where I would find the strength for this struggle, which is so unequal yet so necessary" (interview). Poniatowska is known—in addition to her substantial publications—for her desire to understand and help (physically, at times, as she did after the 1985 earthquake) the disenfranchised people of Mexico. She also recognizes this quality in Rodríguez. Writing about the 47-day encampment on Reforma Avenue and contradicting published reports, perhaps purposefully, of a humorless Rodríguez, she notes: "And the *plantón* ended up being a font of happiness, of happenings and of culture and this we owe, almost in its entirety to Jesusa Rodríguez, who from the first night established herself on the *zócalo* and made people think, sing, dance, laugh, play, recite poetry to those who accompanied us... Jesusa Rodríguez [is] the symbol of the Civil Resistance" ("La sociedad").

While in the work of Berman and Rodríguez one finds the collective legacy of Poniatowska, their political incursions also point to a divide among leftists in Mexico; namely, the position regarding support of López Obrador. Many intellectuals have taken a clear stance on the subject, often making enemies in the process. Through the lens of performance, this difference becomes clearer. To see López Obrador "elected" to the highest office in Mexico is either a fatal farce that will weaken the political left—or a brilliant political play. From photos of López Obrador being sworn in a "president" and riding the subway in full presidential regalia, to videos of his journey to all of Mexico's 3,000 polling districts, the scenes were at once moving and disconcerting (http://www.amlo.org.mx/). As López Obrador stated on Berman and Katia D'Artigues's program Shalalá, his campaign had registered over two million voters who had pledged to join any call to civil disobedience. The never-ending debate in Mexico regarding the national oil company, PEMEX, centers on increased privatization that would generate massive demonstrations, and perhaps interruptions in transportation. While opinions on the parallel government are divided, even on the Left, it is clear that the Mexican authorities are threatened: López Obrador and his campaign have been forbidden to use the term "legitimate president." John M. Ackerman, analyzing this decision by the Federal Elections Institute (IFE), notes that "the authority argues that by using the expression 'legitimate president of Mexico' [coalition parties] 'would be transmitting the idea that (López Obrador) is the president-elect in accordance with the law, [the person] to whom the licit designation of president corresponds, the right president, genuine and true, in opposition to someone who is not'" (50).

The anxiety expressed by the IFE, which many see as bending to the will of the PAN, demonstrates an understanding of the power of performance: as with the abovementioned nuptials performed year after year on Valentine's day, the strength of staging future reality is evident in Mexico, and the legacy of seemingly impractical protests—from hunger strikes to silent marches—have over the years produced results for the Left, as well as for the Right. As Berman expresses in *Un soplo en el corazón de la patria*, the 2006 election is indeed "the stone in the PAN's shoe" (71), and the counter-hegemonic performances of López Obrador, many of which are directed by Rodríguez, can be interpreted as effective performances of power or as self-constructed caricatures. While Rodríguez clearly sees potential in the "legitimate presidency," which she describes as "an act of civil resistance" that is a conscious performance meant to keep pressure on the PAN, Berman wonders if the Left is not heading down the path of a previous "legitimate" president under Porfirio Díaz, Don Nicolás Zúñiga y Miranda (interview). This character, according to Rafael Cardona, named himself the legitimate president of Mexico after losing an election to Díaz, perhaps through fraud: "Zúñiga y Miranda, a *señor* who, in his final days as a theatrical attraction in Centenary Mexico, had the custom of presenting himself as a candidate in each one of the successive reelections of [Díaz]. Some celebrated him, others invited him out to show him off as a curious personage of the Mexican picaresque, and many simply called him crazy."

Berman also worries about what she and others see as authoritarian tendencies on the part of López Obrador. Cuauhtémoc Cárdenas, for instance, wrote the following in an open letter to Elena Poniatowska: "The intolerance and sanitizing worry me profoundly, [as does] the dogmatic attitude that prevails around Andrés Manuel [López Obrador] for those of us who do not unconditionally accept his proposals or who question his points of view and decisions, which is a contradiction of the fundamental principles of democracy—respect for the opinions of others and openness to dialogue." The division on the political left is highlighted by Berman's work with TV Azteca, which is seen by many as part of a television "duocracy," along with Televisa. *Shalalá* provides a platform for a variety of artists, politicians, and others. As the definition on the show's website indicates, *shalalá* means "anything goes," and the stage is the hosts' "house": "[they] invite people into their home to converse with complete freedom, without censorship, without political correctness, without ideological competition. Though there is dinner and wine, of course. Say what you want and do what you will.... We ask you questions to understand you better. The only thing that can irritate us is lying, dissimulation." Although Berman makes it clear that this show is very different from her theater, the stage follows many theatrical conventions—no cameras are visible and the set is designed as a house, with the guest(s) arriving through a door as if for an intimate visit. The guest(s) join D'Artigues on the couch as Berman sits in a modern, rotating chair. Both hosts are congenial, though when López Obrador was on the program there were indeed competing ideologies; even if Berman was playing devil's advocate, her antiauthoritarian persona was evident. López Obrador had turned down over a dozen invitations to appear on the program but had finally decided to talk with the hosts about PEMEX. As Berman asked about the potential positive effects of foreign capital, and questioned whether a state monopoly was the best path for Mexico, López Obrador became agitated, referring several times to the "neoliberal" ideas Berman was presenting. When Berman asked a question about the possibility of a senate position, or a run for the presidency in 2012, the politician turned the table on the hosts, wondering if in 2008 the goal could be to democratize the television industry. While programming in Mexico is indeed controlled by very few people who have often been accused of bias, corruption, insider trading, and pursuing political vendettas, *Shalalá* is a platform that allows for the exchange of myriad viewpoints.

Such was the case, for example, with the two transsexuals who appeared on the program, a choice on the part of the hosts that at first seemed anything but political. Yet in speaking about this program Berman expresses her desire to reach beyond an audience of intellectuals and politicians. The topics covered (the transformation of bodies, the social pressures the guests faced) get at the heart of Berman's political stance: "These are the things I identify with the modern left. I wish López Obrador had won—I voted for him—but he doesn't inspire in me some crazy passion. Because [he represents] a left that is statist, anti-sexual, anti-diversity, and pro-monopoly" (interview). This openness, censured by some as a lack of social commitment, follows the postmodern edge of Berman's theater, a stance that is also seen in *Un soplo en el Corazón de la patria*. Berman closes the book with a sections followed by lines that are to be filled in, literally, by the reader; the last chapter is "Design the Adventure of Your Country" (153). This open ending was, of course, a temporal necessity since the book was published in November—five months after the elections. Yet it also points to Berman's view of the role of intellectuals and to her own view of the position of leftists in Mexico today, which she describes as an uncomfortable situation: "Why do you have to be the artillery of a politician? Isn't that when an intellectual renounces being an intellectual?...It seems to me that [López Obrador] set a very grave trap for intellectuals: 'if you're not with me, you're on the [political] right.' As if he were the Virgin of Guadalupe of the left" (interview).

As a playwright, Berman had reached an unusually large audience. Her play *eXtras*, for example, was seen by almost a million spectators throughout Mexico, and the authors she most admires are those who have wide appeal. With *Shalalá*, however, her work is seen by a million people every week and surpasses the so-called círculo rojo (red circle) of the Mexican media (interview). Jorge G. Castañeda explains this concept, theorized by the controversial chairperson of TV Azteca, as

> the thesis—in the end false—of Ricardo Salinas Pliego on the so-called green and red circles. The first is that of the masses who vote and who are defined based on certain basic criteria: employment, prices, security, education, health, housing. One reaches them through the media: television and, on a smaller scale, radio. From this came the tremendous importance that Fox (and indeed Calderón) placed on governmental advertising campaigns and to their direct appearances on television. In contrast, the red circle is made up of informed Mexicans who read the newspapers and follow the news closely. They are politicized and organized in political parties, union leadership, universities, upper management, NGOs, etc. Communication with this group is produced through print media: headlines, editorial columns, photos, etc.

The ability to reach an audience beyond the elite, even if one questions Salinas Pliego's theory, which has been adopted by the PAN, is paramount to an understanding of the current intellectual reach of Berman and Rodríguez. For Berman, the change relates to the need to escape the circle of intellectual discourse: "It's important to me not to end up trapped in the elite class" (interview). In the case of Rodríguez, her politics represent a move from theory to practice, or perhaps the interweaving of both—what Paulo Freire would call "praxis." Both Berman and Rodríguez underscore that their current political activities are not theater, and while the latter sees the link between the cabaret space and the national stage, she also emphasizes radical change that her work with López Obrador implies:

> More than an extension, I would say that it's an absolute change to go beyond the cabaret—political farce created in an enclosed stage—and to take this work to its true setting, which is the street and the plaza. Then we can really say that it passes from one plane to another—completely

different—where theater has direct political consequences, something that, as much as one tries, is not going to happen in the enclosed space of the cabaret. It's like talking about the map and talking about the land; we have now moved to the land. (Interview)

The accelerated move from the space of the theater or the cabaret provides for dialogue that, if at times uncomfortable and heated, is productive. While Berman and Rodríguez have been heavily criticized for their political stances, they are representative of a diversity of ideas on the Left. For Rodríguez the move from the map provides a grounding that was an intellectual necessity—anything else would make her an intellectual fraud.[11] For Berman, the pressure to support a specific politician, or to take a position on whether or not the election was won through fraud, threatens her position as an intellectual.[12] Both artists are pragmatic, though of course their pragmatism takes different forms. Influenced by the legacies of people like Elena Poniatowska, they are public intellectuals.

One can be an intellectual without taking a political stance, or even attempting to share ideas. Thus, for my purposes the term "public intellectual" seems to offer an important distinction. Public intellectuals reach out to a wide audience, share their opinions and knowledge, and, in questioning the status quo, provide a critical stance that may influence the public and/or government. Public intellectuals are artists, activists, professors, performers, writers, among others, who speak truth to power. Unlike the disenfranchised, however, they generally do so from positions of (relative) strength. To some in Mexico, as mentioned above, the term intellectual by definition includes public involvement. Yet there is something different about the artist who stays in her performance space and one who—through the airwaves, or books, or mass demonstrations—questions the power structures that define, and are at times defined by, intellectuals. Henry Giroux writes that "the best work in...cultural politics challenges the culture of political avoidance while demonstrating how intellectuals might live up to the historical responsibility they bear in bridging the relationship between theoretical rigor and social relevance, social criticism and practical politics, individual scholarship and pedagogy, as part of a broader commitment to defending democratic societies" (14).[13] Giroux's ideas about the academy can easily be extended to Berman and Rodríguez, and while professors and others who communicate their ideas through writing are perhaps the most often recognized as intellectuals, it is clear that in Mexico theater practitioners and other artists are included in the equation.

Berman and Rodriguez are exemplary, at once conforming to and informing what it means to be a public intellectual in Mexico. Dwight Conquergood notes that "de Certeau's aphorism that 'what the map cuts up, the story cuts across'...points to the transgressive travel between two different domains of knowledge: one official, objective, and abstract—'the map'; the other one practical, embodied, and popular—'the story'" (311). Rodríguez's affirmation that she and her business/life/performance partner Liliana Felipe have left the confines of the map, moving closer to embodied experiences (as was the case when Berman and Katia D'Artigues interviewed the two transsexuals on their program, to give one example), points to a way of knowing Mexico and Mexicans that has led to sharp criticism.[14] Indeed, Rodríguez has been classified through numerous and colorful adjectives by those who do not agree with her political stance, her social commitment. These adjectives have, in the end, one meaning: "loca," the feminine grammatical form of "crazy." The friends and enemies who wanted Berman to take a stand regarding fraud in 2006, shortly after the elections and before she felt she had sufficient information—not to mention the people who question her decision to work for TV Azteca—use similar adjectives. As in the case of López Obrador's use of the term "legitimate president," which has Mexican officials worried, there is no better indication of the presence of effective, counter-hegemonic activity than verbal attacks meant de delegitimize ideas that cross the line, leaving established territory.

To be a public intellectual in Mexico is to reach beyond the "ivory towers" of a given vocation, to take a political stance (even if that stance is one of relative objectivity), and to face the intellectual, and potentially physical, dangers of sharing ideas. The division among intellectuals on the political left in Mexico could easily be mapped out based on circles of writers and artists who are aligned with specific media outlets in Mexico, cliques based on alliances created over the years as well as new groupings formed during and after the 2006 elections. Berman and Rodríguez, of course, find themselves on different sides of the issue, and they exemplify a division on the political left. They also offer a glimpse at the variety of legitimate activities that occupy public intellectuals in Mexico. While the work of both artist-intellectuals is in many ways very different that in was in the past, it is true that two of the works mentioned above—*La grieta* and *Misa en Los Pinos*—offered blueprints of what was to come. Both were irreverent, but there was a subtle difference: Berman's text, like other plays she had written (e.g., *Entre Villa y una mujer desnuda*, in which the main character is a woman who finds personal freedom by embracing neoliberalism) emphasized the loss of liberty that an authoritarian leader can imply, in this case for a young poet and his wife; while Rodríguez's text presented more clear, direct messages with an anti-imperialist bent. Of the two authors, both unquestionably committed to social progress, one errs on the side of individual liberty (Berman), while the other (Rodríguez) errs on the side of popular power. Each opinion is crucial to a strong Left in Mexico, of course, despite opinions to the contrary—and each illustrates a performance of the role of "public intellectual."

In 2007, at one of López Obrador's demonstrations, which consisted of a walk from the Angel de la Independencia to the *zócalo* (advertised widely both in the liberal media and, for example, on the back of Mexico City's ubiquitous buses, or *peseros*), I saw the performance artist dressed as Sor Juana, as mentioned above. Also part of the parade—a parade that met approximately 500,000 people on the *zócalo*, where the demonstrators were asked to rehearse the song that would honor López Obrador upon his arrival—was a large yellow bus, with a man sitting on the roof above the driver. He was wearing an AMLO mask and waving to the crowd. The rehearsal to prepare the crowd for López Obrador's arrival, as well as this masked representation of populism, brought to mind the masks of the theater. Somewhere in the interstices between the comedy and tragedy of Mexican politics, between two masks, lie the public, intellectual performance spaces of Berman and Rodríguez, productive in their contrast and, in the end, inseparable.

### Notes

1. All translations are my own. I have attempted to favor original content, opting for cognates that best communicate information even when this results in a lack of fluidity.
2. The documentary film *Fraude* presents numerous cases of irregularities in the election, including many of the same tactics used by the PRI to win the 1988 elections. A review of José Antonio Crespo's book, *2006: Hablan las actas: las debilidades de la autoridad electoral mexicana*, for which the author studied thousands of ballots, indicates that "what [Crespo] considers to be two myths about the 2006 elections have been destroyed: the 'grand electoral fraud,' which the sympathizers of López Obrador maintain, and the 'unquestionable and unequivocal triumph' of Calderón" (Delgado).
3. In his recent article on contemporary Mexican political cabaret artists, Gastón Alzate contextualizes the work of Las Reinas Chulas: "Disciples as much of Tito Vasconcelos as of Jesusa Rodríguez, and at

the same time renovators of the genre, this theater-cabaret company has focused its artistic trajectory on the study and development of a fusion of German cabaret, the Mexican 'teatro de revista' and university acting techniques. For the Reinas Chulas, cabaret means, fundamentally, civil disobedience and resistance, signaling in this way the close connection between their work and social activism" (57).
4. Berman's *El narco negocia con Dios* is, as of the writing of this chapter, on stage at the Foro Shakespeare; there are plans to produce her new play *Testosterona* in November 2013; and LATR Books / El Milagro recently published these two plays in a binational edition.
5. In his interviews with prominent Mexicans, including politicians of different stripes who may not be considered intellectuals, Camp concludes that "the majority of public figures [argue] that the intellectual can and should be a public actor. Those Mexicans most involved in public life vigorously believe the two roles not only are interchangeable, but are one. They do not believe that all public figures are intellectuals, but rather that all intellectuals *should* be public figures" (45. Original emphasis). While for Camp "political activity" often refers to government service, this need not be the case, though it is clear that both Berman and Rodríguez are poised for such possibilities: according to Victoria E. Rodríguez, Berman was one of several people a feminist group presented to Vicente Fox, upon his election, to fill cabinet positions (151); and Rodríguez would likely play an important role in any future, official AMLO government.
6. For information on H.I.J.O.S. (Hijos por la Identidad y la Justicia contra el Olvido y el Silencio), a human rights group in Argentina, see <www.hijos-capital.org.ar>. Of particular interest are the group's "escraches," performances meant to denounce and expose criminals, often from Argentina's *proceso*, or "Dirty War."
7. In March 2007, Berman acted the role of "Godmother" for another politically sanctioned gay union in Mexico City. She declared on that day that there was a bit more equality (and a bit less hypocrisy) in Mexico, and noted that "they have given a kiss with historical significance...in front of a multitude of guests and some or other police officer, perhaps perplexed to be, from this moment on, here to protect their kiss and not to imprison it" (Salgado and Quintero).
8. The "repression" to which Rodríguez refers concerns Felipe Calderón and his political party, the PAN. The "everything that we are seeing" includes, among many other issues, the PAN's attempts to challenge civil unions for same-sex couples in the federal district and the state of Coahuila—not to mention the documented human rights abuses that have come with Calederón's war on narcotraffickers.
9. It is important to note Rodríguez's prior commitment to social justice, a commitment that went far beyond the walls of El Hábito and includes running workshops for sex workers, among many others activities.

10. The political advertisement was pulled, though not before the message got through. Rodríguez is quoted as defending Poniatowska: "they have made a major mistake.... It is clear that, as we have seen throughout this sexennial, the *panistas* look down on intelligence, don't recognize intellectualism, and try to disparage people for their brilliance" (Rodríguez, Palapa, and Castañeda).
11. Berman is open to the possibility that Calderón was elected by outright fraud, and not simply through illegal campaigning on the part of President Vicente Fox and the PAN.
12. Berman explains in *Un soplo en el corazón de la patria* that, as "independent" observers, she and others were to make a public declaration if the election were too close to call. On election day, when both candidates made victory speeches, the group was unsure of what their role was. When they consulted a UN elections observer from France, it was clear that they needed to improvise. "The Frenchman said: 'Act.'" So Berman changed the text, as seen in one example of the revision process: "Where is said 'don't declare yourselves winners' we should put 'they have declared themselves winners.' Our pretension of neutrality had just gone to Hell; at that moment was there anything that could be neutral?" (17).
13. Edward Said asks "whether writers and intellectuals can ever be what is called non-political or not, and if so, obviously, how and in what measure. The difficulty of the tension for the individual writer and intellectual has been paradoxically that the realm of the political and public has expanded so much as to be virtually without borders. We might well ask whether a non-political writer or intellectual is a notion that has much content to it" (20).
14. While not the purpose of this article, at times the work of Rodríguez, especially when she was living in the *plantones*, approaches that of the Gramscian organic intellectual. Brian W. Alleyne states that "the organic intellectual represents the interests of the subordinate in society, variously defined; it must be noted that organic intellectuals need not have been born into a subordinate social class—what is pivotal is their political alignment with such a class. Such intellectuals counteract the hegemony of the ruling coalition of classes and class fractions. A defining characteristic of the organic intellectual is constant engagement with politics: such intellectuals do not only think and write, but they act" (173).

## Works Cited and Consulted

Ackerman, John M. "Presidente legítimo." *Proceso*. July 6, 2008: 50. Print.
Alleyne, Brian W. *Radicals Against Race: Black Activism and Cultural Politics*. New York: Berg Publishers, 2002. Print.
Alzate, Gastón. "Dramaturgia, ciudadanía y anti-neoliberalismo: El cabaret mexicano contemporáneo." *Latin American Theatre Review* 41.2 (2008): 49–66. Print.

Berman, Sabina. *La grieta. Diálogos dramatúrgicos: México-Chile.* Edited by Stuart A. Day. Puebla, Mexico: Tablado IberoAmericano, 2002. 67–121. Print.

———. *Las fronteras míticas del teatro mexicano: Entre Villa y una mujer desnuda, Todos somos Marcos, La mujer que cayó del cielo.* Edited by Stuart A. Day. Lawrence, KS: LATR Books, 2009. 15–53. Print.

———. Personal interview. June 24, 2008.

———. *Un soplo en el corazón de la patria: instantáneas de la crisis.* Mexico, DF: Planeta, 2006. Print.

Bixler, Jacqueline E. "Una introducción al Teatro elusivo de la elusiva Sabina Berman." In *Sediciosas seducciones: Sexo, poder y palabras en el teatro de Sabina Berman.* Edited by Jacqueline E. Bixler. Mexico, DF: Escenología, 2004. 17–30. Print.

Camp, Roderic A. *Intellectuals and the State in Twentieth-Century Mexico.* Austin: University of Texas Press, 1985. Print.

Cárdenas, Cuauhtémoc. "Carta enviada por Cuauhtémoc Cárdenas a Elena Poniatowska." September 14, 2006. http://www.el-universal.com.mx/notas/375156.html. Web.

Cardona, Rafael. "La segunda presidente legítima." *La Crónica de Hoy* June 20, 2008. http://www.cronica.com.mx/nota.php?id_nota=368274. Web.

Castañeda, Jorge G. "Fox y los intelectuales." *Letras libres* June 2008. http://www.letraslibres.com/index.php?art=12977. Web.

Cohen-Cruz, Jan. "Introduction." Part One: Agit-Prop. *Radical Street Performance: An International Anthology.* Edited by Jan Cohen-Cruz. New York: Routledge, 1998. 13–14. Print.

Conquergood, Dwight. "Performance Studies: Intervention and Radical Research." *The Performance Studies Reader.* Edited by Henry Bial. 2nd ed. Routledge: New York, 2004. 369–80. Print.

Crespo, José Antonio. *2006: Hablan las actas: las debilidades de la autoridad electoral Mexicana.* Mexico, DF: Debate, 2008. Print.

Delgado, Alvaro. "Hablan las actas: Calderón no ganó." *Proceso.* June 9, 2008. http://www.proceso.com.mx/analisis_int.html?an=59811. Web.

*Fraude: México 2006.* Dir. Luis Mandoki. Contra El Viento Films, 2007. Film.

Freire, Paulo. *Pedagogy of the Oppressed.* Translated by Myra Bergman Ramos. New York: Continuum, 2001. Print.

Fukuyama, Francis. *The End of History and the Last Man.* New York: Free Press, 1992. Print.

Giroux, Henry. *Impure Acts: The Practical Politics of Cultural Studies.* New York: Routledge, 2000. Print.

Hutcheon, Linda. *Irony's Edge: The Theory and Politics of Irony.* New York: Routledge, 1995. Print.

———. *A Theory of Parody: The Teachings of Twentieth-Century Art Forms.* Urbana: University of Illinois Press, 2000. Print.

Kelty, Mark, and Blanca Kelty. "Interview with Jesusa Rodríguez." *Latin American Theatre Review* 31.1 (1997): 123–27. Print.

Lugo-Ortiz, Agnes. "Letter from the Acting Director." *Latin America Chicago*. The Center for Latin American Studies at the University of Chicago. 26.2 (2007): 1, 7. Print.

Montaño Garfias, Ericka. "Jesusa Rodríguez y Liliana Felipe dan 'pasito adelante en la Justicia.'" *La Jornada*. August 4, 2007. http://www.jornada.unam.mx/2007/08/04/index.php?section=sociedad&article=035n1soc. Web.

Muñoz, Alma E. "Contrajeron nupcias 800 parejas homosexuales." *La Jornada* February 15, 2006. http://www.jornada.unam.mx/2006/02/15/050n2soc.php. Web.

Poniatowska, Elena. *La noche de Tlatelolco*. Mexico, DF: Ediciones Era, 1985. Print.

———. "La sociedad lo hace mejor que los partidos." *La Jornada*. December 3, 2006. http://www.jornada.unam.mx/2006/12/03/index.php?section=opinion&article=a03a1cul. Web.

Preston, Julia, and Samuel Dillon. *Opening Mexico: The Making of a Democracy*. New York: Farrar, Straus, and Giroux, 2004. Print.

Rodríguez, Ana Mónica, Fabiola Palapa, and Adriana Castañeda. "'Atrocidad', el espot donde aparece Poniatowska: intelectuales y artistas." *La Jornada*. April 10, 2006. http://www.jornada.unam.mx/2006/04/10/003n1pol.php. Web.

Rodríguez, Jesusa. *Misa en Los Pinos*. Introduction by Stuart A. Day. GESTOS: *Teoría y Práctica del Teatro Hispánico* 17.33 (2002): 111–41. Print.

———. Personal interview. June 19, 2008.

Rodríguez, Victoria E. *Women in Contemporary Mexican Politics*. Austin: University of Texas Press, 2003. Print.

Said, Edward. "The Public Role of Writers and Intellectuals." *The Public Intellectual*. Edited by Helen Small. Oxford: Blackwell, 2002. 19–39. Print.

Salgado, Agustín, and Josefina Quintero. "Con un beso se acabaron 30 siglos de intolerancia: Sabina Berman." *La Jornada*. March 17, 2007. http://www.jornada.unam.mx/2007/03/17/index.php?section=capital&article=034n1cap. Web.

Scherer García, Julio, and Carlos Monsiváis. *Parte de guerra: Tlatelolco 1968. Documentos del general Marcelino García Barragán. Los hechos y la historia*. Mexico, DF: Aquilar, 1999. Print.

Scott, James C. *Domination and the Arts of Resistance: Hidden Transcripts*. New Haven: Yale University Press, 1990. Print.

Vega, Patricia. "Felices y níveas las contrayentes enlazaron sus vidas: Nupcias de Liliana y Jesusa." February 16, 2001. http://www.jornada.unam.mx/2001/02/16/056n1con.html. Web.

## Chapter 6

# From Accounting to Recounting: Esther Chávez Cano and the Articulation of Advocacy, Agency, and Justice on the US-Mexico Border

*María Socorro Tabuenca C.*

*There is no such thing as a private intellectual, since the moment you set down words and then publish them you have entered the public world.*
                                                          Edward Said, 1993[1]

*When one is propagating truths deeply radical and desperately unpalatable one cannot expect an eager and convinced audience.*
                                           Charlotte Perkins Gilman, 1897[2]

Nuestra obligación es luchar para que desaparezca el crimen, la corrupción y la impunidad y son las autoridades las que deben dar respuesta inmediata a nuestras inquietudes. *(Our responsibility is to fight to make crime, corruption, and impunity disappear, and it is the authorities who should provide an immediate response to our concerns.)*
                                                Esther Chávez Cano, 1991[3]

Esther Chávez Cano was trained as an accountant in Mexico City, where she worked in executive positions for national and international corporations.[4] In 1982 she moved to Juárez to take care of an elderly aunt.[5] It was not until 1985, when she could not adjust to her new life in Ciudad Juárez, that she shifted gears and discovered her real vocation in an ad in *El Diario*,[6] which stated, very simply, *"solicitaban reporteros a quienes se les impartiría un curso de periodismo"*— the paper was looking for reporters they could include in a course in journalism.[7] She could not predict then that a few years later the impulse to write would turn her into an international leader[8] against violence toward women and children in Ciudad Juárez, and, more specifically, against the femicide in the city.

Chávez Cano's first forays into the public sphere came as a concerned citizen writing to the editor about municipal inequalities and injustices. These tentative first steps eventually became the weekly voice of conscience in her column in *El Diario*, and ultimately provided her with the platform to become a public intellectual. While her work in journalism did not turn her into a public intellectual, contradicting slightly the affirmation by Said in my epigraph, it certainly paved the way for her to "speak truth to power"[9] by "[facing] down national, state and local leaders, demanding that they pay attention to the violence against women and children and the conditions that continued to breed violence."[10] My contribution to this collection illustrates Chávez Cano's evolution from concerned citizen and journalist to human rights advocate and public, feminist intellectual. I argue that it was her expansion from a critic of local and municipal issues to a determined defender of human rights that confirms this role.

Before my discussion of her move into the public sphere, I would like to provide a brief presentation of this powerful woman.[11] Esther Chávez Cano was born on June 2, 1933 in Chihuahua City, where she studied through middle school. She lost her father at the age of three and her mother in 1961. Chávez and her eight siblings were raised as orphans. At the age of 19, she was sent to Guadalajara to live with her aunt and uncle, and there she studied high school and, later, accounting. In 1988, she began writing for *El Diario*, where she eventually gained a position on the executive board. In 1992, she ran for mayor as the candidate for the Party of Democratic Revolution (PRD)[12] in Juárez but lost the election. The same year, she started the *Grupo 8 de Marzo*[13] in Juárez, an activist women's rights group that protested new authoritarian abortion legislation proposed by the conservative Partido Acción Nacional (PAN). In 1993, Chávez Cano started recording data on the murdered women in Juárez based on newspaper clippings. She also began, along with the *8 de Marzo*, to complain publicly about the government's negligence in solving the murders and bringing the culpable to justice. In 1998, she joined with 13 feminist activist groups, the *Coordinadora de Organismos No Gubernamentales en Pro de la Mujer* (Coordinator of Non-Governmental Organizations Pro-Women) to work together to advocate for the prosecution and prevention of crimes against women. And in 1999 she cofounded *Casa Amiga A.C.*, the first rape crisis center and shelter for abused women in the city, and sixth in the nation. She died in her bed on Christmas day in 2009 after losing a battle with cancer.

Perhaps the best place to begin the discussion of the emergence of Chávez Cano as a public and feminist intellectual is to examine her letters to the editor, her weekly column in *El Diario*, and her book *Construyendo caminos y esperanzas*. My critical framework for arguing that Chavez Cano was a public intellectual—not only for her role in drawing attention to the femicide in Juárez but also for her tireless advocacy of women's and children's rights—relies on two theorists: Edward Said and Elaine Showalter. This essay will not elaborate on the trope or genealogy of the theoretical category of the "public intellectual";[14] rather, I will focus on Chavez Cano's role in one of the most appalling periods in contemporary Mexican history, taking into account Said's reflections on the public intellectual and Showalter's ideas of the feminist intellectual. Said defined the public intellectual as

> an individual endowed with a faculty for representing, embodying, articulating a message, a view, an attitude, philosophy or opinion to, as well as for, a public, in public. And this role has an edge to it, and cannot be played without a sense of being someone whose place it is to raise embarrassing questions, to confront orthodoxy and dogma (rather than to produce them), to be someone who cannot easily be co-opted by governments or corporations, and whose *raison d'etre* is to represent all those people and issues who are routinely forgotten or swept under the rug.[15]

His words resonate in those of the epigraphs by Charlotte Perkins Gilman and Chávez Cano. She spoke her mind knowing she would not only have public resistance—especially from conservatives—but also institutionalized resistance that might result in her own peril.

Chávez Cano was an interesting character. She did not belong to the stale lineage of Mexican *intelligentsia*; on the contrary, as Showalter helps us to see, she had to overcome invisibility to participate in public dialogue: "Whether the issue is the Gramscian universal intellectual, the Foucaultian specific intellectual, the overall decline of the public intellectual or the rise of a new professional managerial class, feminists are excluded from consideration.... Perhaps for these men the intellectual seems to have vanished or become invisible because they cannot see women playing the role" (1). Considering the historical invisibility of the female public intellectual, Chávez Cano's trajectory is even more astounding: one needs to take into account that she began her advocacy from three different marginalized spaces: the geographic,[16] the "generical"[17] or literary, and the gendered. In this sense she ("inevitably") disarticulates the privileged position and space of the male Mexican intellectual, if we take into account Camp's explanation of Mexican intelligentsia: "The contemporary intellectual's role [in Mexico] has become identified with political activism because of ideological commitments."[18] By "inevitably" I mean because she is an activist involved in political issues with a firm ideological commitment, even if intellectual men—to follow Showalter— intend to vanish women as public intellectuals, which in the case of Esther Chávez Cano is simply not possible because she embodies the Mexican definition of the "contemporary intellectual."

Her coming of age as a feminist advocate was also atypical. She did not have either a feminist or an activist past like her colleagues in the *Grupo 8 de Marzo*, who came from Chihuahua City and had a long tradition of leftist struggles and political participation.[19] Perhaps her experience of patriarchy and "machismo" in the corporations where she worked made her more aware of gender inequalities; or maybe it was her familiarity with cases of abuse, rape, and incest that have had a uninterrupted presence in Mexican media, and the stories she heard during her campaign for public office, that make her a feminist by conviction more than by theory.[20] In any case, she had the experience, the knowledge, and the commitment to reinvent herself and fight for women's and children's rights. As Eve Ensler points out, "she was a fierce activist and a huge part of our V-Day movement. She literally changed the world for women in Juárez, bringing the struggle of the raped, the disappeared, the discarded women and girls to global attention."[21]

Her incipient *"Cartas al Director"* set the tone she would use either when questioning Juárez society for its indifference and lack of solidarity toward social problems or when she questioned authorities for their corrupt and fraudulent practices that fostered violence and impunity. She employed frank language to target a spectrum of audiences. In her letter from July 23, 1998,[22] she talked about two tragedies that had the city in mourning: the death of a woman in a local cinema and the subsequent theft of her property, which made her an anonymous corpse; and the heartbreaking drowning of four children who were playing near a city dam that collapsed and also washed away 40 homes, leaving the same number of families homeless. In her letter Chávez Cano questions and challenges her readers:

> ¿Me podrían informar qué ha hecho la sociedad, qué hemos hecho los que queremos un México donde cada familia viva con seguridad y paz?...No he visto unirse ningún partido religioso o político en una magna manifestación pidiendo justicia por los cadáveres que son

despojados de sus pertenencias, por los desamparados que lloran a sus hijos y parientes que por accidente o corrupción murieron sepultados bajo las aguas de un dique derrumbado.

(Can someone inform me, what has society done? Those of us who desire a Mexico where each family can live in safety and peace, what have we done?...I have not seen any religious or political party come together in a great protest demanding justice for the bodies who are stripped of their belongings; for the defenseless that cry for their children and relatives who, by accident or corruption, have died buried under the waters of a crushed dam.)

Chávez Cano addresses several issues to create awareness in the public. It is obvious that "el Director" as a sole designated recipient of the message grows in numbers according to how many people read her letter to the editor that day. Consequently, she enters into dialectical communication with a broader audience, anticipating how her argument will be received. She speaks for those who have been dispossessed of their personal belongings, their relatives, and of their own lives. She claims for them a place in society, in the same society that has denied them its compassion; a society "[que] se está acostumbrando al asesinato, al robo, a la violación." ([that] is getting used to murder, robbery, and rape.) This phrase—with some variations—will be a *locus* for her various critiques.

Chávez Cano will take the place of insider/outsider of that *juarense* society incapable of demanding justice for one of their own ("gentes sumamente conocidas") (extremely well-known individuals.)[23] On the one hand her rhetorical question implies that society in general—political parties, religious groups, the middle class—is not doing anything to prevent these injustices or to support her call for justice. On the other hand, she suggests that by recounting these events she is not condemning these dispossessed to anonymity and silence, but rather she is granting them a place in history, in her story. Chávez Cano thus positions herself as the Gramscian "organic intellectual" who belongs to the *status quo* but who subverts it at the same time by assuming Said's position of "exile," that is to say "outside the mainstream, unaccommodated, unco-opted, resistant...the state of never being fully adjusted."[24] At the end of her letter, she assumes again her position in/out of society by stating: "La responsablidad es de todos y cada uno de nosotros al guardar silencio por la tragedia...por los miles de jóvenes y niñas violadas, por los atropellos cometidos. Gracias por su paciencia y comprensión" (my emphasis). (Each and every one of us is responsible for keeping this tragedy silent...for the thousands of young women and children that have been raped, for the atrocities committed. Thank you for *your* patience and understanding.) By using the deictic "su" (your), Esther may be well addressing the editor and audience in the "usted" form, but her unspecified public is "ustedes." She does not want to evade her social responsibility but appeals for society to be engaged in civil action by simply giving voice to tragedy and injustice. However, Chávez Cano foresees an anonymous audience that mostly remained as invisible as the victims throughout her years as an activist. As a nascent public intellectual, she anticipates "that strategic silence and/or indifference reproduce/s a common-sense arrangement where critical 'reading of the word and the world' (Freire, 1987) [could be] relegated to the periphery."[25]

Chávez Cano was an informed woman able to "opine on a wide array of issues,...concerned...with matters of interest to the public at large, and [did] not keep [her] views to [herself]."[26] In fact, before devoting herself fully to the cause against violence toward women and children, she wrote about Mexican national and local politics, the environment, social justice, the Mexican economy, Mexico's electoral fraud of 1988, the murder of journalists in the country, the US intervention in Panama, NAFTA, women's and children's struggles and rights, and local and national cultural affairs, among other topics. She was devoted to "the tracking down of prejudices in the hiding places where priests, the school, the government and all long-established institutions had gathered and protected them."[27] She was very passionate when defending democracy. In her column of October 3, 1990 she writes: "Juegan con nosotros prometiéndonos democracia de 'mentiritas' porque tras bambalinas se cuece el fraude electoral." (They are playing around with us by promising us a "make-believe" democracy, while behind the scenes there is an electoral fraud that is taking shape.) She was also very critical of the neoliberal thinking that characterized Mexican governments since the presidency of Carlos Salinas de Gortari: "la deuda externa, la caída de los salarios, la miseria, la guerra, la carencia de buenos servicios, el intento de privatizar los servicios de salud, las universidades y otras graves carencias son culpa del presidencialismo que debemos erradicar (*jueves 12 de enero de 1995*). (The foreign debt, the drop in salaries, the misery, the war, the lack of good services, the attempt to privatize health services, the universities and other hardships are to be blamed on the presidential imposition that we must eradicate.) Aside from her critique of the neoliberal political model, I would like to point out her position of "exile" and her vehement call for action as fundamental characteristics of her style that we can observe dating back to her "letters to the editor" of 1988.

Perhaps her candidacy for mayor in 1992 was a preface for what she was going to become in the near future. Chávez Cano comments:

> Desde el inicio de la campaña me involucré con esas fuertes mujeres que dedican nueve o más horas de trabajo remunerado pero antes han ya realizado la labor de madres desde las 3 o 4 de la madrugada... ¿Y el marido? Preguntaba yo. No, él se fue pal otro lado y nunca volvió. Se fue con otra y nos abandonó. Es un borracho desobligado, eran las respuestas comunes de esas gladiadoras del diario vivir... Las historias de estas mujeres son tan parecidas, que una se pregunta de dónde sacan fuerzas para vivir sin un aliciente laboral y llevando a cabo un trabajo tan agotador (*Construyendo caminos*, 27–28).
>
> (Since the beginning of the campaign I got involved with those strong women who spend nine hours or more of work for remuneration and who prior to that have already performed their labor as mothers starting at 3 or 4 o'clock in the morning.... And the husband? I would ask. No, he crossed to the other side and never came back. He took off with another woman and abandoned us. He is an irresponsible drunk, were the common responses of these gladiators of the daily life... The stories of these women are so much alike that you ask yourself where they get the strength to live without any labor incentive while doing such a strenuous job. [*Construyendo caminos*, 27–28].)

Her internalization of these stories led her into a steadfast advocacy that kept her in the public arena until her death.

After the campaign was over, she initiated the *Grupo 8 de Marzo* along with other women from Juárez[28] at the invitation of Irma Campos, the founder of the *8 de Marzo* in Chihuahua City. The first "official" meeting was on November 2, 1993,[29] and Chavez Cano's house turned into the headquarters from that point until the creation of Casa Amiga six years later, in 1999. Before officially being established, the group had agreed to support a proposal from the Chihuahua organization to amend the penal code to reinforce the laws in cases of sexual abuse and gender violence.[30] However, it was the debate about strict new abortion legislation[31] proposed by PAN representative Teresa Ortuño that placed Chávez Cano definitively in the public eye. The PAN wanted to amend the state constitution—which already affirmed "the right to life"—by adding "from the moment of its conception."[32] As a spokesperson for the *8 de Marzo*, Eshter would denounce this amendment as "anti-Constitutional, unjust, inhuman, and incongruent."[33]

From 1988 to 1992, Chávez Cano's column mostly elaborated on the topics previously mentioned. Yet, by 1993, her tone and preference toward women's rights had become central to her advocacy. In a thorough study of her weekly columns,[34] it became clear to me that she experienced a transformation from being a "professional"[35] to an "amateur" who "go[es] into something much more lively and radical."[36] She went from writing 8.5 percent of articles on women or women's rights from 1988 to 1990, to 31 percent in 1993. Most of that year's editorials were on the right to choose and criticizing Ortuño's position on the issue. One example is her column after a televised panel (which she called PAN-el) on the issue. There were representatives from the PAN and *8 de Marzo*, including Ortuño and Chávez Cano, a priest from the Roman Catholic church, and representatives from "Católicas por el Derecho a Decidir"[37] (Catholics for Choice): "A Tere Ortuño se le olvidó la toga de legisladora y se colocó el muy honorable de mujer cristiana... Los conocimientos médicos de la diputada Ortuño salieron a relucir, no existen casos en que peligre la vida de la madre... Por supuesto a juicio de Tere, a la mujer violada le toca gozar 'a fuercitas' el don de la maternidad. Las garantías individuales ni siquiera fueron mencionadas."[38] (Tere Ortuño forgot her legislator's robe and she donned the very honorable one of a Christian woman... The medical knowledge of representative Ortuño surfaced; there are no instances where the mother's life is at risk. Obviously, according to Tere's judgment a raped woman must enjoy, like it or not, the gift of motherhood. The legal rights of the individual were not even mentioned.) The irony in Chávez Cano's words is blunt and leaves no space for Ortuño to escape (her) dogma and propose an alternative law. As a matter of fact the use of the diminutive in "*a fuercitas*" (whether she likes it or not) instead of being used as a diminutive of endearment serves to emphasize the authoritarian effect of the law: without access to legalized abortion, victims of rape must suffer the effects of forced maternity.

Chávez Cano was attacked by the clergy, pro-life activists, and lay conservatives and was labeled a modern Herod and baby killer. She was aware that the polemics of this issue required a very thoughtful and well-articulated response to contest these groups' orthodoxy. Therefore, in "Prejuicios y Machismo" (Feb. 23, 1993, 5-A) she artfully undermines their discourse when she emphasizes: "Estamos conscientes de que el aborto no debe usarse como medio de control natal y no intentamos aconsejar a las mujeres a que lo practiquen, pero sí vemos la necesidad de que se amplíe la campaña de planificación familiar y se establezcan en las escuelas y universidades programas para la prevención del Sida y desde la educación primaria una clara y profesional información sexual." (We are conscious that abortion must not be used as a means for birth control and we are not attempting to advise women to have them performed; however, we are aware of the need for planned parenthood campaigns to be broader and the creation of AIDS prevention programs in schools and universities as well as clear and professional sex education that starts in elementary school.) Chávez Cano refutes the "abortionist" label given by the conservative wing and also proposes both reproductive rights for women and sexual education for females and males for the prevention of AIDS. In this context, the use of the "we" serves to include her fellow activists from the *8 de Marzo* groups in Juárez and Chihuahua, her audience, and the pro-choice constituency. At the end of the editorial she concludes with a different, inclusive "we," and calls for a feminine alliance: "deseamos unir al sexo femenino para que el aborto y la prostitución dejen de ser sexistas, selectivos y que seamos nosotras las que legislemos lo que conviene o no a nuestros cuerpos y los de nuestras hijas." (We wish to unite women so abortion and prostitution cease to be sexist and selective, and for us to be the ones who legislate what is or is not appropriate for our bodies and those of our daughters.) Her universalizing of the "we" to include all women is a call for women to participate in legislation, particularly that which directly bears on women's rights. This "we" is a call to women's political action through a reaffirmation of self, body, and sexuality. Chávez Cano also appropriates the discourse of motherhood[39] ("nuestras hijas") (our daughters) to position herself in accordance with "all women."

The year 1993 was terrible for women in Juárez. The bodies of nine young women[40] were found on the city's outskirts. All nine deaths were allegedly perpetrated by a serial killer and Juárez society was shocked by the findings but the police had no leads. Because of the police's negligence and the gravity of the situation, Chávez Cano recalls, "no puedo fijar la fecha, exacto el caso más impactante que me llevó, en 1993, a recortar las notas periodísticas e iniciar una lista de los asesinatos de mujeres jóvenes y pobres, por el sólo hecho de serlo, que ahora llamamos feminicidio" (Consruyendo, 84). (I cannot recall the exact date of the case, the case with the greatest impact that led me, in 1993, to clip newspaper articles and to start a list of the murders of young, poor women, just for being such, and that we now call femicide). Once again she champions public a cause, this one even more demanding than the abortion legislation. Without abandoning the cause of women's reproductive rights, she transformed herself into a sociologist, an anthropologist, and an ethnographer. Methodically she began to document the names of every murder victim; the date and nature of their deaths; who found the body (though many are still missing); the name of the person in charge of the investigation, if any; whether or how the death was reported and whether the victims' families were informed or helped. In her many notebooks she also listed the names of the police officers, state prosecutors, or other officials who were, or, more often than not, should have been involved in each case.

That year, and following Chávez Cano's lead, the *8 de Marzo* group, the Division of Gender Studies at the Universidad Autónoma de Ciudad Juárez, and the Independent Committee of Human Rights in Chihuahua City[41] continued to keep track of the women's murders through newspaper clippings. This data later became basis for the *Estudio hemerográfico de mujeres asesinadas 1993–1998* (Newspaper Study of Murdered Women, 1993–1998). The record of those cases was (and still is) of extreme importance because the authorities never made public, have not given, and will never give an accurate account of the dead women, especially in light of the fact that these are sexual serial killings.[42] Chávez Cano exposed the state's callous disregard and silence regarding these marginal, tortured, and raped women whose mutilated corpses were discovered in the desert, left exposed for other predators. Her refusal to allow these victims to sink into oblivion or state-sanctioned anonymity and invisibility illustrates how she "speaks of the power of remembrance" (Mendieta, 224).

As stated above, she did not come from a tradition of activism and struggle, yet she stood up for all women massacred and dumped in the desert. As the leading voice of *8 de Marzo* regarding the crimes against women and the negligence of authorities in solving the crimes, she began to gain notoriety. She put the issue of femicide on the local and state agenda by recording and disseminating the facts. On May 25, 1995, in her column "*Cuento de Hadas*," Chávez Cano refutes the deceptiveness of State judicial power:

> Es un hecho que las oficinas del Departamento de Averiguaciones Previas lucen en mejores condiciones de limpieza...pero el cáncer de la falta de sensibilidad, impreparación y carencia de respeto a los derechos humano, muy poco ha variado de una administración a otra, para muestra los comentarios que ha vertido el Sr. Procurador Francisco Molina Ruiz, sobre los homicidios que alarman a la sociedad y LOS QUE NO. El Señor Hernán Rivera nos presentó un Departamento de Averiguaciones Previas [maravilloso]. Entre las maravillas que lamentablemente no existen está la famosa Agencia de investigaciones Previa para Delitos Sexuales atendida por personal exclusivamente femenino, sueño que hemos perseguido muchas mujeres conocedoras del impacto brutal físico y psicológico que representa la violación.

(It is a fact that the Offices of Criminal Affairs looks cleaner... but the cancer of the absence of sensitivity, the lack of preparation and respect for human rights, have not varied much from one administration to the other, as an example, the statements given by prosecutor Francisco Molina Ruiz, in reference to the murders that alarm society and THOSE WHICH DO NOT. Mr. Hernan Rivera showed us a [wonderful] Office of Criminal Affairs. Among the wonderful things that unfortunately do not exist, is the famous Office of Criminal Affairs for Sexual Crimes, handled exclusively by female personnel, a dream that many of us have been pursuing as women who have an understanding of the brutal physical and psychological impact that is rape.

In this excerpt from her editorial, she emphasizes how the authorities, especially the district attorney and the deputy attorney (Hernán Rivera), try to show another face of bureaucracy. The idea of presenting a "cleaner office" may lead one to believe that they are "cleaning" the force from the inside. However, Chávez Cano is very incisive when she declares that nothing has changed despite the new administration; if the floors are less stained, the personnel is not noticeably more ethical. By using irony, she "speaks truth to power" and condemns and clearly mocks the attorney general when mentioning that he dared to affirm that there are "shocking and non-shocking" crimes. One can infer from her writing that he and/or Juárez society in general are not distressed by the tortured, raped, mutilated bodies of these disposable and anonymous women. Apparently for Molina Riuz, those cadavers are "just corpses in the desert" and not the human beings with names and stories that Chávez Cano was inscribing in her journals and reporting to the public. In this manner, she also criticizes the administration's refusal to meet one of our first demands: a true and professional Special Victims Unit.

By the year 1996, the crimes had escalated to a total of 42 since 1993. The crimes rose from 6 in 1993 to 16 in 1996.[43] Impunity was rampant and the state pretended it was working on the cases. That year, *8 de Marzo* and 12 nongovernmental organizations decided to join forces to fight for justice and founded the *Coordinadora de Organismos No Gubernamentales en Pro de la Mujer*. The group decided to name Esther Chávez Cano as their spokeswoman:

A falta de dinero usábamos la imaginación. Organizamos marchas, plantones, toma de oficinas, todos los eventos fueron importantes... Tanto las activistas del Grupo 8 de Marzo, como las organizaciones de la sociedad civil que formamos la coordinadora, queríamos darles nombre y voz a las mujeres asesinadas y desaparecidas y apoyo a sus familias. Exigíamos justicia, castigo a el o los culpables, cero impunidad, pero nuestro objetivo era y sigue siendo...por los derechos de las mujeres en el ámbito laboral, el hogar, la escuela y la sociedad (*Construyendo caminos*, 91).

(Since there was no money, we used our imagination. We organized marches, sit-ins, took over offices, all events were important...The activists of *Grupo 8 de Marzo* as well as the organizations of the civil society that made up *La Cooridnadora*, we wanted to give a name and voice to the women who had been murdered and disappeared and provide support to their families. We demanded justice, punishment to whoever was/were accountable, zero impunity; but our goal was and continues to be...for women's rights in the work, home, school, and social environments.)

Chávez Cano mentions that because of pressure from *Coordiandora de Organismos No Gubernamentales*, in June 2006 the district attorney, Arturo Chávez Chávez, announced the future opening of a Special Victims Unit in Juárez. "El procurador ofrece a la ciudadanía que el personal contratado garantizará a las víctimas su estabilidad emocional, sensibilidad en el manejo de estos delitos, respeto, seriedad y privacidad." (The prosecutor is offering to the people that the hired personnel will guarantee the victims' emotional stability, and sensitivity, respect, seriousness, and privacy when dealing with these crimes). Another triumph for the *Coordinadora* was the opening of a Special Prosecutor's Office for Crimes Against Women; however, Chávez Cano criticizes both institutions for their lack of professionalism and spirit of service. She objects to the many complaints from the victims due to the lack of privacy, respect, and professionalism from the staff: "Se necesita sobre todo voluntad política porque se ha derrochado mucho dinero en la investigación de los crímenes y el método elegido ha sido la fabricación de culpables, conocido coloquialmente como 'chivos expiatorios.'" (*Construyendo caminos*, 57–58). (Above all here is a great need for political will, because there has been too much wasteful spending of money on the crimes' investigations and the chosen method has been to fabricate accusations, known colloquially as "scape goats.") Chávez Cano never ceased her denunciations and criticism of governmental negligence, waste, and abuse of power.

According to Walden Bello,[44] truth does not simply *exist*; it becomes real and it is ratified by action. One should not allow power to destroy the truth; the role of the public intellectual is to point out truth(s) even if inconvenient from a political point of view. For Bello an "engaged intellectual" needs to combine analysis with action, and that is precisely the value of Chávez Cano as an intellectual. She publicly condemned the state for being an accomplice of the crimes, in editorials that included vehement critiques of the police, the officials in power, and the state in general.[45] Repeatedly, she wrote and gave interviews regarding these women's deaths, despite the state's intention to minimize and obliterate them. Consequently, as Bello suggests, in as much as she voiced the crimes and the state's negligence, they became more real.

Chávez Cano never ceased to work toward her goal and when we noticed that Mexican authorities were not interested in solving the crimes, she started an international campaign using every means possible. The Internet was a tremendous resource through which she was able to reach a broader public. She began to request assistance from various international groups such as Amnesty International, Human Rights Watch, and the Feminists against Violence Network (FAVNET), among others. In an e-mail sent on August 5, 1997 to FAVNET, signed by her and *Grupo 8 de Marzo*, it is clear that she wants to have the facts acknowledged and expose the truth, because locally and nationally very little or nothing had been accomplished. The text I am transcribing is a very similar text to one in later letters sent to AI, HRW, and other organizations (all the spellings are verbatim):

> In this city of Cd. Juárez, in the State of Chihuahua, Mexico, 87 women have veen brutally murdered since 1993, many of them were raped and tortured. We feel thst the cognizant authorities have not given the specialized and urgent attention need in these cases, therefore, we are requesting your help in writing letters to the Governor of the State of Cyihuahua demanding that these crimes be resolved. Aplproximateley 28 of these women had their right breast amputed, and their left nipple was bit off. They were raped and died from strangulation. These murders include 19 girls between 10 and 15 years old, raped orally, anally, and vaginally. An Egyptian man and "Los Rebeldes" gang were arrested and charged for these murders. Nevertheless, in these last few weeks other five bodies have been found in different parts of the city. All these women were young, very poor, and many have not been identified. Thank you for your support. We would appreciate that you pass this information along to other feminist organizations concerned with the violence against gender, and if possible, by establishing contact with international organisms such as ONU and International Amnesty. Thanks you. Esther Chávez Cano. Grupo 8 de Marzo. Cd. Juárez, Chih. Mexico. (Box 16:9)

There are various points we can derive from Chávez Cano's e-mail. One is the importance of telling the truth regardless of how "radical and desperately unpalatable" it may be. The details about the way these women were found and the ordeals they went through are employed to catch the reader's attention and to create empathy with the victims and with the call for justice. Another point is the denunciation (and call for spreading the public condemnation) that the 87 women do not represent a matter of "urgent attention" for the authorities. She suggests that the Egyptian and Los Rebeldes are in prison but that there is still a killer at large. The typos and language errors show that for her it was more important to get her message out[46] than to have it "perfectly" written. Here too, the words of Chávez Cano resonate with those of Said: "Nor is there only a public intellectual, someone who exists just as a figurehead or spokesperson or symbol of a cause, movement, or position. There is always the personal inflection and the private sensibility, and those give meaning to what is being said or written. Least of all should an intellectual be there to make his or her audiences feel good: the whole point is to be embarrassing, contrary, and even unpleasant" ("Representations").

It is obvious that she wanted to get across the message that this was clearly misogynist slaughter through sexual violence. For the situation of Ciudad Juárez, the use of the theoretical term *femicide* arose and was used by activists and academics to establish the difference between types of murders committed against men and women. Jill Radford and Diana Russell (1992) described femicide as the misogynist killing of women by men and a form of continuity of sexual assault. And certainly Chávez Cano was very active in disseminating the term, linking it to the cases in Juárez not only in her editorials but also in her other writings (letters, press releases, e-mails, etc.), as well as in interviews. So here we have an accountant with no training in feminist theory determined to make a difference in her city by denouncing urban problems, who becomes an international spokesperson about some of the most heinous crimes in Mexican history: the femicides in Juárez. Perhaps she was not ready (we were not ready),[47] theoretically speaking, to develop a political agenda against the femicide from the beginning. Yet, she had the determination to start working, recounting the facts, articulating the truth, building advocacy, and exercising agency. She had the ability to empower others and call for action.

The process of empowerment evolved in part through demonstrations, sit-ins, picketing, writing, and confronting authorities. Yet she was already working with battered, raped, and/or abused women and children through *8 de Marzo*, "unofficially." And she was also fortunate to be able help other women through direct action when she was invited to found a crisis center. The idea of opening the first crisis center in Juárez was a dream come true, something for which she advocated when she was running for office and saw the discrimination suffered by women in the city (*Construyendo caminos,* 139). Nevertheless, the creation of *Casa Amiga*[48] on February 9, 1999, caused a schism amongst the groups, especially those of the victim's families.[49] It was the first time that Chávez Cano overtly faced an accusation of "profiting" from the victims' pain. With time, this accusation became a *locus* for Governor Patricio Martínez from the PRI to hide his own impotency and complicity in failing to solve the problem. He started a fierce campaign from Chihuahua City to discredit Esther and the group "Mujeres de Negro."[50] He also used his political power to question the work of *Casa Amiga,* and through actions by City Representative Pamela Franco, *Casa Amiga* was deprived of the subsidy they received from the city administration. She was also attacked in both the local newspapers, *El Diario* and *El Norte.* In fact, she stopped writing in *El Diario* because owner Osvaldo Rodríguez was Martínez's business partner.[51] Despite all the accusations and moral and political damage in Juárez, Chávez Cano continued to bring international attention to the issue of femicide. She was also one of the public faces during the organization of V-Day[52] in Juárez in February 2004. This was the biggest demonstration ever in the history of Juárez. There were more than 10,000 people from different parts of the world and the event information was disseminated in more than 45 countries. There were no longer any doubts by 2004 that the problem of femicide in Juárez had transcended national boundaries.

When Said elaborates on Julien Benda's concept of the role of the intellectual in his lecture "Representations of the Intellectual," he mentions that, for Benda,

> real intellectuals are supposed to risk being burnt at the stake, ostracized, or crucified. They are symbolic personages, marked by their unyielding distance from practical concerns. As such, therefore, they cannot be many in number, nor routinely developed. They have to be thoroughgoing individuals, with a powerful personality and, above all, have to be in a state of almost permanent opposition to the status quo: for these reasons, Benda's intellectuals are, perforce, a small, highly visible group of men—never women, it seems—whose stentorian voices and indelicate imprecations are hurled at humankind from on high.

Even though Benda never imagined women as intellectuals, Chávez Cano clearly embodies Benda's representation. Although there have been other important voices that have fought and will continue to fight for women's rights in Juárez, there is no record, still, of any other woman who has been more outspoken over such a long period of time. There is no record of any other woman who has been the public face of the movement nationally and internationally. Did she make mistakes? Yes. Was she co-opted? No. She faced the representatives of the *status quo* in spite of receiving death threats. And even then, she continued working in *Casa Amiga* and she unceasingly contested the State.

On April 2007 Chávez Cano told geographer Melissa Wright "This silence terrifies me... There are no press conferences. No marches. It's like we're back in 1993." When Wright replied, "no one, anywhere, protests violence against women on regular basis," she answered, "we used to" (Wright, 211). Chávez Cano's discouragement in this instance expresses her concern that the cause we were fighting for—and that she led—was a lost cause. However, if we go back to Said, when talking about the very topic of lost causes, he affirms that

> [the] intellectual vocation, which is never disabled by a paralyzed sense of political defeat, not impelled by groundless optimism and illusory hope... what has been cogently thought must be thought in some other place by some other people. In this way thinking might perhaps acquire and express the momentum of the general, thereby blunting the anguish and despondency of the lost cause, which its enemies have tried to induce. We might as well ask from this perspective if *any* lost cause can ever really be lost. (2003, 553)

Putting Chávez Cano's words in perspective, we can argue that perhaps she was thinking about all the efforts, all the enthusiasm, all the people, all the trouble she went through, all the conferences, the travel, the movement... and all of the sudden... an impasse, a gap, a great silence. Possibly her words come from the frustration of knowing that despite a national Commission to Prevent and Eradicate Violence Against Women in Juárez and a Special Prosecutor's Office created during the Vicente Fox administration to do something about femicide, very little was achieved. Maybe it was because the federal police had dismissed the cases of serial killings and other cases had exceeded the statute of limitations. Or, maybe it was because after 15 years of struggle we were never convinced that the people imprisoned were the true criminals. I don't know for sure and I will never be able to say. Fortunately, Chávez Cano lived to see her efforts recompensed when the news arrived on December 10, 2009, that the Inter-American Court of Human Rights condemned Mexico for violating human rights conventions in three of the cases of murdered women presented to the court. The court ordered Mexico to comply with a set of broad remedial measures, including a national memorial, renewed investigations, and reparations of over $200,000 each to the families in the suit. At least (and at last) a little justice was done.

It is fair to say, and her critics have been very uncompromising about this, that Chávez Cano was not the only voice of protest regarding the violence and the femicide in Juárez, and I can confirm that. However, she was the leading voice and the public face of the movement from 1993 to 1999. She was the one who paved the road for other emerging voices such as those of the victims' families and other NGO leaders and scholars. She was "the one who knew by intuition that symbolic sewers were not street tunnels but Mexican State institutions and circles of men capable to kill for pleasure and power" as Lydia Cacho points out. She was, as Elaine Showalter would have it, a feminist intellectual who exemplified "the experience of women who wished to live a full, serious and meaningful woman's life" (133).

During her funeral mass, the priest mentioned that as in the book of Isaiah, hers was a voice that cried out in the desert, the voice of comfort that will lead her people to the Promised Land. Indeed, Esther Chávez Cano was the voice that opened the issue of femicide to the world. She came, like the prophets, "para destruir y construir, para edificar y sembrar" (to destroy and build, to construct and sow).[53] She weakened the authoritarian voice of the state that wanted to erase femicide and constructed a strong discourse to contest it globally. She built a grassroots movement that led her to Casa Amiga and to harvest hope. Like a prophet, she anticipated the future and registered the present. Her pen never stopped documenting injustices and her voice—as low as it was—remained strong until the day she could not utter a sound. Esther never stopped denouncing impunity and demanding justice; never stopped articulating advocacy, agency, and justice on the US-Mexico border.

### Notes

1. "The Reith Lectures: Representations of the Intellectual," *The Independent*, Thursday, June 24, 1993. http://www.independent.co.uk/life-style/the-reith-lectures-representation.
2. Quoted in Elaine Showalter "Laughing Medusa: Feminist Intellectuals at the Millennium, *Women: a Cultural Review* 11.½ (2000): 131.
3. *"Pollo a la maquiladora" Diario de Juárez*, Cd. Juárez, Chihuahua. (Lunes 9 de septiembre de 1991): 3-D.
4. On page 21 of her book *Construyendo caminos y esperanzas*, Esther elaborates on this issue.

5. I would like to thank Julia Monárrez Fragoso, Lowry Martin, and Willivaldo Delgadillo for their important contributions to this essay.
6. It started as *El Diario de Juárez*, and when the company grew and founded a branch in Chihuahua City it kept the name *El Diario*. Because of this, at times the notes will appear as *Diario de Juárez* and at other times as *El Diario*. At present the newspaper has a branch in El Paso.
7. In *Construyendo caminos*, she comments that the director rejected her but due to her perseverance she not only took the course but was also selected to be part of the team in 1989 (20). In all instances, unless specified, the translations are mine.
8. There were/are other leading voices that emerged from grassroots movements, the victims' families and academics such as Judith Galarza, Mónica Alicia Juárez, Guillermina González, Paula Flores, Norma and Marilú Andrade, Evangelina Arce, Marisela Ortiz, and Julia Monárrez, among others.
9. Said, "Speaking Truth to Power" *The Independent*, Thursday July 22, 1993, ibid.
10. "The Woman Who Dared to Stand Tall on the Border." Memorial by Molly Molloy, December 31, 2009. http://lib.nmsu.edu/exhibits/chavezcano/chavezcanomemorial.pdf.
11. Paraphrasing Kathy Staudt in Justin Monarez, "Women's Right Activist's Death Brings Communities Together" on February 18, 2010. http://borderzine.com/2010/02/women%e2%80%99s-right-activist%e2%80%99s-death-brings-communities-together/.
12. The PRD is a democratic socialist party in Mexico. It was founded in 1989 by prominent PRI members and left-wing politicians. It was announced that Cuauhtémoc Cárdenas had won the presidential election in June 1988, representing a coalition of center-left parties, but he was denied victory through fraud and the presidency went to Carlos Salinas de Gortari from the PRI. The PRD has a good electoral presence in central-south Mexico, whereas in the north its profile is low.
13. The name refers to the International Women's Day celebration
14. For more information consult Russell Jacoby, *The Last Intellectuals: American Culture in the Age of Academe* (New York: Basic Books, 1987); Richard A. Posner, *Public Intellectuals: A Study of Decline* (Cambridge, MA: Harvard University Press, 2001); Edward Said, *Representations of the Intellectual* (New York: Pantheon Books, 1994); Paul Johnson, *Intellectuals* (New York: Harper and Row, 1988); Imani Perry, "Putting the 'Public' in 'Public' Intellectual" in the *Chronicle of Higher Education, The Chronicle Review* http://chronicle.com/article/the new-black-public/657444/; Eduardo Mendieta, "What Can Latinaso/as Learn from Cornel West? The Latino Post-Colonial Intellectual in the Age of Exhaustion of Public Spheres." *Nepantla: Views from South* 4.2 (2003): 213–33; among others.

15. In *Representations of the Intellectual.* http://www.independent.co.uk/life-style/the-reith-lectures-representation.
16. Mexico's northern border has been constructed in the national discourse as a marginal space.
17. I am referring here to the genre of "writing letters."
18. Roderic A. Camp, *Intellectuals and the State in Contemporary Mexico,* quoted in Ignacio Sánchez Prado's "Claiming Liberalism: Enrique Krauze, *Vuelta, Letas Libres,* and the Reconfigurations of the Mexican Intellectual Class." *Mexican Studies/Estudios Mexicanos* 26.1 (Winter 2010): 54.
19. Irma Campos was the daughter of a mason who was prosecuted because of his beliefs; she was a lawyer and until her passing in 2009 she fought for equal and just laws for women in Chihuahua state. Alma Gómez, another lawyer, was the daughter of Pablo Gómez and Alma Caballero, two rural teachers from Madera, Chihuahua. Her father was killed by the army when he and other men attacked the military barracks. Her mother was kidnapped by the government's special forces, and Alma and her siblings were forced to flee and live in hiding. Luz Estela Castro has a long trajectory of struggling for women's rights. She is the coordinator of the Centro de Derechos Humanos de las Mujeres and legal representative for mothers of disappeared and assassinated women of Juárez and Chihuahua.
20. I am not implying that she did not have knowledge of feminist theory. My point is that she started reading more theory after she started writing and fighting for women's rights.
21. In "In Memoriam: Esther Chávez Cano." December 25, 2009, http://www.vday.org/node/1775.
22. All the quotes from her letters or columns are from *El Diario / El Diario de Juárez,* unless otherwise indicated. If no page is given it is because the copy I had access to from A&R Hemeroteca (producción y diseño Alvarado Ríos) did not provide the information.
23. Perhaps she is referring to the assassination of Linda Bejarano, a reporter and anchorwoman on a weekly news journal who was killed along with her mother-in-law and a family friend. Bejarano was pregnant. The police officers who gunned her down claimed that it was a case of "mistaken identity." She was killed the day before Chávez Cano wrote her letter to the newspaper.
24. Reith Lectures: "Intellectual Exile: Expatriate and Marginal: What Is the Proper Role of the Intellectual in Today's World?" *The Impartial,* Thursday, July 8, 1993. ibid.
25. Carmel Borg and Peter Mayo, *Public Intellectuals, Radical Democracy, and Social Movements: A Book of Interviews.* (New York: Peter Lang Publishing, 2007).
26. In Amitai Etzioni "Are Public Intellectuals an Endangered Species?" *Public Intellectuals. An Endangered Species?* Ed. Amitai Etzioni and

Alyssa Bowditch (Lanham, MD: Rowman and Littlefield Publishers, 2006), 1.
27. Kenan Malik (2002, 53) quoted in Amitai Etzoni, ibid., 2.
28. Mónica Alicia Juárez, Cecilia Pego, Laura Jiménez, Yvonne Ramos, and María Elena Ramos.
29. I mention "official" because before this meeting the group had no regular place to meet and meetings were "informal" (I joined the group in early September). Minutes were taken randomly; but in November, minutes were taken and formalized. The record shows the importance of officially constituting the group as an "Asociación Civil" (Civil Association) "en términos de acción política no partidista." For the full record of the minutes, consult *The Esther Chávez Cano Collection* Ms 0471. New Mexico State University Library, Archives and Special Collections Department, Box 16:18. Further quotes referring to Esther's documents will use this citation except for the box number. In 2007, Chávez donated her extensive files to the New Mexico State University located in Las Cruces and continued "feeding" the archives until just before her passing, by sending or giving them to librarian Molly Molloy.
30. The penal code was dated and unfair to women: if a man raped a woman he could avoid prison by paying a bond; otherwise he would get one to three months in prison. If a man stole a cow he could get seven years in prison.
31. In those years, abortion was illegal in all 32 Mexican states but the penal code took into consideration exceptions, including: when there is an accidental abortion or miscarriage; when the pregnancy is due to rape or unwanted or nonconsensual artificial insemination and the abortion is performed within 90 days of conception; when the life of the mother is endangered if an abortion is not performed.
32. For more information on the documents that discuss this issue, refer to the *Esther Chávez Cano Collection* boxes 16:4, 16:18, 18:13, 19:1.
33. "Grupo 8 de marzo ante una propuesta legislativa anticonstitucional, injusta, inhumana e incongruente," ms. Box 16:4.
34. I have a copy of most of her columns that range from 46 to 60 articles each year (except for the year 1997 where I could obtain only 36). María Elena Alvarado supported me in the research and gathered the information in a binder, calling it A&R Hemeroteca (producción y diseño Alvarado Ríos). There is a copy of these materials at the NMSU Collection but it was not yet accessible when I went to do my research there.
35. I am using here the term "professional" in the sense that she took her column and audience very seriously, despite the fact that she did not make a living from her writing. Until she started working full time in Casa Amiga, she continued working as an accountant for a tile and marble company in Juárez.

36. Said, "Professionals and Amateurs: Is There Such a Thing as an Independent, Autonomously Functioning Intellectual?" *The Independent*, Thursday, July 15, 1993, ibid.
37. Catholics for Choice and its international partners work individually at the national level and collectively in the international arena to advance Catholic teachings and thinking that advocate women's moral agency and that enhance the reproductive and sexual health and lives of women and their families throughout the world.
38. For the full argument go to "Moros y cristianos" Ciudad Juárez, Chihuahua (Martes 28 de septiembre de 1993): 3-A.
39. She never had children and was never married.
40. The data was taken from Julia Monárrez Fragoso's article "Serial Sexual Femicide in Ciudad Juarez: 1993–2002." www.womenontheborder.org.
41. The database now has information until the year 2003 and can be found in www.casa-amiga.org.
42. Unfortunately, the Mexican Federal Attorney General's Report on the Women's Murders of 2006 reiterates that the crimes were exaggerated, denies the serial murders, states that family violence was the main cause of these murders, and claims that most crimes were solved.
43. Data from Julia Monárrez Fragoso in "Sexual Serial Femicide in Ciudad Juárez: 1993–2001." www.womenontheborder.org.
44. "*Desafíos y dilemas del intelectual público.*" http://www.rebelion.org/noticia.php?id=66847.
45. By 1999, 40 percent of her editorials refer to women's rights and focus on specific stories of the murdered women and/or include stories from the women who went for help to Casa Amiga, the women's crisis center she directed. By 2000, the last year she participated as an editorialist at *El Diario*, 100 percent of her articles dealt with the topic.
46. A comment from Irasema Coronado during her book presentation at the University of Texas at El Paso on March 9, 2011 was that even though she did not speak English very well, "she made herself understood." Ms. from author.
47. Clara Rojas has mentioned that we were not ready to articulate a political agenda for women in Juárez. And after reviewing Esther's and other activists' achievements I wonder if the achievements could have been greater or if the system/state and corporate world would have let us do more. In "(Re)inventando una praxis politica desde el imaginario feminista," in *Bordeando la violencia en la frontera norte de México*, ed. Julia E. Monárrez Fragoso and María Socorro Tabuenca Córdoba, (Mexico City: El Colegio de la Frontera Norte, and Miguel Angel Porrúa Editores, 2007), 83–114.
48. For more information visit www.casaamiga.org.mx.
49. For more information on this issue refer to *Construyendo caminos*, "Campaña de desprestigio," in *Esther Chávez Cano Collection* box 16:16, the document called "Compendio de campañas en contra de

Esther Chávez Cano," 15:10; and "The V-Day March in Mexico: Appropriation and Misuse of Local Women's Activism," by Clara Rojas, in *Making a Killing: Femicide, Free Trade and La Frontera*, ed. Alicia Gaspar de Alba and Georgina Guzmán (Austin: University of Texas Press, 2010), 201–10.
50. Cultural geographer Melissa Wright has studied this phenomenon in "El lucro, la democracia y la mujer pública," in *Bordeando la violencia*, 49–82.
51. For more information, refer to *Construyendo caminos*, 121–23.
52. Amnesty International was co-organizer with other Mexican and US women's groups including AFL-CIO. This demonstration brought back Casa Amiga and Esther Chávez Cano to the forefront of the movement.
53. Biblical references are taken from *La Biblia Latinoamericana*, XXXIII edición, edición revisada 1995 (Navarra, España: San Pablo-Editorial Verbo Divino, 1995), 31.

## Works Cited

Bello, Walden. "Desafíos y dilemas del intelectual público." http://www.rebelión.org/noticia.php?id=66847. Web.

Borg, Carmel and Peter Mayo. *Public Intellectuals, Radical Democracy, and Social Movements: A Book of Interviews*. New York: Peter Lang Publishing, 2007. Print.

Bové, Paul A. *Edward Said and the Work of the Critic: Speaking Truth to Power*. Durham and London: Duke University Press, 2000. Print.

Cacho, Lydia. "¿Quién mató a Esther Chávez Cano" sandralorenzano.blogspot.com/.../quien-mato-esther-chavez-cano.htlm. Web.

Chávez Cano, Esther. "Cartas al Director," *El Diario de Juárez*, Cd. Juárez, Chih., 23 de julio de 1988. n.p. Print.

——. *Construyendo caminos y esperanzas*. Mexico, DF: Cátedra UNESCO de derechos Humanos UNAM-México, Academia Mexicana de Derechos Humanos, Casa Amiga, AC, 2010. Print.

——. "Cuento de Hadas." *Diario de Juárez*, Cd. Juárez, Chih., 25 de mayo de 1995. n.p. Print.

——. "Moros y Cristianos." *Diario de Juárez*, Cd. Juárez, Chih., Martes 28 de septiembre de 1993. 3-A. Print.

——. "Oye Bartola..." *Diario de Juárez*, Cd. Juárez, Chih., Jueves 12 de enero de 1995. n.p. Print.

——. "Pollo a la maquiladora." *Diario de Juárez*, Cd. Juárez, Chih., Lunes 9 de septiembre de 1991. 3-D. Print.

——. "Prejuicios y Machismo" *Diario de Juárez*, Cd. Juárez, Chih., Martes 23 de febrero de 1993. 5-A. Print.

Ensler, Eve. "In Memoriam: Esther Chávez Cano." December 25, 2009. http://www.vday.org/node/1775. Web.

*Esther Chávez Cano Collection* Ms 0471. New Mexico State University Library, Archives and Special Collections Department. Print.

Etzioni, Amitai. "Are Public Intellectuals an Endangered Species?" In *Public Intellectuals. An Endangered Species?* Edited by Amitai Etzioni and Alyssa Bowditch. Lanham, MD: Rowman and Littlefield Publishers, 2006. 1. Print.

*La Biblia Latinoamericana*. XXXIII edición, edición revisada 1995 Navarra, España: San Pablo-Editorial Verbo Divino, 1995. Print.

Mendieta, Eduardo, "What Can Latinaso/as Learn from Cornel West? The Latino Post-Colonial Intellectual in the Age of Exhaustion of Public Spheres." *Nepantla: Views from South* 4.2 (2003): 213–33.

Molloy, Molly. "The Woman Who Dared to Stand Tall on the Border." December 31, 2009. http://lib.nmsu.edu/exhibits/chavezcano/chavez canomemorial.pdf. Web.

Monarez, Justin. "Women's Right Activist's Death Brings Communities Together." February 18, 2010. http://borderzine.com/2010/02/women %e2%80%99s-right-activist%e2%80%99s-death-brings-communities -together/. Web.

Monárrez Fragoso, Julia E. "Serial Sexual Femicide in Ciudad Juarez: 1993–2002." www.womenontheborder.org. Web.

Radford, Jill and Diana Russell, eds. *Femicide: The Politics of Woman Killing*. New York: Twayne Publishers, 1992.

Rojas, Clara. *Making a Killing: Femicide, Free Trade and La Frontera*. Edited by Alicia Gaspar de Alba and Georgina Guzmán, Austin: University of Texas Press, 2010. 201–10. Print.

———. "(Re)inventando una praxis politica desde el imaginario feminista." In *Bordeando la violencia en la frontera norte de México*. Edited by Julia E. Monárrez Fragoso and María Socorro Tabuenca Córdoba. Mexico, DF: El Colegio de la Frontera Norte; Miguel Angel Porrúa Editores, 2007. 83–114. Print.

Said, Edward. *Reflections on Exile and other Essays*, Cambridge, MA: Harvard University Press, 2003. Print.

———. The Reith Lectures: Representations of the Intellectual, *The Independent*, 1993. http://www.independent.co.uk/life-style/the-reith -lectures-representation. Web.

Sánchez Prado, Ignacio. "Claiming Liberalism: Enrique Krauze, *Vuelta*, *Letas Libres*, and the Reconfigurations of the Mexican Intellectual Class." *Mexican Studies/Estudios Mexicanos* 26.1 (Winter 2010). Print.

Showalter, Elaine "Laughing Medusa: Feminist Intellectuals at the Millennium." *Women: A Cultural Review* 11.½ (2000): 131.

Wright, Melissa. "Femicide, Mother-Activism, and Geography of Protest in Northern Mexico." *Femicide, Free Trade and La Frontera*. Edited by Alicia Gaspar de Alba and Georgina Guzmán. Austin: University of Texas Press, 2010. 211–41. Print.

## Chapter 7

# Mayan Cultural Agency through Performance: *Fortaleza de la Mujer Maya–Fomma*

*Elvira Sánchez-Blake*

Chiapas is a grand stage of coexisting realities and temporalities in permanent collision, an enactment of Nestor García Canclini's definition of hybrid cultures.[1] An observer strolling in Chiapas' center city of San Cristobal de las Casas finds Mayan women and children in traditional garments alongside business executives and tourists. Their particular versions of the Spanish language resonate in the city space, as they sell artful textiles and numerous items that condense cosmologies of ancient cultures. Music of different genres plays everywhere: typical marimba, modern pop, and metallic rock propitiate an eclectic orchestration of sounds. The visitor is engulfed by an environment that pushes a sort of "Mayan consumerism": faces, costumes, glyphs, masks, ruins, art, weavings, handcrafts, flutes, and drum beats—a folklore potpourri announcing an idealized past. Restaurants offer Italian, French, and Indian cuisine along with savory Chiapanecan foods in specially designed heritage scenes and settings. Even the local Burger King displays a Mayan motif. Paradoxically, descendants of the Maya are tacitly discouraged from entering the same restaurants and stores that celebrate their heritage. In such a context the observer is a spectator, part of a staged live spectacle where actors portray multiple identities and roles meant for celebration and consumption of the so-called authentic Mayan experience.

In this setting of vibrant public performance, a group of indigenous women from the highlands are using theater to create awareness, educate, and change attitudes in their communities and beyond. By so doing, they enact pre-Columbian traditions mixed with Spanish theatrical models, and new paradigms of cultural performance as a continuously changing dynamic of the autochthonous and the mestizo,[2] insider and outsider, and tradition and modernity. In this chapter, I explore the work of Petrona de la Cruz and Isabel Juárez from the collective women-based troupe Fortaleza de la Mujer Maya (Strength of Mayan women), who use performance as a sociocultural transformative tool that, among other things, reconfigures the concept of the intellectual in today's Mexico. I propose that performance works as a channel of reflection and refraction that fosters changes of attitude about women and family conditions, community laws, and awareness of indigenous and gender rights in Chiapas.

Petrona de la Cruz Cruz and Isabel Juárez Espinosa, two indigenous women from Tzotzil and Tzeltal communities, entered the public forum of the 90s amidst two competing social revolutions, those of women and of indigenous peoples. The testimonial account of Guatemalan activist Rigoberta Menchú—subsequently laureled with the Nobel Peace Prize—put the Maya and women prominently in the world's gaze. More recently, the 1994 neo-Zapatista uprising drew attention to indigenous rights throughout the hemisphere. De la Cruz and Juárez emerged from this crossroads as the first indigenous women playwrights with a new proposition—to strengthen Mayan women through theater and performance and to create a refugee center for them. Although both the Zapatistas and FOMMA struggle against the exploitation of indigenous people, and for the attainment of human rights, the theater troupe has maintained a position of neutrality, distanced from political confrontation. As Harley Erdman points out, while Zapatista leader Marcos has played a central role in terms of military and political confrontations, in contrast, FOMMA "delves into the personal domestic foundation that supports and perpetuates the exploitative system that spurred the rebellion" (160–61). In other words, while Subcomandante Marcos has been accused of becoming a public media celebrity, FOMMA has arguably used the virtues of performance for its cause without becoming commodified by the system.

FOMMA was founded in 1994 by Juárez and de la Cruz as a center for women and children displaced from highland indigenous communities. Since its inception, FOMMA's mission has been to inspire Mayan women to be independent and to sustain themselves economically. Its services are advertised as a way "to combat shyness, fear and thoughts of inferiority in a world full of poverty, ignorance and hostility by offering cultural, educative, and productive theater workshops" (*Nuestra misión*).[3] Their website promotes their services as "programs that educate women and children in Tzeltal, Tzotzil, and Spanish as well as offering an extensive array of vocational skills such as tailoring, bakery, manual crafts, cultural, and using computer programs. In addition, Fortaleza de la Mujer Maya provides services such as childcare, women's rights education, and healthcare."[4] FOMMA's plays have been presented in Mexico, North and South America, Australia, and Europe. *The New York Times* described Juárez and de la Cruz as "the first female Indian playwrights," recognizing the "quiet theatrical revolution they have spawned" (Myers, 4).

Part of FOMMA's success responds to a balance attained between performance and social drama that challenges traditional structures in Mayan communities practiced for centuries. In "Theater and the Problems of Women in Highland Chiapas" de la Cruz explains, "Through drama we can explore family and social problems that could not be expressed in other ways. People learn to value their mother tongues and virtues of their culture, and they are made aware of the vices and defects of our society, all while being entertained, not feeling attacked nor scolded" (255). This statement summarizes two axes of FOMMA's paradigm: keeping tradition alive and simultaneously raising awareness about the negative aspects of the same traditions. At the same time, theater has familiarized non-Mayan audiences with their ways of thinking and living. As expressed by de la Cruz, "We have observed that they now regard us with respect and even admiration" (255).

In her analysis of contemporary Mayan theater, Tamara Underiner contends that indigenous women constantly play roles offstage and onstage. Offstage, they play themselves for tourists, dressed in traditional attire and posing for the photographic opportunity. Onstage, FOMMA's women-only plays "symbolically reverses cross-gender casting traditions not only in fact but in style...They are able to reclaim for themselves a whole performance tradition that has historically worked to mock and exclude them" (75). Indeed, the revolution spawned by FOMMA transcends the theatrical stage into a permanent living performance that makes these indigenous women from the highlands of Chiapas pioneers in the struggle for gender rights and ethnic pride. After nearly two decades working with FOMMA, they have positioned themselves as new public intellectuals advocating for women's rights and dignity in Mexico.

Following the decentering thrust of this book, Juárez and de la Cruz can be also considered alternative public intellectuals because their influence reaches a nontraditional audience on one hand, and the broader circles of Mexican mestizos and intellectuals on the other. Through a slow process of promoting cultural performance and agency, they have become spokespersons and the moral conscience of women and their social groups as public artists and intellectuals,[5] and it is the intersection of performance and cultural agency that comprise the key elements of analysis in this chapter.

In her book *Stages of Conflict*, Diana Taylor makes a fundamental distinction between theater and performance. In theater, performers are professional players before a public audience. This stage seems to function as a socially accepted boundary between actors and the audience, where players move on a predetermined and finite place called the stage. Performance, on the other hand, is a broader concept that includes practices such as ritual and dance and does not presume the traditional notion of stage (2–3). This type of "stage" expands to an infinite space without boundaries between players and the audience. Taylor considers *performance* a valuable conceptual tool "to trace the ways aesthetic interventions into the political sphere share and contest the underlying assumptions and strategies of more explicit political practices that rely on public spectacles" (21). A classical example of this type of performance is the Argentine Mothers of la Plaza de Mayo's political protests in a public space. Performance has constituted itself in various anti-theatrical forms including performance art, public art, and public performance. Among these competing terms, Taylor theorized the concept of "performing culture" as one "that allows for agency, thus opening the way for resistance and oppositional spectacles" (*Negotiating Performance*, 13–14). Performing culture complements and becomes an ally of cultural agency, defined as "a vehicle for agency through creative actions and reflections that influence collective change" (Sommer, 20). Cultural agency and cultural performance are concepts interwoven with "collective resistance and change," two elements at the core of FOMMA's theatrical project.

By means of the power of "agency" invoked by the theatrical experience, I propose that FOMMA's stagings are intended to transform social realities common to actors and the public. Borrowing Taylor's conceptualization and applying it to the project of de la Cruz and Juárez, we can say that they subscribe to the definition of "cultural performance," where playwrights and actors dismantle codes of signification that reflect and refract shared realities. Cultural performance allows each participant to contest and interrogate the codes of signification instilled by tradition in their own communities. By exposing these codes, actors and spectators mirror their own realities, reacting critically as they become the message and the vehicle for interrogating and transforming the collective social body.

The relationship of FOMMA to revolutionary performative practice has been widely analyzed. Albadalejo, Erdman, Marrero, Steele, Taylor, and Underiner, for example, consider FOMMA a special model that frames social reality from a gendered indigenous perspective without subscribing to any political ideology.[6] While I agree with this definition, I underscore the character of resistance and social transformation of the group. Although FOMMA's plays have been presented even outside Chiapas, including on international stages, it is clear that their messages are aimed at homeland indigenous communities, and to a lesser extent to a supranational audience sympathetic to their plight. In these sociocultural contexts, de la Cruz and Juárez are cultural agents aware of the contexts that fostered the emergence of their theater.

Petrona de la Cruz and Isabel Juárez are products of two factors: a drive to keep heritage traditions alive in their Mayan communities, and the need to change oppressive conditions for women ruled by those traditions. Both women of Mayan descent are bearers of syncretic religious beliefs and practitioners of ceremonial rituals. Both endured domestic abuse and marginalization in their own communities. Both were expelled and survived as single mothers in the city of San Cristobal de las Casas. De la Cruz suffered domestic violence in her hometown of Zinacantán. She attended school and worked as a domestic servant. She later joined the theater troupe Lo'il Maxil, associated with Sna Jtz'ibajom (The Writer's House), where she studied acting and playwriting. Isabel Juárez, a Tzeltal woman from Aguacatenango, was also expelled from her community for having a child out of wedlock. She endured hard physical labor in San Cristobal and started working with Sna Jtz'ibajom in 1990. Three years later, de la Cruz and Juárez joined forces to start their own women-based collective theater group, FOMMA. Both women found their way to empowerment through theater: "Pude gritarle al mundo, al público el dolor que sentía por dentro" (I could scream to the world all the pain I kept inside) says de la Cruz.[7] Through theater, de la Cruz and Juárez recovered their sense of belonging, by creating their own community values and rules (e.g., no men allowed on stage), working for their peers (victims of domestic violence), and inventing their own space (the stage). Through this process, and without realizing it, they began to foster collective change through creative actions.

Theater enabled de la Cruz and Juárez to become political protagonists in their communities by assuming an otherwise unrealized voice. Not only did they use this tool to heal personal pain and trauma, but also to create a device to help others like them. Theater became the inspiration, the channel, a way of life and the conveyor of messages that nurtured and transformed women's conditions in home territory. In this way, they accrued leadership capacities that made them into spokespersons and advocates for their communities and social groups.

Rosana Blanco-Cano points out that "El teatro de Fomma desafía el papel subordinado, ornamental y periférico impuesto por las narraciones y espacios nacionales mexicanos a las comunidades mayas de Chiapas" (78). (Fomma's theater challenges the subordinate, ornamental, and peripheral role imposed by the Mexican national narratives to the Mayan communities of Chiapas.) In addition, as a feminist proposal, according to Blanco-Cano, "de la Cruz disloca las narraciones sobre la feminidad indígena icónica. En lugar de reproducir imágenes tradicionales e inmóviles de los cuerpos femeninas indígenas, los propone como agentes sociales con una capacidad productora de cultura e historia y como una forma de renegociar los valores de lo femenino indígena tanto en el ámbito local como nacional" (78). (de la Cruz dislocates iconic narrations about indigenous femininity. Instead of reproducing traditional and immobile images of indigenous women's bodies, she proposes them as social agents with a capacity for producing culture and history and as a way to renegotiate the indigenous feminine values both at the local and at the national level).

Through this negotiation, de la Cruz and Juárez have been able to convey messages to their people from within. They speak in their own languages through shared cultural codes and with the necessary sensibility to reach women and community leaders. In a way their traditional stage extends from the inside—the private domestic space—to the outside—the public space—enacting daily confrontations between traditional practices and modern influences. Therefore, FOMMA's difference as a theatrical troupe is that cultural agency originates within an indigenous perspective, reinscribing gender roles and transforming social practices.

FOMMA's repertoire illustrates the tensions among tradition, modernity, and cultural survival. Its plays have been called social dramas, melodramas, comedies, and *teatro popular*.[8] While I consider that they do not subscribe to a particular theatrical genre but to their own, they are, broadly speaking, social dramas, where plots revolve around issues of breach, crisis, and redress.[9] These plays have evolved in response to social demands. Early plays focused on domestic abuse, more recent ones confront external challenges: markets, politics, cultural challenges, and migration. Recently, FOMMA started participating in public radio with a regular series.

I examine three categories of plays based on realities on the inside and outside. First are those dealing with domestic issues by Petrona de la Cruz. Next are plays responding to outside realities by Isabel Juárez, and, finally, I explore two collective creations by FOMMA's members. I end with a brief exploration of de la Cruz and Juárez's incursion into mass media.

In *Una mujer desesperada*, first published in 1992, de la Cruz exposes physical violence against women by their own family members. The play demonstrates how women are defenseless victims in a self-perpetuating reality that continues from generation to generation. In the first act a mother, María, is abused and beaten before her daughters by a drunken husband. When a neighbor arrives, the drunkard falls, knocking his head against the fireplace, and dies. In the second act, the mother has remarried to support her family. The second husband, also abusive and alcoholic, wants to have sex with the eldest daughter, Teresa. When Teresa resists, he declares, "It's time that you understood that you belong to me as much as your mother does, because I am in love with you and I'm not going to allow some bum to take my place. You are mine for better or for worse!" (305).[10] Outraged at María's intervention to defend Teresa, the husband kills María. Afterward, Teresa confronts her stepfather, and shoots him to death. Before being taken to jail, Teresa goes to her room and leaves a message, telling her boyfriend that she acted to "protect her honor," and she shoots herself. Teresa summarizes the entire drama on her deathbed, "Maybe it is our fate to suffer" (309).

*Una mujer desesperada* was the first play by an indigenous woman from Chiapas to receive international attention. For this work, de la Cruz was awarded the Rosario Castellanos Chiapas Prize for literature in 1992. This was also the first time a Mayan woman translated personal experience into theater, breaking a long-standing silence about alcoholism and domestic abuse. Although this was a topic frequently addressed by other theater troupes, such as Teatro Petul in the 50s, in indigenous languages with indigenous puppeteers, this was the first time a script was written by an indigenous woman (Castillo). This unprecedented action of breaking silence had a multiplicative effect on women and their communities. Members of the organization started to talk and build confidence. Many women did not even know they had a voice, says Isabel Juárez, but they also received critical reactions from their communities where they were considered "locas" and as "mujeres que no tienen nada que hacer" (women who have nothing to do).[11]

Most remarkable was the reaction to *Una mujer desesperada* by the theater group in which de la Cruz participated at that time. Members refused to perform the play, arguing, "this did not happen here." In her article "Eso sí pasa aquí: Indigenous Women Performing Revolutions in Mayan Chiapas," Teresa Marrero referenced this argument to rekindle the idea of women's resistance through theater. Marrero contends that the group's attempt to silence de la Cruz is reflected by society at large throughout many of political, economic, and social levels in Mexico (314).

After the success of her first play, de la Cruz delved into social dramas related to family and community. Dramas such as *Desprecio paternal* (Paternal disdain) and *Madre olvidada* (Forgotten mother) portray issues of family abuse and domestic violence from fathers and sons against female kin. Both dramas continue the trend of moral responsibility in exposing social conflicts based on breach, crisis, and redress. *Desprecio paternal* depicts a father's complaint about his wife for not engendering sons, and against his daughters for not being male. Verbal and physical violence mark the play from the start. Pedro yells at his daughters without reason, and threatens physical punishment. Tired of mistreatment, two leave home for the city to study and search for a different life. Years later, in the second act, a daughter returns home as the appointed school teacher to the community. She finds a dying father who asks for forgiveness. This open ending signals hope to escape the fate of physical abuse through education and knowledge. At the same time, it poses a question about the value of education for indigenous people. The fact that the school system and bilingual education are addressed in a social drama reflects awareness of the author about theater's effectiveness in reaching a larger national audience. Hence, the play achieves dual purposes: it creates awareness about an internal problem and expresses a community concern to the non-Mayan audience, ultimately the one sector in command of civil regulations and laws.

*Madre olvidada* dramatizes a son's abuse of his widowed mother and sisters, appropriating his father's lands for himself. The fulcrum element is the mother's endorsement of his behavior. She justifies his actions and fiercely defends him against her daughters' complaints. Anna Albadalejo's analysis of this play highlights that "María (the mother) is just teaching the daughters the rules of survival in a patriarchal social model" (64). However, the play also denounces the injustices of land tenure and inheritance prevalent in indigenous communities. The exclusion of women from legal land titles is unconstitutional by Mexican law, but in most communities indigenous laws prevail.[12] In the play, when the daughters are able to go beyond their town's rules and learn that they are entitled to the land, they confront their brother and regain legal possession of the property. The brother is imprisoned and later released when he recognizes his misdoings and begs forgiveness. The play's resolution upon a happy moralizing note idealizes a complex reality that merits scrutiny and reconciliatory actions.

*La tragedia de Juanita* recounts the story of a *cacique* (wealthy landowner) who buys a nine-year-old girl for a wife. Her parents' refusal does not preclude him from forcing/convincing them through alcohol and economic pressure. After taking Juanita home, he rapes and murders her in an act of outrage for her inexperience in killing and cooking a hen. The local authorities are unable to punish the landowner for fear of reprisal, given his power over the village. This play's tragic ending is based on a real case reported in a highland community in 1993.[13]

While most of Petrona de la Cruz's plays focus on domestic violence and abuse of women, Isabel Juárez explores women's survival in a global society affected by complex economic and social issues. Rural-to-urban migration and marketing of local products are the foci of two of her most recognized plays: *Migración* and *Las risas de Pascuala*. *Migración* is a story about a family that decides to sell its land and move to the big city. The play exposes the challenges faced by indigenous people: racism, linguistic difference, ignorance of socially accepted codes, and fundamental questions of survival. A key issue arises when the wife, Catalina, refuses to sell her land. Carlos echoes men's presumption of their right to dominance, "¡Tú tienes que ir a donde yo vaya, quieras o no! ¡Y el terreno, si quiero venderlo, lo vendo!, porque es mío" (you have to go wherever I go, whether you want or not! As for the land, if you want to sell it, I'll sell it because it is only mine) (*Cuentos y Teatro Tzeltales*, 154). The play ends bleakly: the family loses everything and Carlos becomes a depressive drunkard. Jobless and homeless in the big city, the only venue for survival is Catalina's prospective employment as a domestic servant. The moral of this drama is that the despite city's appeal, rural life still offers the basic ingredients for survival and support through a communal existence. As Juárez remarked, *Migración* has been the subject of workshops, round tables, and discussion in several communities, for it discourages moving to urban centers. It also exhorts women to reaffirm their judgment and their position in family affairs. This is only one of several FOMMA plays deconstructing the idea of a better life through migration. At the same time, as many communities disintegrate because of religious and political conflicts, women are left with the task of survival and keeping the communities together.

Again, as Underiner points out, "FOMMA urges coming together, comradeship, and sorority, as key to meeting the challenge" (73).

In *Las risas de Pascuala* (Pascuala's laughter), Isabel Juárez treats a delicate subject about women and child street vendors. This play reveals the hardships of women who produce the colorful textiles, artwork, and ceramics that are hallmarks of the Chiapanecan heritage. It shows the abuses and discrimination experienced by indigenous people in a city where they are subject to alien social codes and regulations. Pascuala portrays an outspoken, self-confident woman who learns the terms of engagement. Tired of abuse, she decides to unionize street vendors to confront the police officers demanding bribes from them. In the end, Pascuala defeats police authorities with her knowledge and assertiveness. As in many FOMMA plays with a moral exemplary tone, Juárez dwells on messages of self-affirmation while maintaining tradition alive.

*Viva la vida* (Long live life), an example of a collective work by FOMMA's members, revolves around the subject of birth control and access to medical health centers. The play is divided in two segments to represent two time periods. In the first part a woman is about to give birth, but her husband does not pay attention to her and instead demands food and attention. She dies after giving birth in her house for not having access to basic health-care services. In the second part, 20 years have gone by and a more modern woman is about to deliver a baby. When she experiences labor pains, her family takes her to the health center where she gives birth to a healthy child. After the delivery the doctor informs her about birth control and reproductive matters. The purpose of the play, as explained by Petrona de la Cruz, is to illustrate to women the benefits of health-care services, which are regarded with mistrust in many communities.

*Buscando nuevos caminos* (In search of new paths), another collective creation, deals with immigration to the United States. The plot depicts the issues involved in the experience, from children abandoned by parents and abused by relatives, to the exploitation by "coyotes" during transit to the United States. This play has had particular impact in communities, schools, and universities, where it has revealed the traumatic experiences of migrants as well as the family members left behind. The purpose, as explained by de la Cruz and Juárez, is to discourage people from leaving their homeland in search of ill-conceived illusions of the American dream.[14]

*Corazón de mujer: el latido que estremece*, a radio series focused on women's issues in highland Chiapas, was a government project commissioned to Petrona de la Cruz and Isabel Juárez. It debuted March 8,

2011 (on Women's Day) and aired weekly to portray and condemn abuse and domestic violence in Chiapas. This radio "soap opera" was broadcast in Spanish, Tzeltal, and Tzotzil, and was widely advertised in billboard spots all over Chiapas, attracting wide audiences from city dwellers to rural communities. As one listener expressed, "people stop their daily routines to listen to 'Corazón de mujer.'"[15] Another listener mentioned the controversy the program aroused in some communities among men who felt indignant about the issues exposed and among women who identified with them.[16] de la Cruz and Juárez were gratified by the public response, which was expressed in debates aired after each segment and by letters in Facebook and comments on Twitter. When I interviewed them in July 2011, the next stage of the program was still in the scriptwriting process and de la Cruz remarked that the continuation of the series depended mainly on audience responses to the storyline.[17] Once again, the private intersects with the public and the dynamics of performance and public response meet in a virtual space that transcends the physical boundaries of the stage.

In a recent visit to Chiapas, I was struck by the heightened recognition—both by insiders and outsiders—about FOMMA. A native Tzeltal woman who owns a textile operation in San Cristobal told me that she had learned her skills at a FOMMA workshop. Another told me she had left her abusive husband, started school, and was now conducting her own successful handicraft business after joining FOMMA. Several troupe members shared stories about overcoming domestic violence and self-affirmation through their work in theater. However, most astonishing was to hear non-Mayan people remark about the works of Petrona de la Cruz and Isabel Juárez and their influence at a societal level.[18]

It is evident that FOMMA's plays and its complementary workshops constitute a dual-purpose vehicle to create awareness and reflection about common topics affecting Mayan communities and the mestizo audience. The plays explored in this chapter address issues of internal community affairs such as domestic violence and family relations alongside exploration of outside realities: marketing, migration, education, and legal issues among others. They also make the non-Mayan audience aware of their own position and misconceptions about indigenous people. Through 20 years of existence, FOMMA has opened the path to a more informed, proactive generation of women. Also, from being an indigenous centered project, it has expanded to a wider area of influence. This is illustrated by numerous invitations to present their plays at schools, universities, and community centers, nationally and abroad.

It is important to note that Juárez and de la Cruz's recognition is due in part for the model they have set as indigenous and as women, two parameters that have attracted international attention from feminists and human rights activists. The fact that the New York University's Hemispheric Institute for Performance and Politics chose FOMMA to set its headquarters in San Cristobal as the Centro Hemisférico[19] with grants obtained from the Ford Foundation is remarkable. Also noteworthy is the reception that FOMMA's affiliates have received through the press and cultural centers. Despite the fact that their work is less appreciated in central Mexico, as Isabel Juárez remarked in her interview, it does not demerit their recognition at international settings, in the academia and in the cultural scope of Chiapas.

Another fact worth mentioning is the awards and recognition they have received as leaders and promoters of culture in the state of Chiapas. After her literary prize in 1992, de La Cruz has been the recipient of several prizes and fellowships. In 1999, FOMMA was awarded a national prize from the Mexican Institute on Research for Family and Population for its work in radio, theater, and education. In August 2013, Petrona de la Cruz was recognized in a public homage by the Center of Scenic Development "The Open Door," at the IV Festival of Independent Theater "Another latitude," in Tuxla Gutieerez, capital of the state of Chiapas.

Special attention is given to FOMMA and its activities by the press in San Cristobal de las Casas, where the organization and its members are often mentioned and considered as public voices. That does not apply to the national press, except for few articles in *La Jornada* (Mexico City). This phenomenon can be explained by the usual omission of central Mexico and its distant regions' cultural activities and figures, but also because, paradoxically, the condition of indigenous and women that makes them so attractive for academics and activists, is less appealing for the ethno-centered perspective of mainstream culture in Mexico. Another reason explained by Juárez was the bureaucratic procedures they need to undertake to be able to perform on national stages.

It is undeniable that the most notable influence FOMMA has achieved has been in local communities in Chiapas, where, as Anabelle Contreras observed,

> Cuando la gente de las comunidades indígenas ve sus dramatizaciones suele haber tres reacciones comunes: el silencio, la burla y el repudio, o las lágrimas y el agradecimiento. Nadie permanece neutral porque ellas no han distinguido el teatro de la vida. Por el contrario, han llevado

la vida cotidiana al teatro...pues como ellas dicen, "cuando la gente ve sus problemas en escena toma conciencia y se atreve a pensar en soluciones." (39)

(When people of indigenous communities see their dramas there are usually three common reactions: silence, scorn and repudiation, or tears and gratitude. No one keeps neutral because they have not distinguished the theater from real life. On the contrary, daily life has been brought to the theater...as they say, "when people watch their problems on stage they become aware of them and dare to think of solutions.")

At the core of this statement is de la Cruz and Juárez's influence in Chiapanecan communities. Thanks to the services they offer associated with their performances, many people have changed attitudes, received support to modify their lives, and encountered myriad forms of physical and psychological assistance. This contribution at the society level is what makes FOMMA's mission effective and substantial after 20 years of existence. In the words of Diana Taylor, "Their theater has helped them fight the fierce discrimination visited on indigenous peoples in Mexico. From not being allowed to walk on the sidewalks in Chiapas, they are now celebrated as guest artists around the world" (*Holy Terrors*, 4, 5).

I have analyzed in this chapter the work of de la Cruz and Juárez as cultural agents and new public intellectuals. As such they are forging new ways of channeling agendas and epistemologies in which class, race, and gender intersect and support each other.[20] Mabel Moraña asks, "What role do intellectual practices play in the social transformation of postcolonial societies, where vast sectors of the population still suffer social marginalization, racial discrimination and political inclusion?" (25). For Moraña, the role of Latin American intellectuals should be "to understand the politics of culture—the politics in culture—and the urgency to produce emancipated knowledge in peripheral, neocolonial societies" (23). Consequently, they need to consider the uses of language and discourse, "in the intricacies of power and resistance, in the voices of organic, public and 'informal' intellectuals, in populism, community organizations and social movements" (23).

de la Cruz and Juárez Espinosa fit the category of new intellectuals from a peripheral ethnic minority representing alternative modes of knowledge. They are pivotal forces in the "politics of culture" but without playing the political game. Their efforts are transforming social realities by helping create and multiply cultural agents among women and in their communities, and by increasing the awareness of civil society. Elements of class, gender, and race intersect in this epistemology by achieving women's respect and dignity. As Isabel Juárez summarized about FOMMA's main achievements: "Se trata del respeto hacia la vida misma" (it's just about respect toward life itself).[21]

FOMMA would likely have been unable to realize its achievements without the catalytic articulation of historical events and the influence of other public intellectuals. Key among them was Rigoberta Menchú, the most internationally visible Mayan woman who broke the silence for indigenous people to declare their existence and the atrocities committed against them. Menchú's story unveiled the world of de la Cruz and Juárez, that of Maya from the Mexico-Guatemala border, a people with a shared cultural origin. It may seem a coincidence that in 1992 Menchú was awarded the Nobel Peace Prize, the same year in which de la Cruz won the Rosario Castellanos literary prize. It is clear that the quincentennial celebration of the Spanish colonization spawned awareness and recognition of indigenous achievements and opened venues of visibility. In addition, this collective was born at the time when feminists and other activists were searching for women leaders and agents of change, especially in marginalized ethnic groups.

FOMMA's success also derives from the combination of performance with education from inside and outside. The collective is constantly attending theater and performance workshops sponsored by New York University's Hemispheric Institute at various sites in Latin America and the United States, alongside guest artists such as Jesusa Rodríguez from Mexico City and scholars such as Diana Taylor from New York University. When presenting at FOMMA's center in San Cristobal or in nearby communities, each show is followed by a workshop where group members discuss the play's messages and implications. Community members mirror themselves in the plot and become more conscious of realities that can be transformed for the better. At the same time, when the audience is a mestizo one, the plays provide fresh understandings of indigenous traditions and other cosmovision and new perspectives that help to refract people's misconceptions and prior attitudes about indigenous people.

Petrona de la Cruz, Isabel Juárez, and their work with FOMMA tackle the big contradiction posed by Cynthia Steele: "What happens when indigenous 'traditionalism' conflicts with human rights?" (11). This is the same dilemma as that expressed by Underiner: "How to maintain tradition when that tradition often serves to subjugate women, and how to reinvent these traditions in order to incorporate new insights brought by a combination of factors, including international feminism?" (15). By dismantling codes of signification through performance, FOMMA's women have fostered new codes and behaviors without breaking traditional values. Quite the contrary, they have fortified them with pride and dignity. This is of course an ongoing process in which many actors and elements are intertwined. Their plays and performances acknowledge the possibilities and potentials for indigenous women to overcome the multiple manifestations of violence and abuse. Therefore, FOMMA conveys the complex intersections of tradition and modernity, the inside and the outside, gender, ethnicity, and agency. They not only permit, but also encourage social transformation. Juárez and de la Cruz's challenge for the future is to multiply their leadership as cultural agents without falling prey to commodification.

### Notes

1. I refer to García Canclini's definition of hybrid cultures as a juxtaposition of indigenous traditions, colonial hispanisms, modern technological systems, and mass media. The result is a society immersed in the conflict among different historical temporalities coexisting in the same present (46).
2. The term "mestizo" refers to the non-Mayan, Mexican population as a whole.
3. The original in Spanish reads: "Nuestra misión es hacer un llamado a las mujeres para que dejen a un lado la timidez, el miedo y sus pensamientos de que no valen en un mundo lleno de pobreza, ignorancia y hostilidad ofreciendo talleres de teatro, culturales, educativos y productivos." For the rest of the chapter all translations are mine unless stated otherwise.
4. FOMMA'S Website: //hemisphericinstitute.org/hemi/en/enc05-performances/item/1392-enc05-fomma.
5. Definition of public intellectuals by Mills cited by Daniel Brower and Catherine Squires in Etzioni's *Public Intellectuals: An Endangered Species?* (34).
6. I am summarizing a general statement expressed in several analyses of FOMMA's theatrical projects.
7. Personal interview. July 7, 2008.
8. I refer to the categories provided by Harley Erdman and Teresa Marrero.
9. Victor Turner's definition of social drama cited by Teresa Marrero (315–17).
10. I am using the translation by Teresa Marrero, "A Desperate Woman," in Taylor and Villegas, *Negotiating Performance*.
11. Personal interview. July 8, 2011.
12. See Guiomar Rovira's *Mujeres de Maíz* for a discussion of women's domestic violence and legal issues in Chiapas indigenous communities.

13. de la Cruz commented on this case in the personal interview, July 7, 2008.
14. Discussion with the audience after the performance at FOMMA's headquarters, San Cristobal de las Casas. July 5, 2011.
15. Conchita Riqué. Personal interview. July 5, 2011.
16. Héctor Sánchez. Personal interview. July 6, 2011.
17. Personal interview. July 5, 2011.
18. Summary of interviews with FOMMA members and people related to the Center. July 5–6, 2011.
19. The center's mission is to promote, showcase, and archive local performance practices and develop research, artistic creation, and cultural programming with and for local, national, and international communities. It presents public performances, visual arts exhibits, workshops, film screenings, and other cultural activities (Hemispheric Institute's Webpage).
20. I am referring to Nanneke Redclift's statement, "Class, gender and race are not merely connected... They do not simply intersect... They stand for each other" (cited by Moraña and Olivera, *El salto de Minerva*, 34).
21. Personal interview. January 8, 2011.

## Works Cited

Albaladejo, Anna. *La risa olvidada de la madre: 10 años de fortaleza de la mujer maya (Fomma)*. Valencia, Spain: Ediciones la burbuja, 2005. Print.

Blanco-Cano, Rosana. "(Re)vision y (re)construcción de los espacios locales y nacionales: tradición, género y poder en el teatro de Petrona de la Cruz." *Letras Femeninas* 33.1 (2007): 73–96. Print.

Castillo, Debra A. "Puppet Theater from Rosario Castellanos to Sna Jtz'bajom." Presentation. XXI Conference of the AILCFH, Barcelona. October 20, 2011.

Contreras Castro, Anabelle. "Chiapas, tan cerca y tan lejos de Centroamérica: escenarios, conflictos sociales y una dramaturgia posible en femenino." *Ístmica*. Universidad Nacional de Costa Rica, N. 13. 2010: 29–40. Print.

De la Cruz, Petrona. "A Desperate Woman: A Play in Two Acts." *Holy Terrors: Latin American Women Perform*. Edited by Diana Taylor and Roselyn Constantino. Durham and London: Duke University Press, 2003. 293–310. Print.

———. *Li svokol Xunka'e/ La tragedia de Juanita*. Tuxtla Gutiérrez: Centro Estatal de Lenguas, Arte y Literatura Indígenas, 2005. Print.

———. *Madre olvidada*. *La risa olvidada de la madre*. Edited by Anna Albaladejo. Valencia: Ediciones la burbuja, 2005. 65–89. Print.

———. "Theater and the Problems of Women in Highland Chiapas." *Negotiating Performance: Gender, Sexuality and Theatricality in Latin*

*America*. Edited by Diana Taylor and Juan Villegas. Durham and London: Duke University Press, 1994. Print.
Erdman, Harley. "Gendering Chiapas: Petrona de la Cruz and Isabel J. F. Juárez Espinosa of la FOMMA (Fortaleza de la Mujer Maya / Strength of the Mayan Woman)." In *The Color of Theater: Race, Culture and Contemporary Performance*. Edited by Roberta Uno and Lucy Mae San Pablo Burns. London: New York: Continuum, 2002. 159–69. Print.
Etzione, Amitai. "Are Public Intellectuals and Endangered Species?" In *Public Intellectuals: An Endangered Species?* Edited by Amitai Etzione and Alyssa Bowditch. New York: Rowman & Littlefield Publishers, 2006. 1–31. Print.
Fortaleza de la Mujer Maya—FOMMA. "Buscando nuevos caminos." Performance. San Cristobal de las Casas, July 5, 2011.
———. *Nuestra misión*. San Cristobal, Chiapas, 2011. Print.
———. "Viva la vida." Video performance. San Cristobal de las Casas, 2008.
———. FOMMA'S Website: //hemisphericinstitute.org/hemi/en/enc05-performances/item/1392-enc05-fomma. Web.
García Canclini, Néstor. *Hybrid Cultures: Strategies for Entering and Leaving Modernity*. Minneapolis: University of Minnesota Press, 1995. Print.
Hemispheric Institute: Instituto Hemisférico de Performance and Política. August 15, 2013. http://hemisphericinstitute.org/hemi/en/centers. Web.
Juárez Espinoza, Isabel. *Migración. Cuentos y teatro tzeltales: A'yejetik sok ta'jimal*. Mexico: Diana CEP, 2002. Print.
———. *Las Risas De Pascuala. La risa olvidada de la madre*. Edited by Anna Albaladejo. Valencia: Ediciones la burbuja, 2005. 99–135. Print.
Marrero, Teresa. "Eso sí pasa aquí: Indigenous Women Performing Revolutions in Mayan Chiapas." *Holy Terrors: Latin American Women Perform*. Edited by Diana Taylor and Roselyn Constantino. Durham and London: Duke University Press, 2003. 311–30. Print.
Moraña, Mabel, and María Rosa Olivera-Williams. *El salto de Minerva: intelectuales, género y estado en América Latina*. Colección Nexos y Diferencias. Madrid; Frankfurt am Main: Iberoamericana/ Vervuert, 2005. Print.
Moraña, Mabel, and Bret Darin Gustafson, eds. *Rethinking Intellectuals in Latin America*. South by Midwest. Madrid; Frankfurt: Iberoamericana/ Vervuert, 2010. Print.
Myers, Robert. "Mayan Women Find Their Place Is on the Stage." *The New York Times*. September 28, 1997. Arts and Leisure: 4 and 12. Web.
Rivera, Fabián. "Petrona de la Cruz, celebrada." *Cuarto Poder*. Tuxtla Gutiérrez, Chiapas, Mexico. August 21, 2013. Electronic.
Rovira, Giomar. *Mujeres de maíz*. 5th ed. Mexico: Ediciones Era, 2007. Print.
Sommer, Doris. *Cultural Agency in the Americas*. Durham and London: Duke University Press, 2006. Print.
Steele, Cynthia. "A Woman Fell into the River: Negotiating Female Subjects in Contemporary Mayan Theater." *Negotiating Performance: Gender,*

*Sexuality & Theatricality in Latin/o America.* Edited by Diana Taylor and Juan Villegas Morales. Durham and London: Duke University Press, 1994. 239–56. Print.

Taylor, Diana and Juan Villegas Morales. *Negotiating Performance: Gender, Sexuality, and Theatricality in Latin/o America.* Durham and London: Duke University Press, 1994. Print.

Taylor, Diana and Roselyn Costantino. *Holy Terrors: Latin American Women Perform.* Durham and London: Duke University Press, 2003. Print.

Taylor, Diana and Sarah J. Townsend. *Stages of Conflict: A Critical Anthology of Latin American Theater and Performance.* Ann Arbor: University of Michigan Press, 2008. Print.

Underiner, Tamara L. *Contemporary Theatre in Mayan Mexico: Death-Defying Acts.* 1st ed. Austin: University of Texas Press, 2004. Print.

## Chapter 8

# María Novaro: Feminist Filmmaking as Public Voice

*David William Foster*

An often heard statement with regard to María Novaro's films is that nothing really interesting takes place in them—they appear to be a collage of images and circumstances, but there is no sustained plot development and whatever action there is really goes nowhere.[1] In the context of such assertions, Novaro would seem to be countering to a second degree the image of film as a representation of the lived (mis)adventure of life. In the first instance, she is countering the whole notion of the action film, with its vivid characters, its vigorous scenes of physical exertion, its vociferous articulation of colloquial language, and its transparent morality: in short, the quintessential formulaic dispositions of masculinist filmmaking. This is the male-centered action model that Hollywood bequeathed to international filmmaking. If Novaro rejects it in a first instance for presumed reasons of irrelevance, disingenuousness, and falsity, she rejects it in a second instance as it became translated into Mexican filmmaking, to serve as the foundational narrative paradigm for an industry that made it impossible for any contrary voice, much less a feminist one, to emerge until well into the second half of the twentieth century.

Novaro (Mexico City, 1951–) is not only currently Mexico's premier feminist filmmaker, but she is quite simply the first Mexican woman ever to have established a career, properly speaking, as a major film director,[2] or been involved in the infrastructure of filmmaking.[3] Only Novaro has attained international stature as the consequence of a significant array of major productions, which include to date six feature films and numerous narrative and documentary shorts. All of her feature work involves the narration of women's lives—repeatedly women on their own and single mothers, typically at a breaking or tipping point in their lives—and those lives are portrayed both in terms of the rejections of conventional women's roles in Mexican society and as contestations of the multilayered power exerted on women by patriarchal men (and, in some cases, patriarchal women).[4]

Of particular note in Novaro's work is the eschewing of feature-length documentaries. Although she has done some documentary shorts, the extent to which she has turned away from the documentary as, perhaps, the most influential form of filmmaking in Latin America is significant. In a society in which there is general consensus among film people that the genre should directly engage sociopolitical and historical issues, the documentary has enjoyed something like an unquestioned privilege as a vehicle for commentary, denunciation, and calls for reform, revolution, and radical social justice. One only need recall the importance of work by Chile's Patricio Guzman or Miguel Littin, Argentina's Raymundo Gleyzer and Fernando E. Solanas, Bolivia's Jorge Sanjinés, Brazil's Eduardo Coutinho, or Mexico's Salvador Toscano, Arturo Ripstein, and Juan Carlos Rulfo. In the case of feminist filmmaking, there is the important work of Brazilian Helena Solberg, whose *Double Day* (1976) is a founding text of Latin American feminism and probably the first Latin American feminist documentary, at least as regards international stature. Cuban Sara Gómez, Brazilian Lúcia Murat, and Mexican-born US Chicana Lourdes Portillo continued Solberg's example of the importance of the documentary mode as a public forum for feminist issues.

One could argue that, in Novaro's case, coming from the extensive Mexican film industry and its emphasis on narrative, such that Mexico has no documentary filmmaker of the stature of Guzmán or Solanas,[5] narrative filmmaking was her most reasonable choice, at least for an immediate Mexican audience. Like Argentina's Maria Luisa Bemberg (1922–1995), who also eschewed the documentary mode in favor of narrative for her singularly important feminist filmmaking, Novaro has evidently chosen not to follow in the path of the recognized international importance of documentary as a dominant international form of feminist analysis. I will not rehearse here the fundamental differences between documentary and narrative filmmaking.[6] What is important to stress is the nature of Novaro's immediate film audience in Mexico, an audience primarily disposed to narrative filmmaking, the consequence of the strong tradition of directors and actors who have given a fictional storytelling Mexican film successes. Moreover, throughout its history but even more so in recent decades, Mexican film viewing has meant Hollywood fare: one only need examine the daily listings in Mexican city newspapers. Few venues regularly project Mexican films (e.g., the Cineteca), and the inventory of Mexican films in video stores in Mexico City is overwhelmed by American consumer products and icons. The result is that documentary films have few opportunities for survival in the Mexican marketplace, and even less so when they deal with feminist or other subaltern topics.[7] Of course, there is superb documentary filmmaking in Mexico, and many important Mexican titles are seen internationally, often directed by women. But none of these titles can aspire to a broad Mexican audience in the way narrative filmmaking does, and the same is true as regards access to foreign screens. It is in this context that one must understand why Novaro would prefer to emphasize narrative films, as have done other major feminist directors in Latin America like Argentina's Bemberg, Peru's Claudia Llosa, Argentina's Lucrecia Martel and Albertina Carri, Mexico's Maryse Sistach, and Brazil's Lúcia Murat (who, as I have mentioned, has also done documentary work, as has Carri).

Yet, although Novaro points toward the preference of Latin American women directors for the narrative mode, it is also important to underscore how, like her fellow feminist directors elsewhere in Latin America, she has little interest in masculinist paradigms of narrative. The latter include fully empowered central characters; transparent plots that adhere to received paradigms of narrative logic, including definitively resolved endings; action sequences that affirm the value and validity of macho heroics; compulsory heterosexist love stories, with concomitant flourishes of homophobia to highlight exceptions to those stories; plain colloquial language, which means highlighting national(istic) norms; and an overarching criterion of overdetermined realism as regards even the most insignificant details of the material culture of the universe of the film.

María Novaro was born in Mexico City in 1951. It was during her studies in sociology at the Universidad Nacional Autónoma de México that she began working with the Colectivo Cine Mujer (Women's Film Collective), and this experience led her to undertake formal film studies in 1979, and she early on participated in filming several documentaries, moving on in 1984 to begin work in narrative filmmaking. Her first notable success was with *Lola* in 1989, which landed her a fellowship in screenwriting and directing at the Sundance Institute in Utah. Novaro's work has won many prizes in Mexico and internationally, and her work has been featured at major international film festivals such in Berlin, Cannes, Biarritz, and New York (see Ciuk, 448 for further details).

In any interview in Lima in 2010 with Gianfranco Farfán Cerdán, Novaro speaks of her difficulties in creating a space for herself in a Mexican filmmaking world very much dominated by male privilege:

*Y esta parte de su biografía de que cuando va a filmar su primera película el 89,* Lola, *¿usted tuvo que pedir permiso al sindicato de cineastas de su país para filmarla?*
   Sí. Había que hacer las películas con el sindicato. Y de hecho no la hice con el sindicato a partir de la primera experiencia. Porque el sindicato todavía tenía cláusulas. A mí me iban a autorizar que siendo mujer dirigiera. Había que hacer la cláusula. Yo no podía llevar una fotógrafa, no podía llevar algunos colaboradores mujeres. Tenía que llevar gente del sindicato, que eran todos hombres. El clima mismo del sindicato era bastante machista todavía, sobre todo que eran hombres mayores. Por ejemplo, te hacían cosas—y yo ya lo había vivido—como trampas. Ponerte trampas con la cámara, a ver si sabías. Cosas así, un poco infantiles y absurdas. En esa época, en los ochentas, se empezó a crear la fórmula de filmar con cooperativas de cine. De pronto (fue) la solución que encontramos varios para no trabajar con el sistema anquilosado, envejecido, del sindicato de cine. Lo pagué muy caro con *Danzón.* Se enojaron porque era la segunda película que iba a hacer sin el sindicato, y al material filmado a lo largo de una semana que filmaba yo en el puerto de Veracruz, en el laboratorio—que estaba controlado por el sindicato—le metieron mangueras de arena en lugar de agua, y me estropearon el negativo de toda una semana de trabajo. Después de una asamblea en la que en el sindicato habían dicho que si se iba a permitir o no que María Novaro se burlara por segunda vez del sindicato. O sea: guerra, mafia. Eso era rudo. Era una cosa entre machista, sindicalista, no dejar a jóvenes con otros esquemas de trabajo. No sabes el dolor que fue entender que toda una semana de trabajo la arruinaban. Hasta me imaginaba a quien se atrevió a meterle arena a las mangueras en el laboratorio para rayar el negativo. Realmente muy duro.
   *And what about this part of your biography, that when you were about to make your first picture in 89,* Lola, *you had to ask permission from the filmmakers union of your country in order to film it?*
   Yes. You had to do pictures through the union. But the fact is I didn't make it through the union after my first experience. The union still had stipulations. They were going to authorize me as a woman to direct. You had to insert the stipulation. I couldn't use a woman photographer and I couldn't have any women collaborators. I had to use people from the union who were all men. Even today the climate in the union is still quite machista, especially since they were all older men. For example, they would do things to you, things I've experienced, like playing tricks on you. Doing something to the camera just to see if you would catch it. Things like that, all a bit childish and

absurd. During that time, in the 1980s, was the beginning of making films in cooperatives. All of a sudden, some us discovered that this was the way to avoid having to work in an outdated, worn-down system that was the union. *Danzón* cost me dearly. They got mad at me because it was the second film I was going to make outside the union. In the lab, which was controlled by the union, they would spray the film I had spent a week shooting in the port of Veracruz with sand instead of water, destroying a week's worth of negatives. That was after a meeting at which the union had asked whether they were about to let María Novaro thumb her nose at the union a second time. It was a war, the mafia. It was all so crude. It was a mix of machismo, the union, and not allowing young people with other ideas to work. You have no idea how it hurts to learn they'd ruined a whole week's worth of work. I even had an idea of who it was who put sand in the hoses in the lab to scratch the negatives. It was really tough to take.)

The way in which Novaro has used her highly successful filmmaking to break with masculinist paradigms is evident in her first great success, *Danzón* (1991), a film that focuses on a woman who lives to perform with her partner, Carmelo, the popular Mexican dance hall step called *danzón*. When Carmelo suddenly disappears, in her desperation, Julia is ready to give up everything to find him. She goes to Veracruz, has a number of significant adventures, but never finds Carmelo. When she must return to Mexico City or lose her real-life job, Julia returns to the dance hall, where Carmelo has reappeared. They dance (she does so revealing some of the things her adventures in Veracruz have taught her, such as a license for women to look directly into the eyes of her partner), and the film ends. For those who have complained that nothing really happens in this film, beyond Julia's somewhat circumstantial adventures in Veracruz, one's response must be that that is precisely the point. What might "really happen," especially were Carmelo the main character of the film in conformance with the masculinist paradigm,[8] is for there to be some momentous secret behind his disappearance and that Julia's journey to Veracruz must lead to the discovery of that secret and some emotion-drenched finale of anagnorisis, vengeance, retribution, reconciliation, or pathetic denouement. But Julia seems to take everything in stride, profiting rather than suffering mightily from her adventures, growing in feminine self-awareness (one might contrast her presence in the opening dance sequence with that of the film's closure). If the basic framework of *Danzón* is reminiscent of an infinite inventory of Mexican soap operas, Novaro defies them all: the film's microhistories never become the stuff of romance heroines. Moreover, the way in which the film ends without ever resolving the plot it appears to have set in motion—why, exactly, did Carmelo suddenly disappear?—and, moreover, there is no heteronormative resolution of the relationship between Julia and Carmelo: Shouldn't their reunion at the end of the film lead necessarily to matrimony? Isn't the dance narrative an allegory of sexual love, and doesn't the recovery of one's partner mean living together (dancing together, so to speak) happily ever after?[9] To extrapolate such a resolution from what is presented might be possible. But the soap-opera paradigm, a subset of the conventional masculinist narrative,[10] requires that we actually hear church bells and see rice being thrown, not the enigmatic gazes exchanged by Julia and Carmelo as the beat of the *danzón* comes to a close and the credits roll.[11]

Novaro's decision, then, to engage in narrative filmmaking, while yet deconstructing the mechanisms of masculinist paradigms, is what has given particular substance to her work. Her films present the daily lives of ordinary Mexican women, usually those teetering on the line between the modest middle class and virtual impoverishment. The extent to which they are able to overcome male obstacles and even harassment (as in *Sin dejar huella* [2000]) and to persist and endure with little in the way of bourgeois opportunities for success (in short supply for all citizens in Mexico, it must be noted) not only provides a model for feminist survival but also constitutes a significant refutation of privileged male-based determined action and predominance. One of Mexico's great cult films is Jaime Humberto Hermosillo's *María de mi corazón* (1979), also starring, like *Danzón*, the ineffable María Rojo.[12] *María* is both a feminist film and it isn't, although Hermosillo's stature as Mexico's preeminent gay director would dispose one toward stressing the feminist potential. In the film, María is a headstrong magician whose survival skills do not quite match her charming sleights of hand. The result is that, through a series of terrible misunderstandings, she ends up in a mental ward from which her partner, believing that she has once more upstaged him, refuses to rescue her. At the end of the film, she has resigned herself to her own (self-) entrapment. From a feminist point of view, the film is grim in charting the way in which woman can never elude the snares of the patriarchy, figured in the film by an oversized actor. The transvestite actor Xóchitl del Rosario plays the priest who marries María and her partner, as well as that of the Big Nurse at the mental ward who blasts her into submission with a high-pressure water hose before injecting her with numbing tranquilizers; Xóchitl also plays the patriarchal role of an investigative police officer. Berg has described *María de mi corazón* as part of Hermosillo's "madwoman trilogy" (81–88), which echoes Sandra M. Gilbert's and Susan Gubar's legendry trope, in their book of the same name, of the "mad woman in the attic."

Nevertheless, just as much as María is a woman who is treated as mad—who is made literally mad by the mental ward to which she is confined—by a punishing patriarchal society that cannot accommodate her free spirit, Hermosillo's film is equally sexist in the way in which it reduplicates the scheme of grand melodramas in which any woman who does not adhere to the carefully controlled model of femininity will come, in the end (of the film), to a bad end. Such is the case of virtually all of the films starring María Félix, where the spectator might experience a secret thrill over her outrageous antics, but where in the end masculinist order is restored when the *devoradora* (of the 1946 eponymous film directed by Fernando de Fuentes) is appropriately punished for her transgressions. *María de mi corazón*, no matter how much it may rhetorically dispose the spectator toward horror in the face of María's final entrapment from which no magician's skill can enable her to escape, cannot in the end escape itself from entrapment within the narrative of a woman punished for her waywardness, justly or unjustly.

By contrast, Novaro, who was just beginning to make films at the time of Hermosillo's enormous successes with films starring María Rojo, was determined to rewrite the existing scripts for Mexican women. I use the term rewrite, because on one level they are the scripts that have previously been used for the representation of women's lives in Mexico: their dependence, their exploitation, their marginalization, their insignificance in terms of the master narratives of action and predominance. However, Novaro rewrites these scripts in the sense that she examines the cause-and-effect plot curve to which they are unassailably subject in hegemonic male filmmaking and proceeds to recast the consequences such that women, while they may not necessarily triumph in the manner of masculinist action and predominance, are able to elude what had come to be seen as the inflexible narrative paradigm of the nature of women's being in the world. If *Danzón* effects this through the turning away from the principles of coherence that control the stories of soap operas, in *Sin dejar huella*, she more directly constructs a narrative universe in which the male threat is systematically evaded, disarmed, annihilated in order to open up a space of virtually lesbian camaraderie in which, significantly, a young man may learn to be a man in non-(hetero)sexist ways.[13]

*Sin dejar huella* is predicated on the risky decision of Aurelia to steal the cash hoard of her dismal drug-running boyfriend and to head from the northern border city of Ciudad Juárez, where she works in a maquiladora, to Cancún in her car with her two small sons. Apparently little concerned by the fact that stealing narco money in Mexico is a self-imposed death sentence, Aurelia is driven by her desire for a new life. There is a glimmer that this may be possible when she meets Marilú, a petty dealer in false archeological objects who is fleeing justice, although more specifically the piggish attentions of a police detective. The film follows their often desperate attempts to evade their male pursuers, and it is with the pursuers' death (abetted in part by the women in self-defense) that they are ultimately able to reach Cancún and, so the film implies, establish a life together. They are rejoined by Aurelia's small son, whom she has left with her sister for safekeeping. The closing promise of the film is that the two women will establish between themselves a new family unit and that Aurelia's two sons will have the opportunity to mature as men in this alternative and non-masculinist environment.

The title of the film has multiple meanings. Certainly, in a society in which women's lives do not count on their own and count only as signs in male fantasies of domination (the drug-dealing boyfriend, the police detective), women drift through life without leaving a trace—or, at least, without leaving any definitive trace that they can call their own. By contrast, Aurelia and Marliú, by virtue of working, with considerable success, to free themselves from the domination of their pursuers, leave no trace of their one-time subjection to male dominance. That is, they have disappeared without a trace as far as the hegemonic order of their society is concerned.

Novaro makes use of a number of interesting devices in the film to affirm the decentering of conventional plot expectations. One of the most notable is to have Marilú "illegally" crossing the border between Arizona and Sonora with her phony archeological artifacts. But where one would expect her to be smuggling them out of the country for sale in the United States, she is in fact bringing them into Mexico for sale to unsuspecting tourists. This reverse in the story of illegal crossing between the two countries is only the beginning of Marilú's deceptions. Bearing a false passport and being a Mexican who speaks with a Castilian accent are only two of Marilú's aspects of incompliance with patriarchal norms: the latter is significant enough to provoke Aurelia's initial distrust. Moreover, Marilú refuses to negotiate with the police in the time-honored fashion of women's survival in a hostile men's world: she rebuffs the police detective's advances rather than exploiting them flirtatiously to her own advantage. Finally, the bond the two women forge between themselves is unquestionably lesbian in nature, at least as regards Adrienne Rich's important proposal regarding a lesbian continuum, such that we understand as lesbian any way in which women engage with each other in a relationship of mutual emotional dependence that excludes a male-centered anchoring. Thus, Novaro's film, while it neither suggests nor represents a specifically sexual relationship between Aurelia and Marilú, systematically forecloses male intervention in their world, with the exception of Aurelia's two male sons, who will presumably profit accordingly in their character formation from exposure to the privileged bond between the two women.

In pursuing the ultimate benefits of the two women's road trip together across the male-dominated Mexican landscape, Novaro eloquently affirms the possibility of empowered women's lives.[14] Previous films like *Danzón*, as well as *Lola* (1989) and *El jardín de Edén* (1994), were significant for their representation of women coping and enduring, but not yet able to be agents of change and survival in their lives and as role models for others, particularly their sons. In *Sin dejar huella*, Novaro is able to portray such agency. In the process, she denounces women's subjugation to heterosexist imperatives and their bondage to dead-end employment, such as the maquiladora or the bar in the tourist hotel in Cancún where Aurelia is also obliged to work for a time. Crime and corruption in Mexico are part of a male-engineered economy, a naturalized system of national life, and the two women's apparently successful attempts to evade that economy are of heroic proportions for the meaning of the film. Finally, the sphere of meaning Novaro creates in her film is a significant forum for entertaining feminist alternatives to the silencing of women's voices in Mexico.[15]

Sociologist Sara Sefchovich complains repeatedly in *País de mentiras* (2009), her exhaustive analysis of the distortion of public discourse in Mexico, of the trivialization of women's voices and the impossibility for women to legitimate their intervention in public discourse in general and much less in one in which they might be allowed to counter the prevailing vitiation of honest attempts at characterizing social truths in Mexico.[16] Sefchovich is herself a major public intellectual in Mexico, through first her own creative writing and, more recently, her insightful sociological essays on national issues, including the role of women in Mexico. As someone who has played important roles in major social and political forums in Mexico, Sefchovich has had ample experience in the limitations that women have yet to overcome in Mexico in order to obtain full access to a serious measure of powerful influence and participation.

Such a circumstance puts into relief the importance of María Novaro's filmmaking as an alternative to the sort of public intervention

Sefchovich finds ultimately so frustrating. One could argue that such an alternative is little more than the customary symbolic, but not real, power accorded to the *feminine*, little more than an alternative to the more conventional opportunities now amply afforded women to express themselves through writing, but which fall significantly short of any meaningful impact in what is still a very masculinista society. Yet, film is quite of a different order than literature, not only because of the larger audience it reaches, but also because of its greater venues of distribution through DVD sales (which in Mexico include sidewalk hawking), television, national and international festivals, and circulation on the international marketplace. Mastery of the complexities of filmmaking brings a large measure of respect in a technologically grounded culture, and successful women directors can aspire to a public recognition that is rarely available to literary authors.

Like literary authors in Mexico, Novaro has focused on major social and political issues and she has done so through a visual medium that complements, as it reproduces them and reinterprets them, the extensive array of visual images provided by news outlets and mass-distributed popular culture: images of the border, images of the spaces where lives in Mexico are lived out, images of the material culture of Mexican social subjects, and images of the situations of confrontation and abuse at the hands of authorities. Novaro's filmmaking, with its emphasis on the texture of daily social life, resonates with viewers who can sense that they or their neighbors are being represented by her work on the screen. When the protagonist of *Lola* transverses a portion of pre-dawn Mexico City with her child in her arms; when Julia in *Danzón* interacts with her coworkers at the telephone exchange; when the widow in *El jardín de Edén* deals with the hard-scrabble realities of surviving in Tijuana; when Aurelia sets out to protect her son from the violence of the narcos in *Sin dejar huella*, Novaro is modeling very real circumstances of daily life in the Mexico of her spectators that is every bit as eloquent as a sociological essay or a newspaper editorial, and while the focus remains resolutely on the lives of women, the fact that they are repeatedly lower middle-class women means that she is addressing, in the first instance of her narrative universe, an enormous demographic sector of Mexican society. In this way, throughout her career, with relatively few but highly regarded feature-length films, Novaro has been successful in effectively constructing an interpretation of women's lives in Mexico and how those lives are part of a major social canvas. Hers is, of course, not a comprehensive sociological study, and the conclusion of *Sin dejar huella,* for those inclined to prize hard data, could be viewed as utopian, the inevitable finale to a charmingly related if somewhat implausible story of two young women's survival against all the marshaled odds of Mexican male hegemony. Yet, Novaro has established for herself an undisputed place in Latin American feminist filmmaking, and she has the distinction of being Mexico's first truly successful woman film director in an industry that, like Mexico as a whole, has had little room for women's voices.

### Notes

1. Novaro addresses this reservation of some viewers at the outset of her interview with Arredondo ("María Novaro," 196–97). I can add anecdotal evidence to this effect from over a decade of teaching Novaro's films, especially as regards male viewers.
2. As one might expect, Isabel Arredondo accords the greatest space to her in her collection of interviews with five contemporary women film directors in Mexico, *Palabra de mujer.* Elissa J. Rashkin provides the first detailed analysis of women film directors in Mexico, beginning with the early part of the twentieth century. The bulk of her study also focuses on five major names; Novaro is examined under the heading of "María Novaro: Exploring the Mythic Nation" (167–91). For an overview of Novaro's career, see Sutherland.
3. I examine the contradictions and problematical narrative voice of Carmen Toscano's *Memorias de un mexicano,* based on the immense film archive concerning the Mexican Revolution amassed by her father, Salvador Toscano, in the chapter on the film in Foster, *Latin American Documentary Fimmaking: The Major Texts.*
4. Robles provides a detailed analysis of the women's roles in Novaro's films and the various feminist issues with which they deal. Haddu focuses on redefining motherhood in *Lola;* she specifically contrasts Novaro's interpretation of Mexican maternity with the stereotype championed by Sara García in the 100-plus films she made through the height of Mexican film's so-called Golden Age (81–114). Yanes Gómez provides little more than plot summaries and some social and political connections for Novaro's films. However, one virtue of her book is the way in which it stresses the collaboration between Novaro and her sister Beatriz, with whom she works in the preparation of her film scripts.
5. Toscano's work is monumental in recording the Mexican Revolution, but he only made one major film from his material, *Historia completa de la Revolución Mexicana (1900–1927)* (1927), followed by his daughter's reformatting of his material in the form of *Memorias de un mexicano.* None of this should be taken to diminish Toscano's importance in founding filmmaking in Mexico or the significance of his many documentary shorts made before the 1910 conflict.

6. By narrative here I understand essentially a fictional mode. Of course, documentaries may be narrative in nature, and documentaries may make use of fictional elements (e.g., Helena Solberg's *Bananas is My Business* [1995], on Carmen Miranda, makes use of fictional bridges at several strategic points in Miranda's life, such as when she falls to the floor and dies in the privacy of her Beverly Hills bedroom. Docudrama, pseudodrama, and mockudrama are more likely to be grounded in fictional narratives than in verifiable, recorded fact (recorded used here in the sense of actually filmed and witnessable by the spectator).
7. For example, with the exception of Daniel Goldberg Lerner's *Un beso a esta tierra* (1995), Mexican filmmaking on Jewish topics has been overwhelmingly restricted to narrative films, such as Gita Shyfter's *Novia que te vea* (1994), Alejandro Springall's *La muerte esta en hebreo* (2007), and Mariana Chenillo's enormously successful *Cinco días sin Nora* (2008). With *Cinco días*, Chenillo is the only woman director in Mexico to have won the annual Best Mexican Film Award.
8. Moreover, Carmelo hardly conforms to the Pedro Infante type: he is a short-order cook, dark skinned, and never speaks.
9. Novaro discusses her decisions to modify the conventions of soap-opera melodrama in her interview with Arredondo ("María Novaro," 200–2). The essential outlines of Mexican cinematographic melodrama are developed by Julian Tuñón and Susan Dever.
10. My comments here are a variant of what I wrote on *Danzón* in Foster, *Mexico City* (100–11).
11. Mora discusses the masculinist matrix of Mexican filmmaking. He specifically cites Novaro as an example of someone who has "rewrit[ten] the *cabaretera* (dance hall) variant of prostitution and melodrama from a woman-centered perspective" (14).
12. Rojo might not wish to call herself a public intellectual, but she has made use of her political career (first as a *diputada*, now as a senator) in ways beneficial to the Mexican film industry. See in particular the material gathered in *Los que no somos Hollywood*, a symposium Rojo put in motion during her tenure as a *diputada*.
13. Traci Roberts-Camps underscores the question of female solidarity in this and other Novaro films, as opposed to the more contentious image of the lesbian continuum, which I mention below.
14. Claire Lindsay discusses *Sin dejar huella* as a female road movie that critiques aspects of modernity in Mexico.
15. As another example of Novaro's use of film to address sociopolitical issues, Andrea Noble discusses *El jardín de Edén* as an intervention in US-Mexico border politics.
16. See Foster, "Charting the Labyrinth" for a discussion of the importance of Sefchovich's essay as her own attempt to intervene in Mexican public discourse. Prior to *País de mentiras*, Sefchovich published *La suerte de la consorte* (1999; rev. ed. 2002), a work dealing with the first ladies of Mexico and their virtual nonexistence in the shadow

of their husband's overwhelming public persona. Only in the case of Vicente Fox's wife, Marta María Sahagún Jiménez, in her fleeting bid for presidential candidacy, has a Mexican consort had her own public voice. But as Sefchovich points out, Sahagún found it necessary to speak in a thoroughly masculinist registry. *Suerte* has on its cover an image of Soledad Orozco de Ávila Camacho, famous for her ceremonial hats. In the image, her head and shoulders are portrayed in a somber black and white, while the detail of her hat, the symbol, so to speak, of her assignment as presidential consort, is portrayed in color, marking the way in which the symbol overwhelms the person; Sefchovich comments specifically on the importance of Orozco de Ávila Camacho's dress (293–94).

### Works Cited

Arredondo, Isabel. "María Novaro on the Making of 'Lola' and 'Danzón'." *Women's Studies Quarterly* 30.1–2 (Summer 2002): 196–212. Translation of the bulk of author's chapter on Novaro in her *Palabra de mujer* (116–64). Print.

———. *Palabra de mujer: historia oral de las directoras de cine mexicanas (1988–1994)*. Madrid: Iberoamericana; Frankfurt am Main: Vervuert; Aguascalientes: Universidad Autónoma de Aguascalientes, 2001. Print.

Berg, Charles Ramírez. *Cinema of Solitude: A Critical Study of Mexican Film., 1967–1983*. Austin: University of Texas Press, 1992. Print.

*Carmen Miranda: Bananas is My Business*. Dir. Helena Solberg. Perf. Cynthia Adler, Eric Barreto, and Carmen Miranda. Channel Four Films. 1995. Film.

*Cinco días sin Nora*. Dir. Mariana Chenillo. Perf. Fernando Luján, Enrique Arreola, and Ari Brickman. Cacerola Films. 2008. Film.

Ciuk, Perla. *Diccionario de directores: 530 realizadores: biografías, testimonios y fotografías*. Mexico: Conaculta, Cineteca Nacional, 2000. Print.

*Danzón*. Dir. Maria Novaro. Perf. María Rojo, Margarita Isabel, Carmen Salinas, Tito Vasconcelos. Macondo Cine Video; IMCINE; Fondo de Fomento a la Calidad Cinematografica; Televisión Española; Tabasco Films; Gobierno del Estado de Veracruz. 1991. Film.

Dever, Susan. *Celluloid Nationalism and Other Melodramas: From Post-Revolutionary Mexico to Fin de Siglo Mexamérica*. Albany: State University of New York Press, 2003. Print.

*El jardín de Edén*. Dir. María Novaro. Perf. Renée Colma, Bruno Bichir. IMCINE; Verseau International; Universidad de Guadalajara; Fondo de Fomento a la Calidad Cinematográfica; Macondo Cine Video; Téléfilm Canadá; Sogic; Ministerio de Asuntos Exteriores de Francia y Ministerio de Cultura de Francia. 1993. Film.

Farfán Cerdán, Gianfranco. "'Soy una defensora absoluta de la diversidad del mundo' [entrevista, Lima, 22-8-2010]." http://entrevistasdesdelima.blogspot.com/2010/08/maria-novaro.html. November 24, 2011. Web.

Foster, David William. "Charting the Labyrinth: *País de mentiras* de Sara Sefchovich." *Cadernos de estudos culturais* 2.3 (2010): 15–20. Print.
———. *Latin American Documentary Filmmaking: Major Works*. Tucson: University of Arizona Press, 2013.
———. *Mexico City in Contemporary Mexican Cinema*. Austin: University of Texas Press, 2002. Print.
Gilbert, Sandra M. and Susan Gubar. 1979. *The Madwoman in the Attic: The Woman Writer and the Nineteenth-Century Literary Imagination*. 2nd ed. New Haven, CT: Yale University Press, 2000. Print.
Haddu, Miriam. *Contemporary Mexican Cinema, 1989–1999: History, Space, and Identity*. Lewiston, NY: Edwin Mellen Press, 2007. Print.
*Historia completa de la Revolución Mexicana (1900–1927)*. Dir. Salvador Toscano. Salvador Toscano. 1927. Film.
*La devoradora*. Dir. Fernando de Fuentes. Perf. María Félix, Luis Aldás, and Julio Villarreal. Producciones Grovas. 1946. Film.
Lindsay, Claire. "Mobility and Modernity in María Novaro's *Sin dejar huella*." *Framework* 49.2 (Fall 2008): 86–105. Print.
*Lola*. Dir. María Novaro. Perf. Leticia Huijara. Macondo Cine Video; Concite II; Cooperativa José Revuelta; Televisión Espanola. 1989. Film.
*Los que no somos Hollywood: memoria, simposio*. Mexico: LVII Legislatura, Cámara de Diputados, Comisión de Cultura, 1998. Print.
*María de mi corazón*. Dir. Jaime Humberto Hermosillo. Perf. Héctor Bonilla, María Rojo, and Salvador Sánchez. Clasa Films Mundiales. 1979. Film.
*Memorias de un mexicano*. Dir. Carmen Toscano and Salvador Toscano. Clasa-Mohme. 1950. Film.
Mora, Sergio de la. *Cinemachismo: Masculinities and Sexuality in Mexican Film*. Austin: University of Texas Press, 2006. Print.
*My Mexican Shivah*. Dir. Alejandro Springall. Perf. Blanca Guerra, Martha Roth, Sergio Kleiner. Goliat Films. 2007. Film.
Noble, Andrea. "'Yéndose por la tangente': The Border in María Novaro's *El jardín de Edén*." *Journal of Iberian and Latin American Studies* 7.2 (2001): 191–202. Print.
*Novia que te vea*. Dir. Gita Shyfter. Perf. Angélica Aragón, Pedro Amendáriz, Jr., and José Avilez. Fondo de Fomento a la Calidad Cinematográfica (Mex). 1994. Film.
Rashkin, Elissa J. *Women Filmmakers in Mexico: The Country of Which We Dream*. Austin: University of Texas Press, 2001. Print.
Rich, Adrienne. "Compulsory Heterosexuality and Lesbian Experience." *The Lesbian and Gay Studies Reader*. Edited by Henry Abelove, Michèle Aina Barale, and David M. Halperin. New York: Routledge, 1993. 227–54. Print.
Roberts-Camps, Traci. "Female Solidarity in the Films of María Novaro: Aqui Solo Encontramos Amigas." *Chasqui; revista de literatura latinoamericana* 42.1 (May 2012). Forthcoming. Print.
Robles Oscar. *Identidades maternacionales en el cine de María Novaro*. New York: Peter Lang, 2005. Print.

Sefchovich, Sara.1999. *La suerte de la consorte; las esposas de los gobernantes de México: historia de un olvido y relato de un fracaso.* 2a ed., reescrita y aum. Mexico, DF: Oceáno, 2002. Print.

———. *País de mentiras; la distancia entre el discurso y la realidad en la cultura mexicana.* Mexico, DF: Océano, 2009. Print.

*Sin dejar huella.* Dir. María Novaro. Perf. Tiaré Scanda, Aitana Sánchez Gijón, Jesús Ochoa, José Sefami. Tabasco Films; Altavista Films; Tornasol Films; Televisión Española. 2000. Film.

Sutherland, Romy. "María Novaro." *Senses of Cinema* 23 (2002). January 30, 2011. http://sensesofcinema.com/2002/great-directors/novaro/. Web.

Tuñón, Julia. *Mujeres de luz y sombra en el cine mexicano: la construcción de una imagen, 1939–1952.* Mexico: El Colegio de México, Instituto Mexicano de Cinematografía, 1998. Print.

*Un beso a esta tierra.* Dir. Daniel Goldberg Lerner. Perf. Moisés Amkie, Zelig Schnadower, and Susana Sevilla. National Center for Jewish Film (NCJF). 1995. Film.

Yanes Gómez, Gabriela. *Una mujer al espejo: el cine de las hermanas Novaro.* Puebla, Dirección del Periódico Oficial del Estado de Puebla, Secretaría de Gobernación, 1999. Print.

## Chapter 9

# The Masked Intellectual: Marcos and the Speech of the Rainforest

*Oswaldo Estrada*

*He risks his life for what he believes [...] It must be hard to be a guerilla. Being Marcos must be harder than all of that. Even if he jokes, even if he's already a celebrity.*

Elena Poniatowska, "Entrevista al Subcomandante Marcos"[1]

With a few notable exceptions, most books, articles, and chronicles on the Zapatistas and their leader, Subcomandante Marcos, tend to frame the indigenous uprising in Chiapas within the extended mural of revolutionary Latin America. More than the particularities of a group of armed *campesinos* who stand against capitalism, oppression, and inequality on January 1, 1994 in the Lacandón rainforest, what seems to catch the attention of several academics and analysts who write at a safe distance from southern Mexico and its peripheral zones is the Zapatistas' resemblance to other revolutionary leftist groups and guerilla movements of the turbulent 60s, 80s, and 90s. Inevitably, then, a good number of studies chronicle the original uprising of 1994 in reaction to the North American Free Trade Agreement (NAFTA); the collectivity of a group that is nonetheless led by a new, charming, and postmodern Che Guevara, whose army unexpectedly seizes San Cristóbal de las Casas, Altamirano, Ocosingo, and Las Margaritas; the central participation of women; and its Marxist ideology, or what is best described as a mixture—as Marcos himself asserts on television, national radio, and the internet—of patriotic values and elements of Mexico's indigenous culture, the historic heritage of the Mexican Left, Mexico's military history, and lessons from national liberation movements.

A good number of studies also pay attention to Marcos's mystique, as it continues to grow with several pieces of biographical information, old photographs that do not necessarily anticipate the birth of a revolutionary intellectual, and improbable accounts of all sorts about his formative years. Through these venues we can imagine that the spokesman for the Zapatista Army of National Liberation (Ejército Zapatista de Liberación Nacional / EZLN) comes from a middle-class family, that he went to a Jesuit high school, studied at the National Autonomous University of Mexico, lectured for a time at the Autonomous Metropolitan University and subsequently became a revolutionary. As it is well known, more than 15 years ago the Mexican government identified the man behind the now legendary ski mask as Rafael Sebastián Guillén Vicente, born in Tampico, Tamaulipas, on June 19, 1957 (Henck, 13). This public unmasking, however, has only contributed to Marcos's success as a public figure, to the extent that another intellectual, Carlos Monsiváis, sarcastically calls him "The great Puppeteer" or, better yet, "The charismatic leader or the new Piper of Hamelin of a hypnotized country" (Monsiváis, 371–72). Regardless of whether we agree with this assertion or not, today Marcos holds on to his status as "the masked symbol of a romantic and clean revolutionary movement," a particularity that Elena Poniatowska already anticipates when she interviews him during the National Democratic Convention of August 1994.

If the public intellectual, according to Edward Said, is someone who appeals to as wide as possible a public, but maintains an ambiguous citizenship, "as exile and marginal, as amateur, and as the author of a language that tries to speak the truth to power" (*Representations*, xvi), in this chapter I analyze the figure of Subcomandante Insurgente Marcos as the Zapatista leader of the Mayan uprising in Chiapas, whose numerous electronic communiqués, letters, written manifestos, short stories, and coauthored novel are always on the move, in constant dialogue with Mexican and international civil society. Intertwining his own narrative voice with the fictional voices of the rainforest beetle and knight-errant Don Durito de la Lacandona, and that of the Mayan Old Antonio, since 1994 Marcos has been crafting a discourse of his own that represents the historically silenced Indians of the Lacandón rainforest. He is, as we know, a master of electronic and print media, and the creator of an image that continues to be marketed nationally and internationally. By paying close attention to his fictional discourse, however, in which he undoubtedly acts "as a combination of scribe and cultural interpreter, lending the EZLN his university education and pedagogical experience, along with his native command of Spanish and knowledge of urban Mexican culture" (Steele, 248), I highlight how Marcos behaves like an intellectual endowed with a faculty for representing the indigenous *Other*, or those who are routinely forgotten by the Mexican government. The fact that *el Sup*—as his comrades and fans call him—writes as the leader of an armed struggle, in disguise and as an outsider, distinguishes him from other intellectuals studied in this volume, for his mysterious figure mixes the private and the public, his own history and that of others.

Following Said's theoretical postulates on various representations of the intellectual in contemporary societies, I speak of Marcos as a revolutionary intellectual who embodies and articulates the Zapatistas' message, attitude, and philosophy to and for a public. His profile is undeniably that of an individual whose *raison d'être* is to stand for marginalized and/or forgotten subjects on the principle that "all human beings are entitled to expect decent standards of behavior concerning freedom and justice from worldly powers or nations, and that deliberate or inadvertent violations of these standards need to be testified and fought against courageously" (Said, *Representations*, 11–12). I study the consolidation of Marcos's intellectual persona as portrayed primarily in his literary communiqués because they embody the historical experience of the Zapatistas with an aesthetic touch that will certainly pass the test of time. Not coincidentally, the man behind the mask attributes his philosophical formation to the literature that changed his worldview. "My parents introduced us to García Márquez, Carlos Fuentes, Vargas Llosa," he admits in an interview. "They set us to reading them. *A Hundred Years of Solitude* to explain what the provinces were like at the time. *The Death of Artemio Cruz* to show what had happened to the Mexican Revolution. *Días de guardar* to describe what was happening in the middle classes. As for *La ciudad y los perros*, it was in a way a portrait of us, but in the nude" (García Márquez and Pombo, 77–78).

Even if Marcos is a "tragic hero," or a "Moses without a Promised Land," as Ilan Stavans depicts him in the mid-90s (50), no one can deny his current standing as a revolutionary intellectual. We can certainly say that he contributes to the creation of his own myth with his never-ending letters and postscripts, but equally true is that he revives the literary intellectual's relationship to revolutionary activity (Henighan, 518). He accomplishes this intricate task with a unique rhetoric that shows how history is fabricated behind the scenes, and how Latin America is still trapped in a network of hegemonic forces, coloniality, and oppression in global and neoliberal times.

## Against Neoliberalism

When reflecting on the accomplishments and failures of the Zapatistas, journalist Alma Guillermoprieto does not miss that Marcos's literary letters are his most effective weapon against the Mexican government, since they have allowed him "to become a faceless stand-in for all the oppressed, an anonymous vessel for all fantasies from the sexual to the bellicose" (212). Leaving aside her comment on Marcos's alleged sex appeal, her assertion is spot on. In the letters that *el Sup* writes on a regular basis and publishes in national journals such as *Proceso, El Financiero,* and *La Jornada,* the rainforest beetle and knight-errant Don Durito de la Lacandona catches our attention with poignant discussions, fables, and tales of marginalization in times of political pretense and new economic agendas. If, to a large extent, neoliberalism can be seen as a set of economic policies that privilege the private enterprise, free trade, and open markets, Don Durito presents it as a new first world strategy to dominate Latin America. In one of the numerous communiqués where Marcos becomes the beetle's metafictional interlocutor, Durito explains neoliberalism not as a theory that is capable of confronting Mexico's and Latin America's economic crisis but, rather, as the crisis itself. With an empowered voice that reflects a revolutionary origin, the wise beetle argues that neoliberalism "hasn't the least coherence; it has no plans or historic perspective"; it is just "pure theoretical shit" (*Conversations,* 54).

After studying theories that in one way or another portray neoliberal Latin America in the midst of an uneven battle between markets and government control; private property rights and community needs; efficiency and social justice; centralized, technical decision making and democratic accountability (Kingstone, 3), Durito protests: "There are no plans; there are no perspectives, only i-m-p-r-o-v-i-s-a-t-i-o-n. The government has no consistency: one day we're rich, another day we're poor, one day they want peace, another day they want war, one day fasting, another day stuffed, and so on. Do I make myself clear?" (*Conversations,* 54). With an explicit language, the beetle vocalizes what cultural theorists recognize throughout Latin America: that both globalization and neoliberalism stand as contemporary incarnations of neocolonialism, and that capitalism, by ruling all aspects of national and international relations, perpetuates coloniality (Moraña et al., 12). His politicized speech confirms not only the power of words as political action but the existence of a writing pad where Marcos mixes ethics and aesthetics, politics, and performance (Corona and Jörgensen, 244). On the surface, Durito's stories might come across as writing exercises or playful reflections that rely on excessive intertextuality, digressions, constant interruptions, and spontaneous metaphors of all calibers. But right beneath the surface the reader finds meaningful and transcendental passages that guard Zapatista ideals of democracy, liberty, and justice (Vanden Berghe, 47). We observe this narrative technique and its high level of effectiveness from the very first communiqué of 1994 up to the most recent letters that have been published in the first decade of the new millennium, where Durito excuses himself for being just a beetle, employs a carnivalesque discourse built on the limits of the serious and the comic (Pellicer, 202), and successfully delivers a profound message against neoliberalism and its lateral damages.

Speaking on behalf of his masked creator, whose intellectual integrity rejects conformism, easy formulas, and ready-made theories promoted by the powerful and conventional (Said, *Representations*, 23), Don Durito de la Lacandona lectures his audience on Mexico's principal obstacles to a democratic transition, denounces his country's budgetary imbalance as well as its system of domination and political deformations due to the corruption of an entire political, economic, and social network that blocks its opponents and its own civil society. Even though Durito writes before the 2000 presidential election, when the opposition party (Partido Acción Nacional / PAN) defeated the Institutional Revolutionary Party (Partido Revolucionario Institucional / PRI) for the first time since 1910, his discourse still speaks for Mexico's irregularities and endemic corruption, one that cannot be solved with a free-market economy but, instead, with a "a new revolution" from inside (*Conversations*, 91). If neoliberalism, according to the knight-errant, is the plague that has infested Mexico and Latin America, the cure to the problem cannot come from "junior politicians" who have learned their lessons abroad. Even if they have good intentions, the problem they face is quite large:

> They arrive with a messianic message that nobody understands. While the respectable decipher it, they make off with their booty, which is to say, power. Once they have that, they start to apply the only lesson they ever learned: "act like you know what you're doing," and they use the mass media to acquire that image. They obtain consummate levels of pretense, to the point of constructing a virtual reality, followed its course, and something had to be done. Then, they started to do whatever occurred to them: this way one day, that way the next. (*Conversations*, 108)

In the same manner that other peripheral societies use aesthetics to convey and promote unorthodox ideologies and anti-conformism (Beverley and Zimmerman, 9–10), in his literary letters and postscripts Marcos denounces racism and authoritarianism, attacks against civilians, and the cynicism of the former leftists and revolutionaries who end up serving the system that they originally criticized. Acting as a true intellectual who tells the government what it does not want to hear with an ironic yet humorous, eloquent and courageous voice (Said, *Representations*, 8), Marcos allows Don Durito to behave like Cervantes's Don Quijote, even at the expense of becoming the beetle's Sancho Panza. In such moments we hear him say:

> In neoliberalism, my squalid squire, history becomes an obstacle because of what it represents of memory, graduate students are promoted into forgetfulness and the meticulous statistics of the trivialities of Power become the object of study and of great and profound dissertations. Power converts history into a badly told tale, and their social scientists construct ridiculous apologies with, indeed, a theoretical scaffolding so complex that they are able to disguise stupidity and servility as intelligence and objectivity. In the tale of neoliberalism, the powerful are the heroes because they are powerful, and the villains to be eliminated are the "expendables," that is to say, Blacks, Asians, Chicanos, Latinos, the indigenous, women, the young, prisoners, migrants, the ones who have been screwed over, homosexuals, lesbians, the marginalized, the elderly, and, very especially, rebels. In the tale as told by Power, the happening that is worth something is the one that can be recorded on a spreadsheet that contains respectable indices of profit. Everything else is completely dispensable, especially if that everything else reduces profit. [ ... ] The ethical balance between good and evil transforms into the amoral balance between Power and the rebel. For Power, money carries weight; for the rebel, dignity carries weight. (*Conversations*, 180)

As we go through similar passages where Durito fights ferociously against neoliberalism, we distinguish an authorial voice that employs a national language not only for obvious reasons of convenience and familiarity but also because the intellectual wants to impress on that language a particular sound, a distinctive accent, and a perspective of his own (Said, *Representations*, 27). While some of these linguistic markers are inevitably lost in the English translation, readers can still identify the intellectual who speaks for and testifies to the sufferings of the indigenous people of Mexico in particular, and of other minorities in general. It is the same strategy that Marcos employs when he describes himself, in the third person, with bits and pieces of *others* who are marginalized and exiled within their respective societies. Although his main focus is Mexico's lack of democracy, injustice, and inequality, Marcos universalizes the crisis of the indigenous Zapatistas and associates their experience with that of others around the world. As he cleverly states in one of his early communiqués of 1994 that continues to travel around the globe:

> Marcos is gay in San Francisco, black in South Africa, an Asian in Europe, a Chicano in San Isidro, an anarchist in Spain, a Palestinian in Israel [...] a communist in the post-Cold War era [...] a pacifist in Bosnia, a Mapuche in the Andes [...] a peasant without land, a marginal editor, an unemployed worker, a doctor without a job [...], a dissident of neoliberalism, a writer without books or readers and, certainly, a Zapatista in the Mexican southeast. (EZLN, 243)

The approach of departing from Emiliano Zapata to the global oppressed not only identifies *el Sup* with other social emancipatory struggles, it also situates the Zapatistas in front of a global audience that should hear the exploited, the underrepresented, and the forgotten (Hiller, 273). Echoing his own creator, Durito will also pronounce that "there's nothing more foolish in all of Mexico today than being indigenous or young or a rocker or a knight-errant or a beetle" (*Conversations*, 85). The act of aligning himself with other minorities through a process of self-deprecation is, of course, not gratuitous. While Durito struggles to emancipate his marginal comrades with eccentric wisdom and from the peripheral position of a small insect that carries the insignificance of *others* (Vanden Berghe, 76), his readers are forced to engage in contemporary discussions of racism and modernity, discrimination and current waves of *blanquitud civilizatoria*, a condition that Bolívar Echeverría describes not *only* in terms of ethnicity, or the civilizing idea of whiteness, but *particularly* as the permanent identity marker of a globalized and capitalist world that excludes single individuals or collective groups from the master outline of a modern society (63–64).

If, according to a postscript, "Durito says liberty is like the morning. There are those who wait for it to arrive while sleeping, but there are also those who stay awake and walk throughout the night to reach it," Marcos complements the metaphor with a message that highlights the permanent state of exile of those whom he represents: "I say that we Zapatistas are addicts of the insomnia of which history despairs" (*Conversations*, 185). As further proof of that marginality, in a subsequent communiqué Durito tells Marcos that the *bolsas* of the poor are quite different than the *bolsa de valores* (stock market) of the rich. "Our *bolsas*," he argues, "are known as bolsas and as the word indicates, they're good for holding things. They usually have holes caused by neglect, but they are mended with hope and embarrassment" (*Conversations*, 207). It is a condition, Marcos implies in another communiqué, shared by the "brown" Latino community of the United States that continues to carry a heroic history: "That of their color, hurt and worked until it is made hope. Hope that brown will be one more color in the rainbow of the races of the world, and it will no longer be the color of humiliation, of contempt and of forgetting" (*Conversations*, 256). This, of course, is also the hope of the Zapatistas whose ongoing hardships seek to grow and bear fruit, like an apple tree (*Conversations*, 315) whose feet "grow large from walking the long night of sorrow to hope" (*The Speed*, 174), and whose sense of liberty make them reject "the nostalgic option, that of forgetting [...] the one being offered to the Mexican indigenous as the most suitable for their idiosyncrasies" (*The Speed*, 197).

In all of these passages, Marcos, the intellectual behind Durito's discourse, depicts himself as an outsider, as someone who feels outside the chatty, familiar world of those in power (Said, *Representations*, 53). If the intellectual as exile transmits unhappiness, dissatisfaction, political disagreement, and historical inequalities, well into the twenty-first century, Marcos's knight-errant continues to point out the flaws of capitalism and defines Mexican politics as "a bad comedy in which no one knows his role" (*The Speed*, 327). With ease, Durito's sentences align themselves with a postcolonial sensibility, denounce truncated modernities, and relate to other codified literatures of Latin America (de la Campa, 437). The beetle speaks and makes us laugh with a discourse that seems too advanced for an insect, but he also reveals an intelligent intermingling of sociopolitical and aesthetic agency.

## The Word of Wisdom

In a new study on the revolutionary public relations of the Zapatista insurgency, Jeff Conant writes that Marcos's writing embodies the force of history, memory, myth, and ancient wisdom thanks to the figure of Old Antonio, the man who speaks with the voice of earthly authority, the voice of the elder and of the aged prophet (72). His assertion is by all means precise. Marcos's Antonio is portrayed on the printed page with a literary language that captivates readers at once:

> Antonio dreams that the land he works belongs to him. He dreams that his sweat earns him justice and truth; he dreams of schools that

cure ignorance and medicines that frighten death. He dreams that his house has light and his table is full; he dreams that the land is free and that his people govern themselves reasonably. He dreams that he is at peace with himself and with the world. (*Shadows*, 50)

Antonio's discourse is powerful not only because it expresses an indigenous world of dreams and myths, but also the weight of colonialism and, most certainly, a revolutionary alternative to corporate capitalism and globalization (Foran, 275). If it is true that in Mexico "everyone dreams," in this portrayal of Old Antonio we become aware that "it is time to wake up" (*Shadows*, 50).

Those who have studied Antonio as a literary figure point out that his tales reconfigure fragments of the Mayan *Popol Vuh* (Vanden Berghe, 120), and that he is the bridge that connects the indigenous Zapatistas with western societies (Valdespino Vargas, 49). This, of course, is exactly what Marcos tells Yvon Le Bot in an interview, where he admits that his now legendary character provides an accurate picture of the indigenous cosmogony so that the outside, urban world can better understand it (153–54). What interests me the most about Old Antonio's stories is the fact that they also reveal Marcos, the writer, as an intellectual who uses the word of the Mayas in order to create innovative riddles of freedom, justice, and democracy. Old Antonio does not dominate Don Durito de la Lacandona's language of contemporary politics and neoliberalism. And yet he manages to convey transcendental messages about the old gods and the creation of the world, the men and women of maize, the living myth of Emiliano Zapata, and the never-ending struggle of his contemporary heirs.

No one knows if Old Antonio is simply a fictional character, or if he was indeed a wise man that Marcos met ten years before the uprising (Le Bot, 153). What we do know is that he delivers his teachings with a quiet poise that encourages his men to continue fighting against oppression. In the still of a dark and cold night, when the future rebels try to find an indigenous translation for the Spanish verb *rendir* (to surrender), with the speech that characterizes him, Antonio tells Marcos: "That word doesn't exist in a true language; that's why our people never surrender and they would rather die" (*Relatos*, 27). Determined to fight with his people, right before the uprising Old Antonio encourages Marcos to go on, with the words: "To die in order to live" (*Relatos*, 40); he accepts that "the ingredients needed to bake the bread we call tomorrow are many" (*Our Word*, 389); and insists on teaching others that they can be as big and powerful as the enemies they choose to fight, or as little as their greatest fears. Playing the role of the student who has successfully learned the lesson from his master, Marcos takes these opportunities to instruct his readers: "The government fears the Mexican people; that's why it has so many soldiers and policemen. It has a big fear. Consequently, it is very small. We are afraid of oblivion, the one we've been reducing with the strength of our pain and blood" (*Relatos*, 68).

As we move from one story to the next, we can see why Carlos Monsiváis would consider that Marcos wraps the indigenous message with an eloquent and poetic breath that speaks for an entire community (374). Antonio's discourse, according to meta-literary Marcos, symbolizes the "ritual of the word" (*Relatos*, 50); when the old man speaks, "he gives warmth and comfort with words that hug like friends, like comrades" (*Relatos*, 63). Aware of what a figure like Antonio represents for the Mayan communities—for being one of their own—Marcos allows him to speak in the narrative with a Spanish language that privileges orality over literacy, in order to transmit an *alter/nativist* discourse of multiculturalism, *mestizaje*, and hybridity (Vanden Berghe, 103).[2] This happens seamlessly. In line with his "oral" culture, Antonio's sentences are formulaic, cumulative, redundant, or copious (Ong, 38–80; De Garay, 198), but in every instance we recognize the intellectual who seeks to stir up debate and controversy, from a solitary position, outside of the established opinion (Said, *Representations*, 69).

Marcos legitimizes diversity, for instance, when Antonio points at a macaw crossing the afternoon sky and explains that the gods painted this bird with all the colors, so that it would always "stroll around in case men and women forget that there are many colors and ways of thinking in the world, and how happy the world will be when all the colors and ways of thinking have a place" (*Our Word*, 375). In "The Story of One and All," Antonio continues to validate the concept of diversity and seeks a productive dialogue that recognizes difference. He says that the first gods

> saw that not one but all are needed to make the world turn. And that's how the first gods became wise, the greatest, the true gods, those who gave birth to the world. They learned how to talk to each other and listen. And they were wise. Not because they knew many things or because they knew a lot about any one thing, but because they understood that one and all are necessary and sufficient. (*Our Word*, 398)

Like an effective teacher who knows how to engage his students with ordinary tales that contain transcendental messages, Marcos emphasizes the same idea of alterity when Antonio argues that "Life without those who are different is empty and dams you to stagnation" (*Our Word*, 390). Ultimately, the old man insists, "the first agreement the very first gods had was to recognize difference and accept the existence of the other [ ... ] the gods agreed it's a good thing that there are others who are different, and that one must listen to them to know oneself" (*Our Word*, 391).

Throughout these stories, Marcos hides behind Antonio in the same manner that he hides his true identity behind his ski mask. In both scenarios, the intellectual resorts to spectacle and theatricality to challenge structures of authority. And just as the mask becomes a subversive strategy, for it simultaneously liberates and empowers, threatens and/or presents itself as dangerous, depending on the perspective of the observer (Jörgensen, 89), Antonio's didactic tales contain seeds of rebellion, nonconformism, a call for action, and a demand for social change. Through Antonio's voice, Marcos maintains a narrative relationship with the indigenous communities that he seeks to represent, but at the same time he establishes a dialogic project as the author and interlocutor of social activism (Herlinghaus, 240). In the story "The Lion Kills by Staring," for example, Old Antonio teaches Marcos that the lion, as the king of the jungle, is strong only because the rest of the animals are weak and they allow themselves to be eaten. This is how it works:

> The lion doesn't kill with its claws or its teeth. The lion kills by staring [ ... ] It stares at its prey [ ... ] The poor little animal that is going to die just looks. It looks at the lion who is staring at him. The little animal no longer sees itself, it sees what the lion sees, it looks at the little animal image in the lion's stare, it sees that the lion sees it as small and weak. The little animal never thought before about whether it was small, neither strong, nor weak. But now it looks at what the lion is seeing, it looks at fear. And by looking at what the lion is seeing, the little animal convinces itself that it is small and weak. And, by looking at the fear that the lion sees, it feels afraid. And now the little animal does not look at anything. Its bones go numb, just like when water gets hold of us at night in the cold. And then the little animal just surrenders, it lets itself go and the lion gets it. That is how the lion kills. It kills by staring. (*Zapatista*, 97–98)

Recreating an indigenous language "from the bottom up" (Vázquez Montalbán, 192), so that it transmits the linguistic and ideological register of the people at the bottom of the social pyramid to those who remain near the top, Marcos crafts a subtle metaphor about the oppressed and the powerful. And just to clarify the not-so-hidden moral of the tale, Antonio wraps it up with a clear message for the Zapatistas:

> A man who knows how to look into his own heart is not afraid of the lion [...], because a man who can look into his own heart does not see the lion's strength. He sees the strength of his own heart, and then he looks at the lion, and the lion sees what the man is looking at. The lion sees, in what the man is looking at, that it is just a lion. The lion sees itself as it is being seen, and is afraid and runs away. (*Zapatista*, 99)

Those of us who are familiar with the Sixth Declaration of the Lacandón Jungle recognize the resemblance between this parable and the words of the Zapatistas that in 2005 still reiterate their permanent commitment to struggle against neoliberalism and for humanity, for "another politics" with the help of the underrepresented "who are afraid but control their fear" (*The Speed*, 285).

In the stories of Old Antonio, Marcos reconfigures the world and its endless struggles from an indigenous perspective that can also reach "workers, campesinos, teachers, students, housewives, neighbors, small businesspersons, small-shop owners, micro-businesspersons, pensioners, handicapped persons," and so on (*The Speed*, 285). Thus, instead of explaining the Zapatista movement with the usual history lesson on "the land, and the injustice, and hunger, and ignorance, and sickness, and repression and everything" (*Our Word*, 413), Antonio takes over the narrative and recites it in mythical terms. Suddenly, *Zapatismo* is explained as a movement that brings together opposite and complementary forces of nature, as exemplified by the duality of the gods Ik'al and Votán. According to this legend, after being together since the beginning of time, the two gods decide to become one in the name of a mythical man: "Votán Zapata and Ik'al Zapata, the black Zapata and the white Zapata, they were both the same road for the true men and women" (*Our Word*, 415).[3] This new version of the revolutionary model can be successfully associated with the history, beliefs, and territory of the indigenous Mayas (Vanden Berghe, 146), from the moment that Marcos presents to the western world an immortal Zapata that has lived for over five hundred years and has been fighting for the indigenous since the arrival of the first conquistadors in 1492 (EZLN, 211). By virtue of these associations, Zapata is presented as a mythical figure that empowers his men, an attribute that is clearly exposed in another communiqué, where the Zapatistas express: "From the first hour of this long night in which we die, our most distant grandfathers say that someone gathered our pain and our oblivion...He is and isn't in these lands: Votán Zapata, the guardian and heart of the people" (EZLN, 211).

Following this ideology, in another story Old Antonio explains that the first three words of all languages have always been justice, freedom, and democracy. "All words come from these three words," says the old man, "it is the legacy of the first gods that gave birth to the world [ ... ] the first gods gave those first three words to the man and women of maize. [ ... ] Since then, true men and women guard these three words as heritage. So that they're never forgotten, they walk them, they fight them, they live them" (*Relatos*, 66–67). Instead of fighting for abstract ideals of plurality, however, Marcos employs Antonio's voice to destabilize the structure of the Mexican State so that it has room to represent more than one nation and different citizenships that are currently nonexistent (Quijano, 329). If memory, according to another tale, is "the key to the future" (*Zapatista*, 130), Marcos fights against historical amnesia with the voice of an aged Antonio who recreates stories of conquest and colonialism that have alternative endings and messages of hope for the Zapatistas. It is true, he tells Marcos, that the conquistadors took over their land. But, ultimately, "the foreigner left. We are here, like the water of the stream we still walk to the river that will take us to the great water where the great gods cure their thirst" (*Relatos*, 74).

Anticipating times of difficulty, Old Antonio reminds *el Sup* that "the sky is not firm," that sometimes it allows death and sorrow to cover the surface of the earth (*The Speed*, 216); he explains that the indigenous people walk as if they were hunched over because they walk collectively, "carrying on their shoulders their hearts and the hearts of everyone" (*The Speed*, 241); and he describes their struggle as a permanent state of seeking, "in order to find ourselves" (*The Speed*, 153). In the end, Antonio, the character, wants what Marcos, the revolutionary intellectual fights for: a nation that respects itself by respecting its own minorities (Monsiváis, 378). To this extent, Marcos's rhetorical reasoning is radically and alternatively democratic: it emerges as a new ethics of social imagination (Herlinghaus, 242), even though it recycles and reconfigures Mexico's revolutionary icons, historical determinism, and various polemics of coloniality that explicitly question the idea of a modern Mexican State and a global, neoliberal Latin America. In any case, what these fictional passages demonstrate is not only that the Zapatistas are enacting what Walter Mignolo considers a "theoretical revolution," but also that Marcos has been their most important mediator, serving as the bridge between the western and indigenous cosmologies, or as the agitator of modernity's long history of coloniality ("The Zapatistas," 245; *The Idea*, 115).

## Uncomfortable Men

In spite of his success as the sole creator of compelling short stories, populated by eloquent and politicized characters that speak of freedom and democracy, human rights, the dark side of modernity, and discrimination at large, most of Marcos's literary critics express their discomfort with his first novelistic incursion, entitled *The Uncomfortable Dead* (*Muertos incómodos*) and written in collaboration with Paco Ignacio Taibo II between December 2004 and February 2005. Originally published as a serial detective drama in *La Jornada* and almost immediately in book form, the novel has consistently been criticized for being overtly propagandistic and carnivalesque, sententious and melodramatic, and structurally uneven, as the product of a creative tactic to counteract the "wearing out" of Marcos's rhetoric and persona since 2001 (Close). Truth be told, the novel does come across as an asymmetrical pairing of two different authors whose narrative styles and literary trajectories are dissimilar. Nevertheless, the odd-numbered chapters penned by Subcomandante Marcos are extremely illuminating, not *in spite of* but *because of* his political narrative, in the sense that it speaks for the masked intellectual who remains true to his original political ideals and shows a permanent commitment to dispute with the guardians of power, capitalism, and neoliberalism. As a reader of Latin American literature, I may not like the aesthetic quality of this coauthored novel, or might even find it of lesser literary strength in comparison to Marcos's short stories. This judgment, however, does not cancel out the fact that Marcos continues to establish his intellectual persona with arguments that reveal his undermining of authority and his defense of human rights, even if authors such as Jorge Volpi consider him a "sad parody" of the Marcos that challenged the Mexican government in 1994, or an "anachronistic" revolutionary that momentarily returned the indigenous to the public space (64).

In perfect agreement with his previous literary endeavors, in *The Uncomfortable Dead* several of Marcos's narrators denounce "the Mexican government's abuse of power, corruption, and political and economic policy of neoliberalism that benefits only mega transnational corporations and harms small indigenous farming communities" (Mato, 105). The "Evil" responsible for Mexico's and Latin America's prevalent corruption and perennial disequilibrium is described not as an entity, but rather as "a perverse and malevolent demon looking for bodies to possess and turn into instruments for creating more evil, crimes, murders, economic programs, frauds, concentration camps, holy wars, laws, courts, crematoriums, [and] television channels" (63). Restating Don Durito's discomfort with contemporary models of economic development, in the novel a Maoist Purépecha Indian nicknamed The Russian raises his voice to complain: "They can't come to me with that crock of shit that globalization is modernity [...] What the hell modernity are they talking about? Go ahead, you tell me. That's old as the hills. First the fuckin Spanish, then the fuckin gringos, then the fuckin French. And now they're all getting together to gang up on us... even the fucking Japanese" (125). Also loyal to Marcos's beliefs in regards to US imperialism, The Russian's tortilla stand in Guadalajara displays the signs "*Say NO to fast food*" and "*We don't accept propaganda for America or any other religion*" (125, emphasis in the original). After all, as he later reminds the main character Elías Contreras, "Them fuckin gringos, they stole half our country in a war and then they persecuted Pancho Villa but couldn't catch him, and now they're tryin to steal the other half of the country with their fuckin transgenic hamburgers and hot dogs and radioactive waste" (127).

In response to a country that marginalizes individuals for being "different" (167), the novel presents us with a "Broken Calendar Club" that supports the Zapatistas' rebellion. It is a diverse club composed of Juli@ Isileko, a gay Filipino mechanic from Barcelona; a German lesbian named Danna May with a Vietnamese last name, Bí Mát, that means "clandestine"; a French woman, whose last name, Prouzakonitost, means "outlaw" in Serbo-Croatian; and Vittorio, an Italian cook whose last name, Nidalote, means "forbidden" in Albanian (48–51). Interestingly, those who have criticized the novel for its "ostentatious diversity" point out that it is built on the surface of "an unmistakable or underlying uniformity" that controls the novel's discourse (Close). What they see as a problem, however, only confirms my hypothesis. As readers we may dislike the fact that Marcos's political agenda saturates the entire narrative, or that we can read *his* polemical pronouncements in every one of his characters. But if those political undertones were absent from the chapters that belong to Marcos, then half of the novel would be completely incongruent with the rest of his literary enterprise. Marcos is polemical and moralizing. He preaches through his protagonists and uses them to undermine authority, to promote diversity, and to include those who are more often than not cut out of various national projects and/or national narratives (Castillo, 47). It is not surprising, then, to read that another character, the transvestite prostitute Magdalena, explains different but closely related types of discrimination with the words "queer," "faggot," "fruit," and "sissy," that together speak for the marginalization of homosexuality, and with the word "Indian," arguably one of the worst insults in Mexico, "which was built on the backs of the indigenous population" (168).

We also recognize a critical attitude of denouncement when Elías Contreras, who has been sent by *el Sup* on a detective mission to Mexico City, walks through the streets of the nation's capital and runs into "people like us Zapatistas, which means people who are screwed, which means people willing to fight, which means people who don't give up" (96). As expected from our previous readings of Marcos, the criminal that is immediately blamed for a generalized situation of inequality is the Mexican government (Guntsche, v; Mato, 109). Employing a humorous voice that does not hide its fierce political stance (Castillo, 47), once again Marcos identifies the government as the great oppressor when Elías gets this message from *el Sup:*

> *We're having some laughs with the crap Fox said on his visit over here. In case you haven't heard about it on the news, he's repeating the same nonsense we heard from Hernán Cortés, Agustín de Iturbide, Antonio López de Santa Anna, Maximilian of Hapsburg, the gringos Polk, Taylor, Pershing, and Eisenhower, and Porfirio Díaz, Gustavo Díaz Ordaz, Salinas de Gortari, and Ernesto Zedillo: He said that we were long gone.*
> (143, emphasis in the original)

It is, indeed, problematic to represent Mexican history "as an unresolved struggle of a mercilessly oppressed people against a series of inherently vicious, exploitative, and treacherous ruling elites" (Close). This Manichean model, as we know from traditional indigenist discourses, has proven to be ineffective and counterproductive. And yet, Marcos goes a step further in a clear attempt to represent the contemporary "colonized," paying attention to various transpersonal and transcultural forces of class and gender, race, nationality, and sexual orientation (Said, *Reflections*, 294–95). In the chapters that belong to Marcos we learn that "the men and women who fight against the Bad are fighting for children, no matter the color of their skin, their last name, age, nationality, race, or language" (171).

Accordingly, at the beginning of Marcos's narrative, a Zapatista woman escapes from her husband's beatings, changes her name from María to April, and seeks protection from the Women's Commission. Later on, acting as an intellectual who is entitled to raise ethical issues of memory and identity formation, or the imposition of norms and standards, in order to induce a change in the moral climate of his particular society (Said, *Representations*, 82–100), in his half of *The Uncomfortable Dead*, Marcos lets The Russian explain the Bad and the Evil as the act of "betraying the memory of our honored dead. Denying what we are. Losing our memory. Selling our dignity. Feeling shame for being Indian, or black, or Chicano, or Muslim, or yellow, or white, or red, or gay, or lesbian, or transexual, or skinny, or fat, or tall, or short. Forgetting our history. Forgetting ourselves" (177).

This is how Marcos's writing continues to impose itself as a literature of otherness. Even if his public appearances have lost their unprecedented impact of 1994, or if Marcos's popularity has decreased dramatically since the *Zapatour* of 2001—when President Vicente Fox allowed the Zapatistas to enter Mexico's Zócalo in the interest of peace and negotiations—his literature stands as living proof of his intellectual views, ideas, and ideologies. For some writers, like Volpi, he might be as passé and harmless as a rock singer of the 70s, a retired boxing champion, or an aged marathon runner (64). For some others, his identity has become a logo, a Mexican souvenir, a T-shirt for tourists, another mask for the Day of the Dead, or the always mysterious and attractive figure of a Latin American revolutionary (Girona, 363). A few others, however, still see Subcomandante Marcos as the intellectual whose political and literary work stands against coloniality in an era of alleged modernization and widespread neoliberalism.

When reflecting on various representations of the intellectual, Edward Said wondered, "How far should an intellectual go in getting involved? [...] How far should one's loyalty to a cause take one in being consistently faithful to it?" (*Representations*, 105–6). Marcos's commitment to the Zapatistas' rebellion clearly exemplifies that, at least sometimes, the public intellectual goes *all the way*. Speaking on behalf of others, today Marcos continues to use the word as a weapon, and from the heart of the Lacandón rainforest, the intellectual of the Zapatista movement still raises his voice to say: "We think, fundamentally, that the future story not only of Mexico but of all Latin America, will be constructed from the bottom. The rest of what's happening, in any case, are steps. Maybe false steps, maybe firm ones, that's yet to be seen" (*The Other*, 155). If that story is still in the making, *el Sup* is definitely contributing to its formation. Like a true intellectual, he leaves us wondering about his future steps or his next communiqués, Don Durito's battle against neoliberalism, Old Antonio's struggles against historical amnesia, the voices that want to be heard, and the masked faces of uncomfortable women and men.

## Notes

1. All translations from Spanish are my own unless otherwise noted.
2. Like Vanden Berghe, I use the term *alter/nativist* following the postulates of Bill Ashcroft, Gareth Griffiths, and Helen Tiffin: "The post-colonial world is one in which destructive cultural encounter is changing to an acceptance of difference on equal terms" (36).
3. For a closer look at the multiple origins of the mythical Votán Zapata, see Valdespino Vargas's *De noches, dioses y creaciones* (95–106).

## Works Cited

Ashcroft, Bill, Gareth Griffiths, and Helen Tiffin. *The Empire Writes Back. Theory and Practice in Post-colonial Literatures.* London and New York: Routledge, 1989. Print.

Beverley, John and Marc Zimmerman. *Literature and Politics in the Central American Revolutions.* Austin: University of Texas Press, 1990. Print.

Castillo, Debra A. "Impossible Indian." *Chasqui. Revista de Literatura Latinoamericana* 35.2 (2006): 42–57. Print.

Close, Glen S. "*Muertos incómodos*: the Monologic Polyphony of Subcomandante Marcos." *Ciberletras* 15 (2006). June 7, 2011. http://www.lehman.cuny.edu/ciberletras/v15/close.html. Web.

Conant, Jeff. "Poetics of Resistance." In *The Revolutionary Public Relations of the Zapatista Insurgency.* Oakland, CA: AK Press, 2010. Print.

Corona, Ignacio and Beth E. Jörgensen. "Introduction." In *The Contemporary Mexican Chronicle. Theoretical Perspectives on the Liminal Genre.* Edited by Ignacio Corona and Beth E. Jörgensen. Albany: State University of New York, 2002. 243–44. Print.

De Garay, Graciela. "Oralidad." *Diccionario de Estudios Culturales Latinoamericanos.* Edited by Mónica Szurmuk and Robert McKee Irwin. Mexico: Instituto Mora; Siglo XXI Editores, 2009. 197–202. Print.

De la Campa, Román. "Postcolonial Sensibility, Latin America, and the Question of Literature." *Coloniality at Large. Latin America and the Postcolonial Debate.* Edited by Mabel Moraña, Enrique Dussel, and Carlos A. Jáuregui. Durham and London: Duke University Press, 2008. 433–58. Print.

Echeverría, Bolívar. *Modernidad y blanquitud.* Mexico: Era, 2010. Print.

EZLN. *Documentos y comunicados 1.* Mexico: Era, 1994. Print.

Foran, John. *Taking Power. On the Origins of Third World Revolutions.* New York: Cambridge University Press, 2005. Print.

García Márquez, Gabriel and Roberto Pombo. "The Punch Card and the Hour Glass: Interview with Subcomandante Marcos." *New Left Review* 9 (2001): 69–79. Print.

Girona, Nuria. "Efectos de identidad y *performance* político del Subcomandante Marcos." *Estudios* 30 (2007): 361–83. Print.

Guillermoprieto, Alma. *Looking for History. Dispatches from Latin America.* New York: Vintage Books, 2002. Print.

Guntsche, Marina. "El vivo y desenfadado éxito de *Muertos incómodos*, del Subcomandante Marcos y Paco Ignacio Taibo II." *Revista de Literatura Mexicana Contemporánea* 33 (2007): i–xi. Print.

Henck, Nick. *Subcommander Marcos. The Man and the Mask*. Durham and London: Duke University Press 2007. Print.

Heninghan, Stephen. "No History to Absolve Them: Spanish-American Revolutionary Discourse after 1990." *Bulletin of Hispanic Studies* 81.4 (2004): 511–20. Print.

Herlinghaus, Hermann. *Renarración y descentramiento. Mapas alternatives de la imaginación en América Latina*. Frankfurt am Main: Iberoamericana/Vervuert, 2004. Print.

Hiller, Patrick T. "Contesting Zapata: Different Meanings of the Mexican National Idea." *Journal of Alternative Perspectives in the Social Sciences* 1.2 (2009): 258–80. Print.

Jörgensen, Beth E. "Making History: Subcomandante Marcos in the Mexican Chronicle." *South Central Review* 21.3 (2004): 85–106. Print.

Kingstone, Peter. *The Political Economy of Latin America. Reflections on Neoliberalism and Development*. New York: Routledge, 2011. Print.

Le Bot, Yvon. *Subcomandante Marcos. El sueño zapatista*. Mexico: Plaza y Janés, 1997. Print.

Mato, Shigeko. *Cooptation, Complicity, and Representation. Desire and Limits for Intellectuals in Twentieth-Century Mexican Fiction*. New York: Peter Lang, 2000. Print.

Mignolo, Walter D. *The Idea of Latin America*. Malden, MA and Oxford: Blackwell Publishing, 2005. Print.

———. "The Zapatistas' Theoretical Revolution: Its Historical, Ethical and Political Consequences." *Review* 25.3 (2002): 245–74. Print.

Monsiváis, Carlos. *Apocalipstick*. Mexico: Debate, 2009. Print.

Moraña, Mabel, Enrique Dussel and Carlos A. Jáuregui. "Colonialism and its Replicants." In *Coloniality at Large. Latin America and the Postcolonial Debate*. Edited by Mabel Moraña, Enrique Dussel, and Carlos A. Jáuregui. Durham and London: Duke University Press, 2008. 1–20. Print.

Ong, Walter J. *Oralidad y escritura. Tecnologías de la palabra*. Translated by Angélica Scherp. Mexico: Fondo de Cultura Económica, 1987. Print.

Pellicer, Juan. "La gravedad y la gracia: el discurso del Subcomandante Marcos." *Revista Iberoamericana* 174 (1996): 199–208. Print.

Poniatowska, Elena. "Entrevista del Subcomandante Insurgente Marcos con Elena Poniatowska." *La Jornada*. 30 Julio 1994–3 Agosto 1994. http://palabra.ezln.org.mx/comunicados/1994/1994_07_24.htm. Web.

Quijano, Aníbal. "El 'movimiento indígena,' la democracia y las cuestiones pendientes en América Latina." *Colonialidad y crítica en América Latina*. Edited by Carlos A. Jáuregui y Mabel Moraña. Puebla: Universidad de las Américas, 2007. 299–335. Print.

Said, Edward W. *Reflections on Exile and Other Essays*. Cambridge, MA: Harvard University Press, 2002. Print.

———. *Representations of the Intellectual*. New York: Vintage Books, 1994. Print.
Stavans, Ilan. "Unmasking Marking." *Transition* 69 (1996): 50–63. Print.
Steele, Cynthia. "The Rainforest Chronicles of Subcomandante Marcos." *The Contemporary Mexican Chronicle. Theoretical Perspectives on the Liminal Genre*. Edited by Ignacio Corona and Beth E. Jörgensen. Albany: State University of New York Press, 2002. 245–55. Print.
Subcomandante Insurgente Marcos. *Conversations with Durito. Stories of the Zapatistas and Neoliberalism*. Edited by Acción Zapatista Editorial Collective. New York: Autonomedia, 2005. Print.
———. *Our Word is our Weapon. Selected Writings*. Edited by Juana Ponce de León. New York: Seven Stories Press, 2001. Print.
———. *Relatos de El Viejo Antonio*. San Cristóbal de las Casas: Centro de Información y Análisis de Chiapas, 1998. Print.
———. *Shadows of Tender Fury. The Letters and Communiqués of Subcomandante Marcos and the Zapatista Army of National Liberation*. Translated by Frank Bardacke, Leslie López, and the Watsonville, California, Human Rights Committee. New York: Monthly Review Press, 1995. Print.
———. *The Speed of Dreams. Selected Writings 2001–2007*. Edited by Canek Peña-Vargas and Greg Ruggiero. San Francisco: City Lights, 2007. Print.
———. *Zapatista Stories*. Translated by Dinah Livingston. London: Katabasis, 2001. Print.
Subcomandante Insurgente Marcos and The Zapatistas. *The Other Campaign. La otra campaña*. San Francisco: City Lights, 2006. Print.
Taibo II, Paco Ignacio and Subcomandante Marcos. *The Uncomfortable Dead (What's Missing Is Missing)*. Translated by Carlos López. New York: Akashic Books, 2006. Print.
Valdespino Vargas, Carla. *De noches, dioses y creaciones. Un acercamiento a* Relatos de El Viejo Antonio. *Textos del Subcomandante Insurgente Marcos*. Mexico: Universidad Nacional Autónoma del Estado de México. 2009. Print.
Vanden Berghe, Kristine. *Narrativa de la rebelión zapatista. Los relatos del Subcomandante Marcos*. Madrid: Iberoamericana/Vervuert, 2005.
Vázquez Montalbán, Manuel. *Marcos: el señor de los espejos*. Madrid: Punto de lectura, 2001. Print.
Volpi, Jorge. *El insomnio de Bolívar. Cuatro consideraciones intempestivas sobre América Latina en el siglo XXI*. Buenos Aires: Debate, 2009. Print.

## Chapter 10

# Javier Sicilia: Public Mourning for the Sons of Mexico

*Javier Barroso*

*Every son who dies becomes a son of this nation.*[1]
                    Javier Sicilia, in one of his first radio interviews after
                                                        his son's murder.

*Not all parents are poets, but all children are poetry.*
                    Banner from one of Sicilia's peace marches.

Since 2006, when former Mexican President Felipe Calderón's term in office began, narco-violence has gone from being considered a peripheral, border issue, to becoming the general public's main concern as it struggles to come to terms with the senseless and daily acts of violence that have permeated the entire nation, including cities once considered symbols of Mexican modernity and high culture, such as Monterrey and Guadalajara. Although figures vary from outlet to outlet, it is estimated that more than 80,000 people have been killed in the three-pronged war waged between the drug cartels and the Mexican military. In 2011 alone, there were approximately 12,000 drug-related deaths, an increase of about 6 percent compared to the previous year (Booth).[2] According to the Instituto de Acción Ciudadana para la Justicia y Democracia, a Mexican nonprofit organization and human rights watchdog that monitors the government's performance, in 2011 71.5 percent of the nation's municipalities were "either occupied or under the control of organized crime" (Gómora). The figure is alarming when considering that the same organization estimates that just six years ago drug cartels had a strong presence in only a third of the country. Although it was one of the bloodiest and grimmest years since the all-out war began, 2011 was also witness to many changes in the way the public reacted to the massacre and the lack of accountability and justice. At the forefront of these new developments is the Movimiento por la Paz con Justicia y Dignidad, a civilian protest group led by Mexican poet Javier Sicilia that has become a symbol of resistance to the violence perpetrated by both the government and the drug cartels. The movement's strength has not gone unnoticed by the large web of criminal groups in Mexico—as of August 2013, five of the movement's members had been killed, including a 73-year-old Michoacan activist, and three had gone missing. Despite the repression, the movement has not only offered a glimmer of hope to the promise of a possible resolution through peaceful demonstrations, but it has also allowed for a rare glimpse into the formation of a public figure in Sicilia's transformation from a somewhat marginal intellectual (and mystic poet) to becoming the face and voice of the war's victims and their families.

The movement's creation and Sicilia's rise came at the highest price: the killing of the poet's young adult son in March 2011. Like many of the thousands of violence victims in Mexico, the deaths of 24-year-old college student Juan Francisco Sicilia Ortega and five more men and a woman who were with him at the time were at first shrouded in mystery. The bodies were found on March 28 inside a vehicle parked near a hotel along the Mexico City–Acapulco highway in the state of Morelos. Three of the bodies were found inside the trunk, and all seven bore the typical signs of having been tortured to death: their heads, wrists, and feet were wrapped in packing tape, their bodies were bruised, and all had died of asphyxia. According to the first reports, the victims were killed simply for reporting to police suspicious activities by a group of men. Later, it was reported that Sicilia Ortega and some of his friends had been in a bar fight with people associated with a drug cartel, and were later killed by hit men. About six weeks after the bodies were found, two suspects were arrested and more details about the possible motive for the murder—police extortion—came to light. According to the suspects' confession, the victims were first robbed by a group of policemen who also stole their personal identification cards so they could extort them. Instead of giving in, Sicilia Ortega and his friends sought help, so the policemen allegedly asked Cártel del Pacífico Sur's hit men to kidnap and kill the victims (Guadarrama). As of August 2013, several suspects remained in different prisons throughout the country pending trial.

The day that his son's body was found, Sicilia was not in Mexico. After returning from an overseas trip for a poetry convention, he not only had to deal with his son's funeral, but also with the media. "I asked the reporters to have some respect; I told them I'd meet them the next day in the city plaza. When I got there I found they'd put a table [for a press conference] out for me, and I realized this was going to be bigger than I'd anticipated" (Padgett). It is telling that the poet acknowledges that suddenly being presented with a public platform to address his situation came as a surprise because Sicilia already was a public intellectual if one follows the ideas on the topic postulated by Edward Said who noted that a public intellectual is somewhat of a redundancy since the mere act of writing and publishing means one has entered the public arena (12). However, I argue that the poet is now a different kind of intellectual, perhaps even anachronistic, because in him both the public and the private intersect, and he can be more easily identified with the accepted definitions and roles of intellectuals from decades past. For example, after his son's death, Sicilia's role in Mexican society transitioned even further from the role of the traditional intellectual, which Antonio Gramsci defined as that of a person who mainly enforced the ideology of the hegemonic powers. Instead, he seems to have become an organic intellectual almost to the letter. For Gramsci, organic intellectuals were "distinguished less by their profession, which may be any job characteristic of their class, than by their function in directing the ideas and aspirations of the class to which they organically belong" (Hoare and Nowell Smith, 3). Gramsci clearly derived this definition from Marxist thought about class struggle, but Sicilia does not represent a particular economic class; rather, he represents a completely new class of Mexicans: the millions who have been directly or indirectly affected by the armed confrontation between cartels and the government. Furthermore, I argue that Sicilia's influence among the public also has a great deal to do with the fact that he personifies the spirit of the moment, or what Raymond Williams identified as the structures of feeling of a certain period. The poet personifies the country's mourning, anger, confusion, and fear, which are arguably the main elements of the zeitgeist of the past few years in Mexico.

Historian—and quite possibly the most visible Mexican public intellectual before Sicilia's rise—Enrique Krauze, in an opinion piece published by the *New York Times*, called the movement and the public's response to it "something amazing" and noted that "its every move was followed by the national media," while thousands showed up for rallies and marches ("Can This Poet"). He also pointed out that Sicilia's movement is not the only recent form of resistance in Mexico, as "it was just one part of a larger awakening of civil society here, which can be seen in the strengthened investigative efforts of the press, a more aggressive application of anticorruption laws, and the formation of voluntary associations, focused on everything from the environment to poverty." While the assertions about the press and the government's efficacy can definitely be contested, the creation of associations that fight for human rights and government accountability has certainly had an impact in Mexico's public arena. And while several of these organizations existed before Sicilia's Movimiento por la Paz con Dignidad y Justicia, the flagship movement has helped the others gain much more notoriety among the general public, especially thanks to their online presence through Twitter feeds, Facebook pages, and blogs. In his opinion piece, Krauze also draws a parallel between the student movements of 1968 in Mexico and the present-day organizing of citizens to resist the current violent state in the country: "Multiparty democracy finally arrived in 2000, but only now, more than four decades after the 'Olympic massacre,'[3] has true protest returned. The government is not involved, and the people are not afraid of the government. The movement is political, but it exists outside politics." Even if one were to agree that the "true protest" was absent in Mexico since the late 1960s, Sicilia's movement is far from being the first instance in recent years of organized protests against the violence and lack of security in the nation. Since 2005, few but key acts of resistance and mobilizations have propelled new activists onto the national stage, such as Isabel Miranda de Wallace and Alejandro Martí, each of whom suffered the kidnapping and murder of one of their sons in 2005 and 2008, respectively.[4] Although not as massive or long lasting as the Movimiento por la Paz con Justicia y Dignidad, these acts of defiance and public protests were in fact "true" in the sense that they were real, organic, and provoked a national response—and they effectively laid the groundwork for a larger movement to finally emerge.

While it would be incorrect to give Sicilia all the credit for creating an environment that fomented resistance to the current state of affairs in the nation, it would also be unfair and simplistic to pin all the responsibility of Mexico's escalation of violence on Calderón's military strategy. Indeed, the country's incursion into the drug underworld has a complicated and decades-long history. The rise of Mexico as the main port of entry and producer of drugs for the United States has its roots in the 1970s, after the French Connection—drug trafficking operations based in Europe[5]—was taken down, according to Emily Edmonds-Poli and David A. Shirk (311). Around that time, cocaine began to emerge as the preferred drug for US consumers, which led to the rise of the infamous and powerful Colombian drug lords. The authors explain that while Mexico historically "had been an important but low-level supplier of drugs to the United States, notably products like marijuana and opium that were home-grown," it was not until the 1970s and 80s that the Colombian cartels began to rely heavily on the northern Latin American country to traffic their product into US soil (311). After the demise of the Colombian cartels in the early 90s, power shifted to the Arellano Félix and Gulf cartels in Mexico. The bloody infighting between these two cartels began in 1997 and lasted for approximately ten years. "Unfortunately, Mexican and US Law enforcement successes against the Arellano Félix and Gulf cartels appeared to strengthen the hand of their rivals.... This resulted in a wave of violence beginning in 2004" (312). While the growth of drug trafficking in the nation was a direct result of external events like the dismantling of Colombian cartels, according to José Luis Velasco, the rise of Mexican cartels also coincided with the transition to true democracy two decades ago: "In the 1990s, as democratic transition took its most decisive steps, Mexico expanded its participation in the international drug market: it consolidated its position as a producer of cannabis and heroin, substantially increased its participation in global cocaine trafficking, and became a major producer of methamphetamine. The arrival of the first non-PRI administration in 2000 did not change this situation" (8). Even before Calderón took office (Velasco published his study on drug trade in the age of Mexican democratization in 2005) it was clear that "together with counter-insurgency, anti-crime policies have led to the worse human rights abuses in Mexico.... Military involvement in Mexico's anti-drug campaigns have put key civilian functions into the hands of the military, reduced civilian control over armed forces, and undercut democratic accountability" (9). It is important to add to the list of negative effects caused by the confrontation between President Vicente Fox's government forces and the cartels is that the capture of several capos and whole drug crime rings led to a nationwide struggle for turf and power among the remaining and emergent drug cartels. The government's intervention effectively led to a three-way confrontation between different drug cartels and federal forces. Writing amid this new wave of violence, Velasco concluded that if Mexico was to decrease the drug business in the nation, it had to "adopt a new anti-drug strategy, relying more on social consensus and less on repression" (121). This, unfortunately, was not the route chosen by Calderón's government.

Shortly after swearing in as the second president in the post-PRI era, Calderón made clear that one of his main priorities would be to take the drug cartels head on. One of his "first moves on taking office was to send military troops to several states to disrupt the drug trade and apprehend narco-traffickers. And while these efforts resulted in the capture of several high-profile cartel leaders, they have also led to human rights abuses and an escalation in violence that has claimed thousands of lives" (Edmonds-Poli and Shirk, 383). Despite the constant calls for a change in strategy from all sectors of the community, in October 2011, nearly a year before he finished his six-year term, Calderón continued to push for the use of the military to fight drug cartels and try to establish peace in key areas. Also, he "stepped up calls for Mexico's Congress to approve stalled initiatives to remake state and local police forces, codify the military's role in fighting crime and broaden its powers, toughen the federal penal code and tighten laws to stop money laundering" (Archibold et al). The former president continued his national security strategy until the end of his term, and the media continued to zero in on the alarming number of violent deaths directly related to drug cartels.

While the murder of Sicilia's son came at a time of unprecedented rates of violence in the nation, it also came at a time when the writer was continuing to establish himself as an important figure in contemporary Mexican poetry. Just two years earlier, in 2009, he received the prestigious Premio Nacional de Poesía Aguascalientes for his book *Tríptico del desierto*, which was the culmination of decades of publishing poetry. His first poetry collection, *Permanencia en los puertos*, was published in 1982, and he has published nine more poetry books throughout his career. Sicilia has also published several novels, including perhaps his best known one, *El Bautista* (1991), and *El fondo de la noche* (2012), his latest one. In addition to fiction, he published two long-form essay books and two collections of his articles in the popular left-wing political magazine *Proceso*. His spirituality and fervent Catholicism, which infuse most of his opinion pieces and speeches, also permeate most of his fiction and poetry. But Jesús Antonio de la Torre Rangel, who edited the poet's first collection of *Proceso* columns in book form, is quick to point out that the author is "un católico laico de pensamiento propio; de fe plenamente adulta; por eso los artículos de Sicilia se inscriben en una línea crítica." Perhaps because of this great element of religiousness in his fiction, which effectively made him a niche writer, and despite the recent poetry award and his numerous publications, Sicilia was not widely read and was definitely not part of the small group of Mexican mainstream authors. He was also ignored by critics and academics who, around this time, began in-depth study of poets born in the 1950s. Even Krauze, who has written at length about the poet since Sicilia Ortega was killed, offhandedly—or inadvertently?—admitted he did not really know his literary work when he wrote in *Letras Libres* "It is my understanding that these intellectual and religious trends guide some of the books and magazines Sicilia has published" ("Haga que"). Perhaps his best known piece of literature is, ironically, what Sicilia announced would be his last poem. In this untitled piece the poet viscerally expresses his pain and helplessness through a vivid image of his son's violent death:

> the world is no longer worthy of the Word
> they drowned it inside of us
> the same way they choked you
> the same way they tore up your lungs. (Vestigios, 61, 2–5)[6]

When he finished reading the original version of the poem during his first public appearance after Sicilia Ortega's killing, he added: "The world is no longer worthy of the word, it is my last poem, I can no longer write any more poetry...the poetry no longer dwells in me" (Morelos).

The decision to not write any more poetry and to completely dedicate himself to activism and to being the voice of the people perhaps also responds to a larger pattern, or a greater change in Mexico, where it is no longer considered permissible or responsible to remain silent. That is, Sicilia's decision could signal a change in the structures of feeling in Mexico. The author himself can be considered a personification of the current structure of feeling, and his movement an emergent element in this structure. Williams, to show that culture is fluid and not static, proposed the concept of the structure of feeling, which he defines as "a particular quality of social experience and relationship, historically distinct from other particular qualities, which gives the sense of a generation or of a period" (131). At the heart of a structure of feeling is the dynamic between what he identifies as the residual and the emergent. The residual is something that was created in the past, but that still exists in the culture no longer as an element from the past but effectively as a present phenomenon (122). On the other hand, the emergent is what is being formed by new practices, values, and relationships in the present. Williams notes that the emergent might be more difficult to identify because there has to be differentiation "between those which are really elements of some new phase of the dominant culture...and those which are substantially alternative or oppositional to it: emergent in the strict sense, rather than merely novel" (123). In short, the structures of feeling announce the embryonic elements of a culture.[7] In Mexico, since Calderón took office, the structures of feeling have been formed by and comprised of fear, indignation, mourning, and anger, all of which are direct consequences of the drug-related violence. It was only a matter of time until all these bottled-up emotions found an escape—the peaceful protests.

The emergence of the protest can also be considered a larger, global structure of feeling, if one considers the peaceful revolutionary movements that have characterized the past few years around the world, specifically in the Middle East. The peace movement in Mexico, and the figure of Sicilia, have not gone unnoticed in the international mainstream media. *Time* magazine named "The Protester" the 2011 Person of the Year, and Javier Sicilia is among the representative people from around the world profiled in the special issue. According to *Time*, before 2011, "street protests looked like pointless emotional sideshows—obsolete, quaint, the equivalent of cavalry to mid-20th-century war" (Andersen, 58). Nonetheless, somehow, "'Massive and effective street protest' was a global oxymoron until—suddenly, shockingly—starting exactly a year ago, it became the defining trope of our times. And the protester once again became a maker of history" (58). Although in 2011 there were numerous, mostly peaceful, protests around the globe, from the United States and Chile to Egypt and Tunisia, Sicilia is adamant about not being greatly influenced by other protesters: "It's obvious there's a civic miracle going on in certain parts of the world, especially the Middle East. But I don't think I and others in this movement were really inspired by anything other than our own pain and suffering. In my case, my heart was simply responding to my son's death more than to anything going on in the Arab Spring" (Padgett).

Regardless of whether the peace movement in Mexico is part of an international trend or whether it is a purely domestic phenomenon, the events that unfolded after the poet read his last poem to the media turned Sicilia into a true organic intellectual, now even at an international level. While during the 60s and 70s it was redundant to say somebody was a progressive intellectual,[8] nowadays it seems equally redundant to identify somebody as a public intellectual, especially in Mexico, where most of the intellectual elite is at the forefront of the public arena, in television, magazines, and newspapers, not to mention their online presence through Twitter feeds, columns published in niche websites and personal blogs. However, somebody cannot solely be a public intellectual, as Said points out:

> There is no such thing as a public intellectual, since the moment you set down words and the publish them you have entered the public world. Nor is there only a public intellectual, someone who exists just as a figurehead or spokesperson or symbol of a cause, movement, or position. There is always the personal inflection and the private sensibility. And those give meaning to what is being said or written. (12)

In Sicilia, it seems that both the public and the personal, or "the private sensibility," mesh into one, which is in part the reason why he has become such a powerful representative of the violence victims in Mexico. His personal inflection became public the moment his son died and he took his grief to the streets. He turned his mourning into a national cause. Thus, he is tightly knit with the large sector of the Mexican population that has been affected one way or another by the nonstop wave of violence. Also, it seems that the poet often identifies himself more with the general public than with the intellectual elite. He appears to stand closer with the "us," the general public that does not belong with the politicians, the criminals, or the intellectuals:

> Among them, the everyday citizens—those of us who do not belong to organized crime nor the political class, and who are not white-collar criminals—, defenseless, fearful, humiliated, with miserable salaries or unemployed, without a present, bearing the weight of the rise in prices, taxes, injustice, insecurity, and in the arrogance of political parties that only seek to govern in order to continue disenfranchising us and administrating misfortune. ("El año que no termina")

Glaringly missing from these words, and from his entire column, is the figure of the intellectual. Sicilia's role in the movement and in the public arena in general is muddled. The leader himself, now neither poet, intellectual, or politician, sides instead with "everyday citizens." While this could be cynically identified as a rhetorical tool to gain more support from the general public, it also signals to his transformation into an organic intellectual who is completely committed to his cause and the violence victims.

Sicilia's personal tragedy made him acutely aware of the struggles experienced by the victims of the violence, effectively giving him a sensibility that few other Mexican intellectuals, if any, possess. His new role in Mexico is akin to Michel Foucault's definition of the specific intellectual, which he differentiated from the universal intellectual, who was "like being the consciousness/conscience of us all" (126). Unlike universal intellectuals, the life conditions of a specific intellectual allow them "a much more immediate and concrete awareness of struggles" (126). Sicilia may have inadvertently referred to his own transformation into a specific intellectual when he looked back at a time before he jumped onto the national stage, during his interview with *Time*:

> I had never thought of starting a movement or being a spokesman for anything. I'm a poet, and poets are better known for working with more obscure intuitions. But in those moments I was reminded that the life of the soul can be powerful too. My chief intuition then was that we had to give name and form to this tragedy and somehow put that into action with real citizens as a way to tell the government, "We need something new, especially new institutions to fight our lawlessness and corruption and impunity, not just that of the drug cartels but the state." (Padgett)

Foucault posited that "the 'specific' intellectual derives from...the savant or expert" (128). What else is Sicilia now an expert of but pain and grief? The poet's move into the particular arena of those not only fed up, but also directly affected by the violence in Mexico paradoxically allowed his position to take a great significance that allows him to "operate and struggle at the general level of that regime of truth so essential to the structure and functioning of our society" (132). According to Foucault, one of the most important roles of the intellectual is his position regarding truth and power, or "the battle for truth," which is "not a matter of a battle 'on behalf' of the truth but of a battle about the status of truth and the economic and political role it plays" (132). For him, the idea is not to free truth from power (since truth *gives* power), but to detach "the power of truth from the forms of hegemony, social, economic, and cultural, within which it operates at the present time" (133). Sicilia's moment of facing this battle for truth came when he first directly addressed the main protagonists in the drug war through an open letter to both politicians and drug cartel members.

The poet published his open letter in *Proceso* on April 3, a few days after his son's murder, and he titled it "Estamos hasta la madre: Carta abierta a los políticos y criminals" ("We Are Fed Up: Open Letter to Politicians and Criminals"). While the first part of the title can simply be translated as "We are fed up," the strength of the Mexican expletive "madre" is lost. Part of the reason why the letter turned so many heads at first was due to its title, not because of the strong demands and questions it was presenting. Sicilia, nonetheless, relates the expletive "madre" to its religious roots: "On the one hand, yes, hasta la madre is Mexican slang, but it has a very religious component as well. The mother, like the Virgin of Guadalupe [Mexico's Roman Catholic patroness], is sacred. To say you're hasta la madre means they've insulted our mother protector; they've committed a sacrilege. It's very strong, very Mexican, but very poetic too in its own way. Anyway, it resonated in ways that exceeded my expectations" (Padgett). The letter's call for action was clear. In it, the poet asks Mexican government officials to do the same thing that José Martí asked of politicians in the nineteenth century, "If you cannot do it, step down," and added: "That phrase should be accompanied by great citizen protests that push them, during these times of national emergency, to come together to create an agenda that unifies the nation" (*Estamos*, 161). If the rest of the country did not emulate this same mobilization, he wrote, the whole nation would continue on a path of no return. Surprisingly to many, including Sicilia, people did follow.[9] Another of the main points in his letter alludes to the corruption in all levels of government, which has led to the citizens' loss of trust in politicians, police forces, and the army: "We are fed up because the corruption in the judicial institutions generates criminal complicity and the impunity to commit it" (160). Sicilia also addresses drug traffickers directly: "Of you, criminals, we are fed up, of your violence, of your loss of honor, of your cruelty, of your senselessness.... Your violence can no longer even be pronounced because, similar to the pain and suffering that you cause, it does not even have a name or meaning. You have even lost the dignity to kill" (160–61). Although the letter was clearly intended as a direct communiqué to the government and criminal groups, it was the general public who was most affected by its powerful message. The letter was widely commented on by the media, but much more importantly, it was reprinted, quoted, read, and even performed in countless online platforms, ranging from personal blogs to YouTube videos. Perhaps what struck a chord with the general public was the fact that Sicilia's main preoccupation, or what seems to keep him going, besides the personal deep pain and indignation caused by his son's murder, is his responsibility as a public figure to not keep quiet any longer.

This same preoccupation was of course evident even before his son was killed. In a May 2010 column in *Proceso* about his love/hate relationship with the church, aptly titled "The Chaste Whore," Sicilia wrote, "The Church pains me so that up until now it had stopped me from writing about its scandals. But keeping silent when one has a public presence is yielding, and I no longer want to yield to anything" (297). This same creed has remained strong in Sicilia, whose speech in Mexico City's Zócalo on May 8, 2011—the culmination of the march from Cuernavaca to the capital—focused on the act of speaking up:

> We are here to tell ourselves and to tell them that this pain in the soul of our bodies will not be turned into hate or into more violence, but into a lever that will help us restore the love, peace, justice, dignity, and the brittle democracy that we are losing; to tell ourselves and to tell them that we still believe that it is possible for the nation to be reborn and come out of the ruins, to demonstrate to the carriers of death that we are still standing and we will not stop defending the lives of all the daughters and sons of this country, that we still believe that it is possible to rescue and reconstruct the social fabric of our towns, neighborhoods, and cities. ("Nuevo pacto")

During this same speech, Sicilia also showed his subversive and nonconformist side through some incendiary statements. For example, he named nearly all of Mexico's political parties and then said that every single one of them had ties with criminal groups and mafias throughout the nation, and added: "Without an honorable cleansing of their ranks and total commitment to political ethics, we the citizens will have to ask ourselves during the next elections, 'For which cartel and for which de facto rulers will we vote?'" Statements like this have made Sicilia an uncomfortable figure in several social spheres in Mexico, a kind of intellectual who is not "there to make his/her audiences feel good: the whole point is to be embarrassing, contrary, even unpleasant" (Said, 12). This unpleasantness is also evident when his discourse turns into what could be described as Christian anarchism, surely due to the influence from the Austrian priest Ivan Illich, with whom the Mexican poet had a very close relationship, as has been noted by Krauze.[10]

The strange marriage between anarchism and religion, especially the highly organized Catholic church, has been quite evident in Sicilia in his opinion pieces and public declarations about the 2012 presidential elections, of which he said he would rather have a no-vote than pick one of the political parties (Mandujano).

The anarchist tones during the poet's speeches and interviews have not gone unnoticed by political analysts such as Carlos Elizondo Mayer-Serna, who on the Televisión Azteca show *Entre 3* tells Sicilia that in his speeches he seems to advocate for the complete removal of the state, which the pundit considers an erroneous solution to the problem because he believes what the nation needs is "more state." During the interview, the activist tones down his public discourse a bit and responds that his position regarding the government has been constantly misunderstood, but still affirms he is an anarchist:

> People sometimes misunderstand me. I would like for the state to be re-established. That is, I am evidently an anarchist, but I live in a republic, and I know the value of a state in a republic. When my son is killed they tell me, "What are you going to do?" Well, I'm going to complain to the state that they did not fulfill the fundamental duty of a republic, which is to take care of the security of its citizens.... But I don't think everything is so muddled that we need to re-establish it. [Change] has to start with the political parties. They need to clean house.

If his anarchist tones seem to bother some of the conservative political analysts, his fervent Catholicism has certainly been uncomfortable to more than one left-wing politician. For example, Sicilia drew a lot of criticism after he published a column in which he criticized PRD 2012 presidential candidate Andrés Manuel López Obrador[11] and his concept of "an amorous republic." López Obrador, as part of his presidential platform, proposed a "new way of doing politics" that would be shaped by honesty, justice, and love: "Honesty and justice to improve living conditions and reach calm and public peace; and love to promote the good and reach happiness." In *Proceso*, the poet opines that a republic can never be amorous because those two concepts are contradictory:

> Love is the opposite of power and in consequence it cannot order or be ordered, nor can it rule or be ruled. It is, as Christ demonstrated, a free act of liberty foreign to any kind of institution. Whoever loves does not impose, does not force, does not make shady dealings, it is pure gratitude and gift; it even is incapable to remedy something—Christ himself, the most obvious face of love, was incapable of avoiding been killed, he did not build any perfect kingdom, and he could not even save one his best friends, Judas. ("¿Es posible")

Perhaps the strongest response he received from PRD came from Senator Carlos Sotelo García, who accused the poet—and "the catholic president" Calderón—of bringing religion into the political arena (79). The senator also noted how in Sicilia the private becomes unapologetically public: "Introducing concepts foreign to the political arena leads us to confuse public life with private life.... your religious concepts are completely respectable, but they are private concepts about your way of living and of assuming your Christianity, which is altogether commendable and worthy of admiration" (79). Careful to not appear to be opposing any of the other ideals that the poet stands for, Sotelo García ends his letter wishing the poet to never let his voice stop resounding for peace and justice. Sicilia, as unfazed as always, responded to the senator through a letter to the editor in *Proceso* in which he tells Sotelo García that he forgets López Obrador is too a catholic, and that love "even in the confusing sense that he uses it" is still a direct descendent from the Gospel. He also, once again, completely distances himself from all candidates and political parties, and adds that due to having received so many insults from López Obrador's followers he is now even more convinced there cannot be an amorous republic. He also chastises the senator for continuing to ignore and never mention, like many other politicians, the victims of Mexico's war (Letter, 79–80).

Sicilia has been an uncomfortable figure even to his own movement. During one of the meetings between the activist and Calderón, the poet hugged the Mexican leader, an action that caused a small uproar among the activist's followers and some of the movement leaders. The poet, unruffled, expressed his sadness regarding those who believe that "entering a dialogue means to give in; that to talk loud and clear, without ending it in the humiliation of the adversary, but with a hug, is to fail" (*Estamos*, 173). Followers and detractors alike have also criticized the activist for simply demanding peace but not offering concrete solutions to the violence problem—as well as for allegedly not achieving any tangible results from his marches. In reality, his movement has certainly had an impact not only among the general public, but with the political class too, including former president Calderón. When during the previously cited *Entre 3* news show a political analyst pressed him about not having concrete goals besides asking for peace or the complete removal of the government, the poet noted that Calderón, as a result of the movement, had finally admitted that the missing persons figures had been underestimated:

> Behind those perverse euphemisms like "collateral casualties," for me there was evidence. It was evident that they were human beings who were suffering. Then when I stepped out with the movement this enormous pain could be visualized, and that is the first thing that the president is faced with, a reality that he had not seen, right? "Oh, they have a name and a last name, and not all of them are guilty. And even if they are guilty they are human beings. What is going on?" And it is only until this dialogue happens that he realizes the dimension of

the victims, that they embody a different kind of pain, right? And that those victims also have a name and a last name, and that they left a huge empty hole because when a son is killed it is awful, incredibly painful, something that will never end. (*Entre 3*)

The criticism that the poet does not offer any concrete solutions other than a complete house cleaning of the government is perhaps moot because all along the movement was created to humanize victims and to organize the public to ask the government and criminal groups for a ceasefire. In his speeches, articles, and interviews, Sicilia often goes back to emphasize the pain suffered by the people. For example, in the *Entre 3* show, the poet tells the hosts that the pain for his son is never going to go away, but at least he knows what happened to him, and he had the chance to have a wake and mourn him. That is not the case with "the abyss" confronted by family members of the "desaparecidos," or those declared missing: "They don't know if they are alive. And if they are alive, they don't know what conditions they are living in. And if they are dead, they don't know where they are or what happened to them or what was done to them." While some of his demands may appear too idealistic and unachievable, he has made it clear that he is willing to risk everything for his beliefs and probably nothing will keep him quiet anymore. Quitting poetry and taking to the streets resulted in him becoming a true organic or particular intellectual, one who is now easily recognized and respected by most Mexicans. He made his grief public and he took under his arm all those affected by the armed conflict.

In the introduction to the book that compiles some of Sicilia's most memorable columns, *Proceso* director Rafael Rodríguez Castañeda writes: "Javier Sicilia's battle is public. In private, we, the readers, can dialogue with his ideas and come together around the pain that is hurting all Mexicans" (10). Sicilia most likely would disagree with the editor's remarks about readers responding to him only in a private arena because he has made it clear that it is no longer a time for keeping the pain and indignation private. Instead, it is time for people to speak up and take their anger and frustration to the streets. During the Ejército Zapatista de Liberación Nacional's marches in Mexico City led by Subcomandante Marcos in the 1990s, one of the most memorable chants was "We are all Marcos." The participants of the current peace movement do not need to proclaim they are all Sicilia. It is already understood. It always was. True leftist or not, poet or activist or both, catholic or anarchist, it does not matter. He is still just a man in mourning. A man who mourns his son and his nation, and who is seeking peace and dignity. He is an intellectual whose private sensibilities openly and unapologetically inform his public discourse. He is asking for accountability and justice, and for that, above all else, is why Sicilia has a following.

**Notes**

1. All translations are my own.
2. By comparison, it is estimated that in 2007 there were less than 2,500 drug-related deaths in Mexico. And although some news outlets reported that in 2011 there was a slight decrease in the number of killings, since 2006 the deaths increased considerably year after year. The death toll has continued to increase even after December 2012, when PRI President Enrique Peña Nieto took office. It is estimated that during the first eight months of his presidency there had been more than 13,000 drug-related deaths.
3. Here, Krauze refers to the October 2, 1968, killing of protesters in the Plaza de las Tres Culturas, in the Tlatelolco subdivision of Mexico City, which took place days before the opening ceremonies of the Summer Olympic Games hosted by Mexico.
4. Miranda de Wallace, the Mexico City schoolteacher-turned-activist, in 2005 began searching for her 36-year-old kidnapped son after authorities showed no real interest, or competence, to solve the crime. Her son was killed during his captivity, but for years the mother continued a relentless search for the kidnappers. She bought billboards in major arteries of the Mexican capital displaying the names and faces of the suspects, and began to stage protests outside Los Pinos and other government buildings until she was finally allowed to meet with President Calderón. By December 2010, thanks to the activist's efforts, police arrested the last of the six suspects. In January 2012, the PAN announced Miranda de Wallace as the party's candidate for the presidency of Mexico City. She lost the election, garnering only 13.6 percent of the votes.

   Martí's son, Fernando, was 14 years old when he was kidnapped in July 2008 on his way to school as he travelled with his driver and a bodyguard in an armored luxury vehicle. Kidnappers asked for a large sum of money in exchange for the son of the Mexican sporting goods magnate, but several days after approximately $2 million were delivered, the teenager's body was found in the trunk of an abandoned vehicle. "In August 2008, the abduction and brutal murder of Fernando Martí... triggered a nationwide series of demonstrations involving hundreds of thousands of people. The Mexican public was particularly outraged upon discovery of the involvement of law enforcement—including federal police officers—in the kidnapping ring" (Edmonds-Poli and Shirk, 383). Since then, Martí has championed stronger sentences for kidnappers and is the president of México

SOS, a nonprofit organization dedicated to promoting better public security in the nation.
5. The French Connection refers specifically, according to Edmonds-Poli and Shirk, to the drug trade in the mid-twentieth century that was "largely controlled by the Cosa Nostra, Italian mobsters with ties stretching from Turkish producers to French refiners and ultimately into US markets" (311). The authors explain that US law enforcement efforts and the relocation of production centers led to the fall of the European-run drug trade.
6. The Spanish original reads: "el mundo ya no es digno de la Palabra / nos la ahogaron adentro / como te asfixiaron / como te desgarraron a ti los pulmones / y el dolor no se me aparta." This is quoted from the definitive version of the poem published by Sicilia in 2013. It reflects small changes the poet made to the version he first read in 2011.
7. To simplify his concept a bit, Williams makes an analogy between language and the structures of feeling. According to him, although there is continuity in languages, throughout time words and expressions are modified, which is why each generation speaks differently. "What really changes is something quite general, over a wide range, and the description that often fits the challenge best is the literary term 'style'" (131), he explains, adding that this same idea can be applied to fashion, architecture, and other social aspects.
8. For an excellent analysis of the role of intellectuals and writers in Latin America during the 1960s and 70s, see Gilman.
9. Although the Movimiento por la Paz did not formally begin until late April—when Sicilia called for the first march—the movement's seed was planted when the writer called for mass mobilizations in his letter. There were two major marches led by Sicilia, one from Cuernavaca to Mexico City in May 2011, and the Marcha del Consuelo, which left Cuernavaca in early June and arrived in Ciudad Juarez a week later. Thousands joined the march, and many more would walk alongside the poet and other participants as the movement passed through several cities and towns on its way to the northern Mexican border. The group has continued to organize marches around the nation, and Sicilia led a march through several US cities in 2012 to protest the trafficking of weapons into Mexico and the Merida Initiative.
10. In its most basic form, Christian anarchists believe in one true source of authority, God. The Mexican historian notes that Sicilia "was a disciple of Ivan Illich, the Austrian Jesuit priest and philosopher who, during the postwar decades, wrote and preached a kind of Christian (and highly socially conscious) anarchism, close to that of Leo Tolstoy and Mohandas K. Gandhi. Illich spent years in Cuernavaca, where he and Mr. Sicilia met" ("Can This Poet?").
11. López Obrador, or AMLO as he is known in Mexico, is considered by many leftists to be the true winner of the 2006 presidential elections. Calderón beat him by less than 1 percent of the vote amid allegations

of fraud, which caused massive protests in support of the leftist candidate. After Calderón officially took office, "AMLO himself refused to stand down, instead establishing a parallel 'legitimate' government, complete with cabinet and policy initiatives" (Edmonds-Poli and Shirk, 381).

**Works Cited**

Andersen, Kurt. "The Protester." *Time*. December 26, 2011: 56–89. Print.
Archibold, C. Randal, Damien Cave, and Elisabeth Malkin. "Mexico's President Works to Lock in Drug War Tactics." *New York Times*. October 11, 2011. http://www.nytimes.com/2011/10/16/world/americas/calderon-defends-militarized-response-to-mexicos-drug-war.html?_r=0. Web.
Booth, William. "In Mexico, 12,000 Killed in Drug Violence in 2011." *Washington Post*. January 2, 2012. http://www.washingtonpost.com/world/in-mexico-12000-killed-in-drug-violence-in-2011/2012/01/02/gIQAcGUdWP_story.html. Web.
de la Torre Rangel, Jesús Antonio. "Algunas líneas teóricas del movimiento por la paz, la justicia y la reconstitución del país." *Crisol Plural*. May 5, 2011. http://crisolplural.com/2011/05/07/algunas-lineas-teoricas-del-movimiento-por-la-paz-la-justicia-y-la-reconstitucion-del-pais/. Web.
Edmonds-Poli, Emily and David A. Shirk. *Contemporary Mexican Politics*. Lanham: Rowman & Littlefield Publishers, 2009. Print.
*Entre 3*. Televisión Azteca. XHDF-TV, Mexico City, October 24, 2011. http://www.azteca.com/capitulos/entre3/76737/javier-sicilia-y-su-marcha-por-la-paz. Web.
Foucault, Michel. *Power*. Edited by James D. Faubion. New York: New Press, 2000. Print.
Gilman, Claudia. *Entre la pluma y el fusil: Debates y dilemas del escritor revolucionario en América Latina*. Buenos Aires: Siglo Veintiuno Editores, 2003. Print.
Gómora, Doris. "Narco controla 71.5% de municipios del país." *El Universal*. January 2, 2012. http://www.eluniversal.com.mx/nacion/192540.html. Web.
Guadarrama, Óscar. "Una extorsión originó el homicidio de Sicilia: autoridades mexicanas." *CNN México*. May 10, 2011. http://mexico.cnn.com/nacional/2011/05/10/una-extorsion-origino-el-homicidio-de-sicilia-autoridades-mexicanas. Web.
Hoare, Quintin and Geoffrey Nowell Smith. "The Intellectuals." Introduction. *Selections from the Prison Notebooks of Antonio Gramsci*. New York: International Publishers, 1971. 3–4. Print.
Krauze, Enrique. "Can This Poet Save Mexico?" *New York Times*. October 1, 2011. http://www.nytimes.com/2011/10/02/opinion/sunday/can-this-poet-save-mexico.html. Web.
———. "Haga que esto dure." *Letras Libres*. May 16, 2011. http://www.letraslibres.com/blogs/blog-de-la-redaccion/haga-que-esto-dure. Web.

Mandujano, Isaín. "Ve Sicilia escenario ignominioso para México en 2012." *Proceso*. January 1, 2012. http://www.proceso.com.mx/?p=293343. Web.
Morelos, Rubicela. "La poesía ya no existe en mí." *La Jornada*. December 3, 2011. http://www.jornada.unam.mx/2011/04/03/politica/002n2pol. Web.
Padgett, Tim. "Why I protest: Javier Sicilia of Mexico." *Time Magazine*. December 14, 2011. http://content.time.com/time/specials/packages/article/0,28804,2101745_2102138_2102238,00.html. Web.
Rodríguez Castañeda, Rafael. Prologue. *Estamos Hasta La Madre*. By Javier Sicilia. Mexico City: Temas de Hoy, 2011. Print.
Said, Edward W. *Representations of the Intellectual: The 1993 Reith Lectures*. New York: Pantheon Books, 1994. Print.
Sicilia, Javier. "El año que no termina." *Proceso*. December 31, 2011. http://www.proceso.com.mx/?p=293305. Web.
———. *El Bautista*. Xalapa, Mexico: Universidad Veracruzana, 1991. Print.
———. *El fondo de la noche*. Mexico City: Random House Mondadori, 2012. Print.
———. "¿Es posible una república amorosa?" *Proceso*. December 22, 2011. http://www.proceso.com.mx/?p=292394. Web.
———. *Estamos Hasta La Madre*. Mexico City: Temas de Hoy, 2011. Print.
———. *La Presencia Desierta: Poesía 1982–2004*. Mexico City: Fondo de Cultura Económica, 2004. Print.
———. Letter. *Proceso*. January 8, 2012: 79–80. Print.
———. "Nuevo pacto o fractura nacional." *Proceso*. May 7, 2011. http://hemeroteca.proceso.com.mx/?page_id=278958&a51dc26366d99bb5fa29cea4747565fec=269046&rl=wh. Web.
———. *Tríptico Del Desierto*. Mexico City: Ediciones Biblioteca Era, 2009. Print.
———. *Vestigios*. Mexico City: Ediciones Era, 2013. Print.
Sotelo García, Carlos. Letter. *Proceso*. January 8, 2012: 79. Print.
Velasco, José L. *Insurgency, Authoritarianism, and Drug Trafficking in Mexico's "Democratization."* New York: Routledge, 2005. Print.
Williams, Raymond. *Marxism and Literature*. Oxford: Oxford University Press, 1977. Print.

# Contributors

Born and raised in Mexico, **Javier Barroso** is a fourth-year PhD student in the Spanish and Portuguese Department at the University of Kansas. He is specializing in twentieth and twenty-first century Latin American literature with an emphasis in Mexican and Southern Cone narrative. His proposed dissertation focuses on representations of World War II and Nazism in the cultural production of the Southern Cone and Mexico. Besides his academic experience, Barroso is a ten-year journalism veteran with experience as a reporter and editor in two major newspapers in Texas.

**Debra A. Castillo** (coeditor) is Stephen H. Weiss Presidential Fellow, Emerson Hinchliff Professor of Hispanic Studies, and professor of Comparative Literature at Cornell University, and has been elected president of the International Latin American Studies Association. Her most recent books are *Re-dreaming America* and *Cartographies of Affect: Across Borders in South Asia and the Americas*. She specializes in contemporary narrative from the Spanish-speaking world, gender studies, cultural theory, and visual studies. She is author, editor, or translator of ten books, including *Talking Back: Strategies for a Latin American Feminist Literary Criticism* (1992), *Easy Women: Sex and Gender in Modern Mexican Fiction* (1998), and (cowritten with María Socorro Tabuenca Córdoba) *Border Women: Writing from La Frontera* (2002).

**Stuart A. Day** (coeditor) is associate professor and chair of the Department of Spanish and Portuguese at the University of Kansas. He studied at Northern Arizona University, the University of Arizona, and Cornell University. His first book, *Staging Politics in Mexico: The Road to Neoliberalism*, was published in 2004. Day has also published anthologies of Mexican plays and coedited, with Jacqueline E. Bixler, *El Teatro de Rascón Banda: voces en el umbral*. He has published book chapters with several presses, as well as articles, play introductions, and interviews in a variety of journals. Day is the managing editor of the *Latin American Theatre Review* and the director of LATR Books.

**Oswaldo Estrada** is an associate professor of Latin American Literature at the University of North Carolina at Chapel Hill, and editor of *Romance Notes*. His research focuses on the rewritings of history, historical memory, gender formation and transgression, and the construction of dissident identities in contemporary Mexico and Peru. He has published numerous articles and book chapters in Latin America, Spain, and the United States on colonial and contemporary literature. He is the author of *La imaginación novelesca. Bernal Díaz entre géneros y épocas* (2009), and the editor and coauthor of *Cristina Rivera Garza. Ningún crítico cuenta esto...* (2010).

**David William Foster** is past chair of the Department of Languages and Literatures and Regents' Professor of Spanish, and Women and Gender Studies at Arizona State University. His research interests focus on urban culture in Latin America, with emphasis on issues of gender construction and sexual identity. He has written extensively on Argentine narrative and theater, and he has held teaching appointments in Argentina, Brazil, Chile, and Uruguay. His most recent publications include *Violence in Argentine Literature; Cultural Responses to Tyranny* (1995), *Cultural Diversity in Latin American Literature* (1994), *Contemporary Argentine Cinema* (1992), and *Gay and Lesbian Themes in Latin American Writing* (1991). He is also the editor of *Latin American Writers on Gay and Lesbian Themes; A Bio-Critical Sourcebook* (1994). *Sexual Textualities: Essays on Queer/ing Latin American Writing* was published in 1997. He is the author of *Mexico City in Contemporary Mexican Cinema*.

**Emily Hind** specializes in Mexican studies at the University of Wyoming and has published a book on Mexican women intellectuals (*Boob Lit*, 2010), a book of interviews with 20 Mexican writers born in the 1970s (*La generación XXX*, 2013), and a collection of interviews with 15 Mexican women writers (*Quince escritoras*, 2003). She has written numerous articles on Mexican literature and film, with concentrations on topics such as children's literature, pirates and celebrity culture, and the genre of the essay. She is currently drafting articles on drug trafficking and the theory of drugs, ageism, and specters, and the Mexican novel and disability studies. Hind's analysis on lesbianism in the work of Rosario Castellanos won the Feministas Unidas Essay Contest 2005.

**María Cristina Pons** is associate professor of Latina/o and American Literature at the University of California, Los Angeles (UCLA). Her main publications include *Memorias del olvido* (1996); *Más allá de las fronteras del lenguaje* (1998), and *Delirios de grandeza. Los mitos argentinos: memoria, identidad y cultura* (2006). She has also published several articles on diverse authors such as Cortázar, Piglia, Monsiváis, del Paso, Saer, and O. Soriano, as well as on neoliberalism and literature, and the Argentinean historical novel (*Historia de la literatura argentina*, 2000). She is currently working on Latinas and Latin American women writers from a comparative perspective.

**Elvira Sánchez-Blake** is associate professor of Latin American literature and culture at Michigan State University. Her interests include Mexican and Colombian contemporary literature and theater. She is the author of *Patria se escribe con sangre* (2000), and coauthor of the critical edition, *El universo literario de Laura Restrepo* (2007). She has published numerous articles in professional journals and magazines.

**Ignacio M. Sánchez Prado** is associate professor of Spanish and International and Area Studies at Washington University in Saint Louis. He is the author of *El canon y sus formas. La reinvención de Harold Bloom y sus lecturas hispanoamericanas* (2002), *Naciones intelectuales. Las fundaciones de la modernidad literaria mexicana 1917–1959* (2009), winner of the LASA Mexico 2010 Humanities Book Award, *Intermitencias americanistas. Ensayos y estudios académicos 2004–2010* (2012), and *Screening Neoliberalism. Mexican Cinema 1988–2012* (2014). He has edited seven scholarly collections and published over 40 scholarly articles on Mexican culture and on Latin American cultural theory.

**María Socorro Tabuenca C.** has a PhD in Hispanic Languages and Literatures at the State University of New York at Stony Brook. She is a professor of Spanish and chair at the Department of Languages and Linguistics at the University of Texas at El Paso. Her publications and articles include her research interests: border Mexican women writers, borders' theory, US-Mexico border's representations in film, and also different representations on the Ciudad Juarez femicide.

# Index

24 Horas, 96

abortion, 140, 145–7, 158
abuse, 135, 140, 142, 145, 150, 152, 167–73, 177, 190, 210, 221–2
academic, 2, 4, 9, 11, 25–6, 30, 39, 46, 65, 97, 104, 108, 237
accountability, 24, 103, 108, 200, 218, 220–1, 232
Acosta, 47, 67
activist, 2, 4, 10, 33, 66, 79, 106, 123, 132, 140, 142, 144, 146–7, 149–50, 152, 156, 159, 161, 164, 174, 176, 218, 220, 229–32
advocacy, 10, 31, 33, 139, 141, 145, 152, 155
agency, 7, 10, 24, 72, 109, 11–12, 139, 152, 155, 159, 163, 166, 168, 177, 179, 189, 204
Aguilar Camín, Héctor, 6, 15, 25, 27, 33, 35–7, 40–3
Aguilar Rivera José Antonio, 19, 40, 102, 108, 114
Alatorre, Javier, 111
Albadalejo, Anna, 167, 170
alienation, 46
AMLO, 113, 117, 128, 134, 135, 233–4
Amor, Guadalupe, 95, 98, 112
anarchist, 12, 203, 228–9, 231 233
Anguiano, Arturo, 36, 41
Arreola, Juan José, 95, 97–8, 112
assassination, 17, 157

autochthonous, 164
autonomy, 18–19, 74
awareness, 51, 54, 143, 163–5, 170, 173, 175–6, 185, 226

Babb, Sarah, 19, 41
Barroso, Javier, 11, 12, 217, 237
Beltrán, Rosa, 24, 41, 115
Benda, Julien, 19, 153
Benítez, Fernando, 72
Berghe, Vanden, 44, 201, 203, 205–6, 208, 214, 216
Berlin, Isaiah, 19, 26, 39
Berman, Sabina, 5, 6, 9, 10, 12, 13, 114, 120, 122, 106, 117–19, 125–38
binational, 30, 34, 120
Bixler, Jacqueline E., 119, 137, 237
Blanco, José Joaquín, 59–60
*Bohemios*, 73, 92
border, 1, 10, 31, 40, 114, 136, 139, 155–7, 159, 161, 176, 187–8, 190, 192, 194, 217, 233, 237, 239
Borges, Jorge Luis, 75
Brito, Alejandro, 80, 89
bureaucratic, 174
Butterfield, Herbert, 25, 41

*cacique*, 171
Cal y Arena, 22, 40–4, 115
Calderón, Felipe, 12, 35, 118, 122, 124, 131, 134–7, 217, 220–2, 224, 229, 230, 232–4

Camp, Roderic A., 2, 13, 19, 38, 41, 121, 137, 157
campesino, 197, 208
caravan, 6, 15
Cárdenas, Cuahutemoc, 18, 23, 113, 129, 137, 156
Cardoso y Aragón, Luis, 61
cartel, 1, 3, 13, 217–19, 221–2, 226, 228
Casa Amiga A.C., 140, 145, 153–5, 158–60
Castañeda, Jorge, 5, 6, 15–19, 22, 30–41, 43, 59, 68, 131, 136–8, 231, 235
Castañeda, Quetzil, 59, 68
Castañón, Adolfo, 71–2, 89, 91
Castillo, Debra A., 1, 7, 8, 45, 169, 178, 212, 214, 237
Catholic, 79, 98, 109, 120, 146, 159, 222, 226–31
*caudillos*, 24, 39, 42
change, 7, 9–11, 18, 20–1, 23, 31, 40, 44, 80, 87, 101, 108, 110, 112, 119, 122–4, 131, 163, 166–7, 169, 176, 189, 207, 213, 221–2, 229
characteristics, 77, 85, 88–9, 96, 121, 144
chauvinism, 72
Chávez Cano, Esther, 10, 139–55, 157–61
Che Guevara, 33, 41, 197
Chiapas, 63, 81, 110, 163–5, 167–70, 172–5, 177–9, 197–8, 216
chronicle, 5, 46, 59, 66, 71, 73–4, 76–8, 80–91, 98, 125, 156, 197, 214, 215–16
Ciudad Juárez, 5, 10, 68, 120, 139–42, 145, 147–60, 163, 187, 239
civil, 3, 15, 18–20, 25–9, 33, 73, 83, 87, 110, 120, 123, 125, 127–9, 135, 144, 149–50, 158, 170, 175, 198, 201, 202–3, 218–19, 221
Civil Resistance Movement, 120

class, 2, 15, 18, 21–2, 31–3, 35, 37–8, 40, 43, 51, 65, 76, 79, 83–4, 98–100, 111–13, 127, 131, 136, 141, 143, 157, 161, 175, 178, 186, 190, 198–9, 212, 219, 225, 230
Clouthier, Tatiana, 33
cocaine, 220–1
COCEI, 48, 58, 68
Colectivo Cine Mujer, 183
Colosio, Luis Donaldo, 39, 40
columnist, 9, 72, 96
commentary, 39, 97, 119, 182
commission, 125, 154, 172, 21
communities, 49, 59, 88, 156, 161, 163, 164–78, 206–7, 210
Conant, Jeff, 204, 214
condemnation, 80, 152
consumption, 48, 50, 65, 85, 108, 115, 124, 163
controversy, 107, 173, 206
Conversations, 200–4, 216
Corona, Ignacio, 200, 214, 216
Coronado, Irasema, 159
corruption, 81, 117, 119, 124, 130, 139, 143, 189, 201, 210, 220, 226–7
Covarrubias, Miguel, 45, 60
credibility, 3, 19, 28, 36, 96, 113
Creel, Santiago, 36
Crespo, José Antonio, 134, 137
criticism, critic, 15, 22–4, 28, 38, 74, 81, 97, 99–102, 104, 111, 119, 122, 127, 132–3, 140, 150, 155, 160, 210, 223, 229, 231, 237
criticize, 6, 12, 35, 81–2, 98, 110, 132, 149–50, 202, 210–11, 229–30
Cruz, Wilfrido, 62
Cuevas, Gabriela, 104
Cuevas, José Luis, 72
cultura mexicana, 45, 195
cultural, 5, 8, 11, 16, 19, 21, 25, 27–8, 34, 36–7, 45–6, 49–51, 58–9, 64–5, 69, 72–4, 76–9, 81–3, 86, 92, 116, 118–19,

125, 132, 136–7, 144, 155, 160–1, 163–9, 171, 174–9, 198, 200, 206, 212, 214, 226, 237–9
*curandero*, 81

Day, Stuart A., 6, 8–10, 12, 13, 117, 136–8, 237
De Iturbide, Agustín, 212
De la Campa, Román, 204, 214
De la Cruz, Petrona, 5, 10, 11, 117, 164, 165–79
debate, 1, 6, 12, 31–3, 37, 43, 66, 72, 90–2, 107, 128, 137, 145, 173, 206, 214–18, 234
Debate Feminista, 72, 90, 92
defeat, 18, 39, 43, 112, 154, 172, 201
degree, 5–6, 8, 19, 29, 61, 83, 96, 100, 181
Del Paso, Fernando, 42, 239
demagogy, 82
democracy, 11, 15, 22, 23, 27–9, 31, 32, 34–6, 39, 41, 44, 79, 119, 127, 129, 138, 144, 157, 160, 201, 203, 203, 209, 210, 220, 221, 228
democratization, 20, 21, 26, 29, 30, 35, 221, 235
demonstration, 58, 121, 123–4, 126, 128, 132, 134, 152–3, 160, 218, 232
desaparecidos, 231
designation, 40
Díaz Ordáz, Gustavo, 212
Díaz, Porfirio, 21, 58, 66, 84, 129, 212
dignity, 80, 97, 165, 176–7, 202, 213, 227–8, 232
discrimination, 153, 172, 175, 203, 210, 212
dispossessed, 143
dissident, 79, 81, 87, 203, 238
diversity, 78, 81, 87, 130, 132, 206, 211, 238
documentary, 47, 67, 120, 126, 134, 181–3, 191, 193

dogma, 7, 15, 21, 28, 30, 81, 129, 141, 146
domination, 20, 23, 83, 138, 188, 201
Don Durito, 11, 198, 200–5, 211, 213, 216
Dworkin, Ruth, 52–3, 64

Echeverría Álvarez, Luis, 27
Editorial Clío, 25
Egan, Linda, 78, 89, 91
*El Día*, 72
*El Diario*, 139–41, 153, 156–7, 159–60
*El Financiero*, 200
*El Norte*, 72, 153
El Paso, 10, 24, 156, 159, 239
*El Santo*, 76
*El Universal*, 72, 88–91, 125, 137, 234
election, 1, 6, 9, 12, 16–18, 20, 29, 32–4, 39–40, 82, 103–4, 106, 109, 113, 117–18, 120–5, 127–30, 132–6, 140, 156, 201, 228, 232–3
elimination, 35
elite, 4, 19, 21–2, 41, 49, 65, 72, 78, 97–8, 131, 212, 224–5
emergent, 221, 223–4
Ensler, Eve, 142, 160
*Entre 3*, 228, 230–1, 234
Epstein, Joseph, 96, 114
equality, 10, 20–1, 29, 32, 79, 81, 123, 135, 197, 203, 212
Erdman, Harley, 164, 177, 179
*Estamos*, 227, 230, 235
*Excélsior*, 72, 100, 114
exile, 143–4, 157, 161, 198, 203–4, 215
EZLN, 198, 203, 208–9, 214–15

FAVNET, 151
Felipe, Liliana, 120, 122–4, 133, 138
Félix, María, 76, 187
femicide, 140–1, 147–8, 152–5, 159–61, 239

feminicidio, 147
feminidad, 168
feminine, 9, 45, 56, 80, 96–7, 99, 101, 103, 112, 133, 147, 168, 185, 190
femininity, 95, 99, 168, 187
feminism, 89–90, 109, 176
Feminist, 3, 10–1, 45, 55, 58, 61, 67, 72, 79–80, 89–92, 109, 135, 140–2, 151–2, 155, 157, 159, 161, 168, 174, 176, 181–3, 185–6, 189, 191, 237–8
feminization, 97, 99
feminize, 9, 95–7, 99–100, 112–13
film, 10–1, 47, 57, 59, 66–8, 83, 86, 96, 105, 134, 137, 178, 181–94, 238–9
folklore, 45, 59, 163
FOMMA, 163–79
Foran, John, 203, 214
forum, 11, 15, 73, 78, 164, 182, 189
Foster, David William, 10, 11, 45, 67, 68, 181, 191–4, 238
Fox, Vicente, 12, 33, 34, 40, 120, 131, 135–7, 154, 193, 212, 213, 221
Franco, Jean, 78, 91
fraud, 12, 20, 32, 83, 118, 126–7, 129, 132–4, 136, 142, 144, 156, 211, 234
fraude, 134, 137, 144
free-market, 21, 34, 201
Fuentes, Carlos, 5–8, 12, 13, 16, 19, 25, 27, 28, 30, 37, 42, 44, 63, 69, 72, 75, 88, 91, 187, 199

Gage, 47, 48, 68
garantías individuales, 146
García Canclini, Néstor, 77, 163, 179
García Hernández, Arturo, 103, 109, 115
gay, 47, 50, 56–7, 66, 78–81, 87, 90, 111, 120, 135, 186, 194, 203, 211, 213, 238
generation, 2, 7, 19, 30, 45, 51, 67, 81, 113, 169, 173, 223, 233

genre, 8, 50, 76–7, 89, 101–2, 126, 135, 157, 163, 168, 182, 214, 216, 238
Girona, Nuria, 213–14
Giroux, Henry, 42, 132, 137–8
globalization, 13, 32, 50, 78, 85–6, 200, 203, 211
González, Luis, 25
governance, 35, 36
government, 3–4, 12, 15, 17, 19–20, 29, 34, 115, 121, 123, 127–8, 198–200, 202, 206, 210, 212, 217–21, 226–7, 229–32, 234
Granados Chapa, Miguel Ángel, 98–9, 113
Grupo 8 de Marzo, 140, 142, 145, 149–51, 158
Grupo Atlacomulco, 36
Grupo San Ángel, 33, 36
guerilla, 197
Guillermoprieto, Alma, 200, 214
Gullén Vicente, Rafael Sebastián, 198

Hall, Stuart, 12, 13
health, 59, 90, 131, 144, 159, 165, 172
Henck, Nick, 198, 215
Henestrosa, Andrés, 5, 7, 8, 45, 46, 48–55, 60–8
Henríquez Ureña, Pedro, 118
heritage, 51, 53, 73–4, 163, 167, 172, 197, 209
Hernández, Felipe, 104, 115
Hernández, Jorge F., 97, 115
heterosexist, 55, 183, 189
heterosexual, 194
heterosexuality, 194
Hidaldo, Miguel, 24
hierarchies, 51, 84–5
Hiller, Patrick T., 203, 215
Hind, Emily, 8, 9, 66–8, 95, 238
*¡Hola!*, 108, 115
homophobia, 79–80, 183
homosexual, 57, 66, 80, 138, 202, 212

homosexualismo, 57
homosexuality, 80, 212
Howitz, Daniel, 97, 115
Huave, 51–2, 67
human rights, 5, 12, 79–81, 86, 123, 135, 140, 148–9, 151, 154, 164, 174, 176, 210, 216–17, 220–2

ideology, 10, 23, 26, 30, 34, 167, 197, 209, 219
IFE, 15, 128, 129
illegitimacy, 52
illegitimate, 100, 103
immigrants, 41
immigration, 2, 35, 65, 172
impoverishment, 186
impunity, 10, 12, 24, 73, 139, 142, 149, 150, 155, 226, 227
incrimination, 80
independence, 18, 26, 36, 49, 50, 54, 56, 67, 74
indigenous, 7, 8, 11, 46, 49–52, 58, 59, 62, 64–5, 78, 81, 86, 110, 123, 163–5, 167–77, 179, 197, 199, 202, 203–11, 212
indignation, 47, 81, 106, 224, 227, 231
inequality, 20, 21, 32, 81, 197, 203, 212
influence, 4, 6, 9, 11, 26, 32, 36, 39, 58, 62, 72, 82, 120–1, 123, 125, 128, 132, 165–6, 168, 173–6, 189, 219, 224, 228
infrastructure, 59, 65, 181
injustice, 10, 106, 135, 140, 143–4, 155, 170, 203, 208, 225
insemination, 158
insurgency, 81, 204, 214, 221, 235
international, 1, 5, 7–8, 10–1, 19, 21, 31, 45–6, 50, 57–9, 61, 65–7, 78, 104, 137, 139, 151–4, 156, 159–60, 167, 169, 174, 176, 178, 181–3, 190, 193, 198, 200, 221, 224, 234, 237, 239
Isthmus, 49, 50, 56, 64, 66–7
Istmeño, 48, 53

Istmo, 49–50
Iturbide, Graciela, 8, 46–8, 54, 56, 59–61, 67

journalist, 1, 15, 30, 47, 56, 60, 72–4, 81, 89, 98, 102, 105, 113, 126, 140, 144, 200
Juárez, Isabel, 5, 10, 164–9, 171–7
Juchitán, 7, 8, 45–50, 53–61, 64, 66–8
justice, 10, 21, 29, 79, 87, 101, 109, 123, 139–40, 143–4, 149–50, 152, 155, 182, 188, 199–201, 204–5, 209, 218, 228–30, 232

kidnap, 9, 157, 218, 220, 232
Krauze, Enrique, 5, 6, 8, 15–19, 24–31, 33, 35–9, 42, 43, 74, 83, 91, 157, 161, 219, 220, 223, 228, 232, 234

La Jornada, 48, 72–3, 90–1, 100–1, 111, 115, 122, 124, 126, 138, 174, 200, 210, 215, 235
La Mafía, 72
lady, 54–5, 61
Lamas, Marta, 79–80, 90–2
Latin America, 12, 26, 39, 42–4, 71, 74, 77, 81, 138, 176, 179, 182–3, 197, 199, 200–1, 204, 209, 213–15, 233, 238
laws, 35–6, 40, 61–2, 106, 123–4, 128, 145–6, 157, 164, 170, 211, 220–2, 226, 232–3
Le Bot, Yvon, 205, 215
Left, 7, 12, 21, 26, 29–34, 38–43, 52, 60, 63, 71, 74, 79, 81–3, 98, 107, 109–10, 112–13, 117–18, 122–3, 125–34, 142, 148, 151, 156, 171–3, 188, 197, 202, 209, 214, 222, 229, 231, 233–4
legacy, 22, 27, 35, 84, 125–6, 128–9, 209
legislation, 16, 140, 145, 147
legislator, 26, 35, 37, 41, 73, 146
legitimacy, 18, 96, 104, 118

legitimate, 32, 52, 96, 117, 125, 128–9, 133, 189, 234
legitimidad, 22, 43
legitimize, 7, 25, 102, 133, 206
Lemus, Rafael, 99–100, 102, 115
lesbian, 3, 56–7, 90, 120, 187–9, 192, 194, 202, 211, 213, 238
Letras Femeninas, 178
Letras Libres, 15, 27, 36, 43, 91, 102, 115, 125, 137, 223, 234
liberalism, 16, 19, 26, 27–9, 38, 39, 43, 157, 161
liberation, 74, 197–8, 216
literature, 6–7, 11, 19, 22–4, 27, 43–4, 61, 73, 76, 78, 81, 99, 112, 116, 118, 169, 190, 199, 204, 210, 213–14, 223, 235, 237–9
Loaeza, Guadalupe, 5, 8, 9, 95–116
Loeza, Soledad, 104–5
Lomnitz, Claudio, 25–7, 43, 59, 65, 68
Long, Ryan F., 23, 43
López Obrador, Andrés Manuel, 5, 9, 36, 48, 49, 113, 117, 118, 120, 124–31, 133, 134, 229, 230, 233
López Velarde, Ramón, 95, 112
Lujambio, Alonso, 36

machismo, 9, 80, 142, 146, 160, 185, 194
machista, 56, 58, 80, 184
macho, 47, 48, 183
Madero, Francisco I, 25
madre, 52, 56–7, 66, 73, 92, 105, 145–6, 170, 178–9, 226–7, 235
marginal, 8, 58, 80–1, 87, 148, 157, 198, 203, 218
marginalization, 81, 167, 175, 187, 200, 212
marginalize, 3, 4, 141, 176, 199, 202–3, 211
marketing, 9, 64, 85, 171, 173
Martí, José, 227
masculine, 58, 96
masculinity, 110, 113

mask, 134, 163, 197–9, 201, 207, 210, 213, 215
massacre, 6, 23, 27, 82, 83, 121, 125, 126, 148, 218, 220
matriarchal, 7, 46–7, 50, 58–9, 61, 69
Maya, 10–11, 68, 163–80, 198, 205–6, 208
media, 1–3, 5, 6, 9, 13, 15–16, 19, 22, 24, 25–8, 30, 65, 72, 79, 80, 86, 95–7, 99, 103, 108, 110–13, 121, 124, 131, 133–4, 142, 164, 169, 177, 198, 201, 219, 222, 224, 227
Menchú, Rigoberta, 164, 176
*mestizaje*, 206
mestizo, 11, 52, 165, 173, 176–7
Mexican culture, 45, 56, 76, 199, 239
Mexican Revolution, 26, 69, 84, 191, 199
Meyer, Lorenzo, 22, 40
migrants, 41, 172, 204
migration, 168, 171, 173
*Milenio*, 37
minorities, 79, 87, 202–3, 209
misogynist, 152
misogyny, 80, 90
mission, 164, 175, 178, 212
modernization, 27, 29, 40, 72, 85, 118, 213
Molinar Horcasitas, Juan, 22, 43
Monsiváis Aceves, Carlos, 5, 6, 8, 19, 33, 36, 38, 43, 58, 68, 71–93, 118, 121, 138, 198, 206, 209, 215, 239
Montemayor, Carlos, 36
Moraña, Mabel, 12, 13, 43, 89, 90, 92, 93, 175, 178, 179, 200, 214, 215
Moreiras, Alberto, 23, 43
Morrero Teresa, 167, 170, 177, 179
Morton, Adam David, 7, 13
mourning, 12, 142, 217, 219, 224–5, 231

movements, 1–2, 8, 11, 20, 30–4, 46, 49, 52, 58, 74, 76, 78–9, 81, 84–7, 110, 120, 124, 142, 152, 154–7, 160, 175, 197–8, 208, 213, 218–20, 223–6, 230–1, 233
Movimiento por la paz, 11, 218, 220, 233, 234
Mudrovcic, 72, 77, 83, 90, 92
mujer, 10, 45, 54–7, 63, 68, 105–6, 111, 114–15, 125, 133, 137, 140, 145–50, 153, 157, 160, 163–5, 169, 172–3, 177–9, 183–4, 191, 193–4
Muñetón Pérez, Patricia, 97, 115
murder, 1, 9, 11, 15, 39–40, 63, 78, 120, 140, 143–4, 147–52, 154, 159, 171, 211, 217–18, 220, 222, 226–7, 232
Myers, Robert, 165, 179

NAFTA, 16, 17, 31, 34, 144, 197
narrative, 10, 16, 20, 26, 39, 42, 44, 59, 63–4, 83, 100–2, 112, 168, 181–3, 186–7, 190–2, 198, 201, 206–8, 210–12, 237–8
nation, 3–4, 18, 37, 44, 46, 64, 119, 121, 140, 191, 199, 209, 212, 217, 220–2, 227–9, 231, 233
national, 2, 4, 7, 9, 11–13, 15, 19–20, 23–4, 26, 31, 43, 46, 48–50, 57–9, 64, 67, 81, 83, 89, 103, 108, 111–12, 114, 117–19, 120, 122, 125, 127–8, 131, 139–40, 144, 151, 153–5, 157, 159, 168, 170, 173–4, 178, 183, 189, 197–8, 200, 202, 211–12, 215–16, 219–20, 222, 225–7
nationalism, 23, 26–9, 31, 34, 41, 44, 68, 80, 83, 84, 193
nationalist, 18, 32–3, 38, 83
nationality, 212
nationalized, 23
nationwide, 15, 221, 232
neoliberalism, 10, 17, 41, 78, 119–20, 134, 136, 200–3, 205, 208, 210, 213, 215–16, 237, 239

Neruda, Pablo, 45, 75–6
New York Times, 5, 165, 179, 219, 234
Nexos, 13, 15, 22, 30, 36, 37, 44, 72, 91, 92, 179
NGO, 131, 149, 155
Niño Fidencio, 81
nomination, 36
Novaro, María, 10, 11, 181–94
Novedades, 72, 126
Novo, Salvador, 5, 73, 80, 95, 96, 98, 112, 114

Oaxaca, 7, 47, 59, 66, 68
Olivera-Williams, María Rosa, 12, 13, 178, 179
organic, 7, 12–13, 17–18, 35, 136, 143, 175, 219–20, 224–5, 231
*Ovaciones*, 111

Pacheco, José Emilio, 72
PAN, 22, 33, 35, 36, 124, 129, 131, 135, 136, 140, 145, 146, 201, 232
paradigm, 18, 19, 21, 23, 28, 34, 36, 165, 181, 185–7
parody, 73, 117, 119, 122–4, 137, 210
participation, 2–3, 29, 78, 107, 120–1, 142, 189, 197, 221
particulate, 231
patriarchal, 58, 170, 182, 186, 188
patriarchy, 142, 186
Paz, Octavio, 4–6, 8, 13, 16, 19, 22, 25, 27, 37, 39, 42, 65, 68, 73, 76
PEMEX, 128, 130
Peña Nieto, Enrique, 1, 17, 36, 232
performance, 9–10, 33, 87, 96–8, 103, 105–6, 108, 112–13, 116–20, 122, 124, 126–9, 132–5, 137, 163–6, 173–80, 200, 214, 217
period, 18–9, 22–4, 26, 55, 67, 89, 98, 106, 109, 141, 154, 172, 219, 223
periodical, 125
periodista, 89, 98, 109, 115

Perkins Gilman, Charlotte, 139, 141
Pitol, Sergio, 75, 88, 92
plagiarism, 62, 95, 102, 103
plantón, 124, 128
playwright, 11, 131, 164–6
plot, 48, 101–2, 108, 168, 172, 176, 181, 183, 186–8, 191
political, 1, 3–4, 6, 9–12, 17–23, 25–30, 32–3, 35–7, 39, 41, 43, 46, 48–50, 58, 60, 65, 73, 75–9, 81, 83–4, 87–8, 90, 98–9, 104–8, 110–14, 118–25, 127–36, 142–4, 147, 150, 152–4, 159, 164, 166–7, 170–1, 175, 182, 189–92, 200–1, 204, 210–13, 215, 220, 222, 225–6, 228–30
Pons, María Cristina, 8, 71, 72, 75, 76, 82, 92, 239
Pop, 74, 97, 108–9, 112, 163
postindependence, 26
postrevolutionary, 20, 23, 29, 34
Pragmatism Unmasked, 39, 43
PRD, 32–3, 35–6, 39, 127, 140, 156, 229
prejudice, 65, 73, 80, 107, 144
preservation, 86
PRI, 1, 20, 21, 28–30, 33–5, 39, 40, 82, 84, 119, 121, 126, 134, 222, 232, 153, 156, 201, 221
private, 139
privatization, 10, 24, 119, 128
*Proceso*, 15, 72–3, 92, 136–7, 200, 222, 226–7, 229–31, 235
PROFECO, 109, 115
professional, 38, 49, 116, 141, 146–7, 149–50, 158–9, 166, 239
progressive, 5, 12, 39, 82, 123, 126, 224
prose, 13, 25, 49, 55, 76, 82, 102
prosecuted, 157
prosecution, 140
prosecutors, 148–50, 154
protest, 1, 3, 48, 105, 111, 122, 124, 143, 155, 161, 218, 220, 224, 233, 235
Protestant, 74, 79

pro-women, 140
purpose, 4, 6, 17, 48, 66, 84, 111, 128, 132, 136, 170, 172–3

Quijano, Aníbal, 209, 215

radical, 3, 13, 20, 32, 80–1, 131, 136–7, 139, 146, 151, 157, 160, 182, 209
Rama, Ángel, 37, 43, 118
rape, 140, 142–3, 146, 148–9, 151–2, 158, 171
Rasgado González, Abraham, 48, 68
rebellion, 17, 110, 164, 207, 211, 213
reform, 18, 21, 22, 24, 30, 32, 33, 35, 182
Reforma, 81, 93, 100, 114, 115
refranes, 76
regulations, 170, 172
*relajo*, 8, 83–5, 87
*Relatos*, 205–6, 209, 216
representation, 111, 134, 153, 155, 157, 161, 181, 187, 189, 215
representations, 28, 43, 152–3, 155–7, 161, 198–9, 201–2, 206, 213, 216
representative, 27, 35, 38, 84, 99–100, 113–14, 132, 145–6, 153–4, 157, 224–5
repression, 2, 111, 123, 135, 208, 218, 221
resistance, 22, 39, 57, 83, 87, 117, 120, 122, 124–5, 127–9, 135, 138, 141, 143, 166–7, 170, 175, 214, 218–20
Revista de la Universidad, 68, 72, 92
revolutionary, 11, 18, 22, 23, 24, 26, 29, 39, 52, 62, 167, 193, 197–201, 204, 205, 208–10, 213–15, 224
Rivas Mercado, Antonieta, 62
Rodríguez, Jesusa, 5, 9, 13, 60, 67, 117, 118, 120, 123, 126, 128, 134, 137, 138
romantic, 55, 95, 108, 198
Rubin, Jeffrey, 60

## INDEX

Said, Eduard, 6, 28, 136, 139, 141, 156, 160, 198, 213, 219
Salazar Escalante, Jezreel, 43, 76, 92
Salinas de Gortari, Carlos, 7, 16, 17, 34, 38, 40, 43, 119, 126, 131, 144, 156, 193
same-sex, 119, 123, 135
Sánchez-Blake, Elvira, 10, 11, 181–94
Sánchez Prado, Ignacio M., 6, 7, 15, 38, 39, 43, 77, 83, 89, 90–3, 157, 161, 239
Sandinista, 30, 31
satirize, 98, 109
Scherer García, Julio, 73, 121, 138
secular, 12, 73, 81, 116
Sefchovich, Sara, 189–90, 192–4
señor, 129, 148, 216
señora, 95, 98, 103, 111
sexist, 80, 105, 112, 147, 187
sexual, 47–8, 50, 54–5, 67, 74, 78, 80–1, 87, 90, 92, 119, 130, 145–9, 152, 159, 161, 186, 189, 200, 212, 238
sexuality, 54, 81, 87, 90, 95, 98, 113, 147, 178, 180, 194
sexually, 48
Shalalá, 9, 120–1, 128–31
Shapiro, Estela, 62
Sheppard, Randal, 26, 44
Sheridan, Guillermo, 102–3
Showalter, Elaine, 141–2, 155, 161
Sicilia, Javier, 1, 5, 15, 217–18, 224, 231, 234–5
¡Siempre!, 72, 107, 115
sindicato, 184
sociedad, 22, 41, 43–4, 68, 73, 91–3, 128, 138, 142, 148–50
Solberg, Helena, 182, 192
Sommer, Doris, 166, 179
sovereign, 24
Spanish, 31, 34, 50–2, 54, 56, 62–4, 68, 75, 78, 90, 100, 118, 163–4, 173, 176–7, 199, 205–6, 211, 214–15, 233, 237–9
specific, 141, 226

stage, 4, 9–10, 30–1, 36, 61, 89, 101, 117–38, 163, 165–8, 173–5, 179–80, 186, 220, 226, 232
stagnation, 1, 207
stance, 4, 28, 31, 128, 130, 132–3, 212
stereotypes, 46, 48, 67, 95–6, 103, 191
Subcomandante Marcos, 5, 11, 81, 90, 91, 110, 137, 164, 197–200, 202–16, 231
subordinate, 136, 168
subversion, 21, 44
supranational, 167
system, 20, 22, 29, 33, 36–7, 58, 80, 85, 87, 90, 106, 123, 159, 164, 170, 177, 185, 187, 189, 201–2

Tabuenca Córdoba, María Socorro, 10, 139, 159, 161, 237, 239
Taibo II, Paco Ignacio, 11, 210, 215, 216
talent, 50, 95–6
Taylor, Analisa, 64, 69
Taylor, Diana, 166–7, 175–80
Taylor, Kathy, 39, 44, 49–50, 67
teatro, 135, 137–8, 168–9, 171, 174–5, 177–9, 238
technology, 85–6
Tehuana, 52
Televisa, 48, 76, 129
The New Republic, 27
The Speed, 204, 208–9, 216
Theatre, 9–10, 117, 120, 136–7, 180
threats, 6, 154
title, 7–8, 28, 37, 54–5, 66, 73–4, 80, 84, 88–9, 96, 100, 103, 108, 112, 170, 183, 188, 199, 226–7
Tlatelolco, 6, 82, 83, 90, 92, 121, 125, 126, 138, 232
Toledo, Alejandro, 21, 44
Toledo, Francisco, 74
trade, 10, 19, 22, 96, 119, 122, 160–1, 197, 200, 221–2, 233

traditional, 2, 4, 11–12, 16, 18, 21, 32, 36, 65, 77–8, 107, 123–4, 163, 165–6, 168, 170–7, 212, 219
trafficking, 1, 10, 135, 220–2, 227, 233, 235, 238
transnational, 10, 30, 64–6, 86, 210
transsexual, 130, 133, 213
Trejo Delabre, Raúl, 22, 44
trope, 100, 141, 187, 224
TV Azteca, 9, 111, 129, 131, 133, 228, 234

UNAM, 43, 72, 92, 115, 138, 160, 235
underdevelopment, 65
Underiner, Tamara, 165, 167, 172, 176, 180
universal, 141, 226
Uno Más Uno, 72, 98, 100
uprising, 78, 164, 197–8, 205

Valdespino Vargas, Carla, 205, 214, 216
value, 7, 9, 18, 24, 27, 29, 35, 46, 53, 58–9, 98, 105, 108, 110, 113, 150, 165, 167–8, 170, 177, 183, 197, 223, 229
Van Delden Maarten, 22, 44
Vanden Berghe, Kristen, 44, 201, 203–6, 208, 214, 216
Vasconcelos, José, 45, 52, 61–2, 66, 89, 134, 193
V-Day, 142, 153, 160
Villamil, Jenaro, 73, 79–80, 89–90, 92–3

violence, 10, 15, 52, 65, 86, 140, 144–5, 151–2, 154–5, 159, 167, 169–71, 173, 177, 190, 217–18, 220–2, 224–8, 230, 234, 238
virgin, 67
Virgin of Guadalupe, 81, 109, 131, 227
virginal, 123
virginity, 58
vocation, 116, 121, 133, 139, 154, 165
voice, 1, 10–1, 15, 28, 34, 61, 76, 79, 83, 98, 100, 107–8, 111–12, 140, 144, 148, 150–1, 153, 155–6, 167, 169, 174–5, 181, 189, 191, 193, 198, 200, 202, 204, 207, 209, 211–13, 218, 223, 230
Vuelta, 22, 27, 43, 44, 68, 91, 157, 161

women, 8–11, 16, 47–50, 52, 54–8, 60, 63, 67–8, 78, 80, 89, 99–100, 103, 105, 109, 111–12, 119–20, 138, 140–61, 163–91, 193–5, 202, 205–6, 208–9, 212–13, 237–9
Wright, Melissa, 154, 160–1

Zabludovsky, Jacobo, 96
Zapata, Emiliano, 25, 203, 205, 215
Zapatista, 2, 11, 17, 164, 197–201, 201–3, 207–16, 231
Zapotec, 5, 7, 45, 47–8, 51–2, 56–7, 59, 61–2, 64, 67–8
zapoteca, 48, 67
zócalo, 87, 117–18, 124, 126–8, 134, 213, 228

CPSIA information can be obtained at www.ICGtesting.com
Printed in the USA
LVOW04*1704191214

419645LV00008B/261/P